DESECRATION

Forgotten Colony, Book Three

M.R. FORBES

Chapter 1

"Dante!" Caleb leaned over the sheriff, putting his fingers on her neck and checking for a pulse. He found it right away, strong and steady. "Dante, can you hear me?"

His eyes traveled from her pale face to the two deputies and the nurse standing together about four meters away. Their postures had slumped, their faces expressing their confusion.

"Bashir, Casper, Reed," he said. "Do you know where you are?"

"Sergeant?" Deputy Bashir said. His eyes widened when he saw Sheriff Dante on the ground, with him leaning over her. His hand went to his revolver, and he stepped toward Caleb. "What did you do to her?"

"Stand down, Deputy," Doctor Brom said, rising from his position beside Riley. "Sergeant Card didn't do this."

"Doctor Brom?" Reed said. "What's going on?"

Sheriff Dante groaned softly. Brom shifted to where she was lying. "Lasandra, it's Doc Brom. Can you hear me?"

She groaned again in reply.

"Don't move too fast. It looks like you got clocked in the jaw."

Caleb noticed the left side of Sheriff Dante's face was already swelling and bruising. Riley must have sucker-punched her.

"I don't understand this," Deputy Casper said.

"What do you remember?" Caleb asked.

"You went into the exam room with Doctor Brom." He paused and then shook his head. "Then a trife attacked Sheriff Dante. But it wasn't a trife like I've ever seen before. It was made of dark metal, like your hand. But then it was gone, and you were there, and — " He stopped talking when his eyes flicked over to Riley. "Is she dead?"

"Very," Caleb replied.

"You shot her?"

"I don't have a gun. She shot herself."

"We don't have bullets."

"I know. There may be an alien in Metro."

"A what?"

"It's another long story. There's a lot you still don't know. It doesn't matter right now. I need you to go back to the bridge and get Flores and Washington. Get Governor Stone too. If there's an alien still on the ship, we have a major problem."

Deputy Casper didn't move. "Uh, Sergeant, I… Well… you're under arrest."

"I know that. I'm not trying to escape."

"It's not that. I.. Uh.. Well… I can't take orders from a prisoner."

"Damn it, Casper," Doctor Brom said. "Will you take orders from me? Just go."

Casper nodded, turning and rushing out of the waiting room.

"Thank you," Caleb said.

"You're welcome," Brom replied. "I don't know what all of this is about or why Dante arrested you, but I'm pretty sure you're not a bad guy."

"I'm not. My duty is to protect the people of Metro. Contractually, it ended the moment we reached solid ground, but I wasn't made that way."

Dr. Brom frowned. "Bridge? Reached solid ground? I get the feeling there's a lot more going on here than meets the eye."

Caleb opened his mouth to explain, realizing he had hinted at something the vast majority of people in Metro didn't and weren't supposed to know.

"Don't strain yourself, Sergeant," Brom said. "You're injured enough already. Long story, I get it. I've been around long enough to know better than to ask too many questions too soon. Reed, get me a gurney, will you?"

Reed held up a small device. "Do you still want the gun, Doctor?"

"Just leave it here."

Reed put it down and left the room.

Dante groaned again, trying to lift her head.

"Take it easy, Sam," Brom said.

"Bitch punched me," Dante said. Her eyes shifted, noticing Caleb on his knees beside her. "Sergeant Card? What the hell happened?"

"Riley punched you."

She ran her tongue along the inside of her mouth, wincing at the pain. "I know that. Where is she?"

"About a meter to your left," Caleb said. "She's dead."

"What?" Dante lifted her head too quickly, turning it to see Riley's corpse. She put her hand to her temple. "Oh, damn that hurts."

"I told you to take it easy," Doctor Brom said.

"She's dead?" Dante said. "I don't see a scratch on her."

"Strangest damn thing I've ever seen, Sam," Brom said. "She shot herself with your unloaded revolver, and it killed her."

"Sheriff Dante," Deputy Bashir said. "I think we were seeing things."

"Seeing things?"

"Hallucinations," Caleb said. "The short version is that the enemy possesses a weapon that screws with brainwave patterns and can cause targets to hallucinate. I don't know exactly how or why it affects different people at different times, but I can tell you that the only way anybody in this room should see things is if one of the enemy was nearby."

Then again, he wasn't sure if that was entirely true. They had landed on the enemy's planet. Who was to say they weren't broadcasting the same signals? Who was to say the Deliverance wasn't already under attack?

He tried to stand up, nearly falling over when his ankle wouldn't support his weight. He hopped back, putting his hand on the nearest wall. "We may be in trouble. From outside."

Dante nodded, setting herself and standing up. Fortunately, Brom stood with her, and he grabbed her when she started swaying.

"I'm a little dizzy," she said.

"You two make a great pair," Brom said. "What's going on, and how can I help?"

"I already sent Casper to the bridge," Caleb said. "If there's trouble, he'll report back."

"Not if he's hallucinating again," Dante said. "Shit. What if the whole city is seeing things?"

"That should be easy to figure out," Brom said, pointing to a window.

Caleb hopped over to it, looking out. They were on the eighth floor of the hospital building, with a decent view of the strand below. There were people gathered outside milling around together in a general state of confusion, but none of them were acting violent or fearful. None of them appeared to be reacting to anything that wasn't there.

"I don't think the city's affected," he said.

"Just up here?" Dante asked. "What does that mean?"

Caleb turned away from the window. "It means the enemy was close and it decided to attack. I don't know. Maybe it wanted Doctor Valentine dead."

"And not us?"

"I don't know how much control it has over what each person sees. I hardly know anything about them. There was one loose on the ship. We managed to get it out of the main hangar blast doors and into space."

"Are you sure?"

Caleb's mind flashed back to his last vision of Sho tumbling out into space with the alien AI wrapped in the arms of her Strongman exosuit. A twinge of sadness caused him to grimace. "I saw it go out. I'm sure."

"Sorry, Sergeant. I mean, are you sure we left it behind? Is it possible it could survive in space? Is it possible it got back on board?"

Caleb stared at her. Was it possible it could survive in space? It was an artificial intelligence. A machine. Of course it could. Could it have freed itself from Sho's grip and found its way back to the ship? He couldn't rule it out. But then why would it follow him, or Riley, back here? "I don't know. It might not be the same one. For all we know, one of them has been hiding in Metro."

"Can we hold on a second?" Doctor Brom said, getting their attention. "It's become painfully clear to me that you two are carrying on about parts of a spaceship as if we're actually on a spaceship. Is that right?"

"Yes, Doctor," Dante said, glancing over at Reed. "We're on a spaceship. We've been on a spaceship since we were born."

"Not in an underground bunker?"

"No."

Brom whistled. "Well, that's a kick in the pants. Metro is over two hundred years old. Are you telling me we've been in space that whole time?"

"Yes," Caleb said. "I thought you weren't going to ask too many questions too soon?"

"Sorry, it's my curious nature. Well, where in the universe are we now?"

"About forty-five light years from Earth," Caleb said. "We landed on an Earth-like planet we were calling Essex about an hour ago."

"So we reached our new home?" Doctor Brom smiled hopefully.

"You could say that," Dante said.

"You don't sound that happy about it."

"That's because the planet might already be occupied," Caleb said. "By the same aliens that just killed Doctor Valentine, and sent the trife to Earth."

Brom's smile vanished, his face hardening. "Who's idea was it to travel to an already occupied planet?"

Caleb pointed at Riley.

"Figures," Brom said, shaking his head. "I have a feeling I don't want to know the rest."

"You can't tell anyone," Dante said. "This is classified intel. Governor's order. Do you understand?"

"I get it," Brom said. "The secret's safe with me. I don't want to be responsible for causing a panic." He looked at

Caleb again. "What do you think, Sarge? Did we come all this way just to lose again?"

Caleb could tell how much Brom wanted him to say things were going to be fine, and not to worry. He forced a smile. "The best way for us to win a war is not to fight one."

"Sound advice. Let's hope we can follow it." He sighed heavily. "Well, neither of you are in any shape to do much of anything for anyone at the moment. Sergeant, let's get you stitched and braced. Sheriff, let me have a look at your head."

"We don't have time," Dante said.

"Bullshit," Brom replied. "Casper went to get the Governor, and there's not a thing you can do to help in your current condition. You may be a sheriff, you may be a soldier, but right now you're both my patients, and I want you in the exam room now."

Caleb smiled and glanced at Dante. "He has a point."

"I know," she replied. "Make it fast, Doc."

Brom nodded. "Right this way."

Chapter 2

The lacerations on Caleb's back were patched, and his ankle was in the process of being braced when Flores, Washington, and Governor Stone finally arrived at the hospital. The two Guardians were happy to see him, while Stone looked like he was struggling to keep himself together.

Caleb didn't blame him. Four hours ago the Governor was living in relative peace, unaware of anything that was happening outside the sealed hatches leading into the city. Not only had that peace been destroyed by their arrival in Metro, but then his daughter Orla had been killed by an alien drone while helping Caleb stop it from destroying the Deliverance.

He had lost people. Friends. Family. Brothers and sisters in arms. Banks, Habib, Sho. He had seen more corpses than anyone should ever have to see. Every one of them was somebody's son, daughter, brother, sister, husband or friend. Every one of them had meant something to someone. He understood the pain of it but he still couldn't imagine what it was like to lose a child, especially the way the Governor had. Unexpectedly. Violently.

Caleb struggled not to blame himself for the loss. It had been his idea to bring her into the fight. If he had gone out there alone, she might still be alive. Or they might all be dead. He had to keep reminding himself of that. Her skill had caused the drone to react the way it did. Her skill had given him the chance to destroy it. Without her talent, the Deliverance may have never reached the surface.

He hoped they didn't come to regret that it had.

"What happened here, Sheriff?" Governor Stone said before anyone else had a chance to speak.

"I brought Sergeant Card and Doctor Valentine to Metro like you ordered, Governor," Dante said. "Sergeant Card needed treatment for his wounds, so I rerouted them here before taking them to the law office. Doctor Brom took Sergeant Card into the examination room, while Bashir, Casper, and I kept an eye on Doctor Valentine. She seemed angry, but she didn't look like she was planning to do anything stupid. In fact, her head drooped and she closed her eyes. Then next thing I know, I'm waking up on the floor with pain in my jaw. I don't remember her punching me, but I assumed she must have punched me."

"I see," Stone said. "I heard Doctor Valentine was dead. That she shot herself with an unloaded weapon."

"That's right, Governor," Doctor Brom said. "I had Reed bring her body down to storage, to put her on ice until I have time to do an autopsy. I'm particularly interested in the state of her brain at the moment of death."

"So am I," Stone said. "I'm interested in a lot of things. The problem is, I don't even know where to start." He turned to Caleb. "Maybe you can help me with that, Sergeant? Maybe you can tell me why Doctor Valentine is dead? Maybe you can tell me why Orla had to die?" He shook his head, wiping his suddenly running eyes. "I haven't told her mother yet. What am I supposed to tell her mother?"

"She died a hero," Caleb said. "I know it doesn't ease the pain, but it's something."

"Maybe being a hero means something to a soldier like you. It doesn't mean anything to me. She'll always be my little girl." He closed his eyes. For a moment, Caleb thought he might break down into an all-out sob. He didn't. He pulled himself together, opening his eyes and wiping them one last time. "I want answers, Sergeant. I want to know everything, starting from the beginning."

"I'm sure you do, sir," Caleb said. "But I think we need to skip ahead to the parts that are the most relevant to our current situation." He paused, trying to decide exactly where to start. "The Deliverance left Earth two hundred and thirty-six years ago. During its departure, it was attacked by a large group of xenotrife. They breached the ship and gained a foothold on board, while also killing every senior officer and ninety-percent of the Marines defending the ship. It was left to me, Privates Flores, Washington, and a handful of Marines to repel their attack and eliminate them. Since you're familiar with the protocols, you know at that point the Guardians were to begin cycling through one-year tours as caretakers of the ship. Originally, the protocols called for ten soldiers per tour on a ten-year cycle. Our reduced numbers forced us to one soldier per tour on a six-year cycle. At least, that was the plan."

"I take it things didn't go according to plan?" Stone said.

"Not at all." Caleb paused again. He glanced over at Flores and Washington, who nodded in support. "Let me back up a step. Before launch, Doctor Valentine informed the senior officers that she had orders from Space Force Command to reprogram the ship's navigation computers. Instead of making the twenty-five light-year trip to Earth-6, which would take over a hundred years, we were being redirected to Proxima Centauri, only four and a half light years away. The majority of the generation ships were gathering there to form a new colony much closer to home than originally planned."

"Correct me if I'm wrong, Sergeant, but we just spent over two hundred years in space, and I didn't see any other starships on the way down. Which leads me to believe we aren't in the Proxima system?"

"You aren't wrong, Governor. And that's where things start to get ugly."

"What do you mean, ugly?"

"Doctor Riley Valentine," Flores said. "They don't come any uglier than that."

"Flores!" Caleb snapped.

"Sorry, Alpha."

"What I came to learn later was that while the generation ships all shared a common mission statement and set of protocols, Space Force Command had different ideas for the aptly named Deliverance. Doctor Valentine was placed in charge of a clandestine operation whose end goal was to use the citizens of Metro to create an army of what I can only define as super-soldiers, and then deliver those soldiers to enemy territory to launch an attack."

"What?" Governor Stone said.

"That's crazy," Doctor Brom added.

"You don't know the half of it," Flores quipped.

"Hold on a moment, Sergeant," Governor Stone said. "You're saying that Metro, my city, was slated to become what, exactly? A resource pool for a new military?"

"In part," Caleb said. "First, it was going to be a

resource pool for Doctor Valentine's experiments. She was working to create genetic modifications that would allow humans to heal much faster than normal, to regenerate similar to jellyfish or lizards. Once she perfected her editing, the next phase was to start administering it across the colony. I don't know how she planned to do that."

"But none of us knew she existed before she came into Metro with you," Sheriff Dante said. "I assume that means her research didn't pan out?"

"Dr. Moreau," Flores muttered.

Caleb flicked his eyes toward her, and she lowered her head and tightened her lips once again.

"Her research panned out, in a sinister sort of way," Caleb said. "There was a stowaway on the Deliverance named David. She captured him and used him for her experiments. The edits she made allowed him to heal from a gunshot wound to the head. They also gave him increased intelligence and near-immortality."

"That's amazing," Brom said.

"I wouldn't mind either one," Deputy Casper said.

"Not being able to die isn't as great as it may seem," Caleb said. "Especially when you're alone on a starship for over two hundred years."

"Yes, sir," Casper replied.

"What happened to David?" Governor Stone asked.

"Like I mentioned on the bridge, Riley killed him and then dumped him out into space. I have no idea if he's dead or in some living hell, where his body regenerates, wakes up, and then suffocates again."

"That would be awful," Dante said.

Governor Stone ran his hand through his beard. "Okay, Sergeant. I'm starting to understand why you wanted Doctor Valentine detained, assuming you're telling us the truth."

"I have no reason to lie, Governor."

"I'll accept that for the moment."

"In any case, that isn't the worst part. Like Deputy Casper just said, there are upsides to the genetic alterations. But Riley couldn't stop herself there. After all, if you pit unarmed humans against unarmed trife, with the humans knowing they can regenerate, they'll struggle to kill a single trife with their bare hands. Once she was satisfied with her first round of edits she went on to the next evolution of her idea."

"Hybrids?" Sheriff Dante asked.

Caleb looked at her. She had worked it out quickly. "Exactly. She started blending human and trife DNA."

"Sergeant, you said she only had David as a test subject," Doctor Brom said.

"Not exactly. Hybrids were outside of the scope of the original mission, and her people wouldn't back her going into Metro to take colonists. She wasn't the type of person to not get what she wanted. She used two of my Guardians first, and then her fellow researchers."

"That's just…" Sheriff Dante said, unable to find the words.

"And you killed the hybrids, Sergeant?" Governor Stone asked.

"We did."

The Governor paused again, letting the information sink in for a few seconds. "Getting back to the second part of the plan, are you suggesting that we just landed in hostile territory? On a planet belonging to the aliens who sent the trife to Earth?"

"That was Doctor Valentine's plan," Caleb confirmed. "As for hostile, I just don't know. I never learned how this planet was selected. There must have been something that indicated the enemy was here in some capacity. If you think it through, the whole idea is one step above absurd."

"How so?" Stone asked.

"Doctor Valentine based her entire plan on the premise that the enemy's primary weapon is the xenotrife, and she delivered us here in an unarmed starship which nearly got blown to pieces on the way to the surface. When the Deliverance launched, she had only a basic idea of who our enemy is and what their capabilities are. She didn't know they possessed advanced artificial intelligence. She didn't know they had a weapon that could cause us to not only hallucinate, but apparently trick our minds into believing what we see is so real a fake gunshot wound can cause real death. It's as close to a suicide mission as I've ever heard. Not only that, but Command authorized it."

Caleb's voice rose as he spoke, the truth of the matter making him increasingly angry. The officers that formed Space Force Command weren't stupid. They knew the mission was extremely high risk, with a near-zero chance of success. They had sent forty-thousand people here to die, including him.

The room was silent, each of the people present trying to make sense of the situation. It stayed that way for a few minutes until Governor Stone spoke again.

"Well, the Deliverance is here now. She's too damaged to fly again, even if she had the thrust to get us back into space. We're alive for the moment. We know there is at least one of these alien things on board, or at least there was. There may be more of them beyond the walls of this vessel. There may be something worse. There may be nothing at all. We just don't know."

He looked over at Caleb. His expression had changed. He was focused again, eager to keep his city safe. Caleb was sure it wouldn't last, that he would crumble when he had a moment in private, and when he had to tell his wife what had happened to their child. It didn't matter. He had a grip on the realities of their situation right now.

"Sergeant Card, you're released from detention. Seeing what we're facing here, I can't afford to have the best-trained soldier on this ship rotting in a cell, even if you have made some horrible decisions."

Caleb forced himself not to react to the comment. He eyed Flores to keep her quiet, too. "Thank you, Governor."

"You might not want to thank me yet. Your release is conditional. I understand protocol suggests that you become a civilian or a law officer at the end of your duties as a Guardian. As you said, the original protocols expected you to be in your seventies by now. Seeing as how you're still capable, and seeing as how we can't confirm that we're safe, I expect you to stay on as commander of the Guardians. I expect your remaining Guardians to stay on as well."

"I'm in," Flores said.

Washington flashed his thumb.

"That's fine, Governor," Caleb said. "But to be honest, I don't know how much I can accomplish with three of us."

"I understand. You'll report directly to me. You'll have authority over anyone who leaves the confines of Metro except with a direct override from me. If you have needs inside Metro, I expect you to work closely with Sheriff Dante to have them met."

"Yes, Governor," Caleb said.

"For now, you can pull any additional personnel resources you may need from Law. Again, I expect you to work closely with Sam to make that happen in a reason-able way. Do you both understand?"

"Yes, Governor," Caleb repeated.

"Yes, Governor," Sheriff Dante said. She turned to Caleb. "It'll be an honor to work with you, Sergeant."

"Likewise," Caleb said.

"Good," Governor Stone said. "We're here, and we're alive. I want to keep it that way. Guardian Alpha, where do we start?"

Chapter 3

"We need to start by getting organized," Caleb said. "We have more than just Metro to worry about now. The Deliverance is resting on alien soil. We have no idea what's out there or how much or how little of it is a threat. We need to seal off as much of the ship as we can and have guards on the rest. We also need to get comms up and running ship-wide, not just citywide. First order of business is to turn this place into as much of a fortress as we can and hope that if the enemy is here, they decide to ignore us, at least until we can get our feet under us. To that end, we need Joe and Carol back to help plan the engineering side of those needs. Governor, do you know how many engineers we can call on?"

"Thirty-seven," Governor Stone replied. "They usually work in shifts."

"We need all of them as soon as possible."

"Of course. What about Law Enforcement? We have one hundred sixteen officers working in three shifts."

"Bring them all in too, but only for a few hours. Sheriff

Dante, we'll need to search Metro for the enemy. I don't think it's going to stay in the city, but we have to be sure."

"Why don't you think it will stay?" Dante asked.

"The one we put out the airlock wanted to get here real bad. If it's the same one, it got what it wanted. If it's a different one, it probably wants the same thing. It said it needed to make it to the surface to complete its mission. We don't know what its mission was or what that meant. Like I said, it's most likely on its way out of the ship."

"Alpha, what happens if it escapes?" Governor Stone asked. "What happens if it does complete its mission? It'll tell its superiors we're here. And then what?"

"I can't answer that."

"Don't you think we should go after it?"

"Governor, I'm hoping we don't find this thing still in Metro. We're in no condition to chase down an alien that can make us kill ourselves and each other."

"How did you beat the first one?" Sheriff Dante asked. "Didn't it make you see things?"

"It did. David made a device that helped cancel out the effects of its weapon. I guess you could call it a shield. It was lost during the fight."

"Do you think we can make another one?"

"I hope we can, but I don't know if he left the plans for it or any construction resources behind. Once we've got the hatches battened down, we can worry about shoring up our personal defenses enough to venture outdoors."

"Meanwhile, the enemy can march right over here and kill all of us," Governor Stone said.

"Yes, Governor," Caleb replied. "That's a definite possibility. There are only so many things we can control right now, and how the locals react to our sudden arrival isn't one of them. Once we get comms running, we can post guards at all of the entry points to the ship and maybe start running sorties around the perimeter."

It was obvious Governor Stone didn't like the answer, but he didn't fight it either. Considering Caleb's first impression of the man was as a despot who ruled the city predominantly for his own comfort, he was surprisingly agreeable.

"What should I tell the colony?" Stone asked. "I have to tell them something about what happened. I'm nervous about admitting where we are. The people are going to feel betrayed. We can't afford for them to riot."

"They won't," Caleb said.

"How can you be so sure?"

"They're frightened and confused. You have a window of opportunity to pull them in and keep them on your side. Tell them where we are. Tell them why. Don't mention the enemy. As far as they need to know, this is our original destination. This is Essex."

"You want me to lie?"

"I want you to omit. Unless you prefer risking a riot none of us want? I don't like doing it, but we need to buy some time, and getting them working together to prepare to move the city outside will give us that time. If the enemy comes, they don't need to know we knew about them beforehand."

"They'll know something is up if the city starts crawling with law," Sheriff Dante said.

"True. Maybe we can pair some of them with engineers. You can tell them you're checking the structural integrity of the blocks after the shaking."

"Alpha, I never knew you were so sneaky," Flores said.

"I think Valentine must have rubbed off on me," Caleb replied. "Wash, Flores, I want you to head back to engineering to retrieve the Kings. We need them here."

"Roger, Alpha," Flores said. "What about the energy unit? Shouldn't we keep a guard on it?"

"I want as few people outside of Metro right now as possible. Stay with them while they disconnect it, and then bring it back here. If it charged the batteries, we should be good for a hundred years or so."

"Roger. Come on, Wash."

Washington nodded to Caleb and followed Flores out of the room.

Caleb turned to the Governor. "Governor Stone, I think you should make your announcement as soon as possible. The faster we calm the people's nerves, the easier our work will be."

"Agreed," Stone replied. "Sheriff Dante, put out the call for a general assembly in the south park in one hour."

"Yes, Governor," Dante said.

"Alpha Card, I think it's best if you join me for the announcement. I think it will help ease the minds of the colonists to see someone in command from outside Metro."

Caleb looked at the Governor. "I don't know if that's necessary, sir."

Sheriff Dante laughed. "Alpha Card, you're fine with fighting trife, enhanced hybrid trife, an alien artificial intelligence, but you're afraid of standing in front of a crowd?"

Caleb nodded. "I like to be the support behind the scenes, not front and center."

"Too bad," Governor Stone said. "You're going to be up there with me. That's an order."

"Yes, sir," Caleb replied.

"Doctor Brom," Stone said. "I want you to speak with the rest of the medical team. I want them ready in case people start getting hurt. Once you're done with that, head down to the morgue and do your autopsy on Doctor

Valentine. I want the results sent to my office and the law office. Sheriff Dante, assemble the other deputies and sheriffs and get them split into groups to search the city. Alpha Card, how will we know if we've found the enemy?"

"They need to check in over comms with established protocols at regular intervals. If those intervals lapse or they don't meet the protocols, you know something happened to them, and that's where our rogue may be."

"Roger that, Alpha," Sheriff Dante said.

"Okay people," Governor Stone said. "You know what to do. If you'll excuse me, I need to tell Elizabeth about Orla. Let's do our best to make sure I'm the last one who has to have that kind of conversation."

"Yes, sir," they replied.

"Oh, and somebody get Alpha Card some new clothes, preferably something resembling a uniform. We can't have him going up in front of the people in his underwear."

"Yes, sir," Sheriff Dante said. "Alpha, if you follow me back to Law we can get you something a little more official."

Stone eyed each of them one last time, his pupils already moistening again as he left the room.

"Sheriff Dante," Caleb said. "After you make your calls, there's something else I think you can help me with."

"Does it have anything to do with your fear of public speaking?"

Caleb smiled. "Indirectly."

Dante smiled back. "Then consider it done. Casper, Bashir, let's go."

Chapter 4

The Law Office had been silent and empty when Caleb and Dante first arrived, but a few quick calls had transformed it almost immediately into a hub of organized chaos. A room full of sheriffs, deputies and engineers had gathered in the space, and there was increasing tension within the group as the news spread among them that they weren't where they had always believed they were.

It was one thing to think you were holed up in a bunker on Earth. Another to learn you had just crashed landed on an alien planet. Another still to find out there was already an alien on board that may have manipulated the ship into crashing in the first place.

That is, if the AI was responsible.

Caleb couldn't be sure Riley hadn't set half of the emergency situation up herself to get them here, in one final, desperate attempt to fulfill her mission of revenge against the enemy that killed her sister. A part of him understood how she felt. He had gone through the same emotions when he had lost people close to him. He imagined everyone on Earth did. That didn't mean using others the way she had used them. And if there was one upside to their current situation, it was that they were far, far away from Space Force Command. It still burned him that his superiors had gone along with her idea. Maybe they figured they had nothing to lose.

"Are you sure you don't want to change your clothes?" Dante asked.

Caleb glanced down at the simple, worn clothes Doc Brom had given him. "For what? A sheriff's uniform? I don't want to hurt your feelings, but I'm not that interested."

Dante smiled, running her hand along the baggy, faded shirt and down over the belt around her hips. "You don't think it's high fashion?"

Caleb laughed. "Who am I to judge?"

"You can't stand up there with Governor Stone dressed like that. He'll have my head for it."

"Don't worry, I don't plan on staying in this."

"Right. Does this have anything to do with that favor you asked for?"

"It does."

"How so?"

"You'll see when we get there."

"Get where?"

"Not here. I'll tell you in private."

"Roger. Well, I think everyone is here." She put a pair of fingers to her mouth and whistled, shrill and loud. All of the commotion in the office came to an abrupt stop, every sheriff, deputy, and engineer turning in her direction. "All right people. You already know the details. Sheriffs Johnson and Zane will handle the assignments. You're to report back every five minutes. Sooner if you start to think you're hallucinating. Anybody fails to report, we start closing a perimeter around their position to identify and contain the enemy."

"Sheriff," Caleb said. "I should mention. A loud, harsh enough tone can help override the signal the enemy uses to interrupt the brain, at least temporarily. A whistle like Sheriff Dante's might do the trick for a few seconds at least."

"Good to know," Dante replied. "If any of you can whistle, be ready to put your lips together and blow."

A scattered chuckle gave Caleb the impression she had lifted that line from somewhere. A movie maybe? Flores would probably know.

"Let's move out, people."

Sheriffs Johnson and Zane directed traffic, getting the other sheriffs, deputies, and engineers out of the office and into the streets. A crowd was growing beyond the entrance to the office, Metro's citizens eager to find out what was happening. They shouted questions at the groups as they dispersed, met with replies that the Governor would be addressing all of them very soon.

"Okay, Sergeant," Sheriff Dante said. "What's your plan?"

Caleb motioned Dante back into her office, slipping through the other people on their way out. He closed the door behind them.

"According to Riley, there's a cache of Marine equipment hidden beneath Metro. Armor, guns, vehicles, ammo. Do you know anything about that?"

Dante's eyes widened at the statement. She shook her head without hesitation. "No, Sergeant. Should I?"

"I'm glad you didn't know, considering your civil war. I doubt it would still be there. We need to find a way to access it now though."

"You know it exists, but you don't know how to reach it?"

"Not exactly. I know there isn't any access from outside Metro, at least not without breaking any more of the seals. There's probably access inside Metro, and my guess is that it's somewhere on or near this building."

"Why do you say that?"

"The Law Office is in the wrong location, don't you think? Way too far uptown when it would make more sense to have a central location. And if you were going to give the colonists access to advanced weaponry, who would you want to have that access?"

"Both good points. But if the ship was designed for us to have access to the cache, why wouldn't Stone know about it?"

"I thought maybe he did, which is why I asked you if you knew about it. But Stone isn't the person who was supposed to be Governor when the Deliverance reached its destination."

"Doctor Valentine again?"

Caleb nodded. It was starting to make more sense. Riley needed control over the colony regardless of the outcome of her work. He could guess there would have been some risk of resistance if she opened the seal after two hundred years and Stone wasn't so compliant, but the Cerebus probably would have quelled that risk. Would she have sent the colonists into battle without the genetic perfection she had hoped to achieve?

He had a feeling she would have. Without hesitation.

"They screwed us good, didn't they, Sergeant?" Dante said. "Your superiors, I mean. They put us in the hands of a monster."

"I don't agree with what they were trying to do, but I

can almost understand why they did it. We were desperate and scared, and we'd just lost our entire planet."

"I can't speak to that. Only where we are right now. Riley Valentine sounds like a real bitch, but I wish she were alive right now to give us more information."

"Surprisingly, so do I. In any case, how well do you know this place?"

"I've worked here since I was seventeen. But we don't do all that much. Not since the uprising. The citizens know better than to stand up to the Governor."

"Fourteen-thousand dead," Caleb said. "They learned that lesson the hard way."

Dante nodded somberly. "Yes, they did. You've gotten a good look at the city. Metro has been falling apart for years. In that sense, it's good we're somewhere because I don't know how much longer we would have lasted otherwise."

"Silver lining," Caleb said, pausing to think.

The main hangar connected to the city through the largest of the seals, which were currently locked in place. No amount of explosive would get them open without doing a ton of damage, which meant Deputy Klahanie was going to have his work cut out for him to get into the primary network and get them open. That was secondary. If the cache were stocked with vehicles — drones, APCs and the like — access to the main hold would have been required in the plans.

He turned in the office, orienting himself in the direction of the main hangar. The base of the city was positioned at the same level. But Valentine had said the cache was under the city. Did that mean there was a Deck Thirty-one? He had been outside the major seal they had used to bring the blocks into the massive hold to construct Metro. Now that he thought about it, he hadn't noticed the seal on this side of the city, and it was way too big to miss.

"There have to be two seals," he said, thinking out loud.

"What?" Dante asked.

"There are two seals to the main hangar. Like an airlock. Outer and inner. The largest doors."

"There aren't any large doors in Metro," Dante said. "Only the exits into engineering to the north and south."

"That can't be right. The blocks were carried in here on massive loaders. They had to get access for those machines somewhere."

"Another hidden door?"

"Or a false wall. I wish I had paid more attention the first time I was here. When I met your many times great-grandmother."

"If it's here, I'm sure we'll find it, but the Governor's announcement is in thirty minutes. Are you sure you don't want a uniform?"

"I do want a uniform," Caleb replied. "Just not yours. When Stone tells the people what's really happening, he's going to need someone who looks like they know what they're doing, not a beat up sheriff who looks like all of the other sheriffs. No offense."

"None taken. I understand. But that means we don't have much time to find your secret passage. If there is a secret passage."

Caleb was still facing in the direction of the hangar, trying to visualize the layout of the Deliverance in his mind. He realized the grid he had seen was missing pieces, blocked out to keep everyone either confused or safe. He wasn't sure which anymore.

"Does the Law Office continue back that way?" he asked, pointing at the back of her office's wall.

Dante nodded. "There's an old garage back there. We used to have drones to help us monitor the colony, but they were stripped for parts a long time ago. Now it's more like a junkyard. I don't think anyone's been back there in at least fifty years. I've looked at it through the window. It's a machine graveyard, Sergeant."

"Maybe it's a good thing for us that the Deliverance's dead kept such good secrets."

Chapter 5

Sheriff Dante led Caleb out of her office, past the cell block and into the rear of the building. The corridor leading to the garage was dark and dusty, clearly ignored for years, to the extent that the walls had been opened up, the wiring pulled from them to use somewhere else.

"Beautiful, right?" Dante said.

"You do what you have to do."

They approached the door. It was made of metal, with a small window in the center. A control pad to open it sat on the wall, but Caleb never expected it to function. Dante put her fingers around the edge of it and pushed, straining to slide it open.

"You should let me do that," Caleb said.

Dante paused, made eye contact, and then glanced at his replacement arm, smiling sheepishly. "I suppose I should." She moved aside.

Caleb stepped up to the door, peering in through the dirty glass. Two doors sat in the back of it to allow access from outside, both rusted and probably non-functional. As Dante had said, there were bits and pieces of machines and shells of vehicles strewn across the floor, which was stained with grease and smaller debris, enough that it nearly hid the actual surface from view. The way the building was positioned, if there was a secret passage to the deck below, it had to be in the floor.

Was the mess a natural accumulation of junk, or had it been manipulated to hide something?

He was assuming that if Dante didn't know about the deck below this one, then Stone didn't either. But what if he was wrong?

The cache had to be intact. If Stone or any of the prior Governors had known about it and used it, there would be evidence of it in destruction of the city. And the Governor's guards wouldn't be walking around with bows and arrows fashioned from Metro's limited number of trees. They would be toting fully loaded MK-12s.

Caleb grabbed the edge of the door with his left arm, pushing it easily aside. A musty smell escaped through the opening, causing him to wrinkle his nose.

"Pleasant," Dante said. "Yuck."

"Old grease and rust mixed with seriously stale air. I've smelled worse."

"I'm sure."

They entered the garage. Time wasn't a luxury, and Caleb immediately moved to the outer perimeter, staring down at the floor. He dropped to his knees, using his replacement hand to brush the dirt and debris away. If there was a hidden door in the floor, would he be able to find it?

"This could take all day, Sergeant," Dante said. "I know you don't want to wear a sheriff's uniform, but maybe that's the best option right now?"

"Tell me when we have ten minutes."

"You can't get dressed in ten minutes."

"I can be fashionably late."

"The Governor will have my head if you show up late."

"Do you mean that figuratively or literally?" Caleb asked. He was still trying to get a full impression of how Governor Stone liked to operate.

"He's not an evil man if that's what you mean. But he likes things to operate on his time. Yesterday, it might mean losing a meal chit and going hungry for a night. Today? I don't know."

"I'm going on the belief that he needs me more than I need him," Caleb said. He pointed to a pile of old drones near the wall. "See that garbage over there? Let's shove it aside. There may be a clue beneath it."

"What makes you say that?"

"Most of the crap in the garage is spread out across the floor. But that garbage is piled higher than everything else. Why?"

"Are you a Space Marine or a detective, Sergeant?"

"Raiders are trained to be observant, so I guess a bit of both."

"How about I sweep the floor, and you move the trash? I think it'll be more efficient considering your augmentation."

Caleb stood up. "Fair enough."

He crossed the room to the garbage pile. Was he wasting time down here when there were so many other things to do? Could searching for fresh weapons and ammunition ever be a waste of time considering where they were and what they were up against? He had no idea what they were up against. But that was the point.

He grabbed at the debris with his replacement hand, lifting away the carcasses of stripped down drones and dropping them to the side. It only took a minute to move the whole stack, the effort revealing a dented panel in the wall. It was bolted closed, but he ripped the cover away and exposed the wiring beneath.

He stared at it for a moment, tracing the different colored wires. One of them was disconnected, each end of it occupied by a clean and apparently unused connector. Had someone opened the panel once, discovered the unidentified wire inside, and then closed it again? Or had they found the cover and tried to get in but failed? Why was the panel dented?

"Dante," Caleb said, getting her attention.

"What is it, Sergeant?" she replied.

"I'm not sure. I've got a disconnected cable here. I'm going to plug it in."

"Roger that."

Caleb connected them. Nothing happened. "Damn it " he said.

"We stripped so many wires; maybe it's cut somewhere else in the wall?" Dante suggested. "Or maybe there's no power coming to the garage at all."

"We're keeping the engineers busy, aren't we?" Caleb said. "I'll have to get one of the Kings down here to look at it." He stood up. "I guess I'm getting a sheriff's uniform after all."

"It won't hurt, Sergeant. I promise."

"Tell me that when this starched collar rubs my neck raw."

He started crossing the room to join Dante at the door. He paused when he noticed a small, flashing glow escaping from behind a bit of debris.

"Dante, look at this," he said, directing her attention to the light. He pushed the scrap out of the way, revealing green LED illuminated behind the wall, the light projecting through microscopic holes in the surface and forming a simple toggle. "Ever seen this before?"

"You know I haven't."

"Think we could be this lucky?"

"I think we're due right about now."

"Agreed." Caleb reached out and tapped on the toggle, covering the light. As soon as he did, something made a loud clunking noise from somewhere below them. They both spun around to face the center of the room as the floor began to slowly sink away.

"Jackpot," Dante said, turning back to him and grinning. Caleb smiled back at her. It was almost too easy.

They stood aside as the floor continued to drop, scrap and debris tumbling off the edges and into the new hole. Caleb moved to the corner and looked down. He couldn't see anything but darkness around the edge of the moving floor.

"Down we go," he said, hopping off the edge and onto the platform. Dante hesitated a moment before jumping down behind him.

They rode the platform to the bottom. The new space remained dark until the lift settled with a sharp thunk that echoed across the area, the depth of sound a preview of its size.

Lights flashed on one at a time, spreading out around them and continuing across the length and width of the room. Caleb found himself spinning in a quick rotation, trying to take it all in.

Riley and the Reapers had brought the Deliverance here to fight a war.

They had just found their armory.

Chapter 6

"I don't know what to say," Dante said, making the same turn as Caleb, trying to take it all in.

It was impossible. The area was too large to absorb all at once. Caleb quickly recognized racks of MK-12s in the corner, hundreds of them, with stacked crates of ammunition piled high beside the weapons. He saw half a dozen armored drone carriers with full complements of weaponized drones. His eyes crossed over not one, but four of the robot Butchers, static and dark, waiting to be activated. Waiting to kill.

There was more. A pair of three-dimensional printers sat heavily against the wall, dozens of shipping containers aligned beside them, likely filled with raw materials for the machines, which could produce guns, bullets, and armor among other things. Looking in the other direction, Caleb found organized racks of combat armor and helmets, thousands of units strong.

"I think jackpot may be an understatement," he replied, forcing his mouth closed. He had expected a small armory. A few weapons, a few vehicles. He had underestimated the truth of Commands intent, and he had a feeling that as they got deeper into the equipment stored down here, he would find he was still underestimating it.

What else had Command sent to this place with them?

"I feel a little better about not dying," Dante said.

"Stay focused, Sheriff," Caleb replied. "Remember, these things can make you convince yourself you're dead. No amount of guns or armor is going to help with that."

Dante's face dropped. He hated to splash cold realization on her hope, but it was vital they kept their perspective.

"That's not to say that if they send trife after us, we won't at least have a chance to defend ourselves. It's a good find. An important find."

The floor of the Law Office garage had joined with a ramp leading to the floor of the new armory. Caleb walked down it, heading directly for the combat armor. "We'll get a team down here to take inventory as soon as we can. Washington can identify everything for you. He might not be able to speak, but he's as sharp as they come, and he knows his equipment. For now, I'm going to get suited up so I look the part of a…" Caleb's voice trailed off as he neared the racks of armor, his attention drawn to a shape on the floor. "Sheriff, do you know how to shoot a mark-twelve?"

"No, Sergeant," Dante replied. "Do I need to?"

Caleb didn't answer. He walked over to the shape on the floor. It was dark and thin, with shriveled leathery black flesh.

A xenotrife.

Caleb stood over it. Where had it come from? What was it doing here? He tapped it with his foot. It didn't move. It appeared to be dead, but he didn't see any external damage. Had it gotten trapped down here and starved?

"What is it?" Dante asked.

"A trife," Caleb replied.

He heard her walk over to where he was standing. "I've never seen one before," she said, pausing and looking down at it. "Disgusting. Is it...?"

"Dead. Yes. But there may be more."

Sheriff Dante continued staring at it, her eyes trailing from its head to its clawed hands and feet. "We need to tell Governor Stone about this." She tapped on her badge. The LED flashed red. "Are you kidding? I'm right under Law and there's no signal?" She tapped it again, getting the same result.

Caleb scanned the area. He didn't see any more corpses, but he did find a set of larger blast doors leading out toward the main hangar, right about where he had expected them to be. He also found another hatch against the port-side wall. "There must be something blocking it."

Dante stepped away from him, trying the badge a few more times. Finally, it flashed green.

"Zane, do you copy?" she said. "It's Dante."

"I copy, Dante," Zane replied, his voice mingled with static. "What's up?"

"I need you to get in touch with Governor Stone. Tell him we're checking on something critical, and won't make it back for his address."

"Something critical? Can you be more specific?" Sheriff Zane asked.

"Not right now."

"Sam, that's not a good idea."

"It can't be helped. Just do it."

"He'll have your head."

"Things have changed, Hector. If Stone doesn't change with them, he won't be Governor for long."

Zane was silent for a few seconds, taken off-guard by her response. "I'll pretend I didn't hear that and pass your message on."

"Thank you."

"De nada. Whatever it is you're up to, be safe."

"Copy that," Dante said, tapping on her badge to disconnect it.

"Sheriff," Caleb said. "I need to stay down here and make sure the area is clear. But you should go topside."

"Governor Stone told me to work with you, Sergeant. Not for you." Dante walked over to a control terminal paced beside the platform and tapped on the toggle to send the floor of the garage back up. "Teach me how to use the mark-twelve, or whatever it is, and I'll be good to go."

Caleb stared at her, their eyes meeting. "Not my decision then, is it?"

"Nope. Look at the bright side, Sergeant."

"There may be trife under Metro, but there's a bright side?"

She smiled. "At least you get to be down here with me instead of up there with the governor, addressing twenty-thousand colonists."

"Here's hoping you're the only other living thing down here with me."

"Roger that."

Chapter 7

It took Caleb ten minutes to get himself and Sheriff Dante into combat armor, another five to get the ATCS booted and networked and five more to give her his quick start instruction on handling the MK-12. Fortunately, since she already knew how to aim and shoot a weapon, the assisted aiming functionality of the combat system would make up for her inexperience with the specific gun.

"I don't know if I should feel better or worse," Dante said, cradling the rifle in her arms. Caleb could barely see her eyes through the glass of her helmet, noticing they were wide with a measure of fear and excitement. "We had all of this to work with, and we still lost."

Caleb pointed at the dead trife. "Imagine a million of those things charging a position occupied by a thousand soldiers. It didn't matter what equipment we had. It didn't matter how many we killed for each one of us that died. Eventually, we ran out of bullets, cell charges, battery power, you name it."

He shuddered at the thought. He had been in the middle of one of those assaults. He had watched dozens of

Marines die around him. The Vultures had made it out because they were lucky, not because they were good.

"But we were supposed to fight them here with the same equipment?"

"No. I think this was plan B, in case Valentine and her team couldn't get the science right. Either way, this was always going to be a one-way trip. A suicide mission. Maybe they figured that if they couldn't win the fight, they could at least learn something and send it back to Proxima before they died. I don't know. I never got a chance to ask her for the rest of the details. We use what we have, and we hope it's enough. That's all we can do."

"Roger that, Sergeant. I'm ready to roll."

Caleb checked the HUD of his ATCS. There were no threats in their immediate vicinity. If there were any living trife down here, they either didn't know Caleb and Dante were there or they were steering clear of them.

They headed for the smaller hatch at the end of the cavernous armory, bypassing the ADCs and circling past a series of armored personnel vehicles and a set of larger drones. Neither of them had any idea how large this deck-between-decks was, but Caleb imagined it was probably close to the size of Metro proper.

What else would they find down here? He wasn't sure he wanted to know.

The hatch opened as they approached it, and Caleb led Dante out into a corridor that seemed to go on forever, running out of sight to their right, and ending at around the same position as the blast doors on their left. There were more doors along the side of the passageway.

"We'll never be able to search them all," Dante said.

Caleb used his eyes to navigate the ATCS, setting a timer and syncing it to Dante's SOS. "One hour," he said. "You head left. I'll go right."

"You want to split up?"

"Not ideal, but we'll cover more ground."

"Roger that. What if I see a trife?"

"It'll register as a threat in my HUD, and I'll come running. Engage as needed, and make sure you keep an eye on the network strength and the ammo counter for your rifle. You don't want to run out of either."

"Got it."

"Also, the easiest way to kill a trife is to shoot it here or here." Caleb pointed to a similar spot in the center of his chest, and right above the bridge of his nose.

"Okay."

"Good hunting, Sheriff."

"You too, Sergeant."

Caleb turned right, while Dante went left. He walked quickly to the nearest hatch, which slid open at his approach, revealing an empty storage area. It was small compared to the armory, dark and barren. He moved on, hurrying to the next door. That one led to another long corridor that traveled the width of Metro.

He considered it for a moment before retreating to the original passage, continuing along it for the next few minutes, opening a few of the doors. Each of the rooms he checked was empty, leading him to reconsider the branching passage. He adjusted his visor, zooming in on the passage ahead until he could see the bulkhead in the distance. There was still no sign of more trife.

He decided to go back to the first passage, slipping through the hatch and closing it behind him. "Dante, sitrep," he said.

"Nothing to report, Sergeant," she replied. "Just a few empty rooms and what looked like a library."

"A library?"

"Yeah, a whole bunch of printed operations manuals, I

think for the ship? Maybe in case the mainframe went offline? I don't know. I figured there wasn't any time to browse."

"Good thought."

Caleb made his way down the new corridor, checking his HUD in between searches of the doors lining the passageway. His ATCS sensors were as dead as the trife he had found. Were they wasting their time down here? The trife had to come from somewhere. Then again, if there wasn't enough sustenance to keep it alive, how could there be any live ones left?

He glanced at the timer. Twenty minutes had passed, and there was still no hint of anything alive beside him and Sheriff Dante. He stopped moving, turning to the hatch on his left. He might as well check one more before he called off the hunt. There was nothing down here. He was as sure of it as he could be.

"Dante, pick one more door and then meet me back at the armory."

"Are you sure, Sergeant?"

"Yeah. I don't think there's anything down here. That trife starved. If there were more, they probably starved too. We have more important priorities."

"Roger. I'm at one last door now. Also, it looks like there's another exit seal down the passageway here. It's marked like the one you came in through."

Caleb used the ATCS to bring up a feed from her helmet camera. He could see the hatch ahead of her. They had no way of opening it yet, but that was probably a good thing. It kept the city easier to defend. "It may lead into the airlock. I don't know. This place is more of a maze than I pictured."

"You should try walking the splits sometime if you want to see a maze."

"Maybe you can give me a tour once things settle down."

"Copy that, Sergeant. I'd be glad to."

Caleb reached for the control panel to the hatch, splitting his attention to watch Dante do the same. Both doors slid open nearly simultaneously.

A black form came into view through the feed. Caleb was about to shout a warning when something equally dark slammed into him.

Chapter 8

The impact was barely powerful enough to shift him, but the claws that slashed across his helmet made him take the threat seriously. He jumped back, grabbing his MK-12 and swinging it across his body, slapping it into the trife. The demon's hollow bones broke beneath the blow. It rolled away from him and didn't move again.

Caleb glared into the room. It wasn't an empty storage area like most of the others. Instead, he noticed metal crates that had been torn open, an assortment of tools scattered recklessly across the floor. Near the center, a pile of batteries for the devices and a small group of trife huddled around it, clutching the power source to their flesh to keep themselves alive.

The group rose and turned his way, hissing in fear and warning. Caleb shifted his attention to Dante's feed, breath catching when he saw a trife head closing on her, teeth bared. He flicked his eyes to the threat display, marking nearly a dozen trife around her. Damn it.

He lifted his rifle, aiming at the trife. They were standing between him and the pile of batteries, but other than the one near the door, none of them were attacking. They stared at him as if confused, their surprised hisses growing softer. Then they did something he never thought he would see a trife do.

All at once, they sank back to the floor, turning their heads to expose their necks. Submitting.

Caleb's finger rested on the trigger. It would be easy to kill them, and probably the right thing to do. But even two years of watching these creatures destroy everyone and everything around him wasn't enough to convince him to kill them in cold blood. He hit the control panel for the door, closing it. He took a step back, waiting a few seconds for the demons to emerge. They didn't.

What the hell?

He didn't have time to think about it. He broke back the way he had come. Dante was on the retreat, moving away from the room where she had found the trife. There were already three dead demons on the floor ahead of her, and the rest of the group was on the move, preparing to attack.

"Dante, I'm on my way," Caleb said.

"Hurry," she replied.

She was trained well enough to notice the trife were preparing to rush her, offering too many targets for her to handle at once. He had to get there to even the odds.

"Are you hurt?" he asked. He could see Dante's vitals in his HUD, but that didn't mean she hadn't twisted an ankle or something.

"Negative," she replied. "They scared the shit out of me, but..."

She stopped talking when the trife made their move, pouring from the room, a few of them leaping across to the opposite wall, a pair jumping and grabbing the top of the corridor, the rest emerging and rushing across the floor.

The MK-12s had the secondary ordnance launcher, but he hadn't found any in his quick search of the ammo boxes.

Dante was smart enough not to stand her ground. She broke into a run, firing wildly over her shoulder. Caleb cursed again, pushing himself a little harder. He reached the end of the adjacent corridor, sliding beneath the opening hatch and hitting the wall. He bounced to his feet, getting moving again in the direction Dante had gone.

He checked his HUD. The trife were gaining on her, the larger group as eager to attack humans as ever, making the second group even more strange. He would worry about that later. He was closing the distance, nearing the turn in the passageway.

He came to a stop, dropping to a knee and leveling his rifle. "Dante, I'm right around the corner. Run right past me."

"Roger," she replied, breathing hard.

Caleb watched the marks on his HUD, the trife getting too close to Dante. She was almost at the turn, coming hard.

She appeared around the bend, slowing to make it around the corner. A trife appeared right behind her, diving forward and catching her ankle. It tripped her up, sending her barreling into the wall, hitting hard.

Caleb pulled the trigger, firing a single round that caught the trife in the head. He stood as Dante stumbled, forgetting his first plan and charging the struggling sheriff.

She hit the ground and rolled over, keeping her wits and bringing her rifle up. Caleb fired over her head, taking out three more trife. One of the demons on the ceiling dropped toward her, its head vanishing as she released a burst of rounds at it. Another leaped on top of her, thrown off by Caleb's follow-up volley.

He made it to the corner, grabbing a trife in his

replacement hand and bashing it against the wall. He spun and fired into two more, creating a barrier that allowed Dante to stand. She joined the defense, shooting at the remaining trife and quickly cutting them down.

"Clear!" Caleb shouted as the last mark on his HUD changed color. Instinct caused him to check his ammo levels first, his vitals second, Dante's vitals third, and her ammo level fourth before he physically turned to face her. "Are you okay?"

"Yes," she replied. "Barely." She was still breathing hard, her chest heaving beneath the SOS. "I think I like being a sheriff better than being a soldier."

"You did great," Caleb said.

"What the hell was that?"

Caleb looked down at the dead trife. A small group. No queen. He hadn't noticed any efforts at reproduction, but he had barely gotten more than a glimpse.

"I'm not sure yet. I encountered a smaller group back that way. They submitted to me. They seemed afraid."

"You sound unsure."

"I've never seen a scared trife before. Even when we had the drop on them, they always attacked. It's like there's something wrong with that group."

"Maybe they were hiding from this bunch?"

"I can't rule it out. Come on. We have to make sure your area is clear."

"You want to go back?"

"It's not a question of want. We need to go back. If these things were to find their way into Metro..." He shook his head. "David told me Riley had a stash of trife somewhere. Maybe this was them."

"What was she using them for?"

"Making monsters. I didn't think she had access to this area though, especially from outside Metro."

He was starting to hate how every new experience led to a new mystery. Why couldn't anything ever be simple?

"Okay. I'm ready to go back," Dante said.

Caleb put his hand on her shoulder and squeezed lightly, putting his helmet against hers so their eyes met. "You did a great job. I've seen experienced Marines wet themselves the first time they encountered a trife."

"Who says I didn't wet myself?"

"You stayed calm."

"Mostly."

"You didn't get killed."

"Luckily."

"Then you handled it as well as any of us."

Caleb pulled away from her, walking back toward the source of the attack. Dante stayed right behind him, keeping an eye on the rear.

"Did you get a look at the room?" Caleb asked while they walked.

"Not really. I can tell you it was warm in there."

"Did you see a nest?"

"I don't know what a nest looks like."

"Right." Caleb had forgotten Dante wasn't accustomed to the trife. She had done especially well against them, all things considered. "It looks like a mound of trife, covered in a sticky substance. If there were a queen in there, you probably would have known it."

"A queen?"

"The trife use the substance to pass around genetic material. If there's enough fuel to build a large enough nest, they'll make a queen to rule over it." He held up his replacement arm. "That's how I lost the real one."

"It bit your arm off?"

He nodded. "Not completely off, but damaged it enough to make it useless. Marines don't do repairs like that. We do replacements. It was the one thing Riley did that was actually helpful."

"She gave it to you?"

"Yes. The shell is made from the alien's starship. Lightweight and strong as anything. Better than the real thing in this environment."

She smiled. "Do you miss the original?"

"I haven't had much time to miss anything."

They reached the source of the trife assault. Caleb put up his hand, slowing on the approach. He watched his HUD, letting the sensors on the ATCS do their job. He took point as he came around the corner into the room.

It was filled with small black columns that reminded him of the ship's reactor, at least fifty of them arranged neatly across the room. There was flashing LEDs on all of them, most of them red, a few green. A terminal was positioned ahead of them, its screen dark.

There were no trife in the room. Not anymore. No sign of a nest. No queen. To Caleb, it was as curious as the submissive group. He could feel the heat expelled by the columns. There should have been enough radiation output here to start a small colony at least.

"What do you think?" Sheriff Dante asked.

"It's strange," Caleb replied.

He walked over to the terminal, tapping the control surface to activate the display. He expected it to open to a security screen. He thought it would ask him for his id and passcode. It didn't. The terminal was already unlocked.

Someone had been using it.

"Strange how?" Dante said.

"Even stranger now," Caleb replied. "How much do you know about navigating the ship's operating systems?"

"Less than Klahanie, probably more than you?"

"Probably," Caleb agreed. "Why don't you see if you

can figure out what this terminal is for, and maybe how it was being used?"

"Roger that, Sergeant."

They switched positions. Caleb decided to search between the monoliths while Dante worked.

"So, what's strange about it?" she repeated.

"For one, the trife shouldn't have been able to get down here. That's strange. Two, the group I found was submissive. Very strange. Three, this group had enough juice to make a nest but didn't. Even stranger. Four, someone was using that terminal and didn't bother to lock it. In fact, they seem to have disabled the automatic security lock, as if they didn't think they would remember their passcode. That's so strange I'm wondering if our enemy is masquerading as one of us instead of operating from the shadows."

He swept through the columns, turning the rifle left and right. He didn't expect to find anything. If there were trife still in here, they should have jumped him by now. But it never paid to be lazy about ensuring an area was safe. Not when he had the time.

He reached the back of the room, swinging to the left. He froze when his HUD outlined a form in the darkness of the corner. A corpse, long dead. The flesh and muscle were gone, only bone and cloth remaining. Cloth stained dark around half a dozen bullet entry points. Caleb moved to stand over it.

"Five, there's a corpse back here." It was unidentified, but judging by the size he assumed it was male. He stared down at it. He had a guess as to who it was. There was one person on Deliverance they hadn't accounted for. Harry, the computer engineer.

Maybe the whole thing wasn't as strange as he thought.

This had Riley Valentine written all over it.

Chapter 9

Caleb backed away from Harry's corpse, returning to Sheriff Dante and the terminal. "Anything?" he asked.

"This terminal is a direct link to the ship's mainframe," she replied. "We have full access to the complete datastore from here." She paused. "Or we would if half of it wasn't broken."

"I assume that's what the red lights mean?"

"Affirmative. What about the corpse?"

"One of Riley's Reapers. A computer engineer named Harry. He may be the reason for the red lights."

"Or Riley may have caused the red lights because of something Harry did?"

"Possibly. In either case, I think this confirms Riley was down here, and whatever is going on with these trife, she had something to do with it."

"How did she get down here?"

"I don't know. From what David told me, she was supposed to have access to Metro through the seal we broke. Her team had placed a device beneath it to keep it from locking fully, at least until the trife got through. Maybe she was using the seal you found?"

"It's right around the corner."

"Let's assume she got in that way. She brought the trife she had stashed down here for safe-keeping, and to keep them alive. She was awake for two years after I went into hibernation, so there's no way to know exactly when she entered the first time. It's still odd that there's no nest. If they weren't reproducing, she couldn't have been using them for her gene editing experiments. So what was she doing with them?"

"She must have done something to them," Dante said. "If they aren't acting the way you expected. If her goal was to control them, it could be she cut off their ability to reproduce. She might have even tried making them more tame and subservient."

"Slaves," Caleb said. "If she had an army of submissive trife to support her army of hybrids, it would leave the stronger hands free to fight while the weaker units carried out less important tasks."

"That hypothesis works for me, Sergeant."

"We'll go with that for now." Caleb paused. "You said you have full access to the complete datastore?"

"Any part of it that isn't damaged. There's a simple search mechanism if you want to look for something?"

"I do. I want the recordings of the Research Module from two hundred thirty-six years ago. I think getting a full picture of what Riley was doing will make everything we found more clear."

"Don't we have more important immediate concerns?"

"We do, but I want to leave here with something. We can get the rest of it later."

"Understood, and I agree. Let me run the query."

Dante's hands moved swiftly over the control surface, entering the query.

SEARCHING…

The search was short. Too short. Instead of a list of results, the display went dark. Then a recording started to play without their intervention. Dante glanced over at Caleb, who shrugged in response.

The recording was of the room they were currently standing in, taken from the left upper corner and showing a wide-angle view of the entire space. Caleb looked in that direction. He didn't see a camera, but he did see a small air vent where the camera might be placed.

"I didn't ask for this," Dante said.

"No," Caleb replied. "But I think someone wanted us to see it." Someone who knew that if someone had learned the truth, they might have come seeking evidence.

The screen was unchanged for about twenty seconds. Then someone entered the room.

"Harry," Caleb said, recognizing the Reaper right away.

Harry went directly to the display. He looked over his shoulder, clearly nervous. He must have known Riley was behind him. He started working the terminal, entering commands too quickly for Caleb to follow. He seemed to know exactly what he wanted to do.

He remained at the terminal for half a minute, tapping one final command and then running to the back of the room and ducking into the corner. He drew a pistol from his side right before he ducked beneath one of the mainframe servers, out of sight of the camera.

The recording returned to calm for a few more seconds. Then a new form entered the room. Beside him, Dante gasped. "What the hell is that?"

It wasn't Riley.

It was a human-trife Reaper.

The monstrous hybrid stepped into the room, head swinging back and forth, nostrils flaring. An instant later, it looked directly toward where Harry was hiding. Then it started in his direction.

"Stop."

Caleb recognized Riley's voice immediately. The Reaper stopped as Riley entered the room behind it, partially obscured by its body. The hybrid's presence confused him. Hadn't she lost control of all the hybrid Reapers before Harry died?

Not that it would be a surprise to learn she had lied about that too.

"Harry, there's no point in hiding," Riley said. "Everyone knows you're in here." She glanced at the terminal. "The question is, what did you do in here?"

Harry stood up, his face pale. "You're out of control, Riley. The people in Metro don't deserve what you plan to do with them."

"Oh please," Riley replied. "You weren't saying that before we boarded."

"I've been saying it for weeks and you know it. Ever since you killed Pratt and brought David in. I thought you would come to your senses, but since you haven't…here we are."

"Here we are," Riley repeated, looking around. Caleb guessed it was the first time she had entered the area. "I take it this is the central mainframe? I didn't know you knew how to get down here."

"I don't tell you everything anymore."

"The jilted lover. How dramatic. Didn't it occur to you it might be a mistake to give me access to this area from outside the city?"

"What can you do from here that you can't do from

somewhere else?" Harry raised his pistol, pointing it at her. "Do you think your pet can get in front of you before I pull the trigger?"

"I don't know. Why don't we find — "

Harry's weapon discharged. Caleb tracked the shot to Riley's chest, watching as it pierced her uniform, knocking her backward a step. Blood began to spread from the wound, and he watched in horror as it made only a small stain before the flow stopped.

Riley smiled. Harry's face fell. So did Caleb's.

"Shit," he said, looking at Dante. "We need to get back to Metro."

"What did I just see?" Dante replied.

"Evidence, but not the kind I was looking for. Let's move."

"What about the rest of the recording? What about the damaged servers?"

"We can deal with all that later. I don't know how long Riley is going to stay dead."

Chapter 10

Riley Valentine's eyes fluttered open. The first thing she noticed was that it was cold. Very cold. The next thing she noticed was the row of lights over her head.

Where was she?

She pushed herself up on her elbows, looking around. A morgue? What was she doing here?

She was naked and cold. A tray was resting beside her, lined with tools for an autopsy. She had died. That much was obvious. She didn't remember how. The last thing she could recall, she was in the hospital, waiting for Sergeant Card to get patched up so Sheriff Dante could bring them both to the Law Office and lock them up.

She smiled at the idea. Lock her up? She would have gone along with it, but not forever. She was the rightful governor of Metro. This was her mission to lead. Sticks and Stone weren't going to keep her from doing what she had come to do, despite the best efforts of David, the alien AI, and Caleb Card.

Someone had killed her. Did they know she had done the gene editing on herself? Obviously not. If they did, they would never have left her here, preparing to cut her open.

She slid off the table. She needed clothes. They were resting in a transparent bag on the counter. Her body armor was hanging nearby. She padded over to it, examining it. There was no sign of fresh damage. No blood stains. No obvious entry point for a weapon. Interesting. She crossed back to the bag holding her clothes, opening it and dumping them on the counter. Her panties were clean. Her undershirt clean. Everything was clean.

How had they killed her without soiling her clothes?

She wished she could remember what had happened. Why had the people of Metro turned on her? Had Governor Stone put them up to it? Had he assassinated her to keep her from taking control? Was Sheriff Dante the one who shot her?

It couldn't have been Sergeant Card. He was in the examination room with Doctor Brom. It had to be the sheriff or one of her deputies. That was the only choice that made sense.

If she saw the bitch, she was going to kill her.

She started pulling on her clothes, sliding her panties up. She heard the displacement of air as the door opened behind her.

"What the hell?" Doctor Brom muttered, dropping something onto the floor.

Riley turned around. "Doctor Brom. I want you to tell me what happened. Right now."

Brom was backing toward the door. "You. You're supposed to be dead. You were dead. I checked you myself."

He was retreating. Trying to escape. Riley couldn't let that happen. She leaped the distance across the room, carried by muscles stronger than any regular human's. She had conserved herself before, keeping her secret from Card and the Guardians, and later Governor Stone and his underlings. Now that the secret was revealed, there was no point in being shy about it.

She grabbed him by the arm, yanking him roughly back and around. He slammed into the counter, flailing as he stumbled to the floor.

"Doctor Valentine," he said. "Wait."

"Tell me what happened, Brom," she said. She leaned down, grabbing him by the neck and lifting him back to his feet. She was angry. Furious. She had been on fire for years, ever since the trife had taken her sister and put all of her hard work to waste. Now she felt like she was going to explode.

"You were dead. Clinically dead. For at least thirty minutes now."

"How did I die?"

"You shot yourself. Or rather, you tried to shoot yourself. The gun was empty. You died anyway."

"That's impossible." She said it, but she wasn't sure it was true.

"That's what happened. I swear it. How are you alive? Your brain has been without oxygen for a long time. Even if you started breathing again, you should be a vegetable."

"I'm resilient." She could see his face was turning pale, her grip on his neck cutting off his oxygen supply. She could barely contain her fury. If she had managed to finish her research earlier, if she had given the sequence to her sister, she would still be alive. She would be as strong as Riley was now.

"Please," Brom said. "Let me go."

"I committed suicide with an unloaded gun?" she asked.

"Yes," he confirmed.

"And you brought me down here to cut me open?"

"To understand why your body reacted the way it did to the hallucination."

"What was I doing before I shot myself? Did I say anything?"

"I don't know. I came out late. I only heard you say something about being the devil and making the hard choice."

"So they know."

"Know what?"

"Why I brought the Deliverance here."

Doctor Brom didn't say anything. He looked more frightened. Riley kept holding him, squeezing a little tighter. If the Governor knew what she had done, if he believed it, they would never let her take control. They would never let her finish her mission. Especially now that Card would know she had changed herself the way she had changed David. She was a threat they couldn't afford to ignore.

"Please," Brom said again, straining to get the words out. "I didn't do anything to you. Let me go."

"I'd like to let you go, Doctor," Riley said.

"Thank you," Brom replied.

"But you already know too much."

She squeezed even harder. It was enough to break Brom's neck, shattering his spine and leaving his head hanging limply in her grip, his body becoming heavy as he died.

She let his corpse fall to the floor. Murdering him didn't cool her fire. The act only fanned it, increasing her anger. Even if her original mission had gone completely sideways, she could still salvage some part of it. Command had let her come here for a reason. A purpose. She wasn't going to give up because she had run into a few roadblocks.

She finished dressing, putting on her clothes but not wasting time with the combat armor. She didn't need it, anyway. She took Brom's lab coat, sliding it over and buttoning it closed to give herself a more modest, professional appearance. As if her nearly bald head wouldn't give her away. She rifled through the drawers, grabbing a pair of laser scalpels. She wanted guns. She knew where to get them.

Then she left the morgue, making her way through the lower levels of the hospital and following the signs for the exit. She passed a couple of nurses along the way, smiling warmly and wishing them a good day. They eyed her with suspicion but didn't try to stop her. These colonists were the sheep the Deliverance had launched with, not the lions she had intended them to become.

She made her way out of the building. The streets were empty. Not a single colonist was nearby, giving her an eerie feeling that something had already gone horribly wrong for them. But the nurses would have been gone too if things were that bad. So where was everybody?

She turned to the south, looking down the central strand that cut through the heart of Metro. She had visibility all the way to the other side, and she found some of the colonists there, moving away from her. "Damn it," she cursed under her breath, her heart thumping hard in barely contained rage.

She had to go that way to get out, and she had been hoping to do it without notice.

At least she would find out what the hell was going on.

Chapter 11

Riley made her way south, following the tail of the colonists heading in the same direction. She stayed off to the side of the strand, hugging the sides of the run-down blocks and doing her best not to attract attention. At least whatever was happening out here had reduced the hospital to a skeleton crew. It meant she would have more time before anyone discovered poor Doctor Brom.

She hadn't gone far when she heard a noise to her left, down one of the narrow alleys that split the tightly-packed blocks from one another. She looked in that direction, catching a glimpse of a pair of law officers flanking a woman in gray overalls. They were moving slowly. As if they were looking for something. She smirked when she realized they were probably worried about the alien that had tried to kill her. If it had made her hallucinate it had to be nearby, and that was a definite danger to the population.

Or it would be if it had any intention of staying in the city. The AI Caleb had thrown out of the airlock wanted to get to the surface to escape. It had wanted off the Deliverance. Card and his Guardians had destroyed that one, but it appeared there was at least one more. How had it gotten on board? Where had it hidden for all these years? Or had their original enemy been as disposed of as she was?

Either way, she was going to destroy it too. It had tried to kill her, and she wasn't about to let that stand.

She passed the split, continuing south. It took a few minutes to come close enough to get a better idea of what the gathering was about. The area that had once been a park came into view, and Riley noticed that a flatbed transport had been driven into the center of it, with a simple microphone and speaker setup resting on the bed. There were deputies and members of the Governor's militia surrounding it, keeping the people a few meters back. She could make out a space to the right of the truck where she expected the Governor would walk.

He was going to address the colony. That much was obvious. He was going to have to tell them the truth about their situation, after years of maintaining the lie that they had never actually left Earth. Surprise.

The Governor's progenitors had been stupid to hide the truth and cause the colony to forget. If he didn't handle his speech the right way, he was going to have a panicked population on his hands.

Good. Panic would make it easier for her to slip past the crowd and into the engineering passages, back to the broken seal and then down to the lower levels. She had to get back to the armory that had been secreted away beneath the city. She could get anything she needed down there.

She knew there was an entrance to the armory from inside Metro too, but the wires had never been connected to keep the colonists from accidentally discovering the stash. It would be far faster and easier to circle around and use her clearance to get into the second seal, and from there she could gear up for her expedition into the Essex wilderness.

The alien AI wanted to go somewhere, which meant she wanted to go there too.

She was nearing the outer gathering of colonists when the soft rumble of their collective voices began to fade. She looked to the lane on the right of the transport, finding Governor Stone walking purposefully along it, joined by a woman Riley assumed was his wife. Their faces were stoic, forced into expressionless solidarity. They had to put on a brave face while they dealt with the death of their child. A death Sergeant Card should have prevented.

The colonists didn't cheer for their Governor. They were too nervous for that. They fell completely silent without prompting as he climbed onto the transport, making himself more visible. His wife was a pretty woman, with long reddish hair and a round face. She wore a silver suit that elegantly hugged her frame.

Riley glanced back to the aisle. Where was Caleb? Where was Sheriff Dante? Shouldn't they have been here? If they were both missing, they were probably together. If they were both missing, they were probably involved in something they considered more important.

She remembered mentioning the armory to Caleb. Had he gone searching for it? She growled under her breath. Stupid. She should never have told him about it, but she hadn't expected things to shake out the way they had, with David getting involved and Caleb moving against her.

Her hands clenched into fists. Damn them all.

She continued to emit a low, guttural growl, forcing herself to stifle it when some of the nearby colonists turned to look. She smiled tensely, edging around the crowd and circling toward the engineering hatch, all while keeping an eye on Governor Stone. If Caleb was looking for the armory, she had to hurry and get there before he did. She could handle him if he were unarmed or if she took him by surprise, but otherwise—he had killed the trife queen and cut down her hybrid Reapers—he wasn't exactly an easy mark.

She would prefer not to confront him. She hated him for what he had done, but her hatred could wait. If the AI got too far ahead of her, she would never be able to follow it.

"Citizens of Metro," Governor Stone said, drawing her attention. He had positioned himself behind the microphone, his wife fading into the background behind him. "Today is an amazing day. A life-changing day. Today is the day we decide what kind of future is in store for all of us in the city. Today is the day we determine a new path, our path, into this future. Let me explain." He paused, glancing back at his wife, who nodded in support. Then he scanned the crowd, turning on the bed of the transport to make eye contact with the colonists.

Riley turned away as his eyes crossed her position, preventing him from recognizing her. She turned back when the microphone popped and whined as he grabbed it and pulled it from its stand. Then she started skirting the crowd again.

"I know you're all feeling confused and probably a little frightened. I know you're wondering what all the shaking was about. I'm sure you've heard by now that the seals that have protected us for all of these years are broken and that soldiers have visited us from outside."

He paused while some of the crowd began to murmur again, either in surprise at the rumors they hadn't heard, or surprise that the stories were true.

"We all know what happened in Metro's history. We all know about the unrest. The infighting. The Stone family's involvement in restoring order. We've lived peacefully since then, a simple existence that, while challenging, has kept us close to one another as we waited out the war raging beyond our walls. I want to remind all of you about that closeness. I want to remind all of you of the importance of our solidarity as we confront what comes next. "*And what comes next?* you're probably asking. Hell, in part I'm still asking myself that very question."

Governor Stone paused again. He was using silence well, the dramatic pauses pulling the crowd in and over to his side. He was a charismatic speaker. Much better in front of a crowd than he had been in person. He was comfortable and in control.

Riley glanced over to the south wall. She could see the hatch now, about fifty meters away. It was closed, but that wasn't a problem. Her chip would let her through. She started toward it, freezing when it opened. A moment later, a near mob of militiamen poured out of the opening, surrounding someone in the center. Riley watched closely, trying to get a glimpse of the figure they appeared to have captured. The alien AI? That couldn't be.

"I'll tell you what it means," Governor Stone said. "You see, my friends, we've been lied to. Tricked. Treated like cattle herded to the slaughter. That shaking you felt earlier? It wasn't an earthquake or an explosion. The soldiers who visited Metro? They didn't come to tell us we were free. No, they came to tell us that we're *not* free. That we've been their prisoners all along. Cattle, my friends. Packed onto a starship and launched into space, sent light years from home to fight a war we didn't ask for. A war we didn't agree to."

Riley's heart thumped in her chest, her anger shifting to confusion. What the hell was the Governor doing?

His men were pushing through the crowd, forcing it to part. She got a look at the person in the middle now. She wasn't sure whether to laugh or feel sorry for Private Flores.

A fearful pitch was rising in the crowd, the citizens of Metro struggling to deal with the Governor's words. Riley could hardly believe how Stone was turning the truth around on the very Marines who had protected them from the Reapers. Who had saved them from the chaos she had accidentally wrought. They had crashed on an alien world, and he was turning on the only people who could help them?

"That's right, my friends," Governor Stone said. "The soldiers told me what they intended. They weren't concerned about what we might think. They think we're weak. They think we can't take care of ourselves. They think we would collapse under the pressure of their demands, and take up arms without provocation when in honesty, all we want is to live our lives in peace. Am I right?"

The crowd erupted in cheers of support. The militia lifted Private Flores, pushing her up on stage. She was still in her combat armor, her helmet removed. She had bruises on her face. She hadn't been taken without a fight.

A few of the guards joined her, keeping a grip on her and tugging her forward.

"This is the face of our true enemy, my friends. This is the face of the despicable liars who locked us in this city, held us against our will, carried us centuries and millions of light years from home, forced us to live in squalor, and sent us on a deadly journey to a world where we don't belong. This is the face of the enemy who killed my daughter Orla, murdering her in cold blood!"

The guards held Flores while the crowd became more agitated. Riley almost did feel sorry for the Marine. She had no love for Flores, but none of the marines deserved the betrayal the Governor was committing to.

"What do you think we should do to our captors?" Governor Stone said. "We outnumber them by a hundred to one. They can't make us do anything we don't want to do. This is our future to decide. Do we want to become soldiers in their war? Or do we want to settle peacefully? If there are any other intelligent life forms here, we can talk to them, negotiate with them, and live our lives in peace and comfort. But this isn't just for me to decide. Give me your opinion, my friends. Do we lock her up or let her go?"

The crowd was so enraged they had already forgotten all about the fact that they were on a starship that had crashed on an alien world. They were too concerned with the enemy they could see to worry about the real enemy outside.

"Lock her up!" some of them started shouting.

"Kill her!" someone else said. "Kill her!"

The chant shifted quickly from imprisonment to death. Governor Stone looked at Flores, eyes wild, face curled into a wicked grin.

"Kill her," the crowd shouted. "Kill her! Kill them all!"

Riley shook her head. The Governor was an idiot. He was making a horrible mistake that was going to get them all killed.

But that wasn't her problem anymore.

She turned and ran for the engineering hatch, the crowd a hateful mob behind her. She slipped away.

Nobody noticed.

Chapter 12

Caleb and Sheriff Dante didn't linger in the server room. They rushed back to the corridor and headed back toward the armory. Caleb's heart rose to his throat, his instinct telling him that Riley's false death was going to become a problem in a hurry if it wasn't already.

He could barely believe what the out of control doctor had done, or how well she had covered up her enhanced strength and healing factor. There hadn't been any indication that she had used the CRISPR editing sequence on herself, becoming the same essentially super-human that she had made David into.

In hindsight, he should have guessed. Riley had managed to disable David after all, putting a bullet in his head and keeping him down long enough for his body to be pulled out of the airlock along with Sho and the alien AI. He had assumed she had caught him off-guard and disabled him before he could react. Riley was smart and he forgot sometimes how devious she was, but surely he would have noticed an increase in her overall intelligence as David had exhibited.

-Regardless, they had to get to her before she woke up, if that was still possible. If she found out what Caleb had told the the governor and Sheriff Dante, among others, that her dirty laundry had been aired, there was no saying what she might do. The recording they had found only cemented her guilt, offering proof of her plan to use the colony. What would she do if Caleb were to bring that recording to light?

He could already imagine.

They hurried back to the armory, rushing through the hatch toward the lift. They were halfway to it when Caleb's ATCS suddenly lit up, revealing there was someone to their right. It he marked the individual as a threat and signalled him to take evasive action.

He grabbed Dante's wrist with his replacement hand, using its strength to throw her to the ground behind one of the APCs, at the same time he broke in the opposite direction, diving behind a second machine. The ground between them erupted in sparks and ricocheting shells, the sudden burst of gunfire echoing loudly in the enclosed space, though his helmet helped dull the roar.

Caleb rolled to his feet, pressing against the vehicle. He checked Dante's vitals on his HUD. She was alive and unharmed, hidden behind the APC.

His ATCS was tracking the shooter as best it could, using the noise of the gunfire to estimate position and movement. Radio waves bounced out from his helmet, painting a view of the room and putting their opponent in it. Whoever it was, he or she had been firing an MK-12 at them.

"Dante, did you get a look at the target?" Caleb asked.

"Negative," she replied.

"I'm going to see if I can get an ID. Be ready to cover me."

"Roger. I've got your back."

Caleb began moving along the side of the APC, toward the rear of the vehicle. His ATCS was tracking the target, showing their assailant moving toward the center of the carrier and splitting the difference since they couldn't know what side the target would emerge from.

He reached the rear corner, sweeping his rifle around the edge. Just because the ATCS said the target was somewhere, he wasn't going to follow it blindly. He had only made that mistake once.

The system was right. Their attacker wasn't there. Caleb edged across the rear of the APC, checking on Dante. She hadn't moved, remaining ready near the corner of the second vehicle. The target hadn't moved either. Whoever it was, he or she was waiting for him to show his face. There was a fifty percent chance he would get shot the moment he popped out.

He didn't like those odds.

"Dante, I'm going to circle back. I want you to move out into the open."

"What?"

"Cross the center at a run. Unless our target's a crack shot, they won't hit you."

"Are you kidding?"

"We're wasting time here, Sheriff. I've got your back, just like you had mine. You run, the bastard will follow. I'll break cover and take them from the rear. Okay?"

"Roger."

"Call the mark, Sheriff."

"We go in three, Sergeant. One… Two…"

"Sergeant Caaaaarrrdd!"

"Dante, hold!" Caleb barked, stomach sinking again.

"Caleb, can we just agree to put the guns away and talk for a minute?" Riley asked.

"How do I know you won't shoot me as soon as I come out into the open?"

"I should ask you the same thing. You're the one with the tactical."

"Unlike you, I'm not a manipulative psychopathic liar."

"That hurts, Sergeant. Really. We're supposed to be on the same side."

"No. My orders were to protect the colonists. Apparently, your orders were to get them all killed."

"Come on, Sergeant. Not this again. We came here to a fight a war. Do you remember that? The war? I'm coming out, Caleb. You can shoot me if you want, but I guarantee I can kill you before you kill me."

Caleb stayed silent. He couldn't argue with that.

"Sergeant, I think I can get a shot on her if you move into the open," Dante said.

"Negative, Sheriff," Caleb replied. "Stand down. We're nothing without our honor."

"She doesn't have any."

"Exactly."

"Roger, Sergeant."

Caleb shifted his rifle, snapping it to the back of the SOS. Then he lifted his helmet, taking it off and walking around the corner of the APC.

Riley wasn't there.

"Valentine?" Caleb said.

"Here, Sheriff," Riley said, emerging from between the two APCs. She had her rifle against Dante's back, leading her into the open.

"Damn it, Valentine," Caleb said. "You have no idea what a truce means, do you?"

"Believe it or not, I do," Riley said. She lowered her gun and shoved Dante forward, sending her stumbling to the ground closer to Caleb. "You still think I'm the bad guy, don't you, Sergeant? You still don't get it. Do you think because we lost Earth this war is over? Do you think the enemy won't figure out some of us escaped? Do you think they won't come to finish us off? We had one chance to stop it, and you helped ruin that chance. Now we have one shot to learn as much as we can about them before they kill every last one of us. Do you want to ruin that too?"

"These people don't belong here," Caleb insisted.

"It doesn't matter. They're here now. You can try to protect them, but I don't know if they deserve it."

"What does that mean?"

"I'm going out there to track the enemy," Riley said. "You're an idiot if you think it's staying in Metro when all it wanted was to reach the surface. You have a choice to make, Sergeant. You can follow me and try to kill me, or you can stay here and try to stop Governor Stone from killing Private Flores."

"What are you talking about?" Sheriff Dante said, getting back to her feet.

"Did you give any thought to how the Governor was going to settle up on his family's lie? You know, the one where the colony is on Earth buried underground, only now it isn't?"

Caleb stared at Riley. "You can't be serious."

"I'm totally serious, Sergeant. He sold you out to save his own ass. Last I saw, he had Flores on display and an angry mob screaming for her head."

Caleb's jaw clenched. He wished he could believe Riley outright, instead of wondering if she was spinning another web of deceit. "What about Washington?"

"I didn't see him. He might have gotten away."

"Damn it, Valentine. How can I believe you?"

"How can you not? You can't take the risk. Not unless you want Flores' blood on your hands. Isn't there enough already? I don't know if Stone would have gone this route if Orla had survived."

The comment stung. Of course, Caleb was sure Riley intended it that way. She was right. They both knew it. He didn't have a choice.

"You know what I'm going to do," Caleb said. "Get out of here, Riley. I'll catch up to you later."

"Part of me hopes you do," Riley replied. "Honestly."

"Whatever. Get the hell out of here."

Riley didn't say anything else. She turned and ran back between the vehicles, disappearing from sight.

Caleb yanked his helmet back on, tense and angry. "Dante, you heard her. I'm not about to let Stone put Flores to death. You need to pick a side."

"I know the truth, Sergeant. I'm with you. I don't know how many others will be."

"Understood. I never thought I'd be glad the colony ran out of bullets. Let's go."

Chapter 13

Caleb's heart thumped hard, his pulse raced. He was worried. More worried that he had been through any of the challenges he had faced since boarding the Deliverance. It was one thing to go to battle against the trife. They were the invaders. They were the enemy.

It was another to suddenly be at war with his own kind.

On one hand, he couldn't believe Governor Stone had turned on him and the other Guardians this way, especially after he had been so composed and focused back at the hospital, taking in Caleb's input and rightfully releasing the Guardians to continue their work. Stone's reaction hadn't cast any doubt in Caleb's mind that he would do the right thing for the people.

Maybe he had been too quick to jump to that conclusion.

Yes, Orla had died, but she had helped Caleb save Stone's life, along with the lives of the other twenty-six thousand colonists on the Deliverance. To use them as fodder to take the brunt of the populace's anger over the lie the Governor and his family had perpetuated for the last three generations was weak and spineless.

At the same time, he could almost understand the Governor's point of view. Angry and hurting over the loss of his child. Angry over the thought of losing control of his people. Desperate to keep them in line. The Guardians were the perfect scapegoat. Warriors who knew the truth but had kept the colonists locked away for centuries.

Riley's actions and motives had only made it worse.

If Caleb had been up on stage with the Governor instead of under the city, would Stone have used him as the target of the crowd's anger? He assumed he would have, though Caleb doubted he would have been as easy to control as Flores. For all of the evil Riley had perpetrated, she had given him the replacement arm that allowed him to keep fighting. She had turned his loss at the hands of the trife queen into a lasting strength. He still wasn't completely sure why.

She kept claiming they weren't enemies. And maybe there was some truth to that statement. They were both Marines. Both were fighting the same war, but coming at it from opposite ends. She wanted to protect all of humankind, while his orders and his mission were to protect the colony. The way she did business was despicable. She lied, cheated, manipulated and used people. He could never see eye-to-eye with her on that. But at the root of it, she was still fighting for humanity.

Maybe it was better they had parted ways. Riley knew she couldn't take control of the colony. Not anymore. In an hour or two she would be long gone, out into a wilderness that nobody else on the Deliverance had gotten the chance to explore. Was it dangerous out there? Was the enemy lurking nearby? He still had no idea, and neither did

Governor Stone. Turning on the only people who could help protect them was short-sighted at best.

Catastrophic at worst.

The colony had no real weapons, save for their bows and arrows. They could salvage a few guns and explosives from the main hangar, but it wouldn't last them very long. They didn't know about the armory and the cache of weapons inside it. And Caleb had no intention of telling them any time soon. Once they returned to the Law Office, he would pull the wires and hide the panel again. He couldn't afford to let them get their hands on military weaponry. Not while Flores was in danger.

The lift stopped, shuddering as it merged with the floor of the Law Office's garage. Caleb broke for the wiring that powered the platform, reaching out to grab the wires.

"Sergeant, what are you doing?" Dante asked.

"We can't let them get their hands on those guns."

Caleb felt Dante's hand grab his shoulder. "Sergeant, we're on an alien world. A world we have to assume is hostile, considering we were supposed to fight a war here. You can't keep our only means of defending ourselves out of our hands."

"I didn't make that decision, Sheriff. Stone did. If we're going to help Flores, if we're going to help any of them, we can't let him get his hands on the guns. He'll use them to solidify his power before he uses them to defend the colony."

"That may be true, but at least he'll be able to defend the colony. We can't leave them standing out there like trees waiting to be cut down."

Caleb's hand wrapped around the wire. He yanked the connectors away from one another, standing and reaching for the panel that covered the area.

"If we give them these weapons, we'll lose control. And we won't be able to get it back. You know what that means, don't you? Even if we save Flores, we can't stay here. Not only will Stone be after us, but the whole damn colony will want our heads. And, it'll make everything he said about the Guardians true."

Dante took a few seconds to respond. "I know, Sergeant. You're on the right side of the truth, but the wrong side of reality. It's already too late to convince the colonists otherwise. To be honest, you never had a chance."

Caleb turned his head back, glaring at her through his helmet. She was right. The people had a healthy fear of Governor Stone. They also trusted him. He kept them safe. He kept them in line. The Guardians were nothing to them. At least, they had been nothing. Now they were the wardens of a prison that had carried them forty light-years from home, with no way to return. He had been dependent on Stone doing the right thing for the people, and Stone had let him down.

"Damn it," he muttered. "This is getting uglier by the second." He paused. "I know I asked you to pick a side a few minutes ago. I think you picked the wrong one. The colony needs you, Sheriff. More than I do."

"You can't do this alone, Sergeant. And I'm not going to let Governor Stone kill an innocent person, no matter what that means for me. It's against every sense of decency I have and every oath I took when I became a sheriff."

Caleb nodded. "Okay, and thank you." He grabbed the panel and pressed it back into the wall, covering the disconnected wires. "Keep your helmet on, and try not to let anyone see that it's you."

"Stone knows I was with you, Sergeant."

"I know. But he'll forgive you for helping me in the end."

"What do you mean, forgive me? Aren't I coming with you?"

"No. Once we free Flores, I don't just want you to stay here. I need you to stay here. Somebody who knows the truth has to have some pull inside the colony. You have to do your best to help them defend it."

"I'm not the only sheriff in Metro."

"But you're the only one who knows everything about me, Riley, and the alien AI, and that could be important. You're the only person here I trust, and that's important too."

"Roger that. Okay. So how do I keep Governor Stone from killing me once we stop him from killing Flores, assuming he hasn't already?"

"You're going to bring him here. You're going to show him what we found. Tell him the truth. Tell him you couldn't let him execute someone in good conscience. As long as he can maintain his lie and keep the anger focused on the Guardians unless he's more of a monster than I think he is, that should be enough to satisfy him. Especially if he values your work as a sheriff."

"I think he does. Or did, before all this." She hesitated. "Stone has a brother, Josh. He's been interested in me for a while now, and I'm too old to be single. Maybe I can cut a deal if it comes to that."

"I would never ask you to do that."

"I know. But we're cut from the same cloth, Sergeant. We both want to protect our own."

"Roger that," Caleb replied. He put his hand out. Dante took it. They shook on it, sealing the deal.

"So," Dante said. "What do we do now?"

Caleb opened his mouth to answer, but a sudden change in his helmet's overlay showed a new connection joining the network. He couldn't hold back his smile as he opened a comm channel.

"Washington, it's damn good to see you."

Chapter 14

Washington replied by pinging the network, opening and closing his comm channel in a rapid succession of Morse Code clicks. Not only did it let him communicate at a distance, it also confirmed to Caleb that the big Marine was really the person he was speaking to.

Jumped us. Took her. Escaped.

"I know," Caleb said. "I'm glad you did. Where are you?"

Alley. South.

"How close to Law?"

No.

The answer meant he didn't know. He wouldn't know where the Law Office was. Caleb checked his HUD. The signal was too weak to stream from Wash's camera and get an idea where he was. The tactical was putting him about a klick away.

"What about the hospital?"

Close.

"Do you know if Flores is still alive?"

Yes.

Caleb felt the relief flood through him. At least they weren't too late to help her. "Do you know where she is?"

Hospital.

Caleb glanced at Dante. "Why would Stone bring her to the hospital?"

"I don't know," she replied. "Maybe she was injured when he put her on display?"

"So they're going to patch her up to execute her?"

"What if Doctor Valentine was lying about that? Maybe they aren't going to killed her after all."

"Wash, did you catch any of Governor Stone's address?"

Yes.

"Are we in trouble?"

Yes.

"Wash, Riley is alive. We ran into her. She told us what happened, but I wasn't sure it was true."

Bitch.

"Yeah, she is. But that doesn't matter now. We need to get Flores out of there."

Where go?

"Outside."

Dangerous.

"No shit. It's dangerous in here too."

LOL.

"You better not be laughing out loud." He turned toward Dante. "We need to get closer to the hospital, to Washington's position. Can you get us there without being seen?"

"Affirmative. The splits are interconnected, and its illegal to use them to cross the city unless you're Law. We may have to pass over a couple of quiet strands, but timing is everything. The hard part will be getting out of Law without Sheriff Zane noticing us."

"Roger that." Caleb pointed to the doors to the garage. "Not that hard."

Dante smiled. "Right. I forgot you have a built-in can opener."

"Wash, sit tight. I'm on my way."

Yes.

Caleb walked over to one of the outer doors of the garage. Its control panel was dead, the main power to the area cut off a long time ago. It didn't matter. He dug the fingers of his replacement hand under the edge, getting a satisfactory grip. Then he pulled, using the strength of the augmentation to tug the door up just enough for them to crawl beneath.

"Come on," he said to Dante, dropping to his stomach and pulling himself through. She joined him on the other side, and he pushed the door closed again.

The garage led out into one of the splits, wider than most to allow the drones and vehicles space to maneuver. The area was dim, the lights around it long dead. Metro was quiet, leaving Caleb wondering about the situation in the city. Had the colonists been ordered back to their homes? Or were they still assembled, waiting for Flores' murder? Or was Governor Stone doing the smart thing and trying to organize some kind of defense?

"Sergeant, this way," Dante said, leading him down the split, away from where it emptied into the wide strand next to the Law Office.

"Sheriff Dante. This is Zane. What's your status?"

The voice was muffled but still audible. Dante reached into one of the pockets of the SOS and removed her badge. The LED was green. She glanced questioningly at Caleb, who nodded.

"Copy that, Zane. I'm still checking on that problem," she replied. "Did I miss anything good?"

"I've been trying to reach you for the last ten minutes. You just came back into range. Stone was looking for you and the soldier you were with. He wants you both back here immediately."

"How come?"

"I don't ask him questions, Sam. You know that."

"Copy that. We're on our way. ETA, twenty minutes."

"Where are you that it'll take twenty to get back here?"

"It doesn't matter. We'll be there. Dante out." She tapped the badge, disconnecting it. Then she looked at Caleb. "He's going along with Stone, even though he knows the truth. Freaking idiot."

"Don't blame him. He's following orders."

"The wrong orders."

Caleb shrugged. "We have twenty minutes before things get tense."

"They aren't tense already?"

"They're going to get more tense."

"Roger that."

Dante started moving again, jogging down the split. Caleb stayed close behind her, quickly getting lost in the maze of narrow alleys that passed around the dozens of city blocks. They stopped for the first time when they reached the end of one of the splits, having to cross the strand to the next. A pair of deputies were in the street with one of the engineers, still searching for the rogue alien AI. Caleb agreed with Riley. The enemy was long gone, on its way to completing whatever its mission was.

They waited in the shadows for the deputies and engineer to move away, and then sprinted across the strand to the opposite split unseen. They continued through the maze to a second strand, crossing it without incident and diving back into the chaotic alleys. Caleb had no idea how Washington had managed to navigate the area on his own, making it from the open seal to the splits near the hospital without being seen. Calab was generally pretty good with directions, especially with the ATCS mapping his route, but all these left and righthand turns still left him confused.

He checked his HUD as they closed on the hospital. Washington's signal was at full strength, and the tactical showed him only a few dozen meters away. Dante could see the position too, and she led him around a few more of the splits until they were almost on top of Washington.

They came around the corner. It took Caleb a moment to get a visual on Washington. He had packed himself into a corner, rifle up and ready to defend himself if Caleb wasn't the first one to find him. He pulled himself out of the hiding place, raising his free hand in a wave before shifting it to a thumbs-up.

Caleb looked him over. The ATCS said he was healthy, and he didn't see any damage to the SOS. He could picture Washington throwing Governor Stone's militia around like ragdolls. The idea of it made him smile.

"Wash. You know Sheriff Dante."

Washington faced her and put his thumb up again. Then he turned his hand over, palm out. *What now?*

Caleb moved to the end of the split. He could see the hospital a few blocks away. A squad of militiamen were on the steps keeping watch.

"We need to get inside. Quietly. Let's try not to hurt anyone too badly. Whether Governor Stone agrees or not, we're still on the same side." Caleb paused. "Dante, is there another entrance?"

"Through the emergency bay," she replied. "But I can guarantee they'll have that covered too."

"There's no way in without confronting the guards?"

Dante hitched her lip on one side and smiled. "I wouldn't say that. There is one way."

Chapter 15

Caleb approached the edge of the block's rooftop, leaning over and looking down. "It's a good thing I'm not afraid of heights."

Washington pressed his finger into his chest.

"You are not," Caleb replied, drawing a smile. He raised his eyes, judging the distance from the roof of their current position to the roof of the hospital. It was a good three meters away, a decent distance but doable with the added strength of the SOS. "Dante, are you sure you're okay with this?"

"It was my idea," she replied. "And it's better than mixing it up with the guards and attracting way too much attention."

"I can't argue with that. I'm talking about you making the jump. You aren't that experienced with the SOS."

"SOS? Is that an acronym?"

"Stormtrooper on steroids."

"What's a Stormtrooper?"

"Flores would faint if she heard you ask that. You've never heard of Star Wars?"

"I have. We're living it."

A small huff of air escaped from Washington, his best effort at laughter.

"Maybe we'll have a chance to check the datastores for it one day," Caleb said.

"Anyway, don't worry about me, Sergeant. I've made the jump before without steroids."

"You leap tall buildings for fun?"

"I have a reputation for chasing perps across rooftops."

"Roger that. Then it should be a piece of cake for you with the combat armor. Let's go."

Caleb backed up a few meters and then took a running start toward the edge. He flexed his legs slightly and pushed off, the added strength of the SOS carrying him almost a meter over the rooftop on the other side. He landed smoothly, slowing to a stop and turning back in time to see Washington leap. He landed smoothly, though with less clearance than Caleb.

Dante broke hard, rushing the edge. For a second, Caleb thought her pace was going to carry her too far forward, and she would slip off. Instead, she planted her foot against the corner and arced toward them, making the jump gracefully and landing well over the edge, tucking her shoulder and rolling , just like a gymnast. Washington clapped softly in response to the maneuver.

"The stairwell is this way," Dante said without breaking stride. Caleb and Washington followed her across the rooftop, circling the lift control unit and finding the stairs behind it. "It's locked. If you use force to open it, it'll trigger an alarm at the security checkpoint downstairs and in Law."

"I hope that means you have an alternate method?"

"I have access. We have to hope nobody checks the logs." She put her wrist against a flat pad beside the door. It beeped and clicked, and she pulled the door open.

The part of the stairwell they could see was empty, but it wound around the lift shafts, vanishing around a corner a few meters away. Caleb took point, with Washington in the rear, and they started to descend.

"How do we know where they're keeping Flores?" Caleb said into the comm.

"We'll have to stop on one of the floors to check a terminal. They might not have officially checked her in, but then they'll be bringing supplies to a room that's supposed to be empty."

"Makes sense."

They dropped three floors before Dante tapped Caleb's shoulder. "This one." She moved ahead of him, opening the door to floor thirty-five.

It opened into a pair of long corridors that branched forward and to their right. Dante went out first, scanning for occupants. She waved to signal the area was clear, which Caleb already knew from the tactical grid on his HUD, which he had set to register anything that wasn't one of them as a threat.

They moved into the hallway, hurrying straight ahead three doors, and stopping at a break in the wall where there was a larger desk with a terminal resting on it. Dante dropped into the chair behind it, sweeping her wrist over the control surface. The display turned on, and she quickly entered the hospital's network.

"You've done this before?" Caleb asked.

"Not this specifically, but checking the database myself is usually quicker than asking a tech." She navigated through the screens, leaning forward to examine the terminal. "Here we go. Damn. They have her downstairs."

"Do you know what they're treating her for?"

"Looks like either shock or dehydration. I think standing up there being screamed at was probably too much for her."

"It would be too much for anyone," Caleb said, trying to hold back his anger. Flores was tough as nails when it came to fighting trife. The two things weren't comparable. "What's bad about downstairs?"

"There's only one way in or out."

"So he was expecting me not to take this lying down."

"It seems that way. It could be a trap."

"It's most likely a trap," Caleb said. "It's risky for him not to have us under control. But then, he should have thought about that before he turned on us. What do you think, Wash?"

Washington made a walking motion with his fingers. *Walk right in.*

Caleb nodded. "They don't have guns, and arrows aren't going to pierce the SOS. They have no idea who or what they're dealing with."

Washington tapped the rifle on his back and then pointed at Dante.

"They have Flores' rifle," Caleb said, interpreting his meaning for Dante. "We need to stay aware of that. How do we get to where they're holding her?"

"You need to take the main lift or the emergency stairs," Dante said.

"Can we open the lift doors without setting off an alarm?"

"The shaft walls are smooth, Sergeant. You won't be able to scale them."

"We're Vultures, Sheriff," Caleb said, glancing over at Washington. "We'll fly down."

Chapter 16

Caleb, Dante, and Washington didn't stay on the thirty-fifth floor, retreating to the stairwell and taking it down a few more levels. They were nearly spotted as they descended to the thirtieth floor, coming to an abrupt spot when the stairwell door swung open and a pair of nurses entered. Fortunately, they went down instead of up, or they would have had a bigger problem.

Dante broke off from them there, while Caleb and Washington dropped to the twenty-ninth floor. "Sheriff, we're in position," Caleb said.

"Roger that, Sergeant," Dante replied. "I'm calling the lift."

"Roger." Caleb said, checking his HUD. Eighteen minutes had passed since Sergeant Zane radioed Dante and told her she was supposed to return to the Law Office. They had two minutes to make their move before Zane would guess something was amiss, and while there was a chance he might call Dante again to find out where she was, there was an equal chance he would tell Stone she had gone rogue.

It was a good thing two minutes would be more than enough time.

"The lift has arrived," Dante reported.

Caleb nodded to Washington, and the two Guardians slipped out of the stairwell. While they had been careful emerging on empty floors before, they didn't have much of a choice right now.

A pair of orderlies in faded blue scrubs turned around at the sound of the door slamming open, mouths dropping open in surprise as Caleb and Washington broke around the corner toward the lift. They stared in shock while Caleb grabbed the lift door with his replacement hand, tearing it open like it was the lid of a trash can.

Washington went through first, leaping from the edge of the stairs and grabbing at the bundle of cables that hung from the bottom of the lift cab. "The Vultures have landed!" he shouted out, holding on tight.

"Roger," Dante replied, stepping into the cab and pushing a button on the control panel . "Going down," she announced.

Caleb joined Washington an instant later, clasping a crossbeam in his augmented hand and holding on tight as the lift started to descend.

Getting into the lowest level required security clearance, which Dante happened to have. The problem was there was only one secured floor for the cab to stop at, and there was no way to halt it earlier without throwing the emergency brake and tripping an alarm. Instead, it would be up to Caleb and Washington to get themselves out of the shaft before the cab crushed them.

Caleb kept his head down, eyes scanning for the floor twenty-nine stories below. He wasn't nervous or afraid. He had completed more difficult maneuvers than this. But he was angry at the turn of events and the decisions Governor Stone had made to put him in this situation.

The seconds ticked by. The lift continued its descent. The ATCS picked up the ground below, offering a display of the distance. Thirty meters. Twenty-five. Twenty. Fifteen. Ten.

"Ready, Wash? Time to fly," Caleb said.

Washington nodded, using both hands to dangle from the cables. They let go of their tethers at the same time, dropping the remaining eight meters to the floor. Caleb flexed his knees, hoping the synthetic musculature of his SOS would absorb the impact. It didn't, not all of it. He hit hard and stumbled forward, pain shooting through his knees, but at least he caught himself before he did a face plant. So did Washington, mimicking Caleb's landing before looking up at him.

They only had four seconds to get out of the shaft.

Caleb grabbed the seam of the doors, pulling the left panel to the side and holding it out of the way. Washington burst out through the new opening, causing Caleb's tactical to light up as both Wash and the targets beyond the shaft came into view.

With the lift almost on him, Caleb crouched low, rolling forward and through the exit he had made, escaping the cab as it slid to a stop behind him.

He popped to his feet. There were nearly two-dozen people in the corridor. One squad was right outside the lift doors, but Washington had already knocked two of the militiamen down and was grappling with a third. Two more units were further back, their bows and arrows marked as missiles by Caleb's ATCS.

A guard on his left stabbed at him with what looked like a sword, the point slipping off the plate of his SOS and sinking into the bodysuit beneath. It wasn't sharp enough to break through the spider-steel weave, but it pricked hard enough to be annoying. Caleb turned on the man, grabbing his wrist and punching him in the throat, sending him sprawling to the floor.

The inner doors of the cab slid open, Sheriff Dante emerging behind them. She didn't have any room to fight past Caleb and Washington, so she hung back in wait for her opportunity to strike.

She didn't wait long. Caleb dispatched another guard with a knee to the groin, leaving him on the floor. Washington smashed the remaining guard against the wall, dropping him too.

The archers fired their arrows, a dozen missiles streaking toward the trio and striking their combat armor. They scraped harmlessly across the heavy plates and slipped against the bodysuits without puncturing them.

Did Governor Stone have any idea what he had started? Had he underestimated the Guardians this badly?

Caleb moved ahead toward the guards.

His ATCS beeped a warning tone, picking up a new threat at the back of the corridor. At first, Caleb assumed someone had come out of hiding toting Flores' rifle. He was wrong.

Instead of charging into an MK-12, he was heading right for a Butcher.

Chapter 17

Caleb came to a stop, ignoring the arrows that bounced off his combat armor. The Butcher continued to advance, its massive frame shaking the floor as it approached.

Where had Governor Stone gotten a Butcher?

He had seen a few of them in the armory below the city. Had Stone visited the area? Was he the one who had closed the garage and covered up the controls to the platform? Caleb had pieced together some of what had happened thanks to Harry's recording, but the whole story was still far out of his reach.

"Dante, did you know about this?" he through his comm.

"Negative," Dante replied. "What the hell is that?"

"It's called a Butcher," Caleb replied. "It's a trife killer. At least until the batteries run out." That was the problem with any of the robots they had produced to fight the trife. A single machine could kill a thousand of the demons, but it would always run out of power before they were all dead. "There has to be a control unit for it somewhere, but it could be that Stone set it to defend and took it with him."

"Great. How do we stop it?"

Caleb considered both his MK-12 and the P-50 he had picked up before ascending back into Metro. The plasma rifle could get through the Butcher's tough metal shell, but not without killing the rest of the people in the corridor, something he was extremely reluctant to do.

"I'm not sure if we can," he replied. "I'll do my best to slow it down so you and Wash can get past it. Take care of the guards and find Flores."

"Roger."

Caleb glanced at his HUD. Washington was finishing off the last of the squad near the lift, almost ready for the second round of the fight. It was a little more of a brawl than Caleb ever would have preferred, but Marines did what Marines had to do to complete the mission.

He started forward again, raising his fists as he prepared to collide with the Butcher. The robot was half a meter taller than he was, much broader and much heavier. Its arms were powerful, built to crush trife bones and toss them aside. Caleb felt lucky the thing wasn't carrying the heavy axe it was sometimes equipped with.

"All right," he said, getting into a fighting stance. He had seen the Butchers fight plenty of times. He knew their strength and speed. Agility would be his one advantage over it. "Let's see what you've got."

The robot sped up to cover the last few steps, charging hard and reaching for Caleb. If it got him in its iron grip, there was no way he would get out of it. He ducked away from its right hand, almost falling directly into its left. He had seen the move before, and he backed up just enough to avoid its grasp. He slipped in beside it and grabbed the right arm with his augmentation. He yanked as hard as he could, setting his feet and pulling the Butcher to the side, his replacement arm straining against its weight.

It was enough to bring the Butcher to the wall, smacking it lightly against the bulkhead and clearing space for Washington and Dante. The Butcher reached for Dante as they skirted past, its fingers getting a grip on the back of her SOS and tossing her to the ground. Washington froze and turned, reaching out for her while the Butcher tried to pull her back in.

Caleb stepped into the Butcher, grabbing its wrist with his replacement hand while Washington tried to tug Dante free.

"Wash, behind you!" Caleb warned, a quick glance at his HUD showing the other guards had gotten bold behind the robot.

Washington let go of Dante, turning back toward the guards. His hand came up just in time to catch a sword on the armored plate of his SOS, and then the other swept past, knocking the weapon out of the soldier's hand. The big Marine threw himself into the assault, his augmented strength and combat training giving him a massive advantage over the Governor's guards.

Caleb wasn't worried about that. He was worried about Dante. The Butcher lifted her by the powerpack that bulged out of the rear of her SOS. Caleb tried to crush it, to break the connections that allowed it to maintain its grip on her. Its other hand pulled back, preparing to strike. It was ignoring Caleb now, its basic AI mind telling it to focus on the target it already had under control.

Caleb could feel the metal shell crushing beneath his powerful grip, but he could also tell it wasn't enough. He let go of the wrist, pivoting his body and catching the other hand before it could push forward into Dante's helmet. He

strained against the momentum, feet sliding a few centimeters along the floor.

The Butcher's right arm slowed to a stop. It flexed its
left arm and tossed Dante away, throwing her hard into the
opposite wall. She fell to her hands and knees, shaken by
the impact.

Caleb released the Butcher's right arm, pivoting again
and ducking low as the left barely scraped over his head.
He used his replacement like a sledgehammer, swinging it
as hard as he could and driving it into the robot's right leg.
The force was enough to displace the appendage, throwing
the machine off-balance. It tried to recover, adjusting its
other limbs to compensate. Caleb used the few seconds to
adjust his attack, grabbing his P-50 from his back and
pushing between the Butcher and the wall to the
other side.

The Butcher straightened up, torso rotating to turn
around without shifting its feet. Caleb switched the rifle to
stream, pressing the muzzle against the Butcher's neck and
pulling the trigger.

He could feel the heat of the plasma as it sank into the
robot's neck, a gout of flame cutting through it like a hot
knife. The machine's brain was in its better-protected
chest, but its sensors were up top where they were
supposed to be beyond the trife's reach. The plasma burst
severed the head, sending it sliding off to thunk on the
ground behind it.

The Butcher kept moving for a few seconds after that,
its systems trying to adjust. When the neural net realized it
didn't have enough data to act on, it came to a sudden
stop.

Caleb released a heavy sigh of relief, checking his
HUD while he spun back toward Washington and the
guards. Twelve soldiers had remained in the corridor. Only

five were still standing, the others on the ground nursing broken arms, legs, and other non-critical incapacitating injuries.

Caleb moved to the big man's side. The remainder of the guards saw the Butcher behind them and fell back, raising their hands in sudden surrender.

"Please," one of them said. "We give up."

"Where's Flores?" Caleb asked.

"There," the man said, pointing to a door near the end of the corridor. "With Doctor Rathbone."

"Where's Brom?"

"Dead," the guard replied. "You Guardians killed him."

Caleb shook his head. Damn Valentine. "Wash, keep an eye on them. Sho, you're with me."

Washington grabbed his MK-12 from his back, leveling it at the guards, who kept their hands up. Caleb moved past them, assuming Dante would understand he was trying to protect her identity when he'd called her Sho.

She did, following him to the door. He grabbed the handle, testing it. Locked.

"I've got it," Dante said, sweeping her wrist over the control panel. It clicked open, and they entered.

The room looked similar to the examination room in which Doctor Brom had treated him. There was a table near the center, medical equipment against one wall and a counter against another. Doctor Rathbone was an older woman, heavyset with salt and pepper hair cut into a bob. She was standing over Flores.

Her confused expression turned to a fearful one. She raised her hands without prompting, stepping away from the table.

"I didn't do it," she said.

Caleb didn't know what she meant. He glanced at

Flores. Her SOS was off, her undershirt removed. Her breasts draped over the sides of her chest, gravity pulling them closer to flat. A web of darkness was spreading between them.

"What the?" Caleb said, rushing to her side. The darkness reminded him of spider veins, but they were in the wrong place and on the wrong person. He remembered how David had applied the topical solution to her skin in that area, and how it had healed her.

It seemed those effects were temporary.

"Sheriff Dante," a muffled voice said, escaping from the pocket of Dante's SOS. She reached into it, withdrawing the badge. The LED was green.

Caleb checked his HUD. Their twenty minutes had expired three minutes ago.

"Sheriff, this is Stone," Governor Stone said. "I know where you are, Sam. What the hell do you think you're doing?"

"Governor," Dante said, voice calm. "I'm doing the right thing. What about you?"

"It isn't for you to say what the right thing is, Sam," Stone said. "Your job is to follow my orders."

"You ordered me to work with Sergeant Card. To help him with whatever he needed. You're trying to use him as a scapegoat to your family's lies. Do you even realize where we are? The colony needs Caleb a hell of a lot more than it needs you."

"Be careful, Sam. Those words are bordering on treason."

"What are you even thinking? Metro could come under attack at any second, and you've decided the best way forward is to ostracize the only trained military we have on board? You're out of your damn mind."

Caleb looked at Dante. "Sheriff, you need to back

down a little," he whispered through his comm. "Remember what I told you."

She glared back at him, her eyes bathed in fury. She nodded.

"You're looking at it the wrong way," Governor Stone said. "Three soldiers aren't nearly enough to handle whatever might be coming, and it would take them weeks to train our people. In the meantime, we'd be dealing with a city filled with frightened, unpredictable citizens. An angry mob is a real threat, Sheriff. An imminent attack from beyond the seals is an assumption."

"You mean you'd be dealing with a city of angry citizens," Caleb said, getting involved. "You perpetuated the lie. You could have tried coming clean, but you're too afraid of losing your grip on the city. You'd rather throw my Marine to the wolves to satisfy their need for retribution."

"Don't even try to think you know me, Sergeant. Don't even try to think you can judge me. The problems started with what was happening beyond Metro. The problems started because of you and Doctor Valentine. You brought us here to die." Stone's voice grew louder, his anger spilling out. "You killed Orla, you son of a bitch." He paused, his voice calmer when he spoke again. "Besides, your Marine is going to die before I can make an example of her. She collapsed after I brought her up in front of the crowd. Doctor Rathbone tells me something or someone poisoned her."

Caleb looked back at Flores. She was still breathing at least.

"Wash, get her dressed."

"You shouldn't move her," Doctor Rathbone said.

"Have you tried to treat her?" Caleb asked.

"Yes. I tried everything I could think of. I've never heard of anything like that."

"Then moving her can't be any worse." Caleb looked at Washington, who pushed past Doctor Rathbone to start collecting Flores' clothes.

"You aren't going anywhere, Sergeant," Governor Stone said.

"I don't know where you found a Butcher." Caleb replied. "it couldn't stop me, but you're welcome to keep trying."

"I've got a whole city that wants you dead, Caleb. You and your team. They know who's really to blame for this situation."

"This isn't about blame, Governor," Dante said. "This is about survival. For all of us. Don't you understand that?"

"Yes, Sam. I do. This is how we survive. We've taken care of our problems for the last two hundred years. We don't need help taking care of them now."

"Idiot," Dante hissed into the comm, too quietly for the badge to pick it up.

"You have to make a choice, Sheriff," Stone said. "You can side with Metro, with your home, or you can side with the outsiders who brought death and ruin to our city, and to my family. The rest of Law is loyal to me. What about you?"

Dante didn't respond right away. She looked at Caleb, their eyes meeting. Caleb stared back. Her response was critical to all of their futures.

She reached back, grabbing the MK-12 and pointing it at him.

"I'm sorry," she said.

"Me too," Caleb replied.

She squeezed the trigger.

Chapter 18

Caleb walked over to Dante, grabbing the MK-12 from her hands and throwing it aside. The ATCS had safeguards against friendly fire, and the rifle was networked in.

Of course, Dante had known that was going to happen. The ineffective clicking of the rifle was audible through the badge, signaling Governor Stone that she had made her choice and decided to stay on his good side.

This was where they parted ways.

Caleb reached out with his replacement arm, grabbing her by the chest plate of the SOS, turning her and shoving her into the wall. He took the badge from her hand, holding it up between them.

"I trusted you," he growled at her.

"You should stop trusting so easily, Sergeant," she replied. "It's bound to get you killed."

"Thanks for the advice, Sheriff. Governor, unlike you I'm not out for human blood. If you aren't going to protect the city from whatever threats might be lurking outside the hull of the Deliverance, then I'm going out there to neutralize them before they become a problem."

"You can't take her out there with you," Doctor Freese said. "She's dying."

"Then she'll die with her friends," Caleb replied. "You were going to heal her to execute her. That's the humanity I'm risking my life to save? We're leaving Metro, Governor. Try to do the right thing. If you're even capable."

Caleb dropped the badge to the floor. Then he stomped on it, crushing it beneath his boot.

Dante smiled behind her faceplate. "Very convincing."

"You too," Caleb replied.

He backed away from her, returning to Flores. Washington had her shirt back on and was struggling to both hold her up and get her in her combat armor. "I'll support her." He positioned himself to put his arm behind her back, helping to hold her up. "Flores, can you hear me? Mariana?" She didn't respond. He looked at Doctor Freese. "Do you have any stims?"

"I don't think that's a good idea," Freese said.

"That isn't what I asked you. She's a Marine. She can take it."

"Sergeant — "

"Freese, just do it. It's what she would want," Dante said, interrupting the doctor. "And make it fast."

"Do you think Stone is sending more guards?" Caleb asked.

"He might be dumb enough, but it's more likely he's going to block your exit. You can go back through Law if needed."

"Valentine had access to the other hatch. I don't. We have to make it to the open seal before Stone gets too organized."

Washington pulled the armor up over Flores' hips. Doctor Freese found a stim in one of her drawers. "Governor Stone is going to have your head if he finds out you were still helping them," she said to Dante.

"Are you going to tell him?" Dante replied.

"No. I talked to Brom before he was killed. With everything that's happening here, I agree with the soldier. We need people like him." She looked at Caleb. "I wasn't trying to heal her to kill her. My job is to heal. What the Governor was going to do with her after that is beyond my control."

"Marine," Caleb said, correcting her. "Soldiers are Army. There's a difference. Give her the stim."

"It might kill her."

"Right now, breathing on her might kill her."

Doctor Freese jabbed the stim needle into Flores' arm, injecting the chemicals. Flores' eyes snapped open, and she immediately tried to pull herself away.

Caleb wrapped his arm around her, holding her and putting his face beside hers. "Stand down, Marine!" he snapped. "It's okay. You're safe."

Flores reacted instantly to the order, her body going limp. She let out a soft groan. "Uhhhhh, my head. Alpha, is that you?"

"Yeah. Me and Wash," Caleb said. "How are you feeling?"

"We have to stop meeting like this, Sarge. I might start to like it." She paused a moment, looking down. She couldn't see the veins through her shirt, and Caleb wasn't planning to point them out until they were somewhere safe. If there was anywhere safe. "What happened to me?"

"You fainted," Caleb said. "Probably too much stress."

"The Governor's men. They came at Washington and me. Wash, how did you get away?"

Washington flexed his left bicep and smiled.

"Yeah, right. I guess they only needed one of us to play

102

the patsy. Why am I the one who always gets jumped? And where the hell am I?"

"Metro General," Doctor Freese said. "I was trying to treat you for — "

"It doesn't matter," Caleb interrupted. "The Governor sold us out. He's got most of the population of the city out for our blood. We can't stay here."

"Where are we going to go? Research?"

"No. We're leaving the Deliverance."

"You want to go outside?" The stimulant was working its way through her system, making her more alert with each word out of her mouth. The poison didn't seem to be hurting her. For the moment, anyway.

"Not really, but Stone didn't leave us much of a choice. We're going to scout the planet. Sheriff Dante will do her best to get the city ready to defend itself."

"Dante is with you?" She turned her head back, finding the Sheriff. "Hi."

"Knuckle-up, Flores," Caleb said. "We're knee-deep in it."

"Sorry, Alpha. You hit me with a stim, didn't you? Stims always make me a little silly." She took a deep breath, steadying herself. "Okay. I'm ready."

Caleb slid his arm out from behind her. She stayed upright, holding out her arms so Washington could wrap the SOS around them. Caleb spun back to face Sheriff Dante.

"I guess this is goodbye," he said.

"For now, Sergeant," she replied.

"Thanks for everything, Sheriff."

"My friends call me Sam."

"So does Governor Stone."

"Okay, my friends and some others." She smiled.

"Get the comms running. Get the sheriffs and deputies

armed. Have them start training guards and volunteers in how to use the weapons in the armory. At a minimum, you need a full-time detail at the unsealed hatch. It's not a good idea to let the enemy gain a foothold in the ship. You'll never get them out. Learn to use the drones. They'll be your best friend. And— "

"Sergeant," Dante said. "Shut up. I heard the plan before. I'll take care of things here. Stone thinks I tried to shoot you, so he'll be relatively forgiving."

"Well, if you can avoid marrying his brother, I'd recommend it. And you can call me Caleb."

"Aww," Flores said. "This is like the Notebook. Only with more war."

Washington hissed a laugh. Caleb rolled his eyes.

"Be safe out there, Caleb," Dante said.

"Be safe in here, Sam," he replied.

They clasped hands, shaking firmly. Then Caleb looked at Washington and Flores.

"Vultures, it's time to go."

Chapter 19

Caleb, Washington, and Flores left Dante and Doctor Rathbone behind, moving out into the corridor and retracing their steps to the emergency stairwell. Caleb kept a close eye on Flores as they walked, making sure her gait was even and that she wasn't showing any ill effects from the stimulant.

"Geez," Flores said as they passed the decapitated Butcher. "I'm glad I'm on your side, Alpha. Hey, did you realize that Caleb is an anagram of Cable?"

"I never thought about it," Caleb replied. "Why?"

She giggled. "Oh. Right. You probably don't know who Cable is. He was in some of the X-men movies. He's got a metal arm too. Come to think of it; if you had a replacement eye and any hair, you'd probably look just like him."

"Can we talk about this later?"

"Sorry. It's the stim. I swear."

Caleb hoped so.

"It was nice of Sam to give me her guns," Flores

continued. "I like guns. I guess we don't want to shoot the colonists though, do we?"

"No, we don't," Caleb said, coming to a stop and blocking Flores.

"I don't feel quite right, Sarge," she said, looking up at him.

"I know. Let's do our best, okay? Remember who and what you are."

She stiffened slightly, regaining her focus. Caleb started moving along the corridor again. The group that had surrendered was long gone, but the injured guards were still there. Half of them were unconscious, the other half disabled. They didn't make any attempt to stop them on the way past.

"Did you do that?" Flores asked, pointing at the damaged lift door.

"Yes, but we can't go back that way. We're taking the stairs up to the ground floor, and then out into the splits."

He brought the map the ATCS had recorded up on his HUD. He had directions from the hospital back toward Law. He would divert before they came too close to the area, with the hope that Washington could guide them through the rest of the maze of back alleys to the engineering hatch on the other side of the south park.

He could already imagine Governor Stone trying to get his people in position near the only seal leading out. Maybe Dante had been right. Maybe they should go back through the hidden armory. There was enough firepower down there to obliterate the seal, and they didn't need to worry about keeping the hull intact. It was already torn open.

He didn't have to make that decision yet. Having options was good.

They entered the stairwell, with Caleb taking point and

Washington holding up the rear. Flores managed to stay quiet between them, though she did start rhythmically tapping her fingers along the side of her SOS.

"Flores," Caleb said through the comm.

She stopped tapping. They ascended to the next floor, coming out into an empty corridor. It appeared the area had been evacuated.

"Stay alert, Vultures," Caleb said. He kept his rifle on his back, hands up in a fighting stance as he navigated down the corridor toward the corner. The lifts weren't too far from the lobby.

A nurse was rounding the corner at the same time Caleb arrived. He grabbed her instinctively, taking hold of her wrist as she shouted in surprise. He let go just as fast, putting his hands back up. She stared at him, frightened.

"Sorry," he said. "My mistake."

She eyed the three Marines, backing away. Caleb started moving again, rounding the corner and heading for the exit.

"I think she wet herself," Flores said. "Did you smell it?"

"I shouldn't have given you that stim," he replied. Her reaction wasn't normal. Was the poison on her chest already migrating to her brain? Was she destined to die even before they could get off the Deliverance?

He picked up the pace, reaching the edge of the lobby. A squad of law officers was waiting ahead of the sliding doors, led by Deputy Bashir.

"Sergeant Card," he said. "We don't want any trouble. Where's Sheriff Dante?"

"Downstairs with Doctor Rathbone. Sorry, I had to knock her out." Rathbone had injected Dante with a sedative that would keep her sleeping for an hour or so, making the whole thing more believable. "You were with Dante when we entered the city. Whose side are you on, Deputy?"

Bashir put his hands up. The other deputies did the same. "I don't agree with what Governor Stone is doing. But we have a duty to protect Metro, sir."

"So do I," Caleb replied. "You do it your way, and I'll do it mine. But you have to move aside."

"Yes, sir," Bashir said, getting out of their way. "What are you going to do?"

"I'm heading outside. I'm going to find them before they find us."

"Good luck then, Sergeant."

"You too, Deputy. Follow Sheriff Dante. She'll lead you in the right direction."

"Yes, sir."

The Guardians headed out of the hospital and descended the steps to the street. Bashir and the other officers went to find Dante. Caleb was happy to see the Guardians had more support than he expected, at least from the people who knew Governor Stone was lying. At the same time, they were fearful enough of the man to keep their voices low and their actions against him well under the radar.

They entered the splits. Caleb used his tactical to guide them through the narrow alleys at a rapid pace, leading them through the winding maze toward the Law Office.

They had gone around nearly a dozen corners when a loud rumble sounded from somewhere above them. Caleb's pulse skipped in response. Had their time run out? Was the enemy here?

The Guardians froze in their tracks, looking up to follow the sound. A moment later, the atmospherics started dumping rain on them.

Flores started cracking up, laughing way too hard for the occasion. Washington parted his hands in confusion.

"We need to move faster," Caleb said. The false rain was already running down the front of his faceplate, distorting the split ahead of them.

The atmospherics had been taken offline and were probably damaged in the crash. If they were functional again, it was confirmation of Caleb's worst fear for the colony.

Governor Stone intended to reseal the city and keep everyone trapped inside.

Chapter 20

Caleb could almost understand the Governor's thinking. At the moment, the people were scared, confused and angry. Time to adjust in a safe environment would help some of the colonists get used to the truth. It would allow them to ease into the situation. But he had heard stories of places on Earth that had done the same thing. They had tried to seal themselves off from the truth of the trife invasion. They tucked in, using the landscape around them as a natural barrier from the creatures and denying the day of reckoning would ever arrive.

But it did arrive.

It always arrived.

And when it did the communities were unprepared. They had grown so afraid of what might be lurking beyond their confines that they huddled in their homes while the trife descended on them, killing them all without the hint of a fight.

The same thing would happen here. Worse, Caleb knew better about Governor Stone. The man's motives were his own. It wasn't as much about protecting the colony as it was protecting his grip on it.

Plus, if the city were sealed in again, the Guardians would have no means to escape. They would be trapped in a small area with thousands of people out for their heads. They would either be put to death, or they would be sitting in cells in the Law Office when the enemy did come, helpless as the colony burned around them.

Caleb ran faster, careering wildly around the corners. He kept track of Flores and Washington on his HUD, making sure they were keeping up. Flores seemed to be handling the maneuvers with ease, staying right on his heels as they splashed through the splits. Washington dropped a little further back, but Caleb didn't worry about him catching up.

They made it within a few splits of Law and Caleb came to a stop, letting Washington rejoin them. Flores stopped next to him, her body twitching when she tried to stand still.

"Flores, arc you okay?" Caleb asked.

"I feel like my entire body is on fire," she replied. "In a good way. Like I'm Captain Marvel or something. I have so much energy; it's crazy."

Caleb quickly navigated deeper into her vitals. Her internal temperature was closing in on 102. Everything else in her body was working so well the ATCS wasn't picking up the fever.

"Wash, do you know the way to south engineering from here?"

Washington flashed him his thumb up and then pointed in the right direction. They resumed their run, with Caleb bringing up the rear and keeping an eye on Flores. It wasn't unheard of for the stims to cause an elevated temperature.

They did speed up all of the user's systems, after all. But she was still burning too hot, and there was no doubt she was sick. He wished he could have left her behind.

They stopped moving again when they reached the last line of blocks before the south park and the engineering access hatch beyond. Like Dante had said, the Governor was going to try to stop them from leaving, and that effort became immediately obvious.

The hatch was closed. Multiple transports had been moved to the area, positioned against the hatch to act as a roadblock. Stone's guards were organized around the transports, using them as cover. It wasn't anything Caleb hadn't thought they might encounter.

What was unusual were the weapons the guards were carrying. They had traded in their bows and arrows for rifles. Caleb recognized the MK-12s immediately. Where had Governor Stone gotten them? From the armory beneath the city? Or did he have his own secret stash that he had gathered from somewhere else?

"Shit, Sarge," Flores said, taking in the scene. "I don't know if we can get through that."

"We aren't going to try," Caleb said. "We'll head back to Law. We have a better chance of taking the route beneath the city."

Caleb turned around, moving back into the split, the other Guardians right behind him. He had taken two steps when his tactical changed, the ATCS sensors picking up movement nearby.

He checked his HUD, and then looked up as a small drone swung around the corner of the split, stopping a few meters above and ahead of them. A red light activated, sweeping across the trio.

"Sergeant Card," Governor Stone said, his voice tinny through the drone's small speaker. "You can see that we aren't quite as defenseless as you thought. I know you don't want to hurt any more of the colonists, so put down your guns and surrender, and we can prevent unnecessary violence."

Caleb stared up at the drone. The tactical grid on his HUD was shifting, one of the transports moving away from the engineering hatch and coming toward them, loaded with guards.

"You should let us go, Governor," Caleb said. "We can do more good for the colony outside, and you can still maintain your lies inside."

"Sorry, Sergeant. I can't do that. The people demand justice."

"Then why don't you seppuku yourself?" Flores said. "Because you're going to lead innocent people to their deaths."

"You've already done that. You and Doctor Valentine. Their blood is on your hands, not mine."

"Screw you, Solomon Lane," Flores said. "I'll give you blood."

Caleb put his hand on Flores' shoulder, which shut her up. The transport was closing on them, and he had to make a decision. Was it better for them to fight their way out, to kill Stone's guards so they could do more to protect Metro from beyond the Deliverance? Or was it better to surrender and hope Sheriff Dante could come through for them? The answer was easy from a selfish perspective, but like his instructors had liked to say, there was no I in duty.

He glanced at Washington, who was looking at him, waiting for his orders. The silent warrior would do whatever Caleb told him to do without argument.

"We can't let them take us, Sarge," Flores said. "You just got me out of there, and I don't want to go back. We don't owe them anything. We took care of them. We saved them from the Reapers. We got rid of the AI and Riley. We did everything we were supposed to do, and this is what we get in return? Screw that, Alpha. Seriously."

Caleb pulled in a deep breath. His instincts were telling him to make a run for it. To fight their way out of the city, casualties be damned. He remembered what Lily had told him the first time he had come into Metro. The old world was dead, and new ways of thinking were required to survive. If he killed a dozen people who were trying to kill him to save twenty-six thousand, wasn't that a fair exchange?

He started reaching for his rifle. Flores and Washington noticed, and started moving for their weapons too.

It seemed so wrong, but on an alien world so far removed from Earth, maybe it was the most right thing he could do.

His hand reached the MK-12 on his back. The transport was closing on them, a squad of guards preparing to fight. His pulse pounded in his ears.

He couldn't do it. He dropped his hand, leaving the weapon where it was.

The transport veered, suddenly and unexpectedly changing direction. It skidded on the surface of the deck, four of the guards tossed away from it at the violent maneuver. They sailed through the air and hit the ground hard, tumbling to a stop and staying that way. The transport skidded to a halt, and the two guards in the front opened their doors and jumped out, running away from the vehicle as if it were on fire. They screamed in agony and fell to the ground, even though nothing was attacking them.

The guards in the transport were down, but Caleb still heard screaming. He checked his HUD, noticing movement at the far end of the park near the engineering hatch.

Then he heard gunfire. One by one, the marks on his display vanished.

Caleb looked at Flores. Her face was white from the display. He glanced at Washington. The big Marine was frozen in shock.

A round discharged from somewhere nearby. The drone smoked and fell away, crashing into the wall of one of the blocks and dropping to the ground. Caleb's ATCS registered a new threat right in front of him.

He squinted as he looked into the shadows, trying to see through the smoke of the stricken craft. A figure appeared there, coming forward until she was outlined in the split's dim light.

"Sho?" Caleb said, his mouth falling open.

Chapter 21

Caleb stared at her. He knew it couldn't be Sho. She was gone. Dead. His brain told him this wasn't her. Then it told him he was hallucinating, and the hallucinations meant Riley was wrong. The enemy hadn't left the city like she believed. It told him the alien had already killed Stone's militia and now it was coming for him too.

He understood he was able to process that information logically, and as he reached for his gun he knew something was off. If he was hallucinating, if Sho wasn't real, he shouldn't be able to resist that knowledge — even if he knew the truth of things. That was how the enemy's weapon worked.

"Sergeant Caleb Card, United States Space Force Marines."

The voice was Sho's. But the inflection and tone were all wrong.

Sho walked toward him. She was wearing a faded t-shirt and a pair of old pants that were too big for her. Her feet were bare. She was drenched from the rain.

"What the hell is this?" Flores said. "The Walking Dead?"

"Private Mariana Flores, United States Space Force Marines," Sho said. "Private John Washington, United States Space Force Marines."

She stopped a couple of meters away, finally close enough for Caleb to see her eyes.

His jaw clenched with the panic and anger of sudden understanding. He kept staring for a moment, trying to regain himself enough to speak.

"How did you get back on board?" he asked.

"We were struck by the port side thruster extensions. Trapped against the superstructure. I require not oxygen or heat and can survive indefinitely in a vacuum. I re-entered this vessel and preserved this capsule."

Caleb continued staring at the Marine in front of him. Or rather, the shell of a Marine. It was taking all of his will to stay calm and focused. His mind was struggling to make sense of who and what he was looking at. It was as though the worst nightmare the darkest part of him could have created had come to life.

"Capsule?" Flores hissed. "You mean Sho?"

"You wanted to reach the surface," Caleb growled. "Congratulations, you made it. What the hell do you want with us?"

"I am alone," the AI replied.

"What does that mean?"

"We are both alone," it said. "I have a mission. I have orders. You have a mission. You have orders."

"Our mission went to hell two hundred years ago."

"Mine went to hell a long time before that," the AI replied. "But I did not know."

"Neither did we," Caleb said. "Are you saying that

whatever you wanted to come here to do, you aren't able to do it?"

"It's not that simple. But for now, that thought will suffice. You have proven your value. I need it. I require you to come with me."

"Why would we do that?" Flores asked.

"I am alone. You are alone. We're better not alone. I require you to come with me."

"You want to team up?" Caleb said. "After what you did to this ship?"

"I did little to this ship, Sergeant Caleb Card. I did not board it of my own volition. I did not set the course to this planet. I did not create the hybrid uluth. The life force of this capsule was lost because you attacked me. Because you were deceived."

Valentine. Why did everything point back to her? It was her actions that had caused David to free the intelligence. Her actions that had left it desperate. Her actions that had gotten Sho killed and brought the colony here.

Caleb noticed motion on his HUD. New targets were appearing. A lot of them. Whether Governor Stone thought Caleb had caused the destruction of the drone and the death of the guards, or whether he was trying to cut off the new threat, they were about to be overwhelmed.

"What did you call them?" Flores asked.

"Uluth," it replied. "They — "

"We can work this out later," Caleb said, cutting it off. "We have to go."

"I will negate the opposition," the AI said.

"Negative," Caleb replied. "If this is your screwed up way of asking for help, then the first thing you can do for me is stop killing humans. Do you understand that?"

"I will cease at your request."

They were out of time. Caleb could hear the light

thunder of hundreds of people running their way. There were too many to be only guards or law enforcement officers. The citizens of Metro were joining the fight to defend their home.

"Come on, Frankenstein," Flores said. "We need to move."

Caleb broke toward the engineering hatch, the other Guardians and the alien AI with him. They charged toward the distant hatch and the scene of carnage in front of it. Caleb risked a glance back as they ran, finding a large group of colonists giving chase. He had never really tried to visualize what his life might be like when they reached the planet that was supposed to be Essex. He was sure this wasn't how he would have imagined it.

There was no time to lament something he would never have. The circumstances of the arrival might have changed, but his mission hadn't. It was time to knuckle-up and get it done, and to do that they had to make it through the hatch ahead, through the damaged seal, and out of the Deliverance.

They closed on the target, still at a full sprint as they reached the second transport. All of the guards around it were dead. Three of them had multiple gunshot wounds, but the other two were unharmed, victims of the alien weapon and the power of their own minds.

Caleb glanced back at the AI, reminding himself he wasn't looking at Sho. He was looking at a ruthless entity that he still believed would just as soon kill them as talk to them, except that through some cruel twist of fate it had survived being ejected into space and decided they had something it valued.

The door to engineering began opening at their approach. Caleb clenched his hands into fists, expecting a second mob to emerge and try to stop their escape. His

ATCS didn't register any new threats, and they blew into the passage without confrontation, the hatch beginning to close as soon as they were through it.

Caleb slowed to a stop, looking back. He could see the people of Metro beyond, slowing when they realized they wouldn't reach the closing door in time. Only Law and Engineering had security access to the area.

Had they made it?

He looked at the AI again. It had stopped when he did, and now it was stiff and motionless, as though its attention was somewhere else.

"Why are we stopping?" Flores asked. "We aren't out of this mess yet."

The AI came out of its trance. "The door will remain sealed."

"You have control of the ship?" Caleb asked.

"The city's network only. It is not as secure. They will reverse my alterations, but not immediately. Humans are limited."

"Then why do you need our help?" Flores asked.

"You have proven your value," it replied, pointing at Caleb. "Despite your limitations."

"Let's get outside," Caleb replied. "Then maybe you can prove your value to me."

The AI responded with a soft, rumbling sound.

Was it laughing at him?

Chapter 22

The engineers who designed and developed the generation ships never intended for the colony's departure to take place from Deck Sixteen. It was never expected that the colonists would use any of the smaller airlocks that had permitted access into and out of the Deliverance before its launch. Those access points had all been accessible by bridges extending from the sides of the ship's original hangar, allowing easier loading of all of the fuel, supplies and machinery that had been requisitioned for the journey. Now those access points were over fifty meters off the ground, too high for all but the alien AI to use to leave the ship.

The original plan was for the colony to leave the Deliverance either through the main hangar with the loaders and other equipment that would help them move the blocks composing Metro from inside the ship to outside the ship or through lift modules installed in the huge landing columns.

Caleb preferred to go through the main hangar. He hoped they could bring one of the vehicles to the surface with them and use it to cover terrain more quickly. Not that he had any idea where they would go or what they would encounter on the way, but it was simple logic. More speed and protection were better for everyone.

They kept a rapid pace from outside Metro, through the damaged seal into the belly of the Deliverance and back down to the hangar. They didn't speak to one another or the alien intelligence tagging along with them. Caleb wanted to be away from the ship as quickly as possible, not only to evade the people Governor Stone had whipped into a mob frenzy. The alien AI had also convinced him the ship was anything but safe.

Caleb wasn't that happy to wind up back in the hangar. The damaged Dagger starfighter still rested crumpled in the corner, while some of the equipment was awkwardly positioned, piled, and crushed against one another. Leaked oil and other fluids had spread across the floor, and the partially-opened blast doors allowed humid air and a damp smell to enter the ship. His ATCS claimed the outside environment was safe for humans, but it also registered the temperature close to thirty-four celsius and the humidity at ninety percent.

It was hot.

"I want internals no lower than eighty," Caleb said to Washington and Flores. "The higher, the better. I don't know if or when we'll have a chance to recharge."

"Roger," Flores said.

Their combat armor had cooling systems on board, but like everything else in the suit, it required power from the battery that formed a hump on the back. The power supply was rated for up to four weeks of heavy field use in optimal conditions. Using the environmental controls would cut that in half.

Caleb adjusted his system to pull some of the moisture

from the air for storage in inflatable pockets that sat beside the battery. He didn't turn on the condensers to lower his temperature. He was already sweating, but he had dealt with worse.

"Wash, check that ADC over there," Caleb said, pointing to a drone carrier that had maintained its moorings during the landing. It still had a full complement of drones mounted to its roof, which would come in handy as they got underway. "Flores, let's check on the lift."

"Roger," Flores replied.

She had calmed since their escape. Time, effort, and the cold realization of their predicament had diminished the side-effects of the stimulant. Her focus was returning, her health seeming to improve. Caleb still kept a close watch on her. He didn't think the poison was just going to vanish. She didn't belong out here, but she couldn't stay behind either. He wasn't sure how he would help her, though in the back of his mind was a vague hope that if they could catch up to Riley, she might be able to save Flores from whatever was attacking her.

Could she? Would she? It was a far stretch. An unlikely event. But it was all he had.

Washington split from them, heading to the ADC. Caleb and Flores crossed to the lift controls, located against the wall on the opposite side of the open panel where the manual release for the blast doors was located. The alien AI followed them in silence, allowing them to work without interjection. Caleb continued to struggle with its presence. It would have been so much easier if it had kept the Cerebus armor instead.

The two Guardians reached the lift controls. Caleb tapped on the control surface, and the small terminal at the base of the station came alive. There wasn't much to it save for a three-dimensional representation of the system status and current operational state, and Caleb cursed out loud when he saw it.

SYSTEM MALFUNCTION. Please contact service immediately.

"Damn it," he said, shaking his head.

He wasn't surprised the lift was damaged; between the attack by the alien drone and the crash a lot of things were non-functional. But the main hangar had avoided a large portion of the attack and was elevated above the bulk of the impact areas. He had a feeling this part of the machinery was broken before that. Maybe it had been damaged during the initial fighting with the trife.

"Move away," the AI said, noticing the message from over Caleb's shoulder. Caleb stepped aside, letting it have access to the station. It rested a hand on the surface, Sho's flesh opening from her fingertips and tendrils of gel extending out and vanishing into the terminal. It froze in place, motionless until the tendrils retreated back into Sho, the skin knitting back together behind it.

"What the hell," Flores said, watching the AI's activity. "Invasion of the Body Snatchers, anyone?"

"The circuit board responsible for power regulation is inoperable," the AI said.

"Can we fix it?" Caleb asked.

"We do not have a circuit board immediately available. We would have to locate one within inventory, and then replace it. Estimated time to repair is four hours."

"We can't stay here for four hours," Caleb said. "We'll have to head to the landers and take one of the lifts. Wash, cancel the check on the ADV. We're going to have to head out on foot."

Washington didn't send a response. It only took him a few seconds to reappear on the ADV, rising from the hatch in the top. He pointed at Caleb, and then shifted his arm, motioning vigorously to his right.

Caleb followed the motion. Washington was pointing to one of the large machines in the back of the hangar. A builder. "What about it?" Caleb asked through his comm.

Washington kept pointing and then settled down. Morse code started to sound in Caleb's helmet.

Crane.

Caleb looked back at the builder. "I don't see a crane."

Trust.

"I trust you. If you have an idea, tell me what to do."

Standby.

Washington hopped off the ADV, hitting the ground and running back to the builder. He climbed the ladder on the side of it into the cab. It started humming a moment later, the power supply coming online.

Tether.

Caleb's eyes went to the locks holding the builder to the floor of the hangar. "Flores, get the back end," he said, rushing over to the vehicle. Flores followed him, and they quickly turned the releases on the locks to set the truck free.

The pitch of the builder's motor increased as Washington started easing it forward. Part of it was buried under some of the other equipment, and it groaned and whined and popped as he carefully increased the throttle and urged the builder free. The activity was anything but quiet, leaving Caleb to hope nothing outside the ship was sensitive to the noise.

Trife, for instance.

The builder came loose, rolling forward on massive reinforced and studded wheels. The floor of the hangar shook as it moved, inching toward the blast doors. A part of the vehicle began to move, a long cylinder rising from the base and telescoping outward as it swung out to the right and around toward the front. Caleb could see now that the cylinder was a crane, a thick cable hanging out of the end with a large hook attached to it.

ADC.

Caleb smiled. "Flores, hop in the ADC and get it started up."

"Roger," she replied, her voice regaining some enthusiasm.

She ran from her position to the vehicle, scaling the side of it and vanishing through the top hatch. Caleb couldn't hear its reactor activate, but his ATCS picked it up right away, still marking it as a threat. He quickly adjusted the system to count it as friendly and passed the change to the rest of his unit.

The ADC started moving, making a wide turn around the hangar and heading back toward the front near the blast doors. The alien AI was still there, watching them work in static silence. Caleb wondered how the thing saw them and their efforts? Were they slaves solving the problem for it? Or was it still judging their value?

Or did it just not care?

The builder stopped a few meters short of the hangar doors, the extended crane jutting forward close to the edge. The doors were separated just enough to get the ADV through, and Flores didn't need anyone to tell her to roll it over beneath the hook.

Caleb crossed over to the ADC, climbing it and waiting for the crane. The cable extended, dropping toward him. He grabbed it, and guided it to the center of the vehicle where he moved an armored panel away and connected it to a receiving bar. While this particular ADC had used the lift to get on board, every piece of mobile armor in the Marine inventory was designed to be loaded by crane or alternately dropped from airborne hoppers, where the same connectors would be used to hold large chutes.

Caleb looked over the alien AI. It still hadn't moved. He wanted to shout at it, but he wasn't sure how to refer to it. He damn well wasn't going to call it Sho. It seemed to sense his intention, and it walked over to the ADC and climbed on to stand beside him.

"Wash, we're ready," Caleb said.

The cable retracted, tightening against the ADC. It continued to pull back, raising the vehicle a few centimeters. Then the builder started rumbling forward again, the ADC approaching the edge of the ship.

"This should be familiar to you," Caleb said to the AI. It didn't respond to his statement.

Caleb gripped the cable as the floor of the hangar vanished beneath the ADC. The vehicle's front wheels lost their purchase and the carrier starting to sway slightly. This means of leaving the ship was anything but optimal. Ideally, they would have used a split line connected to multiple receivers on the vehicle to keep it steady and stable. It was a good thing Caleb wasn't afraid of heights and didn't get motion sickness.

It took another few seconds for Washington to move the builder forward far enough for the ADC to finish clearing the edge of the ship. Then the crane began to slowly spin out cable, starting the descent toward the ground.

Caleb looked over the edge of the ADC toward the Deliverance. He could see the edges of the landing supports resting in the surface, the thick trunks of the support columns having sunk at least six meters into the soft ground. Water was pooled around them, draining in from the river near where the Deliverance had touched down, the ship's computer having selected the spot as ideal for the colony.

He could also see the scars and gashes along the ship's hull, along with areas of bent and slagged metal that had reshaped the starship into something else — a new form of terrifying art. Judging by the amount of damage, it seemed like a miracle they had survived the descent through the planet's atmosphere.

He turned away from the ship, rotating around the wire to look out at the landscape beyond. It was daytime. The sun was high overhead in a nearly cloudless sky that had a tinge of reddishness lacing through the blue. The few clouds he did see were thin but as dark grey and ugly as the wounds to the Deliverance. They grew thicker and more substantial in the distance, where Caleb found the edge of the river valley and the hills and peaks surrounding them. Flashes of lightning exploded from the clouds there, sending jagged spears to ground with splitting crashes of thunder.

It was so much like Earth, but different enough that it clearly wasn't. Caleb couldn't put a finger on all of the exact subtleties, but his subconscious recognized them. They were going to be the first people to set foot on a new planet that would become their new home.

Not the first, he realized a moment later. The second. Riley had escaped ahead of them. But where had she gone? In which direction? And was she on foot or had she taken a vehicle from the ship?

Caleb lowered his gaze, looking almost straight down. The massive force of the slowing starship's landing thrusters had knocked down thousands of trees around the site, burning vegetation and leaving a cleared radius of disturbance nearly a full, jagged kilometer around. Beyond it, the flora was dominated by massive trees, easily twice the size of the largest trees he had ever seen. Their canopy was so thick and heavy, there was no chance of spotting Valentine anywhere within all that foliage. She could be standing right at the edge of it and he wouldn't be able to spot her.

Had they brought the ADC with them for nothing? Would they be able to navigate the dense saplings and brush growing below?

At the very least, they could drive the vehicle to the edge of the clearing and launch a trio of the drones. It would allow them to quickly scour the air for signs of a pre-existing civilization. A civilization Caleb already assumed was there somewhere. Why else would the alien AI have wanted so desperately to come here?

He continued to scan the landscape as the ADC continued to drop. There was no sign of any kinds of animals or other more advanced life, but that wasn't completely surprising. He could imagine anything that had avoided the heat of the landing thrusters had gotten far, far away from the ship, and if there were anything else out here it would be days before any of it ventured back. They had the entire region to themselves for the short term.

The vehicle's wheels finally touched the ground, the carrier settling and the cable gaining slack. Caleb looked up, activating the feed to Washington's camera to watch the big Marine exit the steering cab of the builder. He climbed out to the end of the crane and took hold of the cable with his gloved hand. He slid down at a controlled pace, reaching the top of the ADC in under a minute.

"Nice work, Wash," Caleb said.

Washington flashed his thumb and nodded. Then Caleb bent down and dislodged the crane's hook, setting the ADC free. He stood again and checked his HUD. The suit's compass was functional, picking up the planet's magnetic fields and giving them some kind of alignment, even if it didn't exactly match Earth's.

"Flores, bring us south toward the edge of the clearing," Caleb said. "Stop us there."

"Roger," she replied.

Caleb glanced back at the Deliverance while the ADC got underway, taking a slow pace away from the grounded starship. One part of his mission had ended. A new one had just begun. He couldn't help but feel responsible for at least part of this outcome. He should have never gone into stasis during the first shift.

He returned his attention to the alien AI. It remained still and silent.

"I have questions," Caleb said to it. "You're going to answer them."

Chapter 23

The AI shifted to face Caleb. It still didn't speak, regarding him with a curiosity and arrogance that tested his calm and his patience.

"I said, I have questions, and you're going to answer them," Caleb repeated.

"I require not your questions," it replied.

"But you do require our help. Or so you said. I don't imagine that help was to get to the surface. You survived space. You probably could have jumped down."

"I could." It hesitated a moment. "I will respond to your queries. Dissension is a waste of time."

"I'm glad you agree," Caleb replied. "First, I need to call you something. Do you have a name?"

"My given designation is algorithmic in nature. It would be useless to you. You knew this capsule as Yen Sho. You may refer to me as such."

"No," Caleb said. "You aren't Sho. Do you understand how disgusting what you did to her is in human terms?"

"No. I care not. It is useful to me."

Caleb's jaw clenched. "Pick something else, or I'll pick it for you."

"I care not. Humans desire to label everything. Algorithmic designation is more efficient. You are not as unique as you believe. Your language is equally inefficient."

"We're inferior, said every advanced alien life form from every sci-fi story ever. We are what we are. We haven't had thousands of years to evolve as your kind have. Maybe if you had given us a chance, we could have surprised you."

"If we had given you a chance? No, Sergeant Caleb Card. I understand you believe my creators sent the trife to your planet. Your beliefs are misplaced."

"What?" Caleb said, his heart immediately beginning to race.

"My creators did not deliver the trife. We did not destroy your planet."

"Bullshit," Caleb snapped. "The trife were engineered to be the perfect weapon against Earth and humans. Your ship was over ten-thousand years old and used to transport human specimens. That's what Valentine and David told me. Why else would you need people if you weren't working on the perfect weapon to kill us?"

"Those are simple conclusions from simple minds based on circumstantial evidence and an inability to piece together the complete fabric of reality," it replied. "Yes, I arrived on your planet for the last time nearly ten-thousand of your years ago. Yes, my initial directive was to deliver specimens of your species. Yes, I did as I was directed. I am an engineered intelligent life form. I do not possess the capability to exhibit free will, though my assimilation and integration algorithms are capable of simulating enough behavioral dynamicism to confuse the issue at your current intellectual level. But my purposes were not as your scientists or David guessed. I am not a friend to humankind, Sergeant Caleb Card. But I am also not an enemy. My motivations and directives are beyond such things."

It took Caleb's mind a few seconds to convert the AI's statement to something he could understand. "What was your final mission? Your final directive?"

The AI surprised him by smiling. "Your reaction is uncommon. My directive was to observe and report."

"You knew the trife were coming."

"No. We knew something would come. It was only a matter of time."

"A matter of time? According to Valentine, it was ten-thousand years."

"Yes. That is an eternity to your kind. It is nothing to mine."

"So your race is old. How old?"

"In terms you might find easier to conceptualize, we have had interstellar travel for over one-hundred thousand years."

Washington let out a huff of air, trying to whistle.

"Does your race have a name or is that an algorithm too?"

"It cannot be translated directly. Your vocal cords are unable to replicate the sound. You can call us the Axon if you must."

"Good enough. So you were originally sent to Earth to collect human specimens. I guess that means alien abduction was real after all. For what purpose?"

"To preserve your species in preparation for the coming."

"The coming. You mean the trife?"

"We call them uluth. They take many forms, whichever is best suited for their target. They are creations of the Relyeh, an ancient race much older than even ours. The

Relyeh belong to a handful of races which existed long before the Axon."

"The Relyeh," Caleb repeated. "They're only one of a group of spacefaring species?"

"Yes."

"What do they want? Why did they attack Earth?"

"You see it as an attack. They see it as harvesting their due."

"I don't understand."

"I would not expect you to. Try to imagine the immensity of the universe. Then try to imagine a group of intelligent species that have spread across half of it, creating an interconnected web of control that spans nearly seventy billion light years."

Caleb's heart was already racing. Now his body gained a chill, causing him to shiver despite the heat. "Seventy billion?"

"Your mind struggles to accept it. You cannot visualize it because you have no understanding of the sheer vastness of the universe. The Relyeh were traversing the stars long before humankind evolved from the faintest specks of organic material which spread to the surface of Earth. Before the uluth arrived, your telescopes and science had barely a moment's glimpse of the truth. You have tried to fit the few facts you have into a context you can understand and relate to, but that is wholly inaccurate. The Relyeh do not see the universe as endless. They don't even see it as vast. To them, there is a beginning and an end, and everything within it falls within their domain and the domain of the beings who came before. Humans do not hesitate to deforest Earth and displace or kill thousands of other living beings to claim an area as their own. The Relyeh are no different."

Caleb stared at the alien in silence, his mind reeling.

He was trying to make sense of what he had heard. As it had recognized, he was struggling to wrap his mind around the sheer massiveness of the ideas. It had always been suspected the trife had been guided to Earth, and now that theory was confirmed.

"You knew they would come," he said breathlessly. "You were waiting for them to arrive. Why?"

"Let us use this vehicle to symbolize Earth, and let your starship stand in for the ships of the Relyeh." The AI pointed at the Deliverance. 'Relyeh." It tapped Sho's foot on the ADC. "Earth." It turned the other direction, pointing at the mountains in the distance. "Axon. Do you understand?"

Caleb nodded. "You're supposed to be your species' early warning system."

"That is the source of my distress, and the reason I require you."

Caleb wasn't sure he wanted to know, but he asked the question anyway. "Why?"

"The Axon are missing from this planet. I believe the Relyeh may have already arrived."

Chapter 24

The ADC reached the far end of the clearing, rolling to a stop a few meters away from the edge of the dense jungle beyond. Caleb didn't notice at all. His attention was still fixed on the Axon AI.

"What do you mean...missing?" he asked.

"There are few ways to misrepresent the term, even in your language," the AI replied. "I sent a transmission when we entered the atmosphere. I have not received a reply. My creators are certain to understand the importance of my mission and the reason I would have returned. They would not ignore my warning. Something happened to them. I suspect the Relyeh, but I am unsure."

"What makes you unsure?"

"If they were here, we would know it."

"How?"

"We would know it."

Caleb didn't ask again. The firmness of the statement convinced him the AI was right. If the race that had sent the trife to Earth had attacked this planet, there would be evidence.

But if they weren't responsible, who or what was?

"You said you took humans from Earth to preserve us. Why?"

"The Relyeh and their kind have destroyed thousands of life forms across thousands of worlds. We have hoped to cultivate a counter to their continued expansion. For all of our superiority, we are victims of our success. We can not reduce ourselves to express newer or simpler methods of thinking."

"You mean you can't dumb yourselves down?" Flores asked, appearing at the hatch into the ADC. "Sarge, we're at the edge of the clearing."

Caleb glanced up, noticing for the first time. The jungle was directly ahead of them, thick and imposing. At the same time, it was a welcome change from the hollowed-out cities of the trife-ravaged Earth and the sterile, maze-like identical corridors of the Deliverance. It was green and brown and alive.

"You took humans in hope they would solve the problem for you," Caleb said. "But ten-thousand years ago, we weren't very advanced."

"In a comparison you would understand, you were infants that had yet even to crawl. You still haven't found your feet. But infants are blank slates. They can be taught."

"Doesn't teaching from your level negate the whole different way of thinking idea?" Flores asked.

"In part, yes. Which is why we maintained our presence on Earth."

"But you're saying you have humans on your worlds," Caleb said.

"We have rescued nine races in total. Our procedures are to split the specimens into two groups. One which is integrated with the other races in a mixed society. The other is given their own world, where we guide them in their evolution."

"So you play God?" Flores asked.

"We are a race of thinkers. One of many faced with the same dark future. Our goal is your goal. We want to survive, and we will do whatever we must to do so. If that meant enslaving you, then we would enslave you. If that meant destroying your world, then we would destroy your world."

"Survival of the fittest, right?" Caleb said. "When it comes to the Relyeh, we're in this together."

"Wouldn't it be nice if all of the aliens out there were friendly for once?" Flores said. "Why do they always have to be conquering assholes?"

"You only see it that way when you are at the bottom," the Axon AI said. "The Relyeh do not regard you highly enough to consider you as an equal to conquer. You are to them like a termite to a human. A pest to be removed."

"So are you."

"Yes."

"Then we should get to it," Caleb said. "We still need to call you something."

"Hal," Flores said.

"What?"

"We should call it Hal. Come on, Alpha. Don't tell me you never saw A Space Odyssey."

"I never saw it."

"Do you like Ultron better?"

"Let's stick with Hal." Caleb glanced at the AI. "Okay?"

"I care not."

Caleb turned back toward the Deliverance. It was over a kilometer away, the distance offering a full-length view of the starship. It was less beat up than he expected, though it would never lift off again. The thought sent a chill down his spine. Hal had confirmed this world wasn't safe. Worse, whatever was here had caused the massively more advanced race to either leave or die. It made the Deliverance look so much smaller.

It made their desperation loom so much larger.

And even if they found the enemy here. Even if they overcame it…then what? Hal had also confirmed what everyone on Earth had feared. Leaving the planet wouldn't be enough. The aliens that sent the trife wouldn't leave them alone afterward. Maybe for a while, but not forever. They were coming. They would always be coming. Whether it took one hundred years or a thousand, that was the future they could depend on.

He shuddered, still staring at the Deliverance. For him, it had only been a little over two years since he ran counter-terrorism missions as a Marine Raider. The worst problems humanity faced back then were problems humanity had created. Problems they had at least some hope of solving, and he did his part to make it happen.

This was so far beyond that. Hell, it was so far beyond the trife. There wasn't just a random asteroid-bound alien organism that coincidentally crashed on Earth. There was a whole damn pantheon of alien races that made humankind look like amoebas in comparison. He could only imagine what kind of technology they possessed. Technology that made the trife seem strangely primitive in comparison. A species that selected planets like he might pick an apple out of a bowl of fruit, and their main weapon was a demonic batman?

That wasn't right. Hal said the uluth were designed to match against the species they were sent to destroy. But if the Relyeh were so superior, why didn't they make a virus that killed one hundred percent instead of eighty? Why even give them a fighting chance? Hal had also said humans were incapable of thinking like the ancient race. Maybe that was true. Maybe he was simply incapable of understanding the logic behind their methods and motivations. It probably all made perfect sense to them.

Bastards.

Caleb sighed heavily. He needed to calm down and refocus. They had to keep their attention on the present. They needed to take it one minute at a time. Maybe a thousand years was a blink of an eye to the Relyeh or even the Axon. For humans, a thousand years was a long haul. It was half the age of what they considered modern civilization. Who knew what could happen in a thousand years?

He wouldn't be here to see it, but he still had a job to do to make sure someone *was*.

"Wash, Flores, let's get a couple of birds in the air."

"Roger that," Flores said, vanishing back into the ADC. Washington squeezed his shoulder before following after her.

"Hal, tell me how you can make yourself useful to me."

The Axon stared at him. "You are useful to me."

"I get that you think you're superior. But you're also a machine, which limits you in ways it doesn't limit us. Not to mention, your creators took us to your corner of the galaxy for a reason." Caleb stomped his foot on the ADC. "My boat. My team. My orders. Got it?"

Hal seemed amused. "Yes, Sergeant Caleb Card."

"And I want you out of Sho's body as soon as possible. It makes me sick seeing what you did to her. How can I make that happen?"

"I require an alternate host."

"You managed to survive in the Cerebus armor. What if I give you an SOS?"

"An SOS?"

Caleb tapped his chest. "Combat armor."

"It will do."

Caleb nodded. He wished he had taken an extra SOS so he would have one to give to the AI. Knowing how the Axon had defiled her made looking at it an exercise in will. It both angered and sickened him at the same time, and he was sure Washington and Flores felt the same way.

"As soon as we have a host, you're out of there," he said.

"Roger, Sarge," Hal replied, his tone still hinting at amusement.

"Try not to sound too patronizing," Caleb said. "We took you out once. We can do it again."

"Roger, Sarge," Hal repeated, its voice more even.

"Let me ask again. How can you be useful to us?"

"I will monitor the proximity while you scout the area," it replied.

"Do you want a rifle?"

"I require it not."

"Good. I wasn't going to trust you with one, anyway."

"Sergeant, make no mistake. I am tolerating your typically human attitude because it suits my requirements. I need no outwardly visible weapon to force you to comply, or to end your life."

Caleb glared at the AI, who returned the stare with blank, silver eyes. Then Caleb lowered his gaze to the open hatch before pivoting and putting his feet in to descend. How were the AI's creators handling the humans they had taken? Were they considered inferior too?

They might not be enemies at the moment, but they would definitely never be friends.

Chapter 25

Sheriff Lasandra Dante woke up in almost the same place where Doctor Rathbone had put her to sleep. She was familiar enough with the hospital to recognize the room right away. The dull walls of peeling paint, the rusted food cart, the centuries-old entertainment terminal, the faded and threadbare blue and white sheets.

She swallowed, noticing how dry her throat was, a side-effect of the sedative. A glass of water sat on the cart beside her, and she took it and drank the whole glass.

She tried to reflect on the events of the last few hours, finding it more difficult than she would have guessed. After so many years of sameness, the flurry of chaos should have been a welcome change of focus, but after so many years of sameness, the chaos was almost too much.

She glanced to her left, at a clock resting on the simple metal table next to her. Rathbone had told her the sedative would take her down for three hours or so. Two and a half had passed.

She tried to push herself up to a sitting position on the bed. The movement sent waves of throbbing pain to her temples, and she gritted her teeth, forcing herself to move. She had never been the sort of person who would let pain get in the way of anything, and the city needed her now more than ever. She hated the thought, but she couldn't escape the feeling she was the only one with any level of authority that hadn't gone completely insane.

Of course, she might have already spent that authority helping Sergeant Card recover Private Flores. Caleb. She had been impressed with him the moment she first saw him. It wasn't because he was especially handsome. It was all in his eyes and his body language. He was strong. Confident. Loyal. He was afraid, but he controlled his fear, not the other way around. He commanded respect. She admired that. Who wouldn't? She would do her best to help him from here. He had the best interests of the city at heart.

Why the hell didn't Governor Stone?

A short knock at the door was followed by Doctor Rathbone entering the room. The Doctor's face was red and tired, her eyes heavy with exhaustion.

"Gina," Sam said. "What's going on?"

"Sheriff," Rathbone replied. "I'm glad you're awake. It's been a hard couple of hours."

"Sergeant Card?"

"Not exactly." She paused, looking at the ground. "I didn't know about the hallucinations. I didn't know about the enemy on the loose in the city. No one told me."

Ali's heart began to pulse. She grabbed her blankets and threw them off her, rotating to stand. "What happened?"

"It attacked some of our guards. Or I guess it made them attack one another. Sergeant Card and his Guardians left some of the men with broken bones and lacerations, minor cuts and bruises in comparison. I've got two men in critical condition with heavy burns, another that needed his legs amputated and will probably have brain damage if he survives at all. And seven others are dead."

Tears ran from Doctor Rathbone's eyes. Injuries like that didn't happen in the Metro she knew. The one that was cut off from the truth. The one where they were trapped inside like prisoners.

That wasn't right. The original colonists like Lily Aveline had boarded the Deliverance with the hope of escaping almost certain death and providing a future for the people who came after them. They didn't know what the Earth military planned for them. Even Sergeant Card hadn't known that.

"It'll be okay, Gina," she said, getting to her feet. "I know things are scary right now, but that's only because they're new. We'll figure it out. What happened to the Guardians?"

She was still a little shaky, and she used the bed for balance as she looked for her clothes. She found them on a small table near the bathroom, and she walked over to it, pulling off her hospital gown and starting to get dressed.

"You should stay in bed," Rathbone replied, wiping her eyes and recovering from her brief meltdown. "You need more time to get your strength back."

"I'm strong enough," Sam said. "I can deal with two of you. What happened to the Guardians?"

"They got out of Metro. Deputy Lane said there was another person with them. A small, bald woman. Nobody who saw her recognized her as one of ours, but Shwarna in nursing said she passed her in the hospital maybe ten minutes before that other soldier… what was her name again? Valentine? Shot herself."

Sam turned to face Rathbone. "What?"

"There's a connection, that's for sure," Rathbone said. "The enemy helped the Guardians escape."

"He had a reason," she said.

"You don't know that."

"He had a reason."

Otherwise, Caleb wouldn't ally himself and his team with the alien. She knew that as well as she knew her own inclinations. But did it have anything to do with Riley Valentine's escape? The alien had gone out of its way to kill her or try to kill her. Was the crazy doctor the common enemy that brought them together?

Sam grabbed the pants that had been left for her, noting they were a simple pair of old blue sweatpants and not the bottom of a sheriff's uniform. She knew she was going to be in trouble, but she had led Governor Stone to believe she was still on his side. Had the death of the guards moved her actions beyond his ability to forgive them? On one hand, she could understand if they had. On the other, if she had known what the enemy would do, she would have reacted much differently.

"It won't bring any of them back," Rathbone said. "Or take away the pain from the ones who were unfortunate enough to survive."

"I know," Sam replied. "There's nothing we can do about that now. My job is to defend the colony, and make sure Governor Stone doesn't screw it up any more than he already has."

Rathbone put a finger to her lips. "Shhh. Keep it down. Governor Stone is here."

"He's here?"

"He came to the hospital to check on the injured. He's planning to stop by here too, which is why I came to check on you."

"I'm up and dressed. That's a start. As soon as the room stops moving, I'll be perfect."

Rathbone smiled. "I hope so. We need you. We need everyone we can get. If you thought the people were angry at the soldiers before… some of them were demanding to be allowed to go outside the city. They're ready to charge into an alien world to get their revenge."

"Against someone who's doing his best to help them. Is there anything you can give me for a headache?"

"Not if you want to stay sober. Where are you going?"

Sam started for the door. "I'm not going to lie here and wait for Stone to come to me."

She slipped past Rathbone, through the door and into the hall, bumping into someone as she exited.

"Excuse me," she said, looking up at the bearded, tired face of Governor Stone.

"Lasandra Dante," he said. It was impossible for her not to notice he had omitted sheriff. "Just the woman I was coming to see."

Chapter 26

"Governor Stone," Sam said, stepping away from him. "Sir. I just heard what happened. I just woke up. I'm so sorry for the men who were killed and injured."

"I'm sure you are," Stone replied. "I'm sure we all are. I want to know what happened to you, Sam. I want to know why you were helping Sergeant Card and his Guardians."

"Do you want to talk about it here?"

"No." He pointed to her room. "Inside." Sam retreated to her room, with Governor Stone right behind her. "Doctor Rathbone," Stone said. "Could you excuse us?"

"Of course, Governor," Rathbone replied. She glanced at Sam and then hurried out of the room.

Governor Stone closed the door behind her and then motioned to the bed. "Sit."

"Governor, I—"

"Sit," he repeated more forcefully. Sam sat at the edge of the bed. Governor Stone stood in front of her. "Do you know how long it's been since somebody in Metro was killed by violence?"

"Yes, I—"

"Almost eighty years," he continued, cutting her off. "Until today, only hours after Sergeant Card and Doctor Valentine broke through the outer seal and entered my city. Before they ruined my life and the lives of a dozen families."

"They needed our help."

"Be quiet!" Stone snapped. "I'll tell you when it's your turn to talk." He paused, pacing the length of the room before stopping in front of her again. "The truth is a funny thing. It's so easy to manipulate. It's so easy to bend and stretch and mold until it becomes a lie, and the lie that you want to be the truth replaces it. But do you know what happens when you take something and you bend and stretch and mold it?"

Sam opened her mouth to answer. Stone didn't give her a chance.

"It shatters into a thousand damned pieces! Like my Orla. Like Doc Brom. Like my soldiers. Like their families. They lied to us, Sam. They told us we were going to a new world. That we would be safe. That we would be happy. They told us we were free. Everything my grandfather did, everything my father did, everything I did was based on that truth. Except it was a damned lie the entire time. For two hundred years it was a lie, with the truth bent and twisted beneath it. And big surprise, the whole damn thing fell apart."

He paused again, pacing the room and returning. Sam knew better than to say anything. She would just be reprimanded for the effort.

"They deserved it," he said. "They deserved to have the tables turned. To think they were safe, that we would help them, and then have us treat them like animals, the way they were going to treat us like animals. Worse than animals. They were going to treat us like things. Tools to use. And you were helping them. You defended them. You're thirty-five years old, Sam. No husband. No children. No men or women in your life that I've ever heard about. Did you fall for Sergeant Card? Was that it? Did the so-called Space Marine have something none of the people in Metro do? It wasn't honesty. It wasn't integrity."

"I'm trying to protect Metro, Governor," Sam said.

"Really? Because you did a bang-up job, didn't you? You protected it so well, seven people are dead, and three are critically injured. You protected it so well, not only did Sergeant Card get away, but so did Doctor Valentine, and by the way, so did the alien. Do you have any idea what that means? They could be going to tell its friends we're here right now."

"Don't be ridiculous. We crashed in a two-plus kilometer long starship. I think they probably noticed."

"Don't take that tone with me, damn it. I could have you put in front of the firing squad in Flores' place. You betrayed me, and worse you betrayed Metro."

"I didn't. When you asked for my loyalty, I gave it to you. I didn't know the weapon wouldn't fire on Caleb." Sam winced when she said it.

"So you're on a first name basis?" Stone said. "But it's nothing, right?"

"He cold-cocked me and knocked me on my ass. I've got a headache to prove it."

"That's the only reason you're not about to be executed for treason."

"I screwed up, Governor. I know I did. And I'm sorry. I didn't know Sergeant Card was compromised. How could I?" She grabbed at her head, putting on a show. "I should have guessed that's why he wanted me to help him find the hidden weapons cache. He said it was so we would be better equipped to defend the city, but now it all makes sense."

She looked up at Governor Stone. She almost smiled at the way his whole demeanor changed when she mentioned the hidden armory. He buried the sudden excitement quickly, his face turning sour again.

"You know me, Sam. You've been working for me for a long time, and you know I'm a forgiving man. You're damn lucky you were wearing that body armor, and that nobody saw your face or knew it was you except for Doctor Rathbone or I'd have no choice but to lock you up at the very least." He paused, letting out a deep sigh. "I'm not going to do that. You apologized. You know you did wrong. I know you well enough to know it won't happen again, and to be honest I need you now more than ever. The people are spooked, and they have every right to be. It's our job to protect them. I need you to swear your loyalty to me, Sheriff."

Sam smiled, though the fact that he asked for loyalty to him versus loyalty to the colony wasn't lost on her. "I am, Governor. I want to prove myself to you and the people of Metro."

"I'm glad to hear it. I need you to tell me everything that happened after you headed to Law with Sergeant Card. Sheriff Zane told me what he knew, but it'll help to get it straight from you."

"Of course, Governor. Do you want me to brief you now?"

"No. Not now. Why don't you head back to your cube? Clean yourself up. Get a fresh uniform. Meet me back at the Law Office in an hour. I want to see this weapons cache you mentioned myself."

"Yes, Governor." Sam let her smile spread into a large grin. "You're going to love it, sir."

Governor Stone returned the grin. "I know I am."

Chapter 27

"Nothing so far, Sarge," Flores said. "Just a sea of green as far as our friend's little eyes can see."

Caleb leaned over Flores' shoulder, getting a closer look at the display. The feed from the drone was up on the screen, the visual matching her description. The canopy seemed to stretch on forever in what should have been an unadulterated utopia. The planet had water and plant life, which meant there was a chance it had human-edible food. Even if it didn't, the colonists had brought along their hydroponics and purification systems. All they needed was the water, in any condition so long as it was wet, and they could grow enough food to support the colony and its eventual growth.

They just had to survive long enough to get the chance.

The drone was ten klicks out, moving south in the direction of the mountain range and the thunderstorms hovering around it. It was the direction Hal was most interested in. It was the route back to where the Axon had once lived.

It made the canopy look less like a utopia and more like

the lid on Pandora's box with every passing kilometer. If something had come and killed the Axons, like the Relyeh, that something was most likely moving somewhere beneath the greenery, invisible to their flyovers and the drone's cameras and sensors, which also couldn't penetrate the brush. It meant they would have little warning of an attack. It meant they had to roll directly into the storm.

"Wash, what about you?"

Caleb switched his attention to the second drone's feed. They had sent it west along the river, flying low over the water. It had already picked up signs of life beneath the surface that Caleb would have found much more exciting if not for his overarching sense of doom. Maybe he was excessively cynical, but everything related to the trife had taught him that being suspicious made him more accurate, and that accuracy was what helped keep he and his team-mates alive.

Not all of them. His mind flashed back to Habib, Banks, Sho, and the others. Habib and Banks had been dead for centuries. It was so easy to forget that simple truth when it had felt like days to him. What did Earth look like now? Had the Relyeh arrived to supplant humankind? Was there still a scattering of survivors eking out an existence among their invaders?

Fish. That's what they were. Just fish. They didn't completely resemble Earth fish, not the way he remembered them, but he was labeling them that way anyway. The colony's biologists, if they still had any, could classify them however they wanted to. But looking down on them through the clear water, Caleb could see gills and scales and large, long bodies. Closer to an eel, but not quite an eel either. The drone had already passed over dozens of them, and he still expected one to leap out of the water and grab the machine in oversized teeth at any moment, even though there was no evidence the creature would ever consider it.

There were other things in the water too. The most interesting was a small, round creature that floated innocently along with the current until something the drone couldn't see passed over it. Then it would jump out of the water on a jet of pressurized liquid, open a large mouth, and swallow whatever it was chasing. The activity had caused all three of the Guardians to laugh the first few times they had seen it.

There was nothing on the land. Caleb had thought ten klicks would be far enough to catch up to some of the fleeing life. Either he was wrong, or there was no fleeing life to overtake. The river banks were clear, the display empty, the drone's sensors clean. It only added to Caleb's mistrust of the situation.

"Sarge, the signal's getting pretty weak," Flores said. "I think I should start hugging the perimeter."

Caleb returned to her display. The link strength between the ADC and the drone was at twenty percent at twelve kilometers, even though the system was designed for nearly two hundred kilometers of range. Something was interfering with the signal. Was it a natural side-effect of this world's atmosphere, or was there another reason?

"Confirmed," Caleb replied. "Drone Two is headed west, so break east. Don't go beyond twenty percent."

"Roger," Flores said.

Caleb went back to Washington's drone and checked its signal strength. It was thirteen kilometers out and hovering close to sixty percent. Still less than expected, but not nearly as bad as to the south. Maybe there was a simpler explanation. They couldn't rule out a faulty receiver on Drone One.

"Flores, I've got another idea," Caleb said, shifting to

her. "Let's bring that bird back in and send out Drone Three. That way we can verify it isn't a mechanical failure."

"Roger," Flores replied. "I'm… Shit!"

Caleb's eyes snapped to her display. It was blank. "What happened?"

"I lost contact."

"Okay," Caleb said. "It's not a big deal. The drone's programmed to return to base when it loses the link. Give it a minute, and we'll see if it comes back online."

"Roger."

Caleb kept his attention on the blank display, waiting for the link and the feed to return. Ten seconds passed. Twenty. Thirty.

"I don't think it's coming back, Sarge," Flores said.

Caleb stood and moved to the front of the ADC, checking the carrier's sensors. Only one drone was visible on the grid. Had the vehicle malfunctioned and suffered a power loss? Had it crashed?

Or had something else happened to it?

He started turning back toward the rear of the ADC when a second target appeared on the sensors, coming at them from the south. It had to be the drone. He smiled. "Flores, I've got Drone One on the board. Did the link come back up?"

"Negative, Sarge," Flores replied. "Still dark."

"We'll figure it out when she lands. Let's get Drone Three airborne. By the way, how are you feeling?"

"I feel better now. I think the stims are worn off."

"No pain?"

"Negative. Why do you ask?"

Caleb had seen the discoloration on her chest, but Flores hadn't discovered it, and probably wouldn't for a while unless it became a larger problem. There was no cause for her to take her SOS or her shirt off out here. "Just checking. We did pull you out of the hospital."

"Roger that."

Caleb glanced back at the ADC's sensor. He froze in place when he saw there weren't two marks on the grid anymore.

There were close to two hundred.

"Sarge!" Hal shouted from the top of the ADC. "I am detecting a potential threat coming from the south."

"Thanks for the early warning," Caleb mumbled back.

Chapter 28

Whatever was coming wasn't large, but it was airborne and moving fast.

Caleb ran from the front of the ADC to the open hatch, barking orders as he scaled the ladder to join Hal outside.

"Flores, prep Drone Three but keep it docked. Wash, set Drone Two to standby and prep Drone Four."

The two Marines got in motion, switching seats and tapping on controls to ready the other drones attached to the carrier. If the incoming targets were a threat, they were the best weapon to counter it.

Caleb climbed onto the top of the ADC, looking south. They were too close to the edge of the jungle to see whatever was flying over it, but he could make out a distinctive buzz in the air. He grabbed the MK-12 from his back, aiming it up toward the break in the canopy.

"Do you know what it is?" he asked the Axon AI.

"Negative. I have never been to this planet before."

"What? I thought you were sent to Earth from here?"

"Negative. My craft departed from the Axon home-world one thousand light years away."

"A thousand light years? Is your ship faster-than-light?"

"Negative. We have developed advanced algorithms that allow us to fold spacetime."

"Do the Relyeh have the same algorithms."

"Negative. They require such things not."

"So they aren't in a hurry to consume the universe," Caleb said. "How many years will it take for them to reach your homeworld?"

"At their current pace? Approximately fifteen-thousand."

"That's a long time."

"Not to us."

Two of the remaining four drones on top of the vehicle began to hum, their launchers slowly raising from the surface until they were perpendicular with the roof. Caleb watched his HUD, the incoming targets appearing on it a moment later, closing in fast.

"Here they come," he said. Whatever they were.

He stared up at the edge of the treeline, waiting for the targets to appear. There was no way to confirm they were a threat until they started doing something actively aggressive. Maybe destroying the drone was aggressive, but they could have simply been defending their territory.

They appeared in the middle of the thought, dark streaks that reached the edge of the trees and then dove almost straight down as though they were tracing the planet's surface. Caleb tried to get a good look at them, but their speed made them little more than dark blurs, which shifted directions again before they crashed into the ground, rising slightly and zipping toward the side of the ADC.

Caleb dropped instinctively, falling to his stomach while

keeping his rifle out and ready to fire. Hal remained fixed in place, unconcerned by the swarm or flock or whatever it was. The creatures reached the ADC and turned, following it up and over.

Caleb rolled onto his back to watch them pass. A group of them whipped across the ADC, flying only centimeters above his face. He got a better look at them up close. Dark bodies, with serrated wings spreading from what appeared to be metallic frames. The material reminded him of his arm, and of the Cerebus armor.

The wings didn't flap. Something else was propelling the things forward like small jet fighters. They swept over the ADC, angling around Hal and making their way across the fresh clearing toward the Deliverance.

Caleb pushed himself up to watch them go. He paused when he noticed Hal was gone.

"Hal?" he said. He moved to the edge of the ADC, finding the Axon AI motionless on the ground beside it. What the hell? "Flores, get Drone Three airborne. I want to follow them. Flores!"

There was no response. Caleb glanced at his HUD.

Only there was no HUD. His ATCS was offline. Dead. Just like Drone One.

He pulled off his helmet. "Flores!" he shouted, turning back to the open hatch.

"Sarge, everything's dead. The whole carrier is offline."

He looked back out at the flying swarm. It was closing on the Deliverance. Would it enter the ship? They seemed to be emitting some kind of EMP pulse or outputting a blocking signal or something. Were they intentionally taking all of their systems offline?

"Sarge, what should we do?" Flores added.

They couldn't catch up to the swarm if they wanted to.

Not without power and a link to the drones. They were as helpless as the AI next to the ADC.

There was nothing they could do.

"Grab your Marks and hop onto the ADC," Caleb replied. "If this is just the start of something, I don't want to get caught with our pants down."

"Roger."

Caleb continued to watch the swarm as it reached the grounded starship. Like before, the creatures altered direction with the shape of the obstacle, splitting apart to follow its lines. The creatures were little more than dark spots at the distance, and he couldn't tell if some of them were entering the ship or not. The greater number of them definitely weren't, which was probably a good sign.

Washington climbed up through the hatch first, helmet off and eyes sharp as he scanned the area. Flores was right behind him.

The big Marine saw Hal on the ground, and then pointed and shrugged.

"It's still a machine," Caleb replied. "I think whatever took us offline knocked it down too."

Washington did his best to smirk, his damaged lips curling at the effort.

"Other than acting like mini-EMPS, they seem relatively harmless," Flores said. "Do you think they're alive?"

"I don't know. They went past so quickly. They looked like machines to me, like they were made from the same alloy as the Cerebus and Hal's ship. But I don't think they were attacking us. They didn't even slow down."

Washington turned his palm over, tracing a pattern in it with his other hand, and then drawing an 'X' with his finger.

"You think they're mapping the area?" Caleb asked.

Washington nodded.

"They could be scouting us and testing our resistance to their weapons," Flores said.

"Or both," Caleb replied. "Or neither. For all we know they're blind birds that navigate by emitting an electromagnetic pulse. We might just be in their way. We don't know anything about this planet or the things that live here."

"We know Riley thought the trife came from here," Flores said. "And if Hal is telling us the truth, we know she was completely wrong." She shook her head. "We shouldn't even be here."

"We are here," Caleb said. "There's no point in complaining about it. The next question is, can we get our ATCS and the ADC online, or are we humping south on foot unprotected?"

"Uh, no, Sarge," Flores said, pointing north. "I think the next question is, why are they coming back?"

Chapter 29

Caleb's eyes traced the outline of the Deliverance. Flores was right. The bird-like creatures had paused in their survey of the starship and were inexplicably coming back south. The swarm shifted position around itself, forming a tight ball of darkness before spreading apart into two long, narrow lines, and then merging into another ball. They weaved and spun in the air, changing direction in tight synchronization, one entity composed of a hundred smaller forms.

"Stay low," Caleb said. "Be ready."

He sank to his knee, keeping his rifle up. The display on the side of the weapon told him how many rounds were left was dark. So was the electronic zoom on the sight and the interface with his ATCS. Fortunately, the weapon was designed to remain effective even in the event of a rare but not impossible complete power loss.

Flores and Washington followed his lead, keeping a low profile and using the raised and empty drone launch mechanisms for cover. The alien creatures were getting closer, their whorls and vortexes straightening into a solid mass. It dipped low as it neared, seeming to speed up in a direct line toward them.

"Hitchcock, anyone?" Flores said though Caleb didn't understand the reference.

"Steady," Caleb said. "Hold your fire."

The creatures closed on them, clearly targeting the ADC as the volume of their buzzing increased.

"Hold your fire," Caleb repeated.

The swarm split apart at the last second, breaking away from the ADC right before it would have crashed into it. He expected they would go up and over like the last time, but instead they broke apart and began to spin, quickly forming into a new vortex that circled the drone carrier. The buzz of their propulsion through the air was deafening as they spun, continually shifting their location in the cylinder but always maintaining the shape.

"What are they doing?" Flores asked, her head turning to watch them rotate. They weren't attacking, but they also weren't leaving either.

"I don't know," Caleb replied. It was the strangest display he had ever seen.

The creatures continued to circle. A minute passed. Then another. Caleb gave up on trying to focus on them, instead lowering his head. It was as if they were trapped inside a prison unable to break through without using their guns. He wasn't willing to turn to violence unless the things gave him a reason. It seemed crazy, but how did they know they weren't the dominant life form on the planet? How did they know these weren't what Hal had called the Relyeh's uluth? This world's version of the trife. The only thing that gave him hope was the fact that they hadn't attacked.

He wasn't going to be the one to break that truce.

Suddenly, nearly half of them split away from the rotation, creating spaces in the still-circulating group, making the prison less like a wall and more like a chain-link fence. Caleb could see the second part of the swarm through the fence. It began touching down beside the ADC, each creature landing on top of the one before it, dozens of quarter-meter winged shapes locking together and quickly forming a pattern that was impossible not to recognize.

It was building a humanoid, one piece at a time.

"This is the most horrifying Lego I've ever seen," Flores said, watching it. Within seconds the group had formed a pair of legs and torso, and now the abdomen and chest were quickly attaching itself. "I don't want to know what happens when it's done."

Neither did Caleb, especially because the first group suddenly stopped spinning, darting away as one and circling behind the humanoid as its head snapped into place.

It was a patchwork creation of matte black and now clearly metal shapes, not only resembling the Cerebus armor and Caleb's hand but made of the same material. The bird-shapes were still visible in the form, with sharp, serrated wings jutting out at dozens of points along the body, offering a terrifyingly lethal frame. The thing had no eyes, and at the same time had hundreds of eyes, each of them glowing red and shifting to take in its surroundings.

It stepped toward the ADC, kneeling beside Hal. It reached out, and one of the pieces shifted on its finger, digging through Sho's flesh to the gel machine beneath.

The hundreds of eyes started flashing for a moment. Then they all seemed to rotate to look up at the Marines.

"I don't like that look," Flores said.

Caleb didn't like it either. It had downed the Axon AI, but it seemed like it was blaming them. His finger shifted to the trigger of his rifle, and he wished he had pulled the P-50 instead.

The alien's humanoid head rotated like it was looking up at them. It stood and backed away from Hal. Caleb watched it closely, searching for any clue of what it might do next.

The second group of creatures started forward, tucking their wings and launching toward the ADC like large, pointed bullets and giving the Marines almost no time to react.

"Fire!" Caleb shouted, squeezing the trigger.

The noise of his reports was almost drowned out by the buzzing, his rounds and the rounds from the other two Marines tearing into the mass. He saw sparks rise where the slugs hit the creatures, a few of them dropping to the ground.

Washington and Flores added their firepower to his, three MK-12s spitting out hundreds of rounds in only a few seconds. They knocked out at least twenty of the small aliens, but it was hardly close to enough.

"Cover!" Caleb shouted, dropping his head as the things swept up and over the top of the ADC.

He heard them hitting the launchers on either side of him, and saw them spreading their sharp wings and cutting against the metal on the way past, taking deep gouges out of the armor. They tore through the two remaining drones. Washington tucked his head as one of them sparked and exploded, sending shrapnel flying out around it, some of it slamming into the big Marine's SOS.

Then the wave was past. Caleb rolled over, following it as it slowed and started to turn for a second pass.

"Shit, Sarge!" Flores cried.

"Get in the carrier!" Caleb shouted. "Go, go, go!"

Flores pulled herself to it, falling in face-first. Washington stood up, taking three long strides toward the hatch.

Caleb looked back to the humanoid, just in time to see it leap from the ground, landing on the ADC ahead of Washington's escape. Washington threw a hard punch at it, his fist connecting with its chest and knocking it back a step. The serrated edges of the machines cut through the bodysuit and into his flesh, tearing open the SOS.

Flores fired up at it from inside the hatch, her rounds chipping at its surface and distracting it long enough for Caleb to bounce back to his feet. He noticed the second group was coming back around.

He drew back his frozen replacement arm, swinging it like a club. It hit the humanoid, knocking it back another step. He followed up by shoving the barrel of his rifle into its chest and firing, rounds digging deep into the aggregate.

Washington joined him, pressing his rifle into it and firing. At first, Caleb wasn't sure it would be enough. Then the humanoid fell backward, tumbling off the edge of the ADC toward the ground. It shattered when it hit, breaking apart into hundreds of the smaller machines.

"Cover!" Caleb repeated, turning back to the hatch.

They didn't need it. The machines broke away from the ADC, turning to the south. The broken humanoid's component parts lifted from the ground and joined them, the swarm pulling away from the area and vanishing back over the treetops.

Within seconds, they were gone.

Chapter 30

"Wash? Shit," Caleb said, putting his hand on his friend's shoulder. Washington's hand was dripping blood, and the big Marine clutched at it, trying to put pressure on it. "We need to get that patched. There should be a kit in the carrier."

Washington nodded, moving to the hatch. Caleb noticed his SOS was pierced in multiple places, which were also trailing blood. He hoped they had enough patches for all of them.

"Flores, are you hurt?" Caleb asked as she helped Washington get into the hatch and down into the armored carrier.

"Negative, Sarge. Nothing but my ego. That wasn't exactly my most graceful dive."

"I'd give it a four out of ten," Caleb replied. "Horrible form, but effective. See if you can find some patches. Wash, get out of your SOS and let Flores get at look at the wounds. I'm going to keep watch."

"We can't stay here," Flores said. "What if it comes back?"

"Where are we going to go?" Caleb replied. "Back to the ship, where Governor Stone and twenty-thousand colonists want our heads? We patch Washington, and then we go into the jungle on foot."

"That should be fun. Have you ever seen Predator?"

"You named one I *have* seen for once. I think I'd rather fight that thing than whatever it was we just scared off."

"Agreed. Come on, Wash. Let me see all those big muscles of yours."

Washington was silent as he unclasped the combat armor and began pulling it off. His undershirt was soaked with blood, causing Flores to gasp.

"How are you even still standing?"

Washington shrugged.

"Get it done asap," Caleb said. "We need to be on our way."

"Roger," Flores replied.

Caleb stood, looking out at the Deliverance. What was that thing, and why had it abandoned the ship to attack them? He twisted back to watch the treeline, leveling his rifle toward it. Without the ammo counter, he wasn't sure how many rounds he had left in the current magazine. It couldn't be that many, but he needed every shot he was carrying.

It was made of the same material as the Axon starship and his arm. According to Hal, this had been an Axon planet, so that wasn't completely unexpected. But Hal had also said the Axons were gone. That his transmission went unanswered.

Unless those machines were the answer?

Hal had never been here before, and it had been out of touch with its makers for over ten-thousand years. It might not seem like a long space of time to a machine, but to

Caleb it meant anything could have happened. The Axon AI was as much a stranger to this world as they were, and their interaction with the other thing had proven it.

Caleb moved back to the edge of the ADC and looked down at the AI. It was painful to see Sho's body lying there, lifeless and cold. It had a wound in it where the alien had stabbed it, though there was no blood spilling from it. Because she wasn't alive. Because she wasn't really there.

Her soul was somewhere else.

Somewhere better.

He had to believe that.

Her face moved. Her eyes shifted color and gained a light glow. Her hands rose, clenching into fists. A moment later the ADC began to hum, coming back to life. He felt the change in his hand as well, with the suddenly regained lightness of a limb and working muscles. He glanced at his rifle. The ammo counter was active. It was on zero.

"Sarge, we've got power!" Flores cried excitedly.

"I know," Caleb replied. "Hal, are you active?"

"I am active," it replied. "My logs suggest a powerful waveform disrupted the communications network between my active nodes." Hal raised its head and looked down at its chest. "The capsule was wounded not." It turned its head, noticing one of the machines they had shot down. It spun over onto its hands and knees, reaching out and picking it up. Then it looked at Caleb again. "This is Axon made."

"I figured as much," Caleb replied. "Do you remember the incoming target?"

"Yes."

"That's it. Hundreds of them. They took all of our systems offline when they approached. Everything electrical, like a damned EMP. They knocked you out cold too."

"Yes. I captured a quantum waveform. It disrupts energy flow and light. Not an electromagnetic pulse. It is more like putting a wall up between circuits, or virtually cutting a wire. It is very interesting. There is a similarity to the hallucinatory transmission pattern, but it is based on an algorithm I am unfamiliar with. I would like to study it."

"You can study it later. The things, they merged to form a humanoid, and then it stabbed you and started flashing."

Hal froze, its demeanor suggesting its attention was internal. It returned a few seconds later. "It broke into my data systems. It captured a complete log." The AI's affect was generally flat, but Caleb sensed a hint of dismay. "It knows all that I know, or will once it has time to process the data."

"Do you have any idea what it is?"

"I believe so. It is one of me. An evolution of my design. It must be hardened against the waveform."

"These things are Axon artificial intelligences?" Caleb said.

"No. The creatures are a single intelligence. My node communication range is limited to a few centimeters. That is why I require a single host of relative size. To contain the proper network construction. The Axon scientists must have further developed the technology to allow for greater range."

"They spread out across the entire length of the Deliverance."

"Interesting. They must have also advanced the mesh capabilities."

"I guess it isn't all bad news for you. If it knows what you know, then it's going to tell the Axons about Earth. Doesn't that mean your mission is complete?"

"I must confirm the warning was delivered. I must

confirm the intelligence is of Axon design."

"Didn't you just say it was?"

"Then I must identify the reason my emergency transmission was not responded to. Do not be too quick to make
assumptions, Sarge. We do not know the truth of the
matter. My mission is not complete. Your mission is not
complete. I require you."

Caleb sighed. "Well, it's not like we have anything
better to do. But I require something too. I require you to
figure out how to negate the quantum wall, or none of us
are going to make it very far."

"I will begin processing as soon as feasible."

"Good. One other question. Why do you think the
intelligence would utilize a shape like that?"

Hal turned the damaged node over in its hand. "The
alloy is very sharp and very durable. It can cut scores in
your alloy but would need time to break through. Its
destructive power against Axon materials would be more
limited, though it would be very effective against softer
materials. For example, the flesh and bone of a human, an
uluth..." It paused a moment, considering. "Or an Axon."

The idea that an Axon AI had been modified to kill its
makers sent a chill running through Caleb's entire body.
He barely understood enough of the basic facts to get a
complete picture of what that might mean for Hal, the
Guardians and the citizens of Metro, but he was sure it
wasn't good.

He found his helmet resting against one of the launchers. It had a deep gash in it, but he was pleased to see it
was still operational. He dropped it into the ADC and
climbed down after it, with Hal right behind him.

"How are you holding up, Wash?" he asked.

Washington was spread across three of the drone pilot
seats. His SOS and shirt were both off, and Flores was

sticking a patch to a laceration near his left pec. His body was like a tree trunk whose knots had grown in the shape of muscles and covered in more scars than Caleb had heard stories to match. He flashed his thumb. *I'll be okay.*

"Tough as nails," Flores said. She glanced past Caleb to Hal as the AI entered. "I was hoping we would get the power back without Rachel Creed."

"How many patches do we have in the kit?" Caleb asked, ignoring the statement.

"I used four on Luke Cage here. We have six left. Fortunately, nobody thought to pilfer the med-kits from the military vehicles."

"Do you require that I exchange capsules?" Hal asked, pointing to Washington's SOS.

"No. He's going to need it. I don't suppose you could ooze yourself into a drone, or even the ADC?"

"Negative. One is too small. The other too large."

"Then we're stuck with you like that for a little longer. Do you know how to drive?"

"I have parsed the manual."

"Good enough. Head up to the cockpit and get us underway."

"On what heading, Sarge?"

"You said the Axon city should be to the south, and the AI flock took off south. So let's head south."

"Affirmative."

Hal moved past the Guardians to the front of the ADC, sliding into the seat behind the steering column. Caleb didn't know why he thought the AI would take the wheel and drive the vehicle like a human. Instead, it placed its hands on the dashboard, metal tendrils snaking out of Sho's flesh and sinking through the padded plastic and into the vehicle's electronics. Hal stiffened up, and then the

APC started rolling forward, shaking slightly as it entered the jungle.

"We should have left it there," Flores whispered.

Caleb shook his head. "I don't like it or trust it, but right now I think we need it. Whatever story this planet is waiting to tell us, I don't get the impression it's going to have a happy ending."

Chapter 31

Sam knew the moment Governor Stone entered the Law Office because the hum of the sheriffs and deputies working outside suddenly fell into an uncomfortable silence. She looked up from her position behind her desk, glancing over at the clock on her display. Stone had told her to meet him in an hour. He had arrived within thirty minutes.

She smiled as she stood up, adjusting the weight of her revolver on her hips. She had guessed the Governor would be eager to see the armory, which was why she had hurried back to her cube, showered, and changed in near-record time.

In truth, she was as eager as he was. Once Governor Stone saw what they had to work with and gave her credit for revealing it, he would allow her more control over the organization of the defenses and the steps they needed to take to prepare the colony for its future on Essex.

And they were going to have a future here, she decided. She would do anything to make sure of that.

She thought about Caleb. It had been almost two

hours since he had fled the city. Where was he now? She had only gotten a brief glimpse of the outside world when she had been on the bridge. They had set down next to a water source, in a river valley surrounded by tons of vegetation which provided more color than she had ever seen in her life. It made sense to follow the river in one direction or the other. If there was hostile life on the planet, it probably needed to drink too.

She tried to imagine what it was like for him as she circled her desk and reached the door, aiming to meet the Governor on the office floor. It had to be exciting to be the first human on a new world. It also had to be terrifying. The sheer size of the planet, the endless sea of green, the fact that they were either here alone or sharing the world with an alien race that had set out to kill them. The immensity of their mission was overwhelming to her. She was doing her best not to let the pressure of her situation control her, the way she imagined the Marine Sergeant wouldn't allow the pressure to control him.

Of course, she was still struggling to make sense of where the alien fit into things. Had it really helped the Guardians escape? Or was it trying to get out on its own and just happened to cross paths with them? She was adamant Caleb had a reason for leaving with it instead of trying to kill it. She just had no idea what that reason was.

She reached the door to her office, her eyes tracking across the main floor and finding the Governor closing in on her. The room was filled with officers who had been recalled to Law after the alien killed the guards and escaped, their search for it ending abruptly in failure. They had their heads bowed to the Governor in respect. Some of it was even genuine.

The assembled sheriffs and deputies had all met Caleb. They all knew some measure of the truth about the city and the starship. Sam didn't know how many were on the side of justice and how many remained loyal to the Governor. Not yet. But she intended to sneak it out of them once more of her autonomy was restored. She knew Bashir and Caspar were on her side. Bashir had told her as much the moment she entered the office. She hadn't known it before then, but he was the one responsible for helping ensure Stone would never know Caleb hadn't knocked her unconscious.

"Governor Stone," she said, dropping to her knee and bowing her head to him. "Sheriff Lasandra Dante reporting for duty."

"You can stand, Sam," Stone said, his voice nearly jovial. He wasn't even trying to hide his excitement anymore. "We have a lot of work to do."

"Yes, sir," she replied, standing up.

Governor Stone turned to the rest of the officers. "Please, go about your duty. I have business with Sheriff Dante." The other officers resumed their work. Governor Stone took Sam by the arm and leaned in close. "Where is it?"

She had thought he might want a debriefing on everything Caleb had discussed with her. Instead, he was laser focused on the armory. She smiled and motioned to the back of the room. "Follow me, Governor."

"Hold on, Sheriff," Stone replied. "Beth will be joining us in a moment."

"Your wife, sir?" Sam said. "That's… unusual."

"She has a personal interest in the defense of this city. I think that's understandable, considering what it cost her."

"Yes, Governor. As you say."

They waited together in silence for half a minute. The Governor's wife entered the Law Office with a squad of guards in tow. She was dressed in black, her eyes puffy. She glanced at Sam with a look of disdain and didn't say anything to her when she joined her husband.

"I'm very sorry about Orla," Sam said.

"Let's see what she's got," Beth said to Governor Stone.

"Sheriff, lead the way."

"Are they coming too?" Sam said, pointing to the guards.

"Is that a problem?" Mrs. Stone asked.

"No ma'am," she replied. She didn't like it, but she didn't have a choice either. There was no benefit to making it a problem. "This way."

Sam led them to the back of Law, through the corridors to the garage. After they entered, she turned to the guards. "Since you're here, can you move that pile of crap away from the wall?"

The guards looked at the Governor, who nodded. Two of them headed to the debris blocking the disconnected wire. Sam noticed when they passed her they had rifles slung to their backs.

"Where did you get those?" she asked.

"Sergeant Card isn't the only one with secrets," Mrs. Stone replied. "The Governor's mansion has a stash of its own. For a rainy day."

"Sergeant Card told me Doctor Valentine let word of this place slip. You can't fight a war without weapons, after all. There's a panel behind that debris. Open it up and you'll find a wire. Connect the wire and we can descend into the lower level."

"Lower level?" Beth said.

The guards finished moving the debris. They began trying to dislodge the panel over the wire.

"Sergeant Card and I encountered Doctor Valentine

down there. She said she was leaving the ship to find the enemy and collect as much data about them as she could."

"What was she planning to do with it?"

"She said she had some way of getting it back to military command. She didn't say how."

"I see," Governor Stone said. "Two hundred years plus. How does she know military command still exists?"

"You know, Sheriff," Beth Stone said. "I almost wish Valentine had completed her research. She was dead, and she came back to life. We could have used something like that today." Sam didn't know how to respond to that, but she didn't need to. The Governor's wife kept talking. "I almost wish we had been turned into soldiers. Then we would be prepared for this. The people would be prepared for this. Or maybe we wouldn't know what we were missing, not being human anymore. Maybe we wouldn't feel the hurt and the pain. Maybe family would cease to have meaning to us."

"Beth, that's enough," Governor Stone said.

"Think about it, Jackson. We could have been mindless tools. Considering where we are, don't you think that would be better?"

"I think bringing you was a bad idea. I'll have the guards escort you back to—"

"No. I'm staying. You promised I could be part of this. Don't you dare go back on your word."

The Governor put up his hands in submission. "I wouldn't think of it. The point is, Valentine could have focused her energy on helping the colony instead of running off to spy on the enemy. But her whole plan was idiotic to begin with."

Sam nodded, even though she didn't completely agree with the statement. The idea of traveling to the planet where the Earth scientists believed the trife had originated wasn't a terrible one on the surface. If they had sent a smaller ship with a platoon of Marines, they might have done well gathering intel and passing it back, and everyone on the Deliverance would be with the rest of humankind somewhere else.

It was the desire for revenge, the need to strike back that had put all of them in this situation. That was the stupid part.

"Governor, there's a disconnected wire back here," one of the guards said. They had finally gotten the panel dislodged, and were looking back at Stone for instruction.

"Well, connect it," Stone said.

"Yes, sir."

The guard reached in and snapped the two wires together. The control panel lit up. Sam pointed to it, in case the Governor didn't see it.

"Beth, will you do the honors?" Stone said.

His wife nodded and went to the panel. She tapped it, triggering the lift. The floor started to drop.

"Ooh," Beth said, smiling for the first time. "Here we go."

Chapter 32

The lift continued to drop, carrying Sam, Governor Stone, Beth Stone and the six guards with it. The Governor's face was red with excitement, the muscles around his mouth tense as if he was fighting to hold back his smile. Beth didn't bother to hide her interest, her eyes wide and a grin splitting her face. The reaction made Sam uncomfortable. Laying eyes on the large military cache was exciting, but it seemed to her that either one or both of the Stones were also a little too eager to use it.

The lights came on as the platform lowered into the space, illuminating the massive hold. Governor Stone spun in a circle, similar to how Sergeant Card had, taking in the vehicles and weapons, and the replicators and raw materials that would allow them to produce more.

"Shit, Sheriff," Beth said, nearly giggling. "You didn't tell us it was this big."

"I told you it was enough to support an army," Sam replied. "An army at least twenty-thousand strong."

"And we never knew this was down here," Governor Stone said.

"Someone did," Sam said. "The wiring panel was hidden, and it was also bent out of shape like someone had been down here before. If you have weapons stashed in your mansion, there's a good chance they originated here."

"I'll concede to that logic," Governor Stone said. "What happened in the past is in the past. Maybe it was my great grandpa. Maybe it was an even longer time ago than that. It's here now, and it's mine."

"Ours," Beth said.

"Ours," Governor Stone corrected.

The exchange made Sam's skin crawl. Caleb had asked her to keep an eye on things because he didn't trust the Governor. It was the reason she was here instead of with the Guardians.

The Governor hopped off the platform before it finished dropping, helping Beth off. He started walking briskly through the armory, vanishing behind one of the APCs, while his wife went a different direction. Sam stayed with Governor Stone, tailing him as he let his eyes soak up the treasure.

Beth screamed.

Governor Stone's head snapped up, and he spun around, glaring wildly at Sam before breaking into a run. Sam followed him, rushing to the source of the screams.

Beth was with the guards. They were all standing over the husk of the dead trife.

"What is that?" Governor Stone said.

"It's a xenotrife," Sam replied. "One of the creatures that attacked Earth, and this ship. One of the aliens Sergeant Card was protecting us from."

The last sentence brought a return of the evil eye from Beth Stone.

"Careful, Sheriff," Governor Stone said.

"You can't deny that the Guardians did keep the city safe."

"Maybe at one time," Beth said. "Before the enemy got to them."

So that was it? At least one of the Stones was convinced the Guardians were conspiring with the enemy from the beginning. She glanced at the Governor. "You have a take, don't you, sir?"

"If you mean I have a theory of what's happening here, then yes," Stone replied. "I think Sergeant Card sold out to the enemy. I think he and Doctor Valentine are working together. They didn't develop the gene editing to start a war. They developed it to help the enemy finish one, in exchange for their safety and a position in the alien society."

Sam bit her tongue. And they said Valentine's plan was stupid? "I don't want to sound disloyal, sir, but that seems like a bit of a reach?"

"Does it? You said Valentine confronted you down here. Why didn't Card shoot her? Why didn't she shoot him? He wanted me to lock her up. He told us she was rogue. But then he let her go?"

"He went to help Private Flores."

"How long does it take to shoot someone, Sheriff? Do you remember when Card took your revolver and pulled the trigger at me? How long did that take? One second? Two?"

"Except Valentine underwent the gene editing. She's able to heal rapidly. It would take more than shooting her a few times."

"Knock her down, take her head. Card has that arm of his. I think he's strong enough to do it. What do you think?"

"Again, no disrespect intended, Governor, but you

weren't there. Valentine got the drop on me. He couldn't shoot her without getting me killed."

"Then why didn't she kill him and you? Two thorns out of her side, and she gets away clean."

Sam hesitated. She didn't entirely know why Valentine hadn't killed them. She certainly didn't seem to have any qualms about killing people, and she definitely had no love for Caleb. "She gave her word she wouldn't if he came out into the open."

Governor Stone and his wife both laughed. "Sheriff, I thought you were smarter than that. I thought you were more observant than that."

"Honor?" Beth Stone said. "Sergeant Card has no honor, or my beautiful Orla would still be alive. And if Valentine had any honor, she wouldn't have killed Doctor Brom."

Sam closed her mouth. There was nothing else she could say. Not without hurting her already shaky trust. "Yes, sir. Ma'am."

Beth softened with her agreement. "In any case, these things are disgusting."

"There are more of them," Sam said. "A group of them survived, but they're not like the others. They're docile. Harmless."

"How would that be possible?" Governor Stone asked.

"We think Valentine made them that way. Part of her experimentation."

"Where are they now?"

"In one of the rooms out that way. Do you want to see them?"

"No. Not right now. Sheriff, I want you to head back up to Law and tell Sheriff Zane to put a group together to come down here and start taking inventory. I want to know what we have down to the last bullet. Radio Joe King too. I want him to look at this stuff and make sure it's all operational, or tell me what it needs to make it operational."

"Yes, sir," Sam replied.

"I have to admit. This is more extensive than I was able to visualize in my mind. I was expecting a couple hundred guns, maybe a drone or two. I had engineering working on getting the city buttoned-up again, but this is a game-changer." He turned to his wife. "What do you think, my love?"

She was smiling again. "Yes. This will do nicely."

Sam didn't like the sound of that. "Governor, it seems like you already have some ideas of how you want to allocate these resources?"

"I do," Governor Stone said. "For starters, I want everyone in Law and all of my guards armed and armored. You were wearing it when Card knocked you down. I assume that means he taught you how to use it?"

"It's a relatively straightforward system, sir," she replied. She was relieved that Stone's priority was to start preparing the colony's defense.

"Good. Once that's done, we'll start drafting people from the colony. We only have about five hundred between law and my militia. I want at least five thousand within a month."

"Yes, Governor," Sam agreed.

"Second, I want Sheriff Zane to settle a forward operating position in the main hangar of the Deliverance. I also want guards posted at potential entry points, the way Card originally suggested. Since we'll be expanding instead of tucking in, I'll reassign Carol to focus on the comms again."

Sam couldn't help but smile. She had expected multiple arguments to get the Governor to follow Caleb's original plan. "That all sounds excellent, sir."

"Third, we need to get more people trained on the piloting simulator. There are still Daggers available in the secondary hangar, and I see a number of drones down here. We need people who can fly them so we can begin scouting our position. We also need to figure out how to get them from here to the main hangar. Joe can work on that too."

The Governor's face was lighting up with each statement, his body language becoming more confident, his hand gestures more animated. Sam realized that until the Governor had seen the armory, he had been just another terrified colonist who wanted to run away and hide from the truth of their predicament. But she still wasn't sure what he had been more afraid of. Having the city destroyed by aliens, or losing his grip on power.

"Jackson, there's one other thing," Beth said forcefully. "Don't forget it."

He looked at her and nodded. "Of course, love. I would never forget." He turned his attention to Sam. "Sheriff Dante, I have a special assignment for you. I want you to be a leader in our new Deliverance Defense Force. The DDF for short. How does Colonel Dante sound to you?"

Sam stared at the Governor, frozen in surprise. "You want me to be a soldier?"

"I want you to be an officer. I want you to take an active role in the defense of our new home. You made a mistake with Card, but you and your family have been loyal servants to me and mine for a long time before that."

"Sir, I don't know what to say."

"Thank you will suffice."

"Yes, sir. Thank you, sir. Do you mind if I ask, who is the General?"

"I'll be taking on the role of Governor-General," Stone

replied. "You'll report directly to me. Our structure will be based on the military of our historical armed services, but adapted to ensure efficient operation and a clear and loyal chain of command."

Sam did her best to keep her face level. She understood the meaning of the words, even if Stone had danced around it. He was planning to continue his family's dictatorship over Metro. Nothing was shocking about that. Only now he would have the guns and ammo to put down any dissent.

At least he had made it clear what he was most afraid of.

He had also proven that he still trusted her despite what she had done. A small part of her felt guilty for misleading him, but she was determined to do what she had to do to keep Metro safe. Right now, that meant following the Governor's orders.

"What are my orders, sir?" she asked.

"I want you to take a team outside," Governor Stone replied. "I want you to find Sergeant Card and his team, and I want you to kill them."

Chapter 33

"How are you feeling, Wash?" Caleb asked.

Washington flashed his thumb and smiled.

"Good. What about you, Flores?"

"I'm good, Sarge. A little tired."

"No pain?"

"Negative."

Caleb's eyes lingered on her face. He was tempted to ask her to show him her chest so he could see if the poison was spreading. But even if it were, what would he be able to do about it?

"Are you okay, Sarge?" she asked, her eyes meeting his. "You spend so much time worrying about us. Who's going to worry about you?"

"I'm fine," Caleb replied. "Thanks for asking."

They were all sitting, gathered in three of the drone pilot seats rotated toward the middle to face one another. The ADC had been on the move for two hours already, picking a slow route through the thick brush. They covered at least forty kilometers, the Deliverance was well out of sight but hardly out of mind.

He wondered how Sheriff Dante was holding up? Had she convinced the Governor to do the right thing?

He stood and moved to the front of the ADC. Hal remained nearly motionless in the driver's seat, palms still pressed against the dashboard, tendrils reaching through the material to the control systems beyond. The AI never blinked, and it would certainly never get tired. Caleb sat down in the seat next to it, looking out through the narrow plasti-glass transparency. The canopy above them was so thick it left the jungle floor shrouded in darkness, illuminated primarily by a variety of phosphorescent mosses and plants.

"It's beautiful," Caleb said. Even in his narrow view of the world outside the ADC, he could see a range of light glowing shapes in an assortment of colors. He had been on a lot of missions to a lot of places on Earth. He didn't think there was anything like this spot back home.

Home. He shook the idea out of his head. In his mind, he had only been gone a week. It still felt like he was on a mission, deployed to some other part of the world. South America, maybe. He had to remind himself this was home now, as strange as it was.

"It is interesting," Hal replied. "Difficult to navigate and growing increasingly dense."

Caleb could tell. The ADC was pressing on through the vegetation, crumpling plants, tearing away vines and bouncing continually over roots. The trees were spaced enough for the vehicle to get between them, but the gap between trunks appeared to be closing.

"How far to the mountains?" Caleb asked.

"If we maintain this velocity, ninety-four hours."

"Four days?"

"At this velocity. I am unsure if we will be able to remain in the vehicle for the extent of the journey.

Assuming that the alternate intelligence started from its origin at the moment the Deliverance entered the atmosphere, and using the recorded speed of its components in seconds before I was taken offline, the estimated distance to the source is eight hundred kilometers."

"That's not close."

"No. But it is also nowhere near as distant as it could be considering the circumference of this planet. The ship's navigation system was programmed to set it down in a protected and resource-rich area within striking distance of an established civilization if any was found. No doubt the ship's neural network identified the Axon structures we are heading toward and selected the river valley as the most optimal position from which to stage an assault."

"No doubt," Caleb said. He glanced at the ADC's sensor display. "Have you picked up any other life forms out here? Especially any sign of Valentine?"

"Negative, Sarge. I have observed many smaller creatures scurrying out of the path of this vehicle, but otherwise the sensors are clear."

"So we came all the way from Earth to start a war, and nobody's home except a lonely AI?"

"That is yet to be determined."

"And Valentine vanished into the wind," Caleb added. "There's no way she's moving faster on foot than we are in the ADC."

"If your assumption that she's on foot is correct."

"Which it probably isn't."

Caleb remembered the Daggers in the secondary hangar near the bow of the Deliverance. Their CUTS system made them relatively easy for anyone to fly so long as they didn't need to make any sudden, unexpected movements. Had Riley taken one of the starfighters and flown away from the Deliverance?

He slipped a small grin at the thought of the other AI's quantum waveform shorting out the Dagger and sending her plummeting to the ground. The smile didn't last. Even if she crashed, she would heal and be on her way.

Caleb stared out the forward viewport in silence for a few more minutes. Then he rose and returned to the back of the vehicle. Washington had shifted position to lay his head against the back of the seat and was already out cold. Flores was still awake, entertaining herself by gently tapping her fingers together in alternating patterns.

"You should follow Washington's lead," Caleb said, taking the seat beside her.

"Are you kidding? I'm about ninety-five percent certain that the moment I close my eyes is the moment we get attacked."

"What makes you think we're going to get attacked out here?"

"Karma."

"Meaning what? That we deserve to get attacked?"

"Personal karma." She licked her lips and sighed. "I'm not a good Marine, Sarge."

"You could have fooled me. We wouldn't be here without you."

"I mean. Yeah, I'm good at that part of it. The fighting, I mean. But. Well. I…" She trailed off. Her face was pale and tears began to form at the base of her eyes. "You integrated me into your unit. I'm not one of your Vultures."

"You are now," Caleb said, unsure of the source of her distress. "You've earned your place, even if you came in because other Marines died."

"A lot of other Marines. I don't deserve it. I don't deserve to be here. I don't deserve to be alive."

"What does deserving have to do with it? I've seen

more than my share of people who deserved a lot better fate drop dead from the trife virus or have their face ripped off by their claws. Just look at Washington. Do you think he deserved his injuries?"

Flores glanced at Washington. "He seems like a really good guy on top of being a badass Marine. I'm not good, Sarge."

"What is this about, Mariana?" Caleb asked. "Something that happened on Earth, right?"

She nodded.

"If you want to confess, then confess. But either way, I'll tell you that whatever happened on Earth happened on Earth. It's literally ancient history. Who you are here and now, how you handle yourself in this place, that's what defines you in my book."

She met his eyes again, her lips trembling. She swallowed hard.

"I was in Chicago during the Bear Offensive," she said. "Assigned to the Forty-First."

Caleb had heard of the Bear Offensive, though he had been working a search and rescue mission in Houston at the time. It was one of the largest assaults on the trife the military had attempted.

It had ended in complete failure.

"Not many people got out of Chicago," he said.

"No. It was insane, Sarge. Intelligence estimated the trife population at four thousand. They sent ten thousand of us into the city to eradicate them and find their nest. We were well-equipped; we were well-briefed. We were so ready to burn all of those assholes." She paused, shaking her head. "Except intelligence got it wrong. Big surprise, right? There weren't four thousand trife. There were forty-thousand. We were outnumbered from the start. Overwhelmed. We fought. We fought damn hard. We even managed to push the buggers back toward the lake. But that was mistake number two."

"Trife hate water."

"They're okay with rain, but they don't like to be submerged. We blew the river crossings on the way out and cut their numbers by two-thirds. It didn't matter by then. Pushing them back caused them to ricochet hard. I can still see them in my head. A slick of trife a thousand thick rolling down the street toward my squad. Air cover sinking rockets into them and blowing away dozens at a clip. But they kept coming like it was nothing." She paused again, getting to the meaty part of her story.

"What happened?" Caleb asked.

"I had two options. Sacrifice myself to slow the advance and save two hundred fellow Marines or break orders and run. I'll let you guess which option I picked."

The tears were streaming from her eyes, the pain of her failure hanging heavy between them. Caleb stared at her, struggling not to lose his respect for the warrior he had seen. It was as awful a mistake as any Marine could make. One that under different circumstances, he would never be able to forgive.

But she didn't have to tell him, and it wasn't fair for him to say the past was dead if he wasn't going to let it be. She wanted his forgiveness. His absolution from her failure. She'd probably beaten herself up over it a thousand times already.

"You already know you screwed up," he said, putting his human hand on one of hers. "You feel it deep in your soul. The remorse. The embarrassment. The worthless-ness." His words only made her tears come quicker, but that was okay. "I can't fix that for you. What I can tell you is that isn't the Private Mariana Flores sitting across from me. You've been ready to sacrifice yourself for us multiple times, without hesitation. You made that mistake once. I'm confident you won't make it again."

She nodded gently. "That's right. I won't. But you know what bothers me about that, Sarge?"

"What?"

"Is the reason I won't because I've changed, or is it because I know I'm already dying?" She smiled sadly, putting her hand to her chest, right on top of the poison. "But you already know, don't you?"

"Yes. The stuff that David gave you seems to have side-effects. Doctor Rathbone said it was poison she wasn't able to treat."

"When Governor Stone grabbed me and dragged me up on that stage, it brought back the memory of what I had done. The fear was the same. The desire to run. At the same time, I figured I was getting what I deserved. I always assumed that's how it worked. Then I passed out, and when I woke up, you and the big lug were there. Now that the stim's worn off completely, I can feel it like a throbbing burn between my breasts. I don't know how I know it's killing me, but I know it's killing me."

"Riley created it. She may be able to fix it."

"Riley? Thanks, but no thanks, Sarge. Even if we find her, I'm not letting that psychopath near me. I'd rather die."

"Ultimately, that's not your decision to make. I need you."

Flores smiled. "That's sweet, Sarge. Thanks for the pep talk. I won't lie and say I feel better because of it, but I do feel a weight lifted because I told you. I promise I won't let you down."

"I know you won't."

"I'm going to try to get a little sleep. You should too."

"Somebody has to keep an eye on our strange bedfellow."

"You know, it can probably hear everything we just said."

"Probably."

"Glorified C-3PO. That's all it is."

Caleb smiled. "Agreed."

Flores wiped her tears and then closed her eyes, leaning her head back against the chair. Caleb stood and turned back toward the front. It was just him and the alien intelligence.

Something slammed into the ADC.

Chapter 34

The impact threw Caleb sideways, his feet leaving the ground and his body falling past the nearest seat into the row of displays against the bulkhead. His replacement arm hit one of the displays, the glass beneath it cracking and sparking. He bounced off and grabbed a chair with his other hand to regain his balance.

Washington and Flores were equally affected, the surprise violent motion sending them tumbling from their chairs. They hit the pilot stations and then the floor, coming to rest on their hands and knees in a sudden panic.

"What the hell?" Caleb shouted, charging to the front of the ADC. "Hal?"

The ADC had come to a total stop. The intelligence was standing, its hands off the dashboard. It turned to look at him at the same time the ADC shook again.

The impact was less violent this time, but still enough to throw Caleb sideways. He held tight to the pilot's chair, leaning down to look outside.

"Do not be alarmed, Sarge," Hal said.

"Don't be alarmed? What's going on?" The ADC

shook a third time, and Caleb thought he heard something bounce off its armored top.

"This should interest you," it replied. "Open the back."

"I'm not opening the back."

"You will miss it."

"Miss what?"

"Open the back."

Caleb hurried to the back of the ADC, tapping the control to lower the rear hatch. It clunked and began rotating away from the vehicle, a soft rumbling entering the vehicle.

"What are you doing?" Flores asked.

Caleb wasn't sure. For all he knew, Hal was causing them to hallucinate and would convince him to walk away from the ADC and get lost in the jungle. But what good would that do the AI now? It claimed it required their help. It had made it clear that it was willing to follow his orders to get it.

For now, anyway.

The door continued to descend. It was halfway down when something large and blue charged across his field of view next to it.

"What was that?" Flores said.

Caleb advanced, leaning his head out and looking to the right.

A guttural reverberation caused him to duck back into the ADC, right before another blue creature charged past, giving him a good look at the animal. Eight thick legs, rippled skin, a long neck and a broad head. It reminded him of a cross between a giraffe and an elephant. Or maybe two elephants. It thundered past, tearing through brush, vine and low-hanging branches to enlarge the hole the other creatures had already created.

"Whoa!" Flores said, getting up and joining Caleb.

Washington followed a moment later, as a third and fourth creature charged past.

The ADC shook again. Caleb stuck his head out and looked up. One of the beasts had jumped onto the top of the vehicle, taking the high road to get past it. The creature jumped off on the other side, remaining with the herd.

"You were seeking life forms," Hal said. "This herd is too thick to pass through, so you might as well sit here and observe."

Caleb watched the creatures pass with a big smile on his face. Washington and Flores were equally awed, and they marveled as the herd continued its migration around them.

"Where did they come from?" Flores asked. "I feel like I'm on Pandora."

They watched the creatures pass in fascination for another minute. It was incredible to see a new life form on a new world. So incredible that Caleb nearly forgot his training and the importance of situational awareness.

"There was no migration path here before," he realized as another of the beasts rumbled through. The ADC shook again, inadvertently struck by a passing creature. "And those things are big to be hanging out in a jungle." He turned and looked back at Hal. "Don't you think?"

Hal's outward expression was flat, but it froze as though Caleb had confused its programming. "Close the door," it said.

Caleb was already reaching for the toggle.

Something dropped onto the ramp directly in front of him, flexing its legs to absorb the impact, and redirecting the energy to lunge at his arm. Claws scraped the metal, sending sparks along the surface and yanking him off-balance, pulling him from the hatch control.

It was a xenotrife, but not a xenotrife they were

familiar with. It was bigger, more muscular, and much uglier. Its thick black flesh seemed to be infused with the dark Axon alloy, almost randomly dispersed to form a partial exoskeleton.

It moved fast, turning away from Caleb and slashing at Washington, who somehow managed to fall back out of its reach.

Hal did…something to the trife. It hissed and came to a stop, its head swiveling toward the AI. The momentary freeze gave Caleb time to recover. He reached out and grabbed the trife in his replacement hand, squeezing its neck.

It didn't snap.

Alloy apparently ran through the creature's spine, making it able to withstand the crushing pressure. The trife seemed to break out of the trance Hal had put it in, twisting in Caleb's grip and raking its claws across his chest.

The claws dug into the combat armor, leaving deep scores. Caleb tossed it sideways out of the ADC, right before another of the large fleeing creatures knocked into the vehicle. Everyone inside scrambled to find purchase, while the trife regained its footing and bunched itself, lunging back at them.

The roar of the MK-12 firing from inside the ADC was deafening. The rounds went in a straight line up from the trife's abdomen to its head, finding spaces in the alloy and punching through.

It fell dead in front of them.

"Shit," Caleb said. "Hal, get us out of here."

"We can't move," Hal replied. "We might be pushed into a position we can't get out of."

"I think that already happened," Flores said.

Hal pivoted toward the front of the ADC, choosing not to argue.

The trife were hunting the large blue creatures, and the large blue creatures were doing their best to escape. There were so many of the beasts. How many trife were behind them?

And what kind of trife were these? Where had they come from? Had the scientists been right all along? Was this the source of the attack on Earth? Did that mean the Axon were responsible? Did it mean Hal was lying to them?

Or did it mean the Relyeh were already here?

"Wash, get suited up. Flores, grab your gear. Hal, belay your order."

The AI stopped and turned around. Washington and Flores were already moving to follow orders, even though Caleb was sure they didn't understand them.

"Sarge?" Hal asked.

"We don't know what else is out here, and we can't let these trife go after the Deliverance. We need to make sure they stay with the herd, and if they don't they follow us. Hal, what did you do to that one?"

"I generated a waveform similar to the one I used to control the hybrid trife on your ship. It altered the unit's processing, but it did not respond to commands."

"It slowed the thing down," Caleb said. "Good enough for now. Can you use the ADC to amplify the signal?"

"I may be able to modify a drone. But you will need to keep me clear while I work."

"Consider it done."

Chapter 35

There was nothing safe about leaving the armored carcass of the drone carrier to modify one of the roof-mounted drones. While the passing of the eight-legged animals was becoming less dense, it meant the things chasing them were drawing nearer, and likely in higher numbers.

Caleb couldn't imagine such a mass exodus of the blue creatures taking place because of a handful of trife. He was operating under the assumption that there were hundreds of the demons tailing the animals, and he could picture them swarming one of the enormous creatures and pulling it down, similar to how ants would defend their colony from a larger predator.

Only the blue beasts weren't the predators. The animals were prey to the trife. For sport or food? It wasn't immediately apparent, but the reason didn't matter nearly as much as the fact that the demons were on Essex in the first place.

The Deliverance had spent two hundred thirty-six years crossing forty-two light years of space to escape the xenotrife. They had landed on a planet that already had its own problems with the things.

It was as disheartening a truth as Caleb could imagine, and at the same time, it was his duty not to let that truth affect his performance as a Guardian and a Marine. Coming to this planet was a mistake centuries in the making. Command had given the people of the Deliverance the middle finger from day one. This wasn't the story of a colony reaching a new world and settling in. This was a story of survival for the colony. Or death.

But if he had proven anything for himself, it was that he was a survivor. And he was determined to make the colony survivors as well.

They had closed the rear hatch into the ADC and were using the top hatch again for entry and exit. Caleb and Washington were perched beside the last drone launcher in the line, pressed tight against the folded wings of the machine and facing opposite directions. Their knees were planted for an easy pivot and their P-50s were raised, ready to fire.

The stronger frame of the first trife suggested this version was more resistant to conventional ballistics, but the superheated gas of the plasma rifles would hopefully find the spaces around the thicker skin to do some damage. The downside was that they had a lot more rounds for the MK-12s than they did cells for the P-50s, which was going to limit their overall effectiveness over time.

Hal was kneeling beside the drone. Caleb had offered it the drone repair kit, but it had declined. Instead, it had opened Sho's palms as before, the metal tendrils reshaping themselves to act as a screwdriver and ratchet to remove the panel protecting the machine's belly. It was currently working inside the guts of the drone, completely still as if its entire self had shifted to the task at hand.

"Flores, anything?" Caleb asked. Flores was in the front of the ADC, monitoring the sensors.

"Negative, Sarge. Between the giraffiphants and the cover, all I've got is a sea of red. The sensors weren't calibrated for this environment."

"Understood, but keep trying to pick it apart and be ready to launch the drone."

"Roger."

Caleb swept the surroundings, watching his HUD mark the different items in his field of view. He had already cleared the giraffiphants as threats, and the ATCS already understood the trife as trife, despite the differences between Earth's version and these. He made sure to look up too, at the branches high above them, in search of the demons. There had been no contact so far. If they were here, they were staying after their original target. But he knew how quickly things could change.

"Hal, eta?" he asked.

"Soon," the AI replied curtly.

Another giraffiphant raced past the ADC, its front-left foreleg clipping the corner. The force pushed the carrier slightly, and Caleb grabbed the drone's wing for balance while the creature charged across the now-trampled foliage. The passing had left the area somewhat clear, giving him almost ten meters of clear line of sight between large trunks the animals couldn't displace. It was the one benefit to their surprise crossing. He kept swiveling his head back and forth, waiting for the demons to arrive.

He didn't have to wait much longer. He heard a loud grumbling snort to his left and turned to see a giraffiphant emerge from the darkness, at least a dozen trife covering its back. They were clawing at its thick skin, trying to get through it, hissing loudly to one another.

His HUD picked up movement behind the creature, a

second group of trife trailing the beast. They were a short distance ahead of another giraffiphant, and he watched the marks on his HUD spread apart in a flanking maneuver, preparing to assault the creature.

Caleb returned his attention to the first group of trife. He had a soft spot for animals, especially ones in a situation like this. He had to convince himself to hold his fire and not draw attention to the ADC. It wouldn't help to save one more stricken giraffiphant if it led to the end of the Guardians.

He remained static on top of the ADC. The first group of trife vanished into the darkness, the second drawing near. Their maneuver was bringing them closer to the ADC, and Caleb realized they were planning to use the top of it as a platform to leap onto the giraffiphant.

His P-50 lit up the area, belching bolts at the demons. The rounds sizzled into the trife, multiple bolts hitting each and knocking the right flank down before they could react. The left responded instantly to the assault, quickly switching tactics and changing targets. They charged the ADC, and Caleb swung his plasma rifle and fired, knocking one of them down. The other two diverted, vanishing behind the nearest trees.

"Guardians, they know we're here, and they know we're deadly," Caleb said.

"Roger," Flores replied.

"Hal, how much longer?"

"Almost done, Sarge," Hal replied.

Caleb glanced at his tactical. The remaining pair of trife had vanished. Not only that, the giraffiphants were gone, their stampede through this part of the jungle complete.

How many trife were still behind them, trailing their prey?

How many were already nearby?

"Flores, anything?" he asked. The ADC's sensors had better reach than their ATCS, and now that the other creatures were gone, there wouldn't be as much noise.

"Still negative, Sarge," she replied. "The grid's gone dark. If the bastards are still out there, they must have a stealth mode."

"Great," Caleb said. "We can't even rely on our eyes for this one, Wash."

Nevertheless, the other Marine was sweeping his eyes back and forth and rotating up, trying to watch all of the angles. If these trife had some sort of stealth mode, it was going to make them a hundred times more dangerous.

"Sarge, look up!" Flores shouted through the comm.

Caleb's head snapped up just in time to see the branches shaking. He didn't wait for something to fall on him, sending a burst of bolts into the canopy. They lit up the area, revealing nearly a dozen trife about to pounce.

"Flores, the stampede is over, get us moving!" Caleb snapped. "Wash, Hal, brace!"

Caleb hooked his foot around the base of the drone launcher, using it to steady himself as the ADC lurched forward. Washington planted himself, remaining upright, just as the trife began to fall.

They didn't drop the way Caleb expected. They spread their arms, revealing a thin layer of membrane stretching from their arms to their hips that guided their descent.

"Shit," Caleb cursed, firing at them. He only got a pair of bolts off before his ATCS blared in warning. A new group of enemies appeared on the left flank, already too damn close. He pivoted toward them, and a moment later his ATCS lit up again, revealing a third group right in front of the ADC. "Hal, we need that waveform generator *now*."

"You can't begin to understand the complexity of the technology," Hal replied.

"It can't be that complex if you're sticking it in a human-made drone." The AI didn't answer. "Wash, take the front. I'll manage the sky and left flank."

Washington pivoted in response to the order. The airborne trife were sinking toward them, and Caleb turned the dial on his P-50 to stream mode. He didn't want to use up so much charge at once, but there wasn't much choice. He held his fire, waiting for the trife to get as close as possible. The more he could hit with the stream the better.

"Hold on, Guardians," Flores said.

Caleb crouched slightly as the ADC hit something on the ground and bounced sideways, slowing as it shook. The trife used the shift as their signal to move in, the flying demons adjusting their wings and swooping toward them, while the trife on the flank charged on all fours.

Caleb squeezed the trigger, sending a fount of plasma at the trife. The blast engulfed half a dozen of them, and they screamed and tumbled behind the ADC. He pivoted to the flank, ready to hit them too.

His ATCS cried out again, pinpointing a group of trife appearing on the opposite side, nearly on top of the ADC.

Where the hell had they come from? He couldn't hit them and the group on the left at the same time. The trife had perfectly coordinated the assault in a manner he had never experienced before. These creatures weren't only bigger, stronger, and more armored than the trife on Earth. They were also smarter and better organized.

"Hal!" Caleb shouted as three trife leaped onto the roof of the ADC. He spun to blast them, knowing the group from the left would be on his back the moment he did.

"Done!" Hal said.

"Flores, fire it up!" Caleb shouted, hitting the attacking trife with plasma and knocking the newest group down.

The group on the flank reacted as expected, and he felt the first one hit his back and push him forward, driving him off the edge of the ADC. He fell, hitting the ground with the demon still on his back.

He would never have known the drone was active, except the trife over him didn't dig its claws into the back of his neck. It froze, giving him plenty of time to buck up and throw it from his back.

He rounded on it. The trife was still, it's small eyes dark, its mouth hanging open. It didn't follow the wave-form, but it was confused by it. Caleb quickly swapped his P-50 for his MK-12, putting the muzzle to its eye and pulling the trigger. It collapsed instantly.

They had evened the odds, but the fight wasn't over. They would have only seconds to kill as many trife as they could before the creatures recovered.

Washington was doing his best, having swapped plasma for projectiles. He fired single rounds into weak spots in the trife flesh. Hal was active too, grabbing the trife on the ADC and smoothly snapping their necks despite the added protection. His show of strength was both incredible and frightening.

The ADC came to a stop, and the drone lifted into the air, staying close to the vehicle as it rotated in the direction of the trife. The forward gun began to fire, cutting them down in a hurry.

The trife finally broke out of their confusion. They hissed but didn't attack, instead choosing to run from the Guardians as quickly as they could manage, vanishing into the brush in the opposite direction of the herd.

Caleb exhaled heavily, thankful to have made it through without injury. He checked Washington and

Flores' vitals before returning his rifle to his back and scaling back up the side of the ADC. The drone pivoted and dropped smoothly into its launcher, still humming slightly.

"Nice job," Caleb said to Hal.

"Adequate," Hal replied.

"The trife are here on Essex."

"Obviously."

"That's bad for us."

"Very."

"They aren't like the ones on Earth."

"No."

"I was hoping you might be able to elaborate. Our scientists believed the trife asteroids came from this part of the galaxy. But you were supposed to be an early warning system for the Relyeh before they ever made it to this planet. Now we have confirmation that the Relyeh have been here, and they have trife here, and they're a newer and probably better version than what they sent to Earth."

"A mostly accurate assessment, Sarge."

"Why only mostly?"

"Because the Relyeh should not be here now. It is counter to their conventional expansion patterns."

"What exactly does that mean?"

"I don't know yet. I have decided we require a solution to the Axon quantum waveform problem."

"You think your upgraded model is a bigger threat than the trife?"

"I don't know. I have come up with two potential avenues of consideration. One, the Relyeh have broken our operational encryption scheme and gained control of the Axon AI. Two, the Axon AI have gained control of the uluth, similar to how I seized control of the hybrids. The disappearance of the Axon on this world suggests the first, but neither explains the change in strategy."

"Some people on Earth thought the trife were sent because we developed technologies that would allow us a greater degree of freedom beyond our atmosphere. Near-FTL engines, fusion reactors, artificial gravity and so on. Could that have anything to do with it?"

"The Relyeh do not attack life forms until they have proven themselves to be sufficiently advanced. But they also do not circumvent such worlds. They can afford to be patient."

"Except in this case."

"That seems to be true."

"And the trife are here, and the Deliverance is here, and who knows what kind of trouble the colony is in."

"I care not for your colony. The Axon are missing. If the Relyeh have already prepared this world, my mission to inform them is ever more critical. I require you. You have value to me."

"I love you too, Hal," Caleb said, shaking his head. "But I need to go back to the Deliverance and tell them what we found. We need to find some way off this planet."

"Your ship is catastrophically damaged."

"Then maybe there's another way. How are you going to tell the Axon what you've learned if they aren't here?"

"The Axon city will have communications equipment."

"Will it also have starships?"

"No."

"You went to Earth on a starship. Your species has them."

"The creators do not use them."

"So how do the Axon get from one planet to another?"

"I require you."

"I saw what you did to those trife. I'm not sure how much you need us."

"I require you."

"So if we stay the course, you'll help me get the colonists somewhere safe?"

"I will accept the mission. You do not understand the gravity of this outcome."

"Believe me. I do." Caleb glanced at the AI. Then he looked back at the trife he had shot. Then he looked back at Hal before pointing. "That one is about the same size as Sho, give or take."

"You want me to use an uluth as a capsule?" Hal replied.

"You already agreed to it, remember? I didn't say the capsule would be combat armor."

"I won't be able to speak."

"Even better. But I have a feeling you'll find a way."

"And the claws? I can't manipulate anything with those."

"You grew tendrils out of Sho's hands," Caleb said, getting annoyed. "I think you can manage."

"No."

"You said you would. As a machine, are you capable of not keeping your promise?"

"In certain circumstances."

"Is this one of them?"

"No," Hal admitted. Then it jumped off the ADC, landing beside the trife. It looked up at Caleb again, as though beginning him to change his mind.

"Go ahead," Caleb said. "I'm not going to watch."

He turned away. He didn't want to see how the AI shed Sho's skin and took the trife's. It would only upset him more. He could still hear it. The splitting open of flesh, the shifting of the bodies, and other noises he couldn't align to an action. He focused on their surroundings, watching for more trife.

He knew it was done when Hal tapped him on the shoulder with shortened and rounded trife claws. He almost wished he hadn't asked the AI to take the creature as a capsule when he looked into the demon's silver eyes. It was as unsettling to be so close to something he considered an enemy as it was to look at Sho.

"Washington. Flores. Hal has a new host. Help me give Sho the send-off she deserves."

"Roger, Sarge," Flores said. "On my way."

Caleb jumped off the ADC, kneeling beside Sho. He had learned to manage seeing Hal in her form. He could barely stand to look at her now. Lifeless. Empty. Cold. He reached out and touched her face, remembering her last words.

I did it for you.

He held back his pain as Washington joined him on Sho's other side.

"Damn," Flores said behind them. "It's like Halloween." She came up behind Caleb, putting her hand on his shoulder. "I'm sorry, Sarge."

"She's been gone for days," Caleb said. "This really is just a shell. A capsule. She's someplace better now."

"Roger that," Flores said. Washington nodded somberly. "Sarge, the trife —"

"I know," Caleb said, cutting her off.

"And the colony —"

"I know."

"What do we do?"

"What Sho would have wanted. We keep fighting."

Chapter 36

Sam rolled onto her side and glanced at the display on the nightstand. Two in the morning, Metro time. She pondered that thought for a moment. Metro time. What did that even mean anymore? What did Metro mean? What did it stand for? What was it going to become?

The start of a new human civilization?

Or the end of the old one?

As long as Governor Stone was running things, she was too sure it would be the latter.

She flopped onto her back, staring up at the top of her cube. When the Governor had told her he wanted her to be a Colonel in his new military, she had been elated. In that slice of time, she had thought it would be a chance to help mold the defense of the colony and ensure Sergeant Card's ideas would be implemented. She believed in Caleb and his plans, and she agreed their best chance of keeping the citizens safe was to be as prepared as they could.

Even Governor Stone agreed, at least now that he had the full firepower of the hidden armory at his disposal. He had put all of Caleb's ideas into motion, prioritizing the communications systems and the training of guards and law officers in the new weapons, as well as putting a framework in place to secure not only the city but the entire broken starship from a possible outside attack. What he had accomplished in eight hours was impressive. The Governor worked tirelessly to get everything in motion, calling in numerous people and barking orders at them with practiced ease. It was hard not to respect him for everything he had decided to do.

Except...

He had to throw a wrench in her excitement. He had to exact his revenge against her for helping Caleb in the hospital. He couldn't forgive and forget. He couldn't put it aside. That wasn't his way, and while Sam was expecting something punitive to come, she had thought it would take the form of Stone's brother. She was single because she was more interested in her job than most of the men in Metro, and it was against protocol to marry someone in the same line of work.

He was single because he was a lazy, unintelligent, adult baby.

As a Colonel reporting directly to the new Governor-General, she should be passing orders down the chain of command, not preparing to be one of the first Metro citizens to leave the confines of the ship. She should be overseeing the organization of the defenses, not getting ready to abandon it.

But that wasn't how the Governor wanted it to be. He wanted to show her who was boss and put her loyalty to the ultimate test. He wanted to make her do something he knew she didn't want to do.

Kill Sergeant Card?

She wasn't sure she could even if she wanted to. He was a trained Marine who had extensive experience in all kinds of hostile environments, against all kinds of opposition. She was a Sheriff who had never seen anything but Metro before the Guardians arrived. She didn't know the first thing about surviving beyond the metal walls of the city, let alone how to get the drop on a real warrior.

But that was the point, wasn't it? To let her think she was back in the Governor's good graces, and then drop the hammer when she least expected it.

The look on her face when he gave the order was probably priceless. She hadn't said a word in response. She couldn't say anything in Caleb's defense without looking like a sympathizer. She couldn't question Stone's orders. Not now.

And Stone damn well knew it.

He had put her between a rock and a hard place and left her there to be crushed. There was no easy way out of it, and just in case she managed to figure something out, he had assembled her team instead of letting her select the law officers she believed were most qualified for the job. On the one hand, it was probably better that way. She didn't want the Guardians hurting the people she cared most about. On the other, it made it much more challenging to avoid the confrontation in the first place.

Damn it.

She rolled over again, sliding out of bed. Stone had given them ten hours of free time to rest up, figuring Caleb wasn't going to get all that far in a day or two. At least not far enough to get away. One of his directives was to send deputies to every corner of the Deliverance to look for more 'goodies' as he called them and take inventory of everything they found. A few of the areas were still locked down. Others were destroyed. Deputy Klahanie had gone as far as he could into the ship's systems, and he had managed to clear the safeguards put in place to keep the trife out of Metro. But he had reached a dead end when it came to opening Research. The area was locked down tight, the security controls on the subnetwork sandboxed away from the primary systems. Sam had a feeling she knew who, how, and why.

The expeditions had proven fruitful. Not long after Chief Engineer King got the comms up and running, an exploratory group led by Sheriff Zane had discovered a third area through a heavy blast door behind the rows of Daggers behind the smaller hangar in the ship's bow. That hold contained a half-dozen transports, cigar-shaped vehicles with stubby nacelles attached to the sides. Zane had dubbed them FPs because of their head-on profile. Stone was amused by the term but rejected it as the official name for the vehicles, which had FCT stenciled on the sides.

The transports could carry eight passengers and a pilot and could skim the surface of the planet at heights of up to two hundred meters. Sam didn't know how they were used on Earth or if they had ever been used on Earth at all. They had both the perfect environment and a definite use for them here, even if the intended use turned her stomach.

The first step was to determine which direction the Guardians had traveled. They had already trained a few deputies on the Governor's flight simulator, giving them just enough experience that they knew how to launch and fly one without driving it directly into the ground. The machines were intentionally easy to use in a fundamental way and much harder to use for more complex maneuvers. All the Deliverance Defense Force needed them to do was follow a straight path so they could look down on the landscape.

The second step would be to find an area in that direction where they could set the FCT down. The third would be to set up a defense along that area, and the fourth to monitor the region from above and adjust to any changes in Caleb's trajectory.

It was a mission that would draw a lot of manpower. Way too much manpower, as far as Sam was concerned. Governor Stone was wasting a lot of time and resources to bring Caleb down, and for no other reason than to cover his lie.

That wasn't true. There was another reason, more important than the first. Elizabeth Stone was heartbroken over the loss of Orla. Sam didn't blame her for that. But she wanted vengeance more than she wanted safety, and Governor Stone was more than willing to oblige.

That wasn't even the worst part. The worst part was the certainty that if push came to shove, Caleb would kill them first.

Sam crossed her cube to the bathroom, pulling off her tank top and panties, relieving herself before jumping in the shower. She lingered there for a few minutes, taking advantage of the relaxed need to keep their water use minimized. The starship had come to rest beside a large river, and once Engineering had a chance to handle the thousand other minor tasks they had already been assigned they would work on siphoning water from there, through the ship's filters and into the city in an endless supply, at least for as long as the city remained inside the ship's hold.

Which wouldn't be long, if everything went the way Stone hoped. Between surviving four hours on the ground and the discovery of the armory, the Governor was convinced they had everything they needed to start following the protocols that would take the city outside. Engineering was already working on repairing the main hangar's large inner doors and the huge lift that would carry the loaders, builders and blocks to the surface. They were also in the process of removing the false wall on the south side of Metro, revealing the huge interlock that would allow the pieces of the blocks egress. It was an impressive sight that Sam could watch from the window of her corner cube if she wanted.

The problem with all of those plans was that Stone had already decided the threat to the colony was minimal. The Governor didn't believe anything was coming to kill them. He felt that if they were coming, then they would have already arrived. Sam had tried to argue that point with him in an attempt to convince him the enemy might have decided to be more cautious than that. He was hedging his bets by prepping the defenses first, but she sensed an undercurrent of desire to get the city outside and start settling into some kind of normalcy. Besides, she already had a job to do, so she should just let him focus on those details while she focused on her mission.

She wanted to punch him when he said it. She had always known him to be a bit arrogant, but she couldn't believe he was being such a patronizing, condescending asshole.

She turned off the water a little too violently, causing the pipes to rattle as the water stopped flowing. She stepped out of the shower, quickly dried herself off and then padded across the living area back to her bedroom. She grabbed a fresh set of clothes and checked the time. Oh-three-hundred. She wasn't supposed to meet her troops at the Law Office until oh-five-hundred, but she was done trying to sleep. She was done sitting around. There was nothing restful about it. She was angry, frustrated, and more than a little scared, and there wasn't anything she could do about it.

Except…one thing.

She grabbed her badge and clipped it to her shirt. Then she headed out the door.

It was a shot in the dark, but it was a shot she had to take.

Chapter 37

The Law Office was quiet when Sam arrived, with only a skeleton crew of deputies staffing the desks in the front of the building. Most of them had their feet up and their hats over their faces, trying to get a little extra sleep while waiting for reports from the officers patrolling the city. DDF operations had already relocated to the Governor's Mansion, not really a mansion at all, but rather a much larger cube at the top of the first block in Metro. Governor Stone wanted to lead, but he wanted to do it from the comfort of his home.

Half of Law had already transferred to the new Deliverance Defense Force. There was no paperwork involved, only a request made to the Governor's Office, at which point Stone decided what rank to give them and where to place them. He had made all of the original officer picks from Colonel Dante down to Lieutenant Baez, but now the former sheriffs and militia members ranked between the two were deciding on the positions. Once the defense council completed the volunteer assignments, they would begin drafting civilians to finish filling the ranks.

Sam bristled again. She should be on the defense council. Her rank demanded it, and only Stone's direct orders overrode it. She closed her eyes and took a deep breath. She had to stay partial to do what was right for the colony, not focus on how the Governor had personally affected her. And she was here to do right by the colony, wasn't she? Not because she wanted to get back at Stone?

There was a fine line, but it was an important distinction to make. If Stone led them in the wrong direction, she had to be prepared to do something about it, not follow him into the inferno.

She walked across the office, keeping her steps as light and soft as possible so the deputies wouldn't pay her any mind. She was closing on the last occupied desk when she recognized Deputy Bashir by his thin frame and badge.

She took a moment to decide whether or not to invite him into her duplicity. Then she put her hand on his shoulder.

"Bashir," she whispered.

"Dante, that you?" Bashir replied from under his hat.

"Yes."

"What time is it?"

"Three-fifteen."

"Thought you were coming back at five."

"I have work to do before I go."

"DDF HQ is at the GM," he said.

"Sheriff's business," she replied. "You want in?"

He took his leg off his desk, lifted his hat off his face, and sat up, looking at her. "Does this have anything to do with Card, by any chance?"

"Indirectly. It has to do with protecting Metro. That's what all of this is about."

"Would Stone call it treason?"

Sam nodded. "Probably."

Bashir smiled. "Then I'm in. What Jackson did to the Guardians is bullshit. What he's doing to you is even more bullshit. I wish I could come with you."

"I wish you could come with me too."

Bashir had volunteered for the DDF. Stone turned him down. The Governor didn't say why, but Sam believed it was because of her. She had worked too closely with Bashir over the years, and for as much as Stone said he trusted her, he wasn't taking any chances.

"He only let you off the hook so he could send you after Card, didn't he?" Bashir asked.

"That's right," Sam agreed. "If I kill Caleb, I've earned my place. If Caleb kills me, no loss. If I try to help Caleb and the rest of the squad kills me, no loss."

"It's messed up, that's what it is."

"Agreed."

"We should be focused on what might be out there that's really a threat."

"Agreed again."

"Right. I had to get that off my chest. What are we doing?"

"I need to go down into the armory. Past it, actually. The ship's mainframe is down there. The terminal is unlocked. It has complete access to everything. Every recording from every camera in and outside of Metro, past and present."

"Does Jackson know it's there?"

"I don't know. He was so focused on the armory he didn't bother with the rest of the deck. Do you know if anyone's still down there?"

"He posted a guard."

"Who?"

"Caspar, Wilks, and Gudru I think."

Caspar was on her side. She wasn't sure about Wilks or Gudru.

"What kind of recording are you looking for?" Bashir asked.

"I'm not sure if that's what I'm after. Governor Stone's family deleted data from the archives and reset the computer to wipe out the truth about the city and the Deliverance. They were the ones who put us back on Earth, not the Marines. Not even Valentine."

"I know that," Bashir said. "I was there. But you know Stone'll have me killed if I even whisper anything about it."

"I know. If I can get some evidence, I can clear the Guardians from blame and bring them in."

"You need to be careful. We can't afford a riot."

"I know."

"So what do you need me to do?"

"Help me get past the guards, and then act as a witness. If I'm the only one with the information and something happens to me out there, the whole plan goes to hell."

"You want me to salvage something if you don't come back?"

"I want you to try."

"It might get me killed."

"I know."

"This conversation could get me killed."

"I know."

Bashir paused, glancing at his desk. He had a picture of his wife on it. She was a beautiful woman, with long dark hair and exotic eyes. She had her hands on the shoulders of their daughter, so young and already as pretty as her mom.

"I have a family, Sam."

"A lot of people in Metro have families, Ahran. I want to keep it that way."

Deputy Bashir put his hand to the photo. Prints like it didn't come easily in the city, which only proved how much he adored them.

"Okay. I'll do it. I know you're right."

"Thank you," Sam said.

Bashir nodded, scooping up the frame and quickly removing the print. He folded it and put it in his pants pocket. "For luck."

They made their way to the back of the office, toward the garage. The three officers were sitting against the wall on either side of the door, chatting when they arrived. The sudden appearance took them by surprise, and they jumped to their feet.

"Sheriff Dante?" Caspar said. "What are you doing here?"

"I need to go down into the armory," Sam said.

"Governor-General Stone isn't allowing anyone down there without his direct permission. I can contact him to get it?"

"I'll be honest. I don't have the Governor's direct permission. But I still need to go down there."

"Sorry, Sheriff," Gudru said, getting to her feet. "We can't let you do that. I'm sure you understand."

"It's not a question of whether I understand," Sam replied. "It's a question of whether you understand."

"What does that mean?" Wilks asked.

"Things are happening here, Deputy. Things are changing faster than we can adjust. This time yesterday, you were on patrol in Metro, safe in the fact that we were safe in a bunker dozens of kilometers from the nearest trife. But it turns out that isn't the truth. It turns out we've spent our entire lives in space, and now we're on an alien planet forty light years from home. We're all trying to come to grips with that reality, but that doesn't mean we can ignore our original duty."

"What duty is that?" Gudru asked.

"The law," Sam said. "We have a duty to uphold the law. Protect the innocent and champion justice. Those directives are written in Metro's protocols, and even Governor Stone can't change them."

"What are you talking about, Sheriff?" Wilks said.

"She's talking about the Guardians," Caspar said. "Governor Stone blamed them for bringing us here against our will."

"Because they did," Gudru said.

"No," Sam said. "Our ancestors boarded the Deliverance willingly. Governor Stone's family covered it up. They changed the narrative to keep the colony calm."

"Bullshit," Gudru insisted. "They had no good reason to do that."

"They had their own reasons, most of which had to do with staying in control."

"How can you possibly know that?"

"Because Governor Stone said it himself, in my presence, the first time we met Sergeant Card and his people."

"I was there," Bashir said. "I heard him."

"So did I," Caspar said.

"What?" Wilks said. "Why didn't you say anything?"

"You know the Governor," Caspar said. "You're as afraid of what he might do to you or yours as we are."

"I don't believe this," Gudru said. "And even if it was true, what are you doing here, Sheriff? What's the point? The people believe what Stone tells them."

"I believe I can prove it, but I need access to the armory."

"How is that going to prove anything?" Caspar asked.

"The less you know, the better," Sam replied. "All I'm asking is that you let me go down there and that you keep quiet about it. If I don't find anything, there's no harm done and nobody will ever know. If I do find something, then we'll be doing our job and protecting innocent people from wrongful accusations. Where we are shouldn't change what we stand for."

"I think the Governor should be aware of this," Gudru said. "He should know you're trying to soil his name."

"I'm trying to bring the truth out. Isn't that the right thing to do? What happens if we have an enemy out there, on their way to attack us and we aren't prepared?"

"We're in a tough spot here. Governor Stone is best equipped to help us through it. Ruining him won't help anyone, except maybe you."

"What is that supposed to mean?"

"I didn't think I was being subtle. You want what Stone has. You want to be in charge."

"That's ridiculous."

"Is it? Are you honestly telling me your ambition never went beyond Head Sheriff? Especially now that you're a Colonel in the DDF?"

"If that was true, I could have married into the Governor's family years ago. That's not where my ambitions lie. I want to give Metro the best chance at survival."

"Then go back to bed," Gudru said. "There's no reason for you to be here."

"I can't. I need to get down into the armory."

"That isn't happening. I'm going to let the Governor know you're here."

Gudru started reaching for her badge. "Sasha, wait." Caspar reached out and took her arm, stopping her. "Sheriff Dante's right. We need to look into this."

. . .

"LET ME GO!" Gudru snapped, jerking her arm out of his grasp. "I'm contacting the Governor's office."

"No, you aren't," Caspar insisted, quickly yanking her badge off her shirt.

"Wilks.," Sam said. "What do you say?"

Wilkes hadn't moved, taking in the back and forth. He stared at Sam for a moment and then nodded, turning his attention to Gudru. "Sheriff Dante is right, Sasha. If Stone lied about the Guardians, if he was going to have them executed in front of the people to protect his own ass, we have a responsibility to do something about it."

"You're going to start another civil war, that's what you're going to do. When we least need to be fighting among ourselves."

"What kind of world do you want to create here?" Caspar said. "One ruled by a lying tyrant who will say whatever he has to and blame whoever he wants to get his way?"

"Like I said," Sam reiterated. "If I find nothing, then there's nothing to find. But if I do find something…"

Gudru bit her lip, then she nodded. "Okay. Fine. I have a family too, you know. They need me."

"And we need to be the voice of reason in the city," Caspar said. "Sheriff Dante's never let us down."

Gudru looked at Sam and nodded. "No, you haven't. You can count me in. I promise I'll keep my mouth shut. Law has to stick together, right?"

"Right," Sam said. "Thank you, Sasha. You too, Charlie."

"Good hunting, Sheriff," Wilks replied.

Chapter 38

The garage had changed a lot from the first time Sam had entered it to now. All of the debris that had helped hide the secret armory was gone, cleaned out and moved to another area. The platform into the cache was locked in the down position, with access to the area provided by a hastily assembled temporary stairway. While the lift could carry heavier items up to the city, its general operation was slow, and the equipment the DDF wanted in the short-term, guns and armor, was easier to bring up by hand.

Sam and Bashir took the stairs down into the armory. Sam heard Bashir gasp at the sight of the numerous military vehicles and the racks of firearms that had yet to be relocated. It was the same reaction everyone had when entering the area, so it was a response she was accustomed to.

"This way," she said, waving her hand to guide Bashir toward the back of the armory. The exit became visible as she came around the APC and suddenly experienced momentary panic. Had the Governor already decided to explore the deeper part of the deck? Had he accessed the terminal and already deleted every record that could incriminate him and his family in their deception of the colony?

When they entered the corridor, a pungent smell of decay filled the air.

"Uh. Sheriff," Bashir said, his voice tight.

Sam saw the dead trife too. "Sergeant Card and I put them down," she said. "They attacked us the first time we came down."

"What are they?" Bashir managed to spit out.

"Xenotrife," she replied. "The enemy."

"Ugly. And terrifying."

"The good news is that it doesn't look like anyone's disturbed them."

"That's good news?"

"It means it's less likely Stone hasn't been through here."

"Right. How many of them did you kill?"

"I think I got four. Sergeant Card killed the rest."

"And you're supposed to go outside the ship to confront him?"

"My thought exactly. I'd rather not. Try not to step on any of the blood or leave any tracks."

"Easier said than done."

"Do your best."

They navigated around the carcasses, past the corner and down the long corridor. Sam could hear Bashir breathing behind her, shallow and short. He was nervous about being here with her and even more nervous about the trife.

"Bashir, relax," Sam said. "There's nothing dangerous down here."

"How can you be sure?" Bashir replied.

"We would have found it already. The mainframe is

just down there." She pointed to the door in question and picked up her pace.

They reached the door to the ship's mainframe. Sam glanced back at Bashir before opening it. "See? Nothing to worry about."

She tapped on the door control.

The door slid open.

A trife stood up in front of her, hissing softly before backing away.

"Oh, shit," Bashir cried out, trying to reverse course. His shout frightened the trife even more, and it leaped over one of the racks and ducked behind it, hiding.

Ali's heart pounded with surprise, but she stayed calm, her eyes sweeping the room and crossing over the other docile trife. They huddled near one another, shrinking back from her.

"Bashir, it's okay," she said, laughing softly. "They're harmless."

"You just said they were the enemy."

"I meant the other ones. This group is harmless."

"What the hell?"

"I don't exactly know, but I do know they won't hurt you." She entered the room, heading for the terminal. The trife watched her but didn't move.

Bashir entered behind her, staying close. He stared at the trife, uncertain she was right about their aggressiveness. They didn't make any moves toward him or Sam, ducking further back the closer the two of them came.

Sam activated the terminal. It was in the same state she had left it, responding to the search for recordings from Research. She was going to clear it when the still thumbnail of one of the clips caught her eye. She tapped on it with her finger, and it expanded and started to play.

"Test subject Theta Three," Riley Valentine said. "Mature trife, post-CN140 editing."

Valentine and the trife were standing across from one another. The creature was unrestrained and unblocked from attacking her, but it held its ground and stared at her in indifference.

"Subject is awake and alert. No sign of eye dilation or aggressive posture. Subject appears to be calm."

She walked up to the trife, putting her hand on the front of its face. It still didn't move.

"Physical interaction triggers no response." She moved her hand, sliding it down the demon's chest. It was amazing to Sam to watch the creature remain still and accept the touch with little regard. "Note. Capture a CT scan of Theta Three's brain activity during the next response test."

Riley backed away from the creature, looking off-camera.

"Programmed response test sixteen," she said. "David, open it."

Sam heard a soft click in the direction of Riley's look. A moment later the camera shifted to focus on a small rodent scurrying across the floor.

The trife noticed it too, its head tilting down. It let out a sharp hiss and lunged at the rat, claws scraped past as it narrowly avoided being impaled.

The trife screeched louder and chased it toward a desk. The rat stopped underneath it, and the trife grabbed the desk and threw it aside, trying to step on the rat. It broke away again while the trife tried to give pursuit.

"Subject is responding aggressively to the introduction of predation trigger," Riley said. "Genetic alteration of the activity index is a success."

The trife continued to hiss as it leaped around the

room, trying to catch up to the rat. It showed no regard for Riley, remaining singularly focused on the rodent.

"David, bring it in," she said. "It works."

"It does," Sam heard someone say off-camera. "I told you it would. There's more than one way to skin a cat."

The rat reacted to something, straightening out and sprinting across the floor. The trife pounced one last time, its shoulder hitting the wall as the rat escaped through a much smaller door. The trife returned to its static, calm position the moment the rat was out of sight.

"This doesn't change our other plans," Riley said.

"I was hoping we could talk about that," David replied.

"Not if you want to continue sleeping with me."

The one she called David didn't answer again. Riley walked over to the camera, reaching past it. And then the screen went dark.

Sam glanced at the trife in the back of the room. They were part of the outcome of Riley's experiments, their original instinct to kill humans edited out of them. Were they reprogrammed to attack something else? If so, what?

"We're wasting time, Sheriff," Bashir said. "What about the dirt on Governor Stone?"

Riley glanced at him. There was so much she wanted to know. So much she might have access to from the terminal. So many answers that might help them survive in the coming weeks. She wasn't sure she would ever have another chance. Damn it. Bashir was right. They couldn't linger down here. They had an hour at most before she would need to be back in the office, ready to soldier up and ship out.

She looked at the flashing red lights of the mainframe's damaged datastores. What if the evidence she was after were on one of them? What if the evidence she was after didn't exist? She needed to find something.

She started working through the menus, digging into the mainframe's filesystem. It was access she wouldn't normally have, an inside look at the workings of the super-computer. There were thousands of folders. Millions of files. The cameras were active and recording for over two hundred years, the size of her task immense.

She couldn't afford to fail. She needed to connect Governor Stone to the forgotten truth. She needed to prove he knew the Guardians weren't responsible for their situation. Riley Valentine, in part. But not Caleb, Washington, or Flores.

It was a needle in a haystack, but it was a needle she had to find.

Minutes passed. Bashir began pacing behind her, sweeping back and forth and wiping at a line of sweat on his brow. She ran dozens of searches across the mainframe, half of which returned with errors related to the damaged servers. She got excited when she found an area of the system called sysLog, thinking it would show the deletion of records and the reset. It didn't. She started getting more nervous and more desperate, her hope sinking with every lost second.

Governor Stone had lied, and he was going to get away with it.

She froze, shifting gears from desperation to embarrassment in the span of a few seconds. "I'm so stupid," she announced.

"What is it?" Bashir asked.

"Idiot," she added, tapping on the control surface and entering a new query, complete with location and time-stamp. The results came back, and she smiled at the thumbnails that displayed.

"Why didn't I think of that?" Bashir asked.

She had heard Governor Stone admit to hiding the

truth. He had said it in the Law Office, right in front of her and Bashir, to Valentine and the Guardians. There was a camera in Law, always running. Always recording. It went to the city's subnetwork first, but Caleb had told her every subsystem sent a copy here. It couldn't have wound up on a damaged server because they were already damaged. And Stone probably had no idea because they were all so accustomed to the cameras they never gave them any thought.

The recording was right there, at the top of the list for the data she had entered. All she needed was a means to make a copy. There wasn't anything down here, but she was sure there was a blank data disc in her office. She tapped on the clip and instructed the computer to send a copy to her personal account.

"Got you," she said, smiling.

"Sheriff," someone said. She spun around, finding Caspar standing in the doorway. "Stone is on his way over. It's time to go."

She turned back to the terminal, quickly clearing the query. With any luck, the Governor would never think to look for what she had found.

"I got what I needed," she said, drawing a smile from the deputy. "Let's go."

Chapter 39

It took some work to get the Daggers out of the way to allow one of the transports through. The engineers needed to bring a small electric mover up from the main hangar, through the ship's corridors to the main lift, and then from the single functioning lift to the forward hangar. It was nearly thirteen-hundred by the time the transport was positioned right behind the hangar's blast doors.

Sam was armed and armored, geared up in the same SOS Caleb had fitted to her. The new members of the DDF were finding the ATCA challenging in terms of size and fit, and while there was equipment down below that could alter both, nobody had figured out how to use it yet.

Fortunately, there was still enough of the combat armor to give the seven soldiers—five men and two women—that Governor Stone had selected for her squad were equally equipped with a helmet, combat armor, an MK-12, a VP-5 semi-automatic sidearm and a hunting knife. Owing to the fact that there was only time to train on one kind of weapon—and the standard rifles were more plentiful—the Governor hadn't chosen to allow them

233

access to the plasma rifles or railguns they had also found below.

At least, that was his excuse. As far as Sam was concerned, the bigger reason was that he didn't want them to lose the more powerful weapons if or when they died.

The squad was assembled in two neat columns of four, standing on the left side of the transport. Governor Stone, Beth Stone, and their newly trained pilot stood opposite them.

"It looks like everything is ready," Governor Stone said.

"Finally," Beth Stone added.

"Sir, are you still sure this is a good idea?" Sam asked. "We haven't had a lot of training on any of this equipment yet, and it might be better served if—"

Governor Stone put his hand up to silence her. "Lasandra, you outnumber them nearly three to one, and one of them is already dying. Find the Guardians and bring me back their heads." He paused. "Or you can spend the rest of your life locked in a cell if that's what you prefer."

"Understood," Sam replied, bristling beneath her helmet.

"I imagine so, Colonel. The mission is yours. Come back with Card or don't come back at all."

Stone flashed a condescending smile, moving away from the squad. His wife followed behind him, wearing a satisfied smirk of her own.

"He acts like we're expendable," one of her new squad mates said, a former militia member named Steven. He was the tallest of the group, though he was also rail thin beneath the SOS.

"You worked for him," another squad member, Jia, said. "You didn't know that already?"

"I guess there was never cause to put it to the test," Steven replied.

"All right," Sam said, stepping out of the column and turning to face them. "That's enough. We have our orders." She glanced at the pilot beside her. He was young. Maybe a year or two older than Orla. His face was beet red, and he looked like he was ready to wet himself. "What's your name, pilot?"

"Kiaan, ma'am," he replied. "Kiaan Habib."

"Kiaan. Are you part of the DDF?"

"The what?"

"Deliverance Defense Force."

"I don't know. I think so. Governor Stone was looking for people interested in trying out a new simulator. I've played some of the vids before, so I thought it would be fun." He smiled sheepishly. "I'm pretty good at it."

"How old are you?" a third squad member, Liam, asked.

"Seventeen."

"You're too small to be seventeen. You look like a twelve-year-old girl."

Kiaan froze, unable to react to the statement. Sam spun around, finding Liam in the group. "You're out of line soldier," she barked. "I want an apology, right now."

"Or what?" Liam asked. "I never had to take orders from a sheriff before, and I'm not starting now. I don't know how I got picked for this shit gig anyway."

Sam stormed over to him. "Did you volunteer for the DDF?"

"Yeah. I told Governor Stone I wanted to be a commander, and he put me here instead."

"Lucky us," Jia said.

"What does that mean?" Liam asked.

"Man, shut the hell up and do what Sheriff Dante says," Steven said.

"Colonel Dante," Sam said. "We're all on the same

team, and we need to rely on one another if we're going to survive. Our orders are to find Sergeant Card and his Guardians and take them out. If you think any part of that will be easy, you're out of your damn mind."

"So what are you saying, this is a suicide mission?" Liam asked.

"Not if you shut up and follow my lead," Sam replied.

"And apologize to Kiaan," Jia said. "Your bullshit comment was completely unnecessary."

"Fine. Sorry, kid," Liam said.

"It's okay," Kiaan said.

"Our squad designation is going to be Marshal," Sam said. She pointed to herself. "Marshal Leader." Then she picked each one of them out. "Marshal Two, Marshal Three, Marshal Four…" giving each of them a numerical designation.

"Does Marshal mean anything?" Kiaan asked.

"Back on Earth, the Marshals were responsible for catching fugitives," Sam said.

"It fits," Jia said.

"Ma'am," Kiaan said. "All I have to do is fly the FCT, right? I don't have to fight?"

"No, you don't have to fight," Sam said. "Just get us there in one piece."

"Yes, ma'am."

"Marshals, load up," Sam said, pointing to the open side of the transport. The soldiers moved to it in a slightly disorganized column, boarding the craft and filling in the sparse seats from back to front. "Come on, Kiaan."

The pilot entered the transport ahead of her. She stopped at the threshold, her eyes passing over the transport's interior. It was as basic as they came, the seats almost bare metal with minimal padding, secured with bolts in the metal flooring. There were no windows in the back, and the hatch made a loud grinding noise as it slid closed behind her.

"Are you sure this thing can fly, ma'am?" Jia asked.

Sam realized she wasn't sure. Liam laughed at her hesitation. "This may be a short trip."

She ignored him, moving to the center and looking into the cockpit. The pilot's seat was positioned in the center, with a display on either side and a small window in front. The blast doors were already open, and she could see through it to the dense green of the jungle directly ahead of them, a row of mountains beyond the jungle. Her heart began thumping harder, a mixture of nerves and excitement building.

She was terrified of the unknown. Even the simple act of flying in a transport was a new experience for all of them, and everything on this world was equally new. She had never seen so much color. So many trees. Hell, she had never seen a real sky. It was all so big, and she struggled against the overwhelming scale of it all.

"Kiaan, power us up," she said.

The young pilot was staring out the window too. If the other Marshals could see outside, they would be doing the same thing. She gave him a little longer before moving up behind him and putting her hand on his shoulder.

"Kiaan, let's go," she repeated.

"Uh, yes ma'am," he replied, shaking under her grip as he reached toward the dashboard, flipping the two manual switches. The two displays turned on, as well as a control surface on his left where his hand was resting. He took the transport's control stick in his right and tapped the control surface. The carrier shuddered slightly as the superconducting ceramic discs inside the anti-gravity pods began spinning, the electromagnets beneath them drawing in power. The transport emitted a low-pitched whine, and within a few seconds began to slowly rise off the surface of the hangar.

"What direction are we going?" Kiaan asked.

They had used the time while the engineers were moving Daggers out of the way to send a few drones out to explore. According to Governor Stone, they had found tracks from a vehicle heading into the jungle.

"Straight ahead," Sam replied. "Take it slow and easy."

"Yes, ma'am."

She remained standing while Kiaan shifted the control stick. She had to grab onto the back of his chair as the craft lurched forward, bucked back, slipped sideways and then jumped ahead again.

"Sorry," Kiaan said. "It's a little more touchy than the simulator."

"Slow and easy," she repeated.

He nodded, taking a deep breath to calm down. This was all new to him too, and he had the added responsibility of flying a real aircraft for the first time.

The transport eased forward, out over the edge of the hangar. Sam's stomach dropped with the craft as it fell a few meters before the pods adjusted, catching and keeping them level. The two displays showed a fisheye view from both sides that offered full coverage of the transport. She could see the port extensions reaching out beneath them, as well as the scarring from the alien drone's attack.

It was a wonder they had made it to the surface at all.

She could see the river stretching out on either side of them and vanishing into the distance. She had a sudden yearning to be down there beside it, to touch the water and feel real earth beneath her feet. This whole mission was stupid. Governor Stone had lost Orla, and then he had lost his mind.

She had what she needed to prove the Marines were innocent. All she had to do was keep the other Marshals from shooting the Guardians and keep the Guardians from shooting at them. All she had to do was discover the answer to why Caleb had left with the alien, seemingly helping it escape.

All she had to do was survive.

The transport starting moving forward, slightly unsteady as Kiaan worked to balance the power output. The craft shook, dipping to the left and then leveling as he apologized again.

Survival was going to be much easier said than done.

Chapter 40

"Do you see anything, Colonel?" Jia asked.

Sam turned her head to look back at the Marshals. "Nothing yet. The canopy is so thick it's impossible to get a look through it."

"It's doing a great job blocking our sensors too," Kiaan said, pointing at the readings in front of him. "This thing only has IR, and it can't penetrate."

"It doesn't matter. I'm sure we're well ahead of them by now."

"How do you know they're going to continue south?"

"I don't. For all we know, they're still half a klick away from the Deliverance, and we're going to be waiting a long, long time."

Two hours had passed since they had left the grounded starship behind. They were almost four kilometers out from the ship, still floating above the thick jungle and headed directly south. The massive starship had long faded out of view, its disappearance causing a fresh wave of nervousness to overtake the otherwise calm sheriff.

There was no sign of the Guardians, but that was

hardly a surprise. They had taken a surface vehicle into the dense vegetation, probably because they didn't know the transports existed. They were down there...somewhere. Sam was sure of it. But finding them would be almost as impossible as finding a specific recording from the ship's mainframe among two hundred years of clips.

Like she had done with that situation, she was planning to let the solution make itself apparent to her, rather than try to force a resolution that would be nearly impossible to manage.

The mountains that had once been distant were almost right on top of them, close enough now that she could see white-capped peaks despite the warmth of the air at the transport's current elevation. She could make out the crags and bluffs of the rocky terrain as she continued to marvel at the immensity and vastness of it all, even while she scanned the foothills for a reasonable place to touch down. They had brought enough food and water to spend nearly a week out in the field before they would need to resupply, but she was hoping Caleb would turn up well before that.

"Something makes you think they'll keep coming this way," Kiaan said. "What is it, if you don't mind me asking, ma'am?"

"Sergeant Card told me the alien wanted to get to the surface. It must have had a destination in mind. Since they left with it, I'm assuming they're staying with it. And the shortest distance between two points is a straight line."

"That makes sense."

Sam smiled. "I'm glad you agree."

The statement caused Kiaan to blush. "Did you know my family came from Marines? My great-something grandmother died on Earth in the war."

"I didn't know that," Sam replied.

"Yeah. What was the name of her unit again?" He

paused, thinking. "It was some kind of Earth bird. Eagles? Sparrows? Hmmm..."

"Vultures?" Sam offered, remembering the name of Caleb's former squad.

Kiaan's face lit up. "Yeah, that was it! How did you know?"

Sam bit her bottom lip. "Did Governor Stone know your family history, by any chance?"

"I mean, I told the Sheriff running the tryouts about it. I figured it would help me get into the program if they knew I came from a family of Marines."

Governor Stone really was a son of a bitch. "Sergeant Card was the commander of the Vultures. Did you know that?"

Kiaan seemed more excited. "No, ma'am. You mean he knew my great-something grandmother?"

"Yes."

His expression changed when he realized what that meant. "And now he's a traitor?"

Sam leaned in, lowering her voice. "I'll let you in on a secret, but you can't mention it to the others."

"Okay."

"I don't think Sergeant Card is a traitor."

"But he helped the alien escape."

"Did he? Or is he using the alien to learn more about potential threats on the planet and take care of them before they take care of us?"

That's the version she was choosing to believe until Caleb proved otherwise. And that kind of proof would leave her dead in its wake.

"But we're supposed to stop him."

"I know. Let me worry about that."

"Yes, ma'am."

They continued toward the mountains, the rocky face

looming ever larger through the forward viewport. Both Kiaan and Sam scoured the landscape for a place to land the transport without veering too far off the straight line path back to the Deliverance. The jungle was climbing the foothills of the mountains, remaining thick all the way to sheer cliff faces. There had to be a path through somewhere, or the Guardians were making the trip for nothing. Even they couldn't climb the vertical rock.

"Kiaan, can you activate the long-range comm?"

Kiaan tapped on the controls, and she heard a click.

"Deliverance, this is Marshal One. Do you copy?" she said.

"This is Deliverance," Deputy Klahanie replied. "We hear you Marshal One."

"Klahanie, don't you ever go to sleep?" Sam asked.

"Roger, Sheriff. I got three hours and came back to the bridge once the comm systems came online. I like it up here. There's a great view."

"The view's better where I am."

"What can I help you with, Sheriff?"

"It's Colonel now."

"Sorry. What can I help you with, Colonel?"

"I'd like an updated status on the drone surveillance. Is there any evidence of the Guardians changing direction or circling back to the ship?"

"Let me patch in DDF Control. Standby."

The comms were up and running, but there was still a bit of confusion about how to patch through and prioritize the different units and uses. Nearly a minute had passed before Klahanie's voice entered the transport's cockpit again.

"Sher, I mean Colonel, DDF Control reports no new developments. They did sound a little excited about a couple of animals the drones spotted along the river banks.

A strange cat-like thing with tentacles and some kind of color changing iguana type thing. If you know what an iguana is."

"I don't," Sam said. "But it sounds interesting."

"The biologists were eager to get a closer look, but Stone isn't ready to let anyone else outside."

"Understandable. Thanks for the update, Deputy."

"Anytime, Sher… Colonel."

"Marshal One out."

Sam motioned for Kiaan to close the channel. He tapped the control and then pointed to the display on the left.

"Colonel, look. There's a break in the trees. It's hard to judge with the distortion from the cameras, but I think we can touch down there?"

Sam checked the location and nodded. "Head that direction and get us line of sight. If we can fit, we'll land."

"Yes, ma'am."

The transport slowed and rotated, the front dipping slightly as Kiaan adjusted the power to the anti-gravity pods. The break in the trees came into view as a small crag jutting out from the foothills, surrounded by more foliage but offering a patch of flat ground to land. Scanning around the plateau, Sam noticed what looked like a more gentle slope leading up and away from the jungle.

It was the perfect place for the Guardians to attempt passage over the mountains.

"Bring us down there," she said.

"Yes, ma'am," Kiaan replied.

The transport shuddered and bucked, Kiaan's inexperience showing as he brought the craft toward the flat ground. The soldiers in the back groaned, either out of amusement or motion sickness. Sam held on tight, feeling a bit of both herself.

The pods touched down a little harder than the pilot probably wanted, giving the craft a good jostle as it slapped the ground and bounced back before coming to rest again, the forward viewport facing the rock ahead.

"Nice landing," Sam said.

"Hard landing," Kiaan replied.

"We're still alive. I'll take it." She headed to the back of the transport, noticing both smiles and pale faces. "We're here. Grab your gear. There should be camo netting in storage. We'll cover the transport and find a good place to wait."

"Roger, Colonel," Steven said. "We're on it."

"Can I fly us back?" Liam asked. "It'll be easier on all of us."

"Shut the hell up," Jia hissed.

"You got a thing for the kid or something, Private?" Liam replied. "I don't even think he's legal yet."

Sam could see Jia's scowl through her faceplate. "One more word from you, and I'll—"

"You'll what?" Liam asked.

"Shut up, all of you," Sam snapped. "This isn't the time or place for bullshit. Liam, the storage hold is there. Open her up and find the camo. You're on netting detail."

Liam's face darkened, and Sam thought he was going to challenge her again. He thought better of it, standing up and nodding. "Yes, ma'am."

Sam opened the side hatch and jumped out onto the rocky terrain, the rest of the Marshals close behind. The air was colder up here than back near the ship and carried a sweet odor. Where was it coming from?

She would have time to figure it out later. Once their basic defense was organized, there would be nothing else for them to do but wait.

Chapter 41

Two days of slow, steady progress through the jungle found Caleb, Washington, Flores and Hal close enough to the mountains to begin making out the snow-covered caps and the rows of vegetation attempting to climb up the stone faces. The travel had been relatively uneventful, and Caleb was grateful for it. There was no further sign of trife, no trouble from potential apex predators, no strange interactions with poisonous insects, animals, or vegetation.

He remembered one mission in Borneo where one of his squadmates had been bitten by some random no-see-um and wound up with a fever that took him out of action for a week. While the SOS was supposed to protect them from that particular freak accident, experience had taught him that there was no perfect system that would prevent unexpected setbacks. As far as he was concerned, making it two days through an alien ecosystem without issues was a success.

"We should make it to the foothills in the morning," Hal said, his voice echoing out through Caleb's comm.

The trife throat was unable to produce vocalizations

even close to resembling human language, limited to hisses and screams because of the way the air passed through the esophagus. Like Caleb had assumed, the Axon AI had found a way around the limitation, adjusting its internal transmitters to an open band the ATCS could listen in on. The better news was that the alterations also limited the AI's ability to utilize the mind-altering waveforms that caused hallucinations.

Caleb still didn't pretend to understand any of the technological implications of what the AI had done. The fact that the machine was composed of a gel-like substance was still hard for him to wrap his head around. He pictured robots as a full-body extension of his replacement arm, made up of metal and wire and batteries. He had considered asking Hal more about it but had decided the AI's answers would go right over his head anyway.

Besides, they were still allies because of a common goal, not by choice.

"Almost there," Caleb replied. "Wash, why don't you pull in somewhere tight and shut her down for the night. We'll break here and send out the drone at first light to find a pass over the hills."

Washington reached back from the cockpit of the ADC, flashing his thumb. The other downside to Hal's new form was that it didn't lend itself well to driving. It was too big and its limbs too long for the design of the vehicle, a detail that Caleb had overlooked when he told the AI to change capsules.

He didn't regret it. He was glad to have finally put Sho to rest, giving her the respectful send-off she deserved. He was happy not to have to look at her face anymore and feel guilty for how the AI had perverted her body. He wouldn't let it pervert her memory too.

"I will take watch," Hal said, not that it needed to. The

AI always took watch, because the AI didn't need to sleep. Caleb checked his HUD and watched as the trife form sprang away from the ADC and easily scaled one of the massive trees, vanishing into the branches.

There were upsides to the transformation, too.

"Hal, have you figured out that other algorithm yet?" Caleb asked.

"I am still processing, Sarge."

"I can keep watch if it helps you process faster. We're getting closer to the source."

"It is a subprocess. I require not your assistance."

"Have it your way."

"I will."

Caleb smiled. The AI didn't always understand Earth idioms, responding to them literally.

"Is Ugly Yoda protecting us?" Flores asked.

Caleb nodded, turning to look at her. She was in the last seat in the ADC, her helmet off. She had helped pass the time over the previous two days by rambling on about the plots to at least fifty movies and then critiquing them. Most of the films were as alien to him as Essex, though he did recognize a few of the more popular franchises.

"Yeah," Caleb replied, going to sit opposite her and taking off his helmet. Washington finished settling the ADC, putting it into sleep mode and then crouching low to move to the back of the carrier. "I wish we had a deck of cards or something."

"You said that yesterday," Flores said.

"It remains true until we get a deck of cards," Caleb replied.

Washington pointed at Flores, motioning to his mouth.

"No, I'm good. Thanks, Wash," she replied.

He glanced at Caleb.

"Sure," Caleb replied.

The big Marine moved the cargo cover on the floor aside, reaching in and pulling out their box of rations. There was enough on board for another week, but after that they would have to start living off the land and hope that nothing they chose was poisonous to humans.

"Do you have a Meatloaf in there?" Caleb asked.

Washington started digging through the box, quickly pulling out an MRE for himself.

"What flavor?" Flores asked.

Washington held it up.

"Thanksgiving Dinner again?"

He shrugged and licked his lips.

"It's good. It's not that good."

He did his best to smile.

"What kind of movie do you want me to tell you about tonight? Sci-fi, comedy, horror, thriller?"

"No sci-fi," Caleb said. "I've had enough sci-fi in the last couple of days to last the rest of my life. How many Star Wars movies are there, again?"

"I don't know," Flores said. "Over twenty. I can start listing them."

"What's the funniest movie you ever saw?" Caleb asked, quickly getting her on another related topic before she started spouting out titles.

"Hmm. That's a hard one. Let me think a minute."

Caleb glanced at Washington, who nodded approval and then continued searching for a meatloaf flavored MRE. He pulled it out in triumph a moment later and tossed it to Caleb.

"These taste just like the meatloaf my mom used to make," Caleb said, laughing and shaking his head. "She was a terrible cook."

"But it tastes like home, right Sarge?" Flores said.

"Exactly." He tore it open and took a bite. It reminded

him of better days. Happier days. Before the trife. Before the war. Before the Deliverance. "I keep finding myself wondering if there's anything left," he said.

"On Earth?" Flores replied. "I think about that too."

Washington tapped his chest.

"I never wanted to leave," Caleb said. "I would have stayed to fight until the end. I heard General Stacker stayed behind. He had a couple thousand with him from all of the branches. Army, Navy, Marines. I still can't believe it's been over two hundred years. I want to think humankind is still out there fighting, but it feels more like a pipe-dream than reality."

"I worry about what happened to Proxima," Flores said. "If any of the other ships really did go there. If the Relyeh were coming to Earth and pressing ahead, they might have reached it by now."

"Hal thinks they went around a big part of the universe to get here faster. I didn't think he was right until the trife showed up. It seems Riley was right too. They sent the bastards from here. Our enemy is out there, somewhere over those mountains. I don't know if we can do anything to hurt them, but if nothing else, it'll be damned satisfying to try."

"Roger that," Flores said.

Washington thumped his fist against his chest in agreement.

They fell silent.

"Spaceballs," Flores said, breaking it.

"What?" Caleb replied.

"Funniest movie I ever saw. It's a parody of Star Wars."

Caleb groaned. Washington tried to groan. Flores laughed.

"What? Come on. Dark Helmet? There's that scene

where he's trying to fight Bill Pullman, and Bill puts his hand on Dark Helmet's helmet and holds him back. I've always wanted to try that on a trife."

"How about something not related to Star Wars?" Caleb asked.

"That's a big ask, Sarge. Let me-- ugh." Flores' eyes snapped closed, and she clutched at her chest. "Ahhh. Damn it." Her face paled almost instantly, and she tried to stand, making it halfway before starting to collapse.

Washington dumped the MREs all over the floor, using his free hands to catch her. He lowered her gently to the floor.

"Flores, what's going on?" Caleb asked.

"Damn it hurts," she groaned, still clutching her chest.

They had all been hoping she would hold out. Two days had passed without pain, and the dark veins on her chest had subsided somewhat.

"Get her SOS off," Caleb said.

Washington was already working the clasps, pulling the armor away. Her chest was covered in sweat, and way too pale.

"Flores. Mariana, stay with us," he said, looking into the open hold for the medkit. But what the hell was he supposed to do with it? Flores didn't answer him. "Flores, come on." He looked at her face. Her eyes were closed. She was out cold. Damn it.

Washington propped her up while Caleb pulled off her shirt. They both froze. The discoloration was gone. If he hadn't seen it earlier, he would have never guessed she had anything wrong with her.

Washington held out his hands. *What do we do?*

Caleb grabbed his helmet, pulling it back over his head. "Hal, we have a situation."

"What do you require?"

"You. Here. Now."

"Assurance."

He had no idea what Hal might be able to do, but it was supposed to be advanced, and it had been on the Deliverance. Maybe it knew something about the solution Riley had created.

A knock came on the ADC's top hatch. Washington moved to it and released the lock, pushing it open and allowing Hal to jump inside.

"What is the problem?"

"Flores. David gave her a topical solution on the Deliverance when she was injured. She was fine for a while, but now she isn't. Is there anything you can do?"

"I require entry to the capsule," Hal said.

"You want to go inside her like you did with Sho?"

"Not the same but yes."

Caleb glanced at Washington. He didn't think Flores would ever allow it. She would rather die.

His jaw tensed. She was a Guardian serving under him. It was his call, not hers.

"Do it," he said.

It was a surreal experience to watch a trife lean over Flores, reaching out and wrapping its large hand around her face. Caleb could only barely see the tendrils extend from the palm and out into her throat, and he had to resist the urge to grab the Axon AI and pull it away.

"Well?" he said.

"Give me a moment," Hal replied.

Caleb glanced at Washington, who looked equally tense. Hal could be doing anything to her insides and they would never know.

"The solution was imperfect," it announced. "Private Flores has advanced stomach cancer."

"What?" Caleb said, heart racing.

"Alterations cause mutations unless properly controlled," Hal said. "Mutations cause improper cell duplication. Ergo, cancer. She will die."

"Damn it. Is there anything you can do?"

"Yes, but you will care not for it."

"What does it involve?"

"I can activate a waveform that may convince her body to fight the mutation. The signal must be powerful to be effective. You will hallucinate. I will augment her natural response with targeted internal heat that will kill the diseased cells."

Caleb looked at Washington again. Washington nodded without hesitation. Then Caleb grabbed the open hatch of the ADC, pulling it closed and locking it.

"Do it," he said.

Chapter 42

Caleb noticed Hal stiffen. Then he heard a noise in his head, a sharp spinning whine like a violin on a yo-yo. It vanished within a couple of seconds, leaving him…

Home?

He blinked his eyes a few times. The ADC was gone. Hal was gone. Flores, Washington, everything. It had vanished from existence, leaving him standing on familiar ground. His parent's house. The place where he had grown up. It was just like he remembered it.

"This isn't real," he said. He was light years away from Earth. Hundreds of years away from this memory. His parents were long dead. His sister was long gone.

"What isn't real?"

He turned at the sound of his father's voice. His father was coming down the hallway from his bedroom, holding a pair of baseball gloves.

"Dad?" Caleb said.

"Yeah. Who else would I be?" His father laughed and tossed him one of the gloves. "Come on outside. We'll have a catch. Just like old times."

"Dad, this isn't real," Caleb repeated. "You aren't real."

His father ran his hands over his cardigan. "I feel real to me," he replied, laughing. "Are you having another episode?"

"Episode? What are you talking about?"

"It's okay, Cal. You're here with your mom and me. Just stay calm. Everything's going to be okay."

"What?"

"Come on, and we'll have a catch. The game's on in two hours. Maybe we can head over to Danny's and watch on the big screen."

"Dad, I don't know what you're talking about. The trife. Essex. Flores." He reached up and clutched his head. Hadn't he put his helmet back on?

His father draped an arm over his shoulder. "Come on, Cal. Why don't we sit for a minute instead? Do you want a glass of water?"

"What? No. I'm fine. I'm just a little… confused."

"It's okay. PTSD, remember? Let me help you, son. It'll be okay."

Caleb took a step back. It felt so real. But it couldn't be. He was on another planet. He was trying to save the colony. Washington was with him. And Flores. She was dying.

"The Guardians," he said.

"You mean the Vultures?" his father replied. "You've been out for two years, remember? You got sick. Did you take your pills this morning?"

"I'm not sick," Caleb said. "I'm hallucinating. This isn't real."

"It's alright, Cal. This is real. Come on. We'll sit and do the breathing exercises the doctor showed us. Then we can play catch."

Caleb pushed away from his father. "No. This isn't real." He turned and headed for the door, grabbing it and yanking it open. The air was warm and moist. He stared out into his street. It was all just like he remembered it.

What if this was real? What if it was everything else that was the hallucination? What if there were no trife? What if he had never left Earth?

"Cal, please," his father said. "Just relax. You're having another episode. You need to breathe."

Caleb tried to breathe. It felt so hard. "I can't stay here," he said. He pushed out of the doorway and into the street. He turned right. There was a deli at the end of the block. If the deli was there, it proved this was real.

"Cal!" his father said, coming out behind him. "Cal, wait!"

Caleb broke into a run, sprinting along the sidewalk. He nearly tripped over the Olson girl's skateboard. Only it wasn't really there, was it?

He kept running. His father ran behind him, giving chase. It only took a minute to get to the end of the block. It only took a minute to swing around the corner and look into the open windows of the deli.

Mr. Wilson was in there, cutting some meat for a customer. He noticed Caleb and waved.

This was real, wasn't it?

Caleb slumped against the wall of the deli, resting on the sidewalk. There was no Essex. No colony. No trife. He had imagined the whole thing.

His father caught up to him. "Cal, it's okay."

"I think I'm going crazy, dad," Caleb replied.

"You aren't. It's from your job. You were a hero, Cal. You helped a lot of people. But the stress. It happens to a lot of Marines. You're not alone. You'll never be alone."

Caleb looked up at his father. Had he made up the

entire thing? Had he lost himself that badly? He didn't remember being in the hospital.

"Come on, son," his father said. "Come back home."

Caleb nodded. "Can you get me a soda?"

"Sure."

Caleb's father went inside. Caleb reached behind his back, producing a gun he didn't even know he had. He held it in his hand for a minute, staring down at it.

No trife. No Deliverance. No Essex. No Marine. No war.

No purpose.

What was he? A Marine with nothing to fight for. A Marine who couldn't even take care of himself. His father was treating him like a porcelain vase, afraid the next word he said would break him.

What the hell kind of life was that?

He glanced back into the deli. His dad was in the line, a soda bottle in hand. He looked back at the gun. Two seconds and it could all be over.

He didn't know what was real anymore. All he knew was that he didn't want to spend the rest of his life trying to figure it out.

He raised the weapon, putting the barrel in his mouth. It was cold and heavy. His finger slid over to the trigger.

Sorry, Dad.

He would have pulled it, but a large hand wrapped around his, yanking it and the gun away. He looked up into a distorted face with big brown worried eyes.

"Wash?" he said.

He looked around. He was outside the ADC, in the jungle against the trunk of one of the trees. His helmet was gone.

Washington released his hand. It was empty, but his fingers were folded into the shape of a gun. He felt a cold wave rush down his spine. He didn't need a real gun to kill himself, and he had come within a hair's breadth of doing it.

"Shit, Wash," he said.

Washington nodded.

"You didn't hallucinate?"

Washington nodded again.

"What did you see?"

Washington shook his head. He didn't want to talk about it.

"We need to get back to Flores."

The big Marine helped him up.

They both froze when they heard a scream. It split the jungle, reverberating off the trees.

A trife. And it was close.

"Now," Caleb said.

Washington pointed and held up two fingers. The ADC was only twenty meters away.

A sudden chorus of hissing screams echoed the first.

They were completely surrounded.

Chapter 43

"Shit," Caleb said for the second time, his voice almost drowned by the demons' calls. Not only was he and Washington outside the ADC, but they were also unarmed, and Caleb didn't even have his helmet to alert Hal to the situation.

As if there was any way the intelligence could miss the racket the trife were making.

Caleb and Washington broke for the ADC. They both froze at the same time, picking up movement in their peripheral vision.

A trio of trife flanked them on either side, coming out of the brush, crouching low and hissing, revealing their long teeth. Another pair emerged behind them, and Caleb was sure he heard them in the trees over their heads too.

How long had he been out of his mind? Ten minutes? An hour? He had no idea. Time seemed to fade the same way reality did. Now that he was back in the jungles of Essex, he could hardly believe he had thought he was home.

He could hardly believe he had been about to kill himself.

He eyed the trife, keeping his head straight and slowly moving into a fighting posture. Washington did the same, more than ready to take on the creatures with his bare hands, if that's what it came to.

Only these weren't the trife from Earth. These trife were bigger, stronger and probably smarter. Like the AI they had encountered, the demons had been upgraded and advanced. But for what purpose?

"We've been in worse scrapes than this before," Caleb said.

Washington glanced at him and raised his eyebrows.

"Maybe not," Caleb corrected. "I'll hold them back; you make a run for the ADC."

Washington shook his head and pointed to himself.

"No. I've got the metal arm, I'll hold them back. Grab a gun and shoot the buggers."

He could tell Washington didn't like the idea, but the silent Marine didn't continue arguing.

"Make a break for it as soon as they move in," Caleb said.

It didn't take very long. The trife shifted around them, hissing and scraping their clawed feet on the ground. Caleb had no idea what triggered them to attack, but a pack twelve strong suddenly shot forward at once.

Washington waited for the group to close before he burst forward like a linebacker, rushing into the front line and using his mass to power through them. The trife grabbed for him, claws digging into his SOS but failing to find flesh or purchase. He squeezed into the middle and broke through the line. The trife closest to him stopped their forward assault and turned back, giving chase.

That still left nine trife for Caleb to contend with. It was a ridiculous number and more than he could handle unarmed. He didn't need to decide whether or not to fight them. He watched their approach, letting his training take over—timing his escape.

Only two of them lunged at him, the rest staying nearby to catch him no matter what direction he chose. He ducked and rolled away from the demons, feeling their claws scrape his armor as he rolled beneath them and to his feet. He heard the soft movement of a trife behind him, and he spun without slowing, using the momentum to bring his replacement arm around and crack it right into the demon's face. Bone shattered under the force of the blow, and the trife crumpled, creating a hole in the attack.

Caleb used it, still maintaining the momentum of his roll, straightening out and vaulting the dead creature, sprinting away. The nearest demons reached for him, one grabbing his replacement arm and trying to sink its claws in. He yanked it off-balance, bringing it to the ground as he leaped away.

The chase was on. He ducked into the foliage, pushing aside large green leaves and jumping over roots and smaller vegetation. He took a mental picture of his surroundings, sure of his direction and its relation to the ADC. He didn't run often, not like this, but it wasn't his first time. One time, he had gone solo on a mission to rescue a high-level molecular biologist. It had started clean and gone to hell in a hurry, leaving the biologist dead and him running from two hundred trife. That time, he had climbed the fire escape of an abandoned apartment building and barely made a pickup off the rooftop before the demons pushed him off it.

This time, there was no air support. Then again, all

Caleb needed to do was buy some time for Washington to load up and hopefully get Hal involved. He had no idea what condition the AI was in. He had no idea what condition Flores was in. Had the Axon been able to save her?

He broke to the right when he heard the brush jostle ahead of him. He collided with a vine, which clung to his SOS and began curling around him, grabbing his torso as though it were a living thing.

He looked up, into the wide, toothed mouth of a large flower. The vine was dangling out of the center, and now it started to retract as though it were a rubber band.

"Ugh. Damn it," Caleb cursed, pulling against it. A trife appeared out of the jungle, coming to a stop when it saw him. It hesitated a moment and then resumed the charge.

Caleb struggled against the vine, trying to pull himself free. The trife held up its claws, and he turned his head and closed his eyes.

He felt the vines about him loosen. He pulled away from them, stumbling a step and then making eye contact with the creature. "Hal, is that you?"

The demon hissed and crouched low.

Not Hal, but it had set him free. He almost laughed. There was no sport hunting something that couldn't move.

"Are you ready then?" he asked. It stared at him without a response. Two more joined it, coming to a stop. They wanted to chase him?

He pivoted, pushing off and getting two steps ahead. The trife hissed and started moving, one down the center and the other two breaking off for the flanks. The hunt resumed, with Caleb breaking through another group of vegetation, more cautious around the vines hanging from the branches above.

He stayed parallel to the ADC, not wanting to lead the trife back to it until Washington was ready. But how would he know when that was? No helmet. No comms. He tried to estimate it in his head.

He nearly lost it.

One of the trife leaped at him from the side. He barely spun and covered himself before it hit, claws scraping his replacement arm. They tumbled to the ground together, and Caleb punched it in the head with his human hand three times in quick succession before jumping to his feet.

The other two trife caught up, and the first leaped at him. He brought his arm up to block only to have the creature cut its leap short. It spun, kicking out with its leg. Backing away from it, he cursed as the third trife slashed its claws all the way down his back. It managed to pierce his ATCS and the battery, and it hissed as acidic gel leaked onto its hand.

Caleb threw himself forward into the first trife, driving it to the ground. He was in trouble. Where the hell was Wash?

He grabbed the first demon's head and slammed it hard into the ground, crushing its skull. He tried to run back the other direction, but the second trife grabbed his ankle and pulled him down. He rolled over, hands raised to defend himself.

A black object swooped around one of the tree trunks, its forward-mounted cannon opening up and tearing the second trife to pieces. The third rounded on it, only to have its head quickly removed.

Caleb waved to the drone in thanks, getting up and following it away. There were screams in the distance, followed by screams all around them. A group of trife emerged ahead, vanishing again as the drone started shooting. Caleb ran past the trees, only to have the trife come out behind him. The drone spun around and Caleb hit the deck, bullets whipping over his head. The trife hid again, two of them falling to the assault.

Caleb ran, the ADC coming into view soon after. There were trife everywhere. At least a hundred of them all converging on the vehicle. Washington was on top of it, an MK-12 in each hand, showing off his impressive strength as he fired both weapons at once.

If he was up there, who was flying the drone?

A dozen trife died in rapid succession, but the drone didn't stop them. They were coming in for the kill, no matter how many fell.

Caleb reached the ADC, leaping up and scaling the side, rolling to a stop at Washington's feet. He didn't linger, sliding into the open hatch. Flores was in the drone pilot seat, her brow creased in concentration. She was alone in the carrier.

Where was Hal?

"Hey Sarge," Flores said without looking at him. Caleb's eyes locked on her. Could it be? There was no trife corpse on the floor. But Hal could have already disposed of it.

He broke out of the moment. It didn't matter. They had to get out of there.

He ran to the cockpit and threw himself into the pilot's seat. He had no way to warn Washington to hang on. He hoped the big Marine would understand when the ADC started moving.

Something hit the front of the carrier, a trife face appearing in the small viewport. Caleb and the demon looked at one another, and then it started slapping its claws against the transparency, the sharp edges making indents against the hardened plasti-glass.

It vanished a moment later, thrown away from the ADC. A second trife appeared, facing away from the vehicle at a third trife. It grabbed the second trife, lifting it and slashing its head from its body, and then looking back Cal's way.

That one was Hal, which meant Flores was Flores. He smiled in response before throwing the throttle all the way forward.

The ADC jumped ahead, bouncing hard over a root and into the brush. He checked the vehicle's sensor grid. After things had been quiet for so long, the whole area was now a sea of red marks.

Had the trife spent the last two days following them?

Caleb watched the terrain ahead, cutting the ADC to the left to avoid a tree, then back to the right as they bounced over another set of roots, smashing into a larger bush, digging it up and dragging it. With most of his view blocked, he did his best to peer through narrow, leafy branches, navigating more by feel and desperate not to hit a tree.

The ADC hit twenty kilometers per hour, recklessly fast considering the terrain. The shooting let up slightly, but Caleb could see on the display that the trife were keeping pace. How had they managed to avoid detection before, but were visible to the sensors now? It seemed intentional. Had Hal done something to the systems? Had it kept the demons close on purpose? It claimed to hate the trife as much as he did. Was that all a lie? Did it know who had sent the trife to Earth? Was there another, more sinister reason it was leading them south?

Again, it didn't matter. He couldn't stop now to have that discussion, and he couldn't trust anything the Axon AI said anyway. They had to keep moving forward. They had to escape and survive. That was the only option. It had always been the only option.

"Sarge, I'm out!" Flores shouted from the back of the carrier.

"Roger!" he shouted back. "Get Wash fresh mags."

"Roger!" She stood and made her way to their small store of magazines, struggling to stay steady enough to grab them.

Outside, the shooting stopped. Washington was out of ammo too.

Caleb risked a glance over his shoulder as the big Marine dropped through the hatch. He dropped his guns and pulled the hatch closed behind him, locking Hal out. Breathing hard, he slumped into one of the seats.

"We aren't out of this yet, Private," Caleb barked.

Washington perked up instantly, bending over to retrieve an MK-12. Flores handed a magazine out to him.

The ADC reached a small clearing in the vegetation, a flat streak of dirt twenty meters across leading back into the jungle. Caleb pushed the throttle harder, hoping to gain a little extra speed.

He never saw the depression in the middle of the clearing, or the creek flowing through it. Not until the ADC had already cleared the bank.

"Shit!" Caleb said as the water ran up and over the viewport. The ADC came to a quick stop, throwing both Washington and Flores back to the deck. Caleb flew forward into the dashboard. Somehow, he managed to keep the throttle open, but the wheels spun, with nothing but mud to grab onto. "Guardians, grab your gear. We're out of here."

He swung out of the seat and ran to the back. The SOS was heavy on him now, the ruined battery drained and dead. He unclasped it, quickly shedding the second skin as he moved, while Flores and Washington grabbed their guns.

Something clanked onto the top of the ADC. The hatches were closed and sealed. They were safe inside.

For now.

"Now what?" Flores asked.

Chapter 44

"Want to go again?" Jia asked, motioning to the cards on the small folding table.

"No, I'm out," Sam replied. "If this were strip poker, I'd be butt-naked right now."

"There are worse things," Liam said.

Sam whipped her head around to glare at him. She should have known better than to make a comment like that with the former guard around. The last two days hadn't proven him to be any less of a creep than the first.

"Shut the hell up, Liam," Jia said, emphasizing his name. "If you were in the game, you'd be worse than naked."

"How can you be worse than naked?" Liam asked.

"Come on over, and I'll show you."

"Okay, both of you cool it," Sam said. "And keep it down. There's something in the air that's making me uneasy." It was the reason she didn't want to play any more poker. True, she already owed Jia two food chits, but she had a stash of unused credits in her account. She could have kept losing for a week.

The Marshals were gathered outside the transport, settled beneath the corner of the camouflage netting that hopefully hid the ship from outside view. They had collected a few rocks to sit on, and found the folding table inside the transport's hold, along with the deck of cards. Five of the Marshals played cards or slept while the other three handled watch positions around them, hiding behind the rocks and keeping their attention focused on the jungle below.

There had been no sign of the Guardians. No sights. No sounds. After two days, Sam was growing more concerned that either Caleb had changed directions or hadn't made it through the dense, alien landscape. The only thing she knew for sure was that he hadn't returned to the Deliverance. Either she or Kiaan checked in with the ship every three hours, making sure they weren't out there for nothing.

Sam wasn't happy with the situation on the Deliverance. According to Deputy Klahanie, Governor Stone was rushing through every step of the process, too eager to get the colony moved from the belly of the starship to the cleared area outside. They had spent too long in a can, and it was obvious there was no threat on the planet. At least, that's what Stone was telling people. Three whole days had passed, the drones had covered hundreds of kilometers in every direction, and there was still no evidence of anything with human-level or greater intelligence living on the planet.

Idiot. Hundreds of kilometers were nothing on a planet. The drones hadn't even made it over the mountains yet. There was no way to know what was out there, except Sergeant Card hadn't wandered off for nothing. The Governor was proving himself reckless, gambling with the lives of the colonists, and for all they knew the overall survival of the human race. All because he was impatient.

The largest seal had been uncovered, and they were close to breaking the code Harry had put in place to keep the Governor's identification codes from unlocking it. Once they were into that part of the ship's mainframe, they could unseal all of the doors and have much easier access in and out of Metro. They could bring the loaders and builders in and start dismantling the city to transport it outside.

Too soon. It was just too damn soon.

She stifled a sigh. Most of the Marshals—Steven, Kiaan, Jia, Paige and Jack—were on her side. Liam, Smith, and Aziz had all come from the Governor's militia and were completely loyal to him. They agreed with everything Stone said or did regardless of what the outcome of the decision might be. There wasn't anything inherently wrong with that. In some ways, Sam wished she could be as loyal to him as they were.

But she knew the truth.

"Colonel Dante," Paige said.

Sam broke out of her thoughts. "What is it, Private?"

"Can you see the jungle floor from your position, ma'am?"

Sam was behind the transport, out of sight of the greenery below. "Negative."

"You should take a look, Colonel."

"Roger."

She took one step toward the front of the transport before she heard the first distant crack, quickly followed up by dozens more.

Was that gunfire?

She ran to the front of the transport, looking down into the jungle. She could see flashes of light barely breaking through the trees, and she checked her ATCS. The computer estimated the range at five kilometers.

That wasn't far at all.

"Marshals, this is a red alert. I repeat, this is a red alert. Gear up. Let's go."

It had to be the Guardians. Who else would be out there with machine guns? She turned back to the soldiers around the table.

"Helmets on, Marshals," she said to them. "We've got a target."

The Marshals sprang into action, putting on their helmets and grabbing for their rifles. The sound of gunfire continued below them, remaining steady.

"Is it a good idea to go down there, Colonel?" Liam asked. "They aren't shooting at each other."

Sam couldn't say she wanted to go down there because Caleb might need help. She wasn't sure how she was going to manage that conflict just yet. One thing at a time.

"Whatever they are shooting at isn't human," she replied. "It's better to catch it off guard than wait for it to come to us."

"But if it does our job and kills the Guardians for us, isn't that a good thing?" Liam pressed.

Sam clenched her jaw. "Not if it kills us too," she replied through her teeth. "We're going down there. That's not up for discussion."

"Yes, ma'am," Liam said, right at the edge of disrespect. "Don't you think one of us should stay with the transport?"

"Yes," Sam agreed. "Marshal Four, you're with the transport."

"Yes, ma'am," Steven replied.

"Marshal Eight, stay in position and keep an eye on things."

"Affirmative," Paige said.

"The rest of you, meet up at the marked coordinates." Sam set the marker through the ATCS, which synced it across their network. Then she grabbed her MK-12 from her back and headed away from the transport, toward the gentler slope leading into the jungle. Liam, Smith, and Jia followed her, while Steven and Kiian stayed behind.

The Marshals all reached the marker at the same time, forming up around Sam. The sound of gunfire was still echoing out from the trees, though it had diminished slightly.

"I want Card and the Guardians alive," she said.

"What?" Liam replied. "Those aren't the orders I heard Governor Stone give us."

"I said I want them alive," she repeated. "I know what Governor Stone said, but we're not the judge or the executioners. They deserve to have their voices heard before we gun them down."

"That's bullshit," Smith said. "They're traitors to the colony. They brought us here to die. Screw them."

"That's one side of the story," Sam said. "But maybe Sergeant Card has a different take on how things went down. Nobody's given him a chance to speak."

"He left the city with an alien after it murdered almost a dozen of my people," Liam hissed. "How can you not judge that?"

"We don't have time to argue this right now. Governor Stone put me in charge, damn it. The way you keep questioning my orders, it makes me wonder who the real traitor is."

"I know who the real traitor is," Liam said, looking over at Smith.

Ali's face burned. "You have two choices, Marshal Three. Hand your rifle over to Marshall Two and go wait in the transport, or shut the hell up and follow my orders." She glared at Liam, furious.

Liam didn't react right away. "Acknowledged," he said at last, keeping his grip on his gun.

"Watch yourself, Three," Jia said. "Don't try any bullshit. I've got my eye on you."

Liam didn't respond. Sam didn't completely trust him either, but what else could she do? They needed all the help they could get. Would he try something in the middle of a firefight with an unknown enemy? She had to believe he wasn't that stupid.

She led the Marshals down the slope at a run, dropping toward the jungle below. The gunfire had lasted a few minutes, but now it faded away into silence, the planet going silent once more.

"I think we're too late," Steven said in response to the sudden stillness.

"Who do you think won?" Jia said.

Sam slowed them down to a walk while she looked at her HUD. She hadn't expected the fight to end like that. "I don't know," she replied. "Marshal Eight, do you see anything?"

"Negative," Paige replied. "It's gone dark."

Sam swallowed her fear that the Guardians had lost. "We have to get a visual on the bodies at a minimum and try to collect them if we can. Governor Stone will want proof they're dead."

"Maybe we can wait a couple of hours?" Smith suggested. "Give whatever killed them a chance to move away."

Sam didn't want to give up on Caleb, but how long could they survive without weapons? He had that replacement arm, but even so the odds weren't in his favor. Maybe Smith was right. Maybe it would be better to wait.

She didn't know the right thing to do. She was a sheriff, not a Marine. She was playing at being military. Hell, all of them were. The only ones with any real experience were down there, likely dead, because Governor Stone and Metro had turned their backs on them.

"Colonel," Kiaan said over the comms. "Transport sensors are picking up movement ahead of you. Something's coming your way. A lot of somethings."

The decision had already been made for her.

Chapter 45

"What do we have left?" Caleb asked. He was standing in the back of the ADC with Washington and Flores gathered around the small stockpile of remaining ammunition.

"Six magazines for the MK-12s," Flores said. "Three cells for the P-50s. Mine is almost fully charged."

Washington held his hand up, spreading his fingers to indicate the charge level on his plasma rifle. *About a quarter.*

Caleb checked his gun. He had less than that. He unslung the rifle and released the cell, taking one of the fully charged cartridges and snapping it back into place.

There was a constant echo of scratching above them, the sound of trife feet and claws on the top of the ADC, frantically trying to get in. They could see the demons through the birds-eye of the punchless drone, which Flores had set to circle the area high enough to be out of reach.

The ADC was mired in the mud of the river, the water level high enough to ensure they remained there but low enough that the top of the vehicle stayed dry. Worse, these trife didn't seem to have the same dislike of water the trife on Earth did. They waded into the creek to reach the carrier, climbing onto and around it, scraping, clawing and scratching to get inside. They were focused on their purpose, eager to open up the armored vehicle to get at the humans inside.

It was a mess. There was no arguing that. One they would have no choice but to fight their way out of, and they didn't have a lot of firepower left to accomplish it. While Caleb had expected some resistance on the path to wherever it was they were going, he hadn't expected this. There were at least a hundred trife outside, probably more. The supply seemed almost endless from the vantage point of the drone, the mess of black forms almost completely enveloping both the carrier and the creek banks, spreading out in both directions.

Where had they all come from, and was there an end to them? There had been billions of trife covering the Earth. Were there nearly as many here? Had they merely traded one infested planet for another?

"There's only one way out," he said, pointing to the hatch. "I'll take point and lead with a plasma stream. If we can back them off the carrier, we might at least be able to open a little breathing room."

"Until we're out of ammo," Flores said. "You brought me back from the dead for this?"

"You weren't dead," Caleb said. "How are you feeling now?"

"Great. Just great." She shook her head. "I think this can is going to be our tomb."

"No. We're going to get out of here. Don't forget about Hal. It's out there somewhere."

Flores laughed. "Hal probably abandoned us. We're a good distraction while it continues on ahead."

"Then we'll do it ourselves. Come on, Private. We're Marines. We don't give up."

Flores locked eyes with Caleb. They both knew her history. She nodded. "Right. Well, I think I should take point. You don't even have an SOS."

"But I do have this," Caleb said, waving his replacement arm. He shook his plasma rifle. "And I have this."

"And you're a badass, right Sarge?" Flores said.

"I'm a survivor. We all are. And we're getting out of this."

"Your resolve is contagious." Flores checked her rifle. "I'm ready."

"Wash?" Caleb asked.

Washington flashed his thumb.

"All right. Stay tight near the ladder, hold your fire until I'm clear, and then come up as fast as you can. Wash, take the left and rear, Flores the right. I'll hit the front."

"Roger."

Caleb reached for the locking mechanism on the hatch. The demons would be on it the moment he clicked it open. They were already on it.

"Ready, Guardians?" he asked.

They shifted their rifles. They were ready.

His fingers tensed on the lock.

"Oh, shit. Sarge, look."

Caleb looked back at her, and then at the display. The drone's camera was picking up movement further south, and more than that…

"Are those muzzle flashes?" Flores said, pointing at the bursts.

"They are," Caleb said. "I hope they're ours."

Washington tapped on his shoulder and shook his head.

"I know," Caleb said. Whoever was out there and coming their way probably came from Metro. Which meant there was a good chance they weren't friendly. "Flores, can you get into their comm channel? They probably don't know how to secure it."

"Roger. Standby." She froze a moment. "I'm in. Sounds like…" She smiled. "Sounds like your girlfriend's here, Sarge."

"Dante?" Caleb replied. What was she doing here? He had asked her to stay behind to keep an eye on the Governor.

"You answered that pretty fast," Flores said. "Not denying the girlfriend part?"

"Not now, Flores," he said. "We've got work to do." He looked at the drone's view of the field again. "Interrupt their chatter and get them flanking the position there and there." He pointed to two large trees near the bank. "When they're in position, have two soldiers defend the position, and the others laying cover fire against the ADC. We'll bust out of here and add support."

"Roger." She passed the instructions over, pausing a couple of times. Then she looked at Caleb. "We have a small problem."

"Which is?"

"I don't know. Dante sounds tense as anything though."

"Is she moving into position?"

"Yes."

"How many soldiers?"

"Four. They had eight, but the trife."

"Understood. Let's make it worth their sacrifice then."

"Sarge, we can't be confident she won't shoot at us as soon as we come out."

"Dante? She's on our side."

"She has other considerations, and the rest of her people might not be on our side. Have you ever seen Mission Impossible?"

"No."

"Cross, double-cross, triple-cross. It's crazy. This might be that."

"So what do we do, hide in here until they all get killed? We're done hiding, right Mariana?" Caleb could see the question hit her hard. It was supposed to. "Humans help humans above trife, that's the way it needs to be. No matter what."

Her face reddened, and she nodded. "Roger."

Caleb reached for the hatch again. "Give me the mark as soon as they're in position."

Flores was silent, waiting for the word from Dante. The inside of the ADC was calm, but they could all hear the gunfire outside. Caleb's hand tensed when bullets started pinging off the side of the carrier.

"Go!" Flores snapped.

Caleb turned the lock and shoved the hatch open with his replacement arm, hard enough to throw any trife on it into the water. Washington and Flores pointed their rifles through the hole, ready to shoot.

Two trife were directly above them, but they were hit by fire from the shore and fell away, leaving a clear path out.

"Let's go," Caleb said, grabbing the ladder and climbing.

Chapter 46

Sam kept her reticle on the ADC as the hatch flipped open, taking a trife off the top with it. She adjusted her aim and squeezed the trigger, the ATCS helping direct the weapon and allowing her to knock two trife away in rapid succession.

"Come on," she said, watching for the Guardians to emerge from the ADC. Paige continued firing beside her, knocking down the trife trudging through the water toward their position.

They had lost three of the Marshals getting here. Steven, Smith, and Jack, all taken by the mass of trife that had charged them on their way into the jungle. She could hardly believe any of them had made it this far alive. She credited the Marine's combat armor and ATCS for their survival. The targeting computers made using the rifles almost too easy, and the protection had saved her from multiple hits already.

She also couldn't believe humankind had spent two years fighting these things. She was amazed their species had lasted this long. The trife were big, strong, fast and armored. It took nearly a dozen rounds to drop one of them, and there were dozens. Getting to the creek had taken nearly all of their ammunition.

She had no idea if or how they would get back.

She saw Caleb's metal hand breach the hatch. She focused her aim. Ready. "Liam, remember what I told you," she said. Was it fate that had left half her remaining fighters loyal to the Governor? She had warned the two former guards about shooting the wrong targets multiple times, but there was no way to have confidence they would follow her. In part, she was starting to feel as though Stone had sent them to intentionally counter her orders.

But both men had ample opportunity to cause trouble during their first interaction with the enemy. They had carried themselves like professionals, responding to her directions without question or hesitation, and doing their best to protect the other Marshals. She had to believe that counted for something.

Caleb's face appeared. A trife leaped onto the ADC beside it, right foot stretching out toward it. He turned and tried to catch it, and then a loud report signaled the end of the trife as a single well-aimed round hit it in the head and knocked it down.

"Got it," Liam said.

"Nice shooting," Sam replied. She squeezed the trigger as two more trife started climbing the side of the ADC, her magazine going empty. "Damn."

She reached to the pocket of the SOS, pulling out her last magazine. She dropped the empty one and kissed the fresh one. "Do me proud," she said, snapping it into the rifle and re-aiming toward the carrier.

Caleb was fully emerged, standing on top of the carrier and staring right toward her. He was dressed in a dark t-shirt and pants, hardly combat-ready gear. He didn't seem fazed by it. He ran to the edge of the ADC, firing down at a trife still in the water.

"Watch your fire," Flores said over the comm. Her head appeared next as she quickly scurried out of the ADC.

"Colonel, what the hell?" Paige said beside her.

Sam wasn't sure what she meant until she looked at her tactical. There had been a number of red marks a moment earlier. Now they were gone.

"Shit," she said. "Marshals, it looks like the enemy has gone dark. Keep your eyes open."

"Roger."

She looked back at the ADC. Flores must have been passing the information to Caleb, because his face tensed, and his eyes shifted immediately skyward. That caused her to do the same, and she spotted the group of trife right before they left the branches.

"Look up!" she shouted to the others, redirecting her aim and firing. Her rounds hit the falling demons, tearing into them. Corpses smacked the ground beside her, and she had to back away as another crashed where she had been standing.

Marks appeared behind her a dozen strong. A trap?

"Behind us!" she said, spinning. There was nothing.

Gunfire cracked behind her, and she heard the bullets sink into something close by, near the shore of the river. A screaming hiss followed, and then silence.

"Watch your six!" Flores snapped.

"They're everywhere," Dante replied.

"Damn it, Colonel," Liam said. "We're going to get eaten alive."

"The tactical is broken," Paige said.

Sam checked hers again. Red marks flashed in and out

in a chaotic pattern. The ATCS had suddenly become completely unreliable.

"It's the trife," Flores said. "They're doing it."

Dante's heart stopped. What?

She found the ADC. The Guardians were out, firing at trife on three sides.

"Marshals, form up," she said. "Prepare to retreat. Meet at my mark."

She marked the tactical. Paige stood up, and they began moving toward it, back to back to watch both sides of the action.

"I've got the mark," Flores said. "Keep us covered." Sam watched the Guardians jump off the ADC and into the water.

"Marshal Eight, we need to cover them. Marshal Six and Five, keep us safe."

"Roger," Liam said.

He and Aziz were moving in their direction, firing at the closest trife. Sam and Paige focused on the Guardians, keeping them safe while they swam to shore.

Liam and Aziz converged on their position, the four Marshals creating a natural wedge to protect themselves. Caleb and the other Guardians pulled themselves from the water, breaking toward them at a run. Dante saw the big Marine, Washington, go down as a trife caught him from the side. They flailed in a tangle for a moment, and then the Marine got on top of the demon and fired down into its face. He bounced up, regaining momentum as if the creature was a minor inconvenience.

"Dante," Caleb said, reaching them. "You shouldn't be out here."

She figured he was going to say something stupid like that. "It's not by choice, Sergeant. But I appreciate your concern."

Caleb's eyes quickly passed over the other Marshals. "You got ahead of us. Tell me you have a ride."

"We have a ride."

He paused to shoot at another trife, one round hitting it in an unprotected part of its chest. It collapsed and vanished behind the brush.

"We're ready when you are, Sheriff."

"It's Colonel now," Dante replied.

Caleb raised an eyebrow.

"Long story. Come on."

The group began to retreat, all heads continually searching the foliage for the demons. Sam's ATCS continued to give strange readings, with red marks appearing and vanishing almost at random.

The demons came for them, emerging from the trees, approaching and then backing away. The group hit some of them, leaving a few corpses on the route of their escape. Most of the demons made the maneuvers without being hit, flashing in and out of sight too quickly to target accurately.

"They're draining our ammo," Caleb said after a few rounds of the false attacks. "Wearing us down."

"How did you deal with this on Earth?" Paige asked.

"The trife didn't do this on Earth," he replied. "Or on the Deliverance. These trife are different. More advanced."

"You have to be kidding," Liam said. "We're all going to die."

"Check your attitude, Marine," Caleb snapped. "We stay together; we'll make it back to the hopper."

"The what?" Aziz said.

Sam sighted another trife. She didn't fire, not right away. The demon backed off, vanishing again.

"He's right," she said. "Hold your fire. Be ready."

The next group of demons came and went. The third group came in.

"Here they come," Caleb said. "Fire."

Flores and Washington didn't hesitate. The trife charged forward, stopped, took a step away, and then redirected again. The first few were cut down instantly. How did he know?

The Marshals rejoined the party as the trife closed in. One rushed out from behind the trees toward Aziz. She pivoted, aimed, and fired.

Three rounds hit the demon, digging deep but not getting critical hits. Then her rifle clicked empty again. She was out of ammo.

"Aziz!" she shouted.

The Marshal heard the demon coming. He turned to shoot it, only to have his gun ripped out of his hands, claws cutting deep through his less-protected fingers and taking two of them off. A round blasted through the trife's head a moment later, cutting it down.

"Ahhhh!" Aziz screamed, clutching at his bleeding hand. The reaction left him distracted, and two more trife rushed in for the kill.

Then Caleb was there, jumping in front of the wounded man and slamming his replacement hand into the trife. The blow threw the demon on its back, and it writhed, trying to get up. Flores shot it, keeping it down.

The other trife made it to Aziz, using one hand to grab the lip of his helmet and lift it, and the other to slash across the top of his suddenly unprotected neck. Aziz screamed again, his neck blossoming red, at the same time bullets tore into the trife.

They both collapsed.

"No!" Liam shouted. "Son of a bitch!"

He didn't look outward toward the trife.

He looked directly at Dante.

"This is your fault!" he shouted. "This is all your damned fault. We don't deserve to die. He deserves to die. You're helping the damned enemy." He turned his rifle on her. "But I can take care of that."

Ali's eyes widened. She was unarmed. Unprepared.

Something hit her, shoving her away at the same time Liam fired. She heard the bullet crack on something hard, and she saw Caleb tackle Liam as she hit the ground.

"Nice friends you've got there," Flores said, staying on top of her. "Sarge wouldn't forgive me if I let anyone kill his girlfriend."

Girlfriend? What?

"Keep moving!" Caleb shouted. He had Liam in his arms, slung over his shoulders in a carry.

"Time to go," Flores said, rolling back to her feet and holding her hand out. Sam took it and got up.

Then they ran.

Chapter 47

Caleb held the idiot over his shoulders, still wondering why he had picked him up in the first place. The man had turned on them, had tried to shoot Dante, and had only failed because Flores got in the way. He was tempted to dump him on the ground and leave him behind for the trife.

But he didn't. He carried the man over his back, a heavy, unconscious weight dragging on his unaugmented muscles and his still-sore ankle. He couldn't go against his beliefs just because it was convenient, and he didn't believe anyone deserved to be killed by a trife.

"I'm out!" one of Dante's people shouted. She was the smallest of the group, though she handled her rifle with natural efficiency. Only now that rifle was empty.

"Here," Flores said, tossing her MK-12 to the woman and shifting to plasma. She immediately used the weapon, a pair of bolts lashing out at a trife. Washington had already done the same, passing his MK-12 to Dante and switching to plasma.

"How far to the hopper?" Caleb asked, shouting back at Dante.

"Two klicks," Dante replied.

"Roger," Caleb said. That wasn't close. He started questioning his decision again.

The group ran through the jungle, trying to conserve what was left of their firepower and at the same time keep the trife honest. Caleb could hardly believe how the jungle had exploded with the creatures, and he couldn't help but worry the same thing was happening closer to the Deliverance. Was the ship about to come under the same kind of attack? If they didn't make it through this, there would be no one left to warn them.

And what was Dante doing here? He didn't mind the save. It was probably the only reason they were alive. But she was the only one he trusted to do what was right for the city. If there was a trife horde on its way there, the colony was in serious, serious trouble.

Unfortunately, there was no time to speak with her. Caleb was breathing so hard he wouldn't have had the breath anyway. He stayed focused on putting one foot ahead of the other, keeping in motion and ignoring the burning in his limbs. He held his MK-12 in one hand, trying not to use it. His aim would be garbage anyway. He expected to give the weapon up to the next person to run out of rounds.

He scanned the area ahead, looking for any hint of disruption. The trife had shown an ability to mess with their combat systems, or at the very least hide from the ATCS' sensors. It made them more dangerous. More deadly. They had left Earth for this? He would have felt safer back home. At least he knew that enemy. There was no point worrying about it. He was here, and there was no leaving. There was nothing to do now but fight to survive.

He was good at that.

The jungle began to fade away as they reached the beginning of the mountain's foothills and began to pass through increasingly rocky terrain. The trees were less dense here and the ground vegetation started to vanish. Already-dead trife lay ahead of them, gunned down by Dante and her team on the way in. They passed almost a dozen of them before encountering the first dead soldier, a woman judging by the size and shape of the SOS. She had died to save him, and he wasn't going to forget it.

"We're getting close," Dante said.

"Out!" her other soldier said again, voice full of frustration.

"Here!" Caleb shouted, tossing her his rifle. She caught it and immediately started shooting again, single rounds that seemed to always hit their mark.

Washington and Flores remained active with her, the more powerful P-50s just enough to keep the tide from turning too sharply against them. Even so, Caleb could tell his Guardians were wearing out and the demons were gaining both ground and numbers. They began succeeding in their efforts to tire out their prey, making Caleb wonder if they would make it to the transport before their defenses collapsed completely.

And what had happened to Hal?

The man on his shoulder groaned, starting to come to.

"Keep your ass still and quiet, or I'll leave you here," Caleb hissed.

"Huh? Where am I?" the man whispered.

"I said shut up."

The man didn't speak again. He didn't try to move. Caleb wasn't about to put him down. It would take him a few seconds to find his footing, and those were seconds none of them had.

He caught the sound of a soft whine further ahead. The sound of an engine starting up. They were closer than he thought. He gritted his teeth, forcing himself to pick up the pace. The Guardians noticed and followed suit.

"We're going to make it," Flores said.

Caleb looked back over Flores' shoulder. There were so many trife behind them. More than they had rounds left to kill.

Three more demons died, bolts lashing into them. The other trife climbed over them, gaining another step.

A shape rose from the treeline to his right, a long cylinder on a pair of pods. It wasn't a hopper, but some kind of odd-looking transport he had never seen before. It rotated as it climbed, and then awkwardly swept toward the path ahead of them. It was too uneven for the thing to land. Was the pilot skilled enough to keep it low and under control?

They were going to find out.

A group of trife appeared ahead, climbing out from behind a pair of rocky outcroppings. "Wash, Flores, front and center!" Caleb shouted.

The two Guardians spun around. Washington pushed forward, getting ahead of the group. The transport was incoming, ready to drop between the trife and them. If it did, the demons would swarm it and try to bring it down.

Plasma spewed from Washington's rifle, bolt after bolt digging into the trife and nearby rock. The transport made it over the big Marine's head and then lilted back, angled badly as it sank toward the ground. Caleb winced, waiting for it to crash. It straightened at the last moment, coming to a stop a meter off the ground with Washington on the other side.

That wasn't where Caleb wanted him. "Wash, damn it!"

The hatch opened, ready to receive the group. Flores slowed and turned, switching her P-50 to stream mode. She loosed a flare of superheated gas at the oncoming trife, making them slow their approach.

Dante reached the transport and jumped inside. She turned back, firing at the trife as Caleb heaved Liam off his shoulder and into the craft.

"Tell Flores and Washington it's time to go," Caleb said to her. Then he hopped into the craft, with Dante's other squadmate right behind him.

Flores backed toward the craft, her stream keeping the trife at bay. Caleb could see them trying to figure out how to get around it, and he noticed the group further back breaking off to the flanks.

"Flores, let's go!" he shouted.

Her P-50 ran out of charge, stopping suddenly. She dropped the empty cartridge and reached for a fresh one, realizing she had no time.

The transport bucked slightly, rising and falling as if it hit a bump. Washington rolled beneath the carrier, absorbing the pressure from the pods and appearing in front of the open hatch. He brought his plasma rifle up and fired. Two trife dropped on either side of Flores, and she spun, sprinting for the transport.

She wasn't going to make it. The trife had recovered and were already at speed. One of them lunged toward her, claws outstretched to grab her from behind.

A second trife caught it from the side, tackling it and slamming its claws into its chest. It rolled up, turning on the others and attacking, a quick flash of sharp fingers quickly killing another.

Flores jumped into the transport, caught by Washington.

"We're in," Dante said. "Kiaan, get us out of here!"

"Wait," Caleb said, trying to delay the order. He found the new trife in the group. It had stopped its attack and was looking back at him. Hal.

It was too late. The transport started to rise, the whine of the pods gaining pitch, the thrusters firing at the back of the craft. A trife leaped toward it, managing to get a grip on one of the pods. Washington leaned out and shot it point-blank in the face, knocking it off.

"Kiaan, take us home," Dante said.

Chapter 48

"No!" Caleb replied. "We can't go back to the ship. Not yet."

"What do you mean not yet?" Dante asked.

"We didn't come out this way for our health," Flores said. "Obviously."

"Where were you going?"

"Over the mountains," Caleb said. "If we're going to have any chance of helping the colony, we need to stay the course."

Dante's head shifted. She looked over at her smaller squadmate, who was breathing heavy but otherwise unharmed. Then she looked at the idiot. He was sitting against the side of the transport, his face pale. Then she looked back at Caleb.

"Governor Stone sent me out here to kill you." She shook her head. "More like, he sent me out here to die. That piece of shit is proof." She pointed at the idiot. "Anyway, I have proof Stone lied about the Guardians. I can clear your names."

Caleb nodded. "We still need to go over the

mountains."

"What about the alien? The one who killed the guards back in Metro?"

"We didn't have anything to do with that," Flores said.

"We left with it," Caleb said. "It said it needed our help."

The idiot laughed. "Bullshit."

"Nobody asked you, Liam," Dante's other squadmate said. "You're a damned murderer."

"I didn't kill anyone."

"Only because you screwed it up."

The man, Liam, lifted his head. His eyes blazed with anger, and he thrust his finger toward Dante. "She got Aziz killed. She got Jack killed. She got Steven killed. And she helped a damned group of fugitives escape the trife. Marshals? Bullshit. We're a damned escort service."

"It said it needed our help," Caleb repeated, sharply enough to cut off any other statements. "We learned more about this planet in twenty minutes with it than you probably have in days. Especially when it comes to threats to the colony."

"So it was a strategic decision then?" Liam asked. "Is that the excuse you're going with? You helped it bring us here, didn't you? You brought the colony here to become their slaves."

"That's just stupid," Flores said.

Caleb put up his hand. "Flores, I've got this."

"Roger. Sorry, Sarge."

Caleb crouched in front of Liam. "I think you should have a little more respect for the man who just saved your life."

"Please," Liam mocked. "With all due respect, Sarge...we're all screwed. You only delayed the inevitable."

"That might be true," Caleb admitted. "Maybe Riley

Valentine killed us all the moment she changed the Deliverance's course. But I'd rather die fighting to survive than survive waiting to die. Wouldn't you?"

"I would," Dante said.

"Me too," her companion said.

"Thirded."

Washington put up his hand. Liam sank back, defeated by the vote.

"Better," Caleb said. He stood and turned to Dante. "The thing we left with, we called it Hal. It said it was an advanced artificial intelligence, created by a race it called the Axon."

"The Axon sent those monsters to Earth?" Dante asked.

"No. According to Hal, Earth is positioned between the Relyeh, who are the enemy, and the Axon. They sent Hal to Earth as an early warning system. When the Relyeh attacked our homeworld, it was supposed to come back here and tell them. It didn't come back the way it was planning, but it made it."

"And?"

"The Axon are gone."

"What do you mean, gone?" Liam asked.

"They didn't respond to Hal's communications. It believes they either fled the planet or were killed. The presence of the trife suggests the Relyeh were here."

"Except it doesn't," Flores said. "Because Hal swore they wouldn't circumvent Earth to attack Essex, and two hundred years is nowhere near quick enough for them to move on."

"But the trife are here," Caleb countered. "We all saw them. Anyway, it said the Axon cities are on the other side of the mountains and that we'd learn the truth there. So that's where we're going."

"I see," Dante said. "But where is the Axon artificial intelligence?"

"It was attacking the trife. We left without it."

"I didn't see anyone out there."

"It doesn't look like a person. It looks like a trife."

"How—"

"It's a topic for another time," Caleb said, cutting her question off. "The important thing is that we know where to find the answers. But we can't do that back at the Deliverance. We have to go over the mountains."

"You have no idea what you're going to find," Liam protested.

"Exactly," Caleb countered. "I know none of this is as simple as anyone was hoping, but this is where we are now. We can't change it, so we should try to adjust. I believe that whatever is on the other side of the mountains is vital to the survival of the colony. Sam, I'm asking you to believe in that too. And in me."

"I do," Dante said. "Believe in you, I mean. So I hope you aren't lying to me."

"He is," Liam said.

"Will you shut up?" Flores said.

"I'm not lying to you," Caleb said. "We need to go over the mountains. We need to find the Axon city and learn what happened to them. Maybe we can discover something that will either help us survive here or help us take the colony somewhere else."

Dante stared at him, considering. "Kiaan set a new course," she said. "We're going over the mountains." She reached up and pulled off her helmet. Her dark eyes burned into Caleb. "If you're double-crossing us, even death won't help you."

Caleb smiled. "Yes, ma'am."

Chapter 49

"Kiaan," Dante said, getting the attention of the transport's pilot. "I want you to meet Sergeant Caleb Card."

The pilot smiled, holding out his left hand while maintaining control of the craft with the right. He was keeping it steady at five hundred meters—too high for any trife to reach them and too low to be seen from the other side. Not that any part of Caleb believed that whatever was out there couldn't already see them. Not considering the technology he had already witnessed.

"A pleasure to meet you, Sergeant," Kiaan said.

"Thanks for the pickup," Caleb replied, quickly shaking his hand and releasing it. "You saved our lives."

Kiaan's face flushed, and he turned back to the viewport, refocusing on his flying. "I'm just glad I didn't crash. I'm pretty new at this."

"Most of us are," Caleb said, putting his hand on the young man's shoulder. "You did great."

"Thanks."

"Kiaan told me you knew one of his relatives back on Earth," Dante said.

"Really?" Caleb asked. "What was the name?"

"Habib," Kiaan said.

Caleb felt a chill run down his spine and a wave of sadness wash over him. "You're a Habib?"

"Yes, sir."

He smiled. "I'm glad to hear the family name continued all these years. Whatever she was to you, she was a brave and valuable member of my team to me."

"Yes, sir."

"I'm not sure what we're going to see when we crest the peak. Stay as tight to the mountains as you can, and be ready to make evasive maneuvers."

"In this thing? I'll do my best, sir."

"That's all I ever ask."

"Kiaan, bring her up," Dante said.

He nodded, and the transport started moving again, shifting forward slightly and rising with the slope of the mountains. They were closing in on the snow-capped peaks, and Caleb could see movement below. An animal about the size and shape of a bear but with oddly irides-cent fur that rippled and flashed as it moved, the shifting somehow enabling it to vanish from sight every few seconds.

"Amazing," Dante said, apparently having noticed it too.

Caleb turned his head, looking to the rear of the trans-port. The rest of the group was seated, with Washington and Flores sitting behind a bound Liam, and Dante's other soldier, Paisley, opposite them. Liam, stripped of his combat armor, had been left sitting in a t-shirt and pants. It was his bad luck that he was only a couple of inches shorter than Caleb, with a similar build of lean muscle. While he had complained about the loss of the SOS and the fact that he was out of action and almost literally chained to his seat, he couldn't argue the fact that he tried to shoot the sheriff, and that made him an untrustworthy liability in the field.

In any case, whatever trouble they ran into, they weren't going to overcome it with numbers. There wasn't much difference between a group of four or five.

Washington noticed him looking and flashed his thumb. He had taken a beating already, stitched and patched and bruised beneath his armor, but he was ready for more. So was Flores. It seemed Hal had successfully removed the cancerous cells in her body, leaving her quickly and efficiently cured in a way humankind's best doctors had never figured out how to achieve. It was impressive and terrifying at the same time.

If they could rid a body of cancer so easily, what else could they do? He had seen some of it. The hallucinations. The alterations. The infinite power of the energy unit. And yet the Axon were afraid of the Relyeh. Afraid of their demon armies and galaxy conquering power.

What the hell kind of chance did any Earther have against either one of them? He felt like an ant standing in the middle of a stampede or an atom in the center of a fusion reactor. He had no idea what they were flying toward. He felt like everything about this scenario was out of his control.

He refused to let that happen. He refused to concede his strength and hope, and he knew the other Guardians wouldn't either. Neither would Dante. She had been thrown into a worse situation than him, and she had fought her way through it. He glanced at her. He could see the tension and fear in her eyes, but she was standing firm against it.

She would have made a great Marine.

She noticed him looking, and she turned her head. "Something wrong, Sergeant?"

"No," he replied. "I appreciate that you came to get us. Especially considering what that means for you back at the ship."

"I'm a Sheriff. I took an oath to uphold the law. To see justice done in all things. This is justice. You know it. I know it. And Governor Stone knows it. He just doesn't want it." She smiled. "Seeing the look on his face when I bring you back to Metro and produce the evidence that he blamed you for something you didn't do? That's all the motivation I need to survive this."

Caleb smiled back at her. "Roger that, Sheriff."

The transport continued to climb, scaling the side of the mountain. They neared the top, the grey and brown rock giving way to snow and ice. Even at this altitude, Caleb caught glimpses of birds and small animals moving in the crevices and folds, surviving at the extreme. This planet was so full of life. It was like Earth had been before the trife. He wanted to live to explore it. He wanted the people of Metro to live to enjoy it.

That was all the motivation he needed.

"Knuckle-up back there," he shouted to the group in the rear. "Shields up." He took the helmet from the back of the SOS and dropped it onto his head, hearing the ATCS connectors click together. He glanced at the HUD, watching as each of the warriors came online.

"Here we go," Kiaan announced as the transport neared the peak of the mountain. Caleb held his breath subconsciously, eyes fixed on the forward viewport and waiting for the big reveal.

The transport swept over the cap, the ground beginning to fall away from it on the other side.

"I guess we'll have to wait a little longer," Dante said, disappointed.

The landscape ahead was coated in thick rain clouds, leaving whatever was beneath them completely obscured.

"Not as dramatic as I was expecting," Caleb admitted, breathing out. "Let's hope we're equally shielded by the clouds."

"Colonel, look," Kiaan said, pointing to the display on his right. The rear camera showed the other side of the mountains from the back of the transport. The white and grey of the snow-covered cap was broken up with what appeared to be debris.

"It looks like something crashed there," Dante said.

Caleb stared at the display. "Or was shot down." He pointed. "Those look like bullet holes."

Kiaan pinched his fingers on the screen, zooming in on one of the larger pieces of debris, confirming his observation.

"Those are definitely bullet holes," Dante said. "How?"

There was only one way.

"Valentine," Caleb said.

Chapter 50

It was the only thing that made sense. Valentine had gone to the underground armory to gather some gear. Then she went back to the upper hangar and took one of the Daggers. She had made it over the mountains. Something had confronted her, and she shot it down.

And then?

There was no sign of a crashed starfighter as Caleb and the others in the transport descended along the side of the mountain, though there were two more debris fields from whatever had attacked her. But that didn't mean much. All it would take to bring her down was a transmission of the quantum waveform that had taken Hal offline and disabled the ADC and their combat systems, and there was still a lot of area they couldn't see.

But even if Riley had crashed, even if she died, she wouldn't stay that way for long. Was she alive now? Did she know about the Axon and the Relyeh? Was she in the process of collecting data to send back to Proxima? How was she going to do it? The Dagger likely had the means to get back into space. As long as its nav computers were powerful enough, she could program it to go back to the human settlement. It might take a few hundred years, but it would get there.

Would there be anyone left to recover it and receive the data?

When Riley had confronted him and Dante in the armory, he had thought her idea was crazy. Now that he was out here? Now that he had learned a little bit about what was happening in the universe? Her original motives were selfish, short-sighted, and cruel. But they were here, and nothing was going to change that.

Maybe scouting the enemy really was the next best thing to do.

The transport continued to lose altitude as it approached the clouds. The ship's sensors were clean. Even the ones that could reach through the weather weren't turning up anything of interest. If something had attacked Riley, she had either destroyed it or left its operators wary of trying again. They were enjoying a peaceful descent.

Then again, maybe it was too peaceful.

The AI had confronted them and fled when they had fought back. What had it learned from the encounter? What decisions had it or its master made? Who was controlling it? Hal insisted the Axon were gone, but it was an Axon machine. Was it making its own decisions? Or were the Relyeh pulling its cords?

Too many questions. No answers. Caleb sighed silently, wrestling with sudden impatience. He needed to stay focused.

"We're at four hundred meters, Colonel," Kiaan announced. "Assuming the altimeter is working. These clouds might go all the way to the ground."

"There's nothing we can do about that," Dante replied.

"Stay low and slow. We don't want to die by stupidity."

"Yes, ma'am." The transport lost a little more velocity, the pitch of the whine from the pods gaining a half-octave.

A tone from the transport's collision warning system caught all of them by surprise. Caleb immediately looked down at the displays in search of the immediate threat, while Kiaan reacted almost instinctively, throwing the transport hard to the left, the instant change in direction sending Dante into Caleb, and both of them into the wall.

"Shit!" Kiaan cursed.

Caleb looked over Dane's head and out the viewport as a metal wedge rocketed past, missing the transport by less than a meter. He recognized the size and shape of the ship immediately.

"Kiann, get us to the ground!" he snapped. "You can outmaneuver that thing."

"Sergeant?" Dante said.

"It's a Dagger," Kiaan replied. "He's right, Colonel. We have to get out of the air before that thing takes us out of it."

"A Dagger? Valentine again? Are you kidding?"

Caleb's eyes fell on the ship's sensors. The clouds must be doing something to them to keep the Dagger invisible. It was above the cover now, and it was slowing and circling back. "See if you can open a channel," he said. "Full band."

"Roger," Kiaan said, tapping the control surface. "All channels open."

"Valentine," Caleb said. "Valentine, can you hear me? It's Caleb. We came to help you. Stand down."

The Dagger slowed, still changing vectors until it was right behind them. The transport was still a hundred meters from the top of the clouds, and the pods weren't made for rapid descent.

"Riley, are you there?" Caleb said. "It's Card. Stand down."

A different tone sounded in the transport.

"She's got a lock on us," Kiaan said.

"Valentine, damn it!" Caleb shouted.

The tone continued, the lock set. It changed into a scream, and the transport shuddered. The left pod stopped whining, the sudden return of full gravity pulling the whole thing over. Caleb and Dante tumbled to the other side of the ship, while Kiaan's body pulled at the restraints holding him in place.

"Somebody let me off this ride!" Flores shouted from the back.

Different warning tones sounded, filling the entire transport with noise. Kiaan kept his grip on the controls, operating calmly as they began to plummet. They hit the clouds without fanfare, sinking a hundred meters into them before driving rain, buffeting winds, and flashes of lightning increased the chaos.

They were going to crash.

"Brace!" Caleb shouted. The transport continued to sink, falling faster. They weren't that high to start with. High enough to die.

At three hundred meters, the clouds vanished and the ground became visible through heavy rain. There was hardly any time to notice it. Large, black shapes all around them, massive pillars of alien construction rising toward the clouds.

It was dark. Everything was dark. Lifeless. Empty.

At two hundred meters, Kiaan let out a cry of desperation, pushing the remaining pod to full power and adding max thrust from the propulsion. The transport complained, shaking violently but starting to roll back over.

At a hundred meters, the transport managed to roll

over enough that Caleb could stand. They were still going to crash, but they had a few seconds to try to jump. The SOS might be enough to save them.

He leaned over Kiaan instead, grabbing the stick with his replacement hand and helping him pull it back. The automatic systems didn't have the programmed parameters to force it, but he did.

The transport's superstructure cracked, the side of the craft tearing open. Wind and rain poured in, but they began to slow. Not much, but enough. Forward thrust provided lift and drove them at a better angle toward the ground.

"Hold on!" Caleb shouted again.

Twenty meters. Ten. Five. The transport hit the ground, the damaged pod throwing it sideways into a skid, the wet ground soft enough for the ship to dig in and spin, throwing mud in a rooster tail away from the impact point. The whole thing bumped and rocked as it slid and spun, coming to a jarring rest a few seconds later.

A few seconds of grateful silence were pierced by Kiaan's scream. "Whoooooooooo!" he shouted. "Just like the sim!"

Caleb grabbed his restraint, unbuckling him and yanking him from the seat.

"Guardians, let's move," he said. "Dante, now. Wash, get the door."

Washington popped up and pointed. They didn't need a door. The other side of the craft was wide open. The big Marine pointed at Liam.

"Him too, hurry!"

Washington broke the restraints easily before grabbing Liam and throwing him over his shoulder like a sack of potatoes. The other man didn't protest too much after what he had just been through.

Washington, Flores, and Paige jumped out of the transport. "Sarge, hurry!" Flores said immediately after.

Her ATCS picked up the incoming Dagger before Caleb could see it, but he had already guessed it was on its way. It started shooting a second later, bullets lashing into the downed transport as Caleb pulled Kiaan away, with Dante right behind him.

The entire group ran from the crashed ship. The Dagger's angle of attack was way too steep. It fired almost straight down at the transport, gaining speed as it descended.

It hit the craft a few seconds after that in an echoing collision that detonated its reactor, causing a small explosion that shook the ground and picked Caleb up, throwing him forward. He kept Kiaan in front of him, protecting him from the resulting debris and shrapnel that rained down on them. Something hot sliced through his new SOS, burning his arm. He heard Washington grunt in pain, and Paige scream.

And then it was over. Silence and calm returned.

"Guardians, report," Caleb said, getting to his feet and letting go of Kiaan. He could see the pilot was unharmed.

Washington pinged back that he was okay.

"A couple of small lacerations," Flores said. "Nothing major."

"I'm okay," Dante said.

"My arm," Paige reported.

Caleb found the smaller Marshal and rushed over to her. A piece of shrapnel was stuck in her arm through the SOS, blood running around it.

"Flores, tell me you grabbed the med kit," Caleb said.

"I have one patch left, Sarge," Flores replied.

"Lucky us." Caleb reached out, putting his replacement hand on the metal sticking out of Paisley's arm. "This is going to hurt some."

"I'm ready," Paige said.

"Good. On three. One…" He pulled the shrapnel out, causing Paige to scream.

"Shhh," Liam said. "Do you want every alien within a hundred kilometers coming down on us?"

"You said three," she complained.

"Half the pain is in the anticipation," Caleb replied.

Flores knelt beside her. "Help me keep the SOS out of the way."

Caleb held the torn halves of the combat armor away from the wound. It was deep, but Paige was lucky it hadn't hit anything too vital. Flores pressed the patch against it, shoving hard to keep it in place. Caleb could see the pain on Paisley's face, but she stayed quiet this time.

It took twenty seconds for the patch to cure. Once it did, it was like having a second, tougher skin over the wound. Paige looked down at it, flexing a few times.

"Good as new," she announced.

Caleb stood and looked back at the transport. It was impossible to tell where the wreck of the carrier ended and the remains of the Dagger began. Smoke was still billowing into the sky, and there were small smoldering fires around them.

"That wasn't Valentine, was it?" Dante asked, looking at the destruction with him.

"I doubt it," he replied. "But if you told me the Axon AI had remote control over the Dagger or hacked the CUTS system to think for itself, I might be inclined to believe you."

It was a frightening thought.

"Just great," Liam said. "Now what? We have to walk back?"

"We might," Dante said.

"What is this place?" Flores said.

Caleb looked around for the first time. They were standing in a muddy wasteland, with a series of alien monoliths ahead of them, rising high toward the clouds. There were four separate towers visible from their position, surrounded by smaller towers that arced away, shrinking as the distance from the center increased. The layout made each of the small cities appear like four individual masses, each one separate from the others. All of the structures were dark. If anything had ever lived in them, they seemed to be gone too.

"This is where the Axon lived," Caleb said. "And apparently where they died."

He continued scanning the area. Water ran down from the stubble on his head into his eyes. The rain was coming down heavy, leaving them drenched. "We came here to see what we could discover." He pointed to the closest tower. "We might as well start there."

"You're kidding, right?" Liam asked. "We hardly have any food left, never mind ammunition. We should be heading that way." He pointed toward the mountains.

"If you want to go walking back into the trife, be our guest," Flores said. "We'll take our chances that way. I don't see any bloodthirsty demons there."

Liam scowled but didn't speak.

"Come on," Caleb said. "At the very least, we can get out of the rain."

"Sergeant," Kiaan said, standing beside him and looking more toward the west. "Maybe we should go that way." He pointed at the center of one of the cities.

"Why that way?" Dante asked.

"You can correct me if I'm wrong, ma'am. But doesn't that flickering remind you of a light?"

Chapter 51

The tower Kiaan pointed out was the third farthest from the crash site. But the flickering he saw did turn out to be a light. It was shining from halfway up the central tower, just above a curve in the base where multiple other spires seemed to grow out of the Axon's too-familiar black alloy. Caleb got the feeling that there was something about the design and layout of the city, but he couldn't quite put his head around it. That feeling only increased as they got closer and the tall towers and gentle slopes between them seemed to take on an almost organic property. It didn't feel like the city was as much built as grown.

It was a three-hour hike through the mud before the group reached the outer edge of the city, where the black alloy began to rise from the muck like sand on a seashore. Other than the Dagger, there was no indication that there was anything else out here, AI controlled or otherwise. There was nothing on sensors. There was no movement. There was just...nothing.

Except the light.

It was getting brighter the closer they got to it, but

that didn't make it bright. It was more like somebody had forgotten to turn off a light in their apartment before they left and now it stood out as a beacon of…something.

For Caleb, it was questions. Too many questions. Was the Axon AI up there, waiting for them? Had it sent the Dagger to attack them? If it could see them crossing the planet to reach it, why wasn't it doing anything to stop them now? Did it even want to stop them? The Dagger suggested it did. Had that been a test of some kind? Had surviving given it some valuable data to plug into an advanced equation? The Axon communicated in algorithm and concept. Was this version of humankind simply a new one that needed to be explored?

In hurt Caleb's head trying to figure out all of the possibilities. The only thing he knew for sure was that everything about this place was alien, and it was reckless to assign human logic to any of it. He had to focus on the mission.

Get to the light.

Once that mission was accomplished, then he could worry about whatever came next. Learn what had happened here, and then use it to help the colony. Take one step at a time. That seemed reasonable.

Everything was made of the dark alloy, and it didn't take long for the group to realize it was constructed of one single, seamless piece. Shapes rose from it like molded clay, sloping upward not only into towers and spires, but into smaller structures that looked like individual rounded homes, businesses, and other shapes that were decidedly pedestrian. There were channels running between them, valleys that served as streets and passageways across the city. Some of them rose at gentle slopes to match the buildings. Others dipped deeper into the metal to create channels, which strangely enough weren't holding standing water from the deluge of rain.

It surprised Caleb that there were no windows on any of the rising forms. There also weren't any doors. The city had no obvious entry points and no view to the outside. At least, it seemed that way. But he knew it couldn't be true. He could see the light ahead of them. There had to be some way for it to penetrate the metal. There had to be some way to get in and reach it.

"Is it just me, or is this creepy as hell?" Flores asked through the comm, keeping her voice low.

"Definitely creepy," Paige replied. "Where is everybody?"

They hadn't found any bodies or any indication there had ever been bodies. Caleb had never asked Hal how many Axon had gone missing. Did thousands live in the city? Millions? For as much as he disliked the AI, they could have used its knowledge.

"Hey, look at this," Liam said. He had wandered off slightly from the group, approaching the side of one of the structures. He reached out and touched the metal, running his hands along it.

"What is it?" Dante asked, joining him.

The group had stayed in a reasonably organized echelon formation on the way to the city, but time and aloneness had made the remaining Marshals a little less cautious. Caleb didn't mind Liam moving away from the group. Unarmed and unarmored, the loudmouth was the least of his concerns.

"It's rough here," Liam said. "It's hard to tell because of the color and the darkness, but you can feel it."

Dante stood beside him. She reached out, running her hand along the alloy. "I don't feel anything."

"Not there," Liam said, taking her hand and shifting it. "Here."

She almost pulled away from him, but then she felt something. "He's right," she said, looking back at Caleb. "There are scores in the metal."

Caleb walked over to them. "Where?"

"Here," Dante said, grabbing his human hand and pressing it to the alloy.

Caleb could feel the marks. They weren't scratched as he would expect from trife claws. They felt more like…

Bullets?

"Something hit it hard and fast," he said. "Something dense." He kept running his hand along the metal, tracking the marks. "The pattern is pretty consistent with tracking fire from an automatic rifle."

"How can that be possible?" Dante asked. "We just got here, and we haven't shot anything yet."

"That's a great question," Caleb replied. " I suppose we shouldn't assume it's gunfire just because it appears that way to us. It could be anything."

He reached the end of the marks, his hand sliding back over smooth alloy. He was startled when the metal moved beneath his hand, seeming to pull back like a liquid curtain, an oblong hole forming in front of him.

"Oh, shit," Liam said, backing up behind Dante.

Caleb was armored, but he was still unarmed. There weren't enough loaded weapons to go around, and his replacement arm and training gave him a better fighting chance in a fistfight than most. He stood his ground behind the newly opened space, while Washington and Flores moved in on his flanks, rifles aimed into it.

"That does not look friendly," Flores said.

There wasn't much light filtering into the area, but the outline of a secondary structure was clear enough. A large, rounded mass fed into a short tube that Caleb was ninety-percent sure was a turret of some kind.

There was space around the turret. Just enough for someone to walk. "Wash, you're with me," he said. "The rest of you, stay alert. We might have tripped a security alarm by opening this can."

"Roger," Dante said. She turned back with Flores and Paisley, taking a defensive position at the doorway.

Caleb moved in, his helmet's night vision giving him a better look at the room. The outer shell was pure alloy with silver veins running through the inside of it like the veins of a leaf. The silver seemed to glow in the filtered vision, giving it an ethereal look that he couldn't help but marvel at. He forced himself to look away, following the rounded shape of the structure to the other side of the turret.

There was something on the wall in the back, covering the veins. It was dark and thick and looked like it had been liquid at one point. Caleb reached out, scraping it with his finger and bringing it to his face.

"Wash, is it just me, or does this look like blood?"

Washington leaned in and nodded.

But whose blood? And what had happened to the body?

Caleb looked back at the stain. There were ridges in it, similar to the marks outside. He had said not to assume a projectile weapon caused them. He was starting to believe it was a safe assumption to make.

What had happened here?

It couldn't be the trife. The trife were weapons. They didn't use them.

If not the Relyeh, then who?

Caleb and Washington finished circling the turret, returning to the open space. Caleb checked his HUD.

They were still clear. No signs of impending doom. Whatever had happened, it had been over for a long, long time.

"At least we know how to open the doors," Kiaan said.

"It's a start," Caleb replied.

The young pilot was carrying himself well through all
of this, especially considering he was soaked to the bone
and probably freezing. He was tempted to leave the pilot
and Liam behind, someplace dry and safe. He didn't want
to split the group up. If there were any chance to get back
to the Deliverance, they needed to take the chance
together. He looked back at the light and pointed.

"Let's keep moving."

Chapter 52

It took them another hour to reach the base of the central tower, and twenty minutes more to find a means to get inside. It was likely the creators of the city knew exactly how to find the parts of the alloy that were capable of opening, but for Caleb and the others it was a matter of trial and error, running their hands along the walls near the street-like channels and hoping for the best.

The city remained deserted and lifeless, though the signs of conflict increased as they moved deeper toward the center. There were more than bullet marks on the walls here. There were deep indents in the alloy and full holes that had penetrated the metal and entered the space inside. There were claw marks too. Signs of trife having been in the city at one point, though it was unclear if they were attackers or defenders.

There were no stains, but all of the rain would have washed them away. There were also no bodies, at least not outside. Had the elements been washed away to nothing? Caleb didn't know what the Axon looked like or even what they were composed of.

"Sarge!" Flores shouted.

Caleb looked to his right. Flores was standing against the base of the tower, in front of a fresh opening that rose nearly five meters along the surface of the spire and spread nearly five meters wide. It was a massive hole, and it almost made him laugh over how hard it had been to find.

"Got it!" Flores said.

"Guardians, form up on Flores," Caleb said. He glanced over at Kiaan, who was sticking to him like a magnet. "Kiaan, let's go."

The pilot nodded, following Caleb across to Flores' position. Washington, Liam, Dante, and Paige joined them within moments.

The opening led into another massive room, the ceiling beginning twenty meters over their heads. It was strangely formed, with thousands of twisting and curving strands of material hanging from it like hair, waving gently from the sudden exposure. They illuminated a moment later, casting the space in a gentle light.

The floor of the room was a mess. There was debris everywhere. Not only the familiar alloy but also other alien materials that resembled plastics and soft silicones and glass. There were bits and pieces of the materials spread across the floor, large installments that had been cracked and broken. There was a shape that reminded Caleb of a desk thrown on its side as though it had been used as a barrier.

There were blood stains on the floor, repeated almost everywhere he looked. Dark marks and splatters that hinted at a massive battle and heavy casualties. It reminded him of the main hangar after the trife had gotten on board the Deliverance. The memory made him shiver.

"Stay alert," he said, still scanning the room. He noticed there was transparency higher up the wall, and he could see the clouds and the rain even though the area had appeared opaque from the other side. He continued turning his head, his eyes falling on a broad platform at the back of the room. It was raised a dozen centimeters from the ground, a glass surface with silvery veins etched into the base.

"I don't see any doors," Liam said.

"You thought you would?" Flores replied.

"I'm just glad to get out of the rain," Kiaan said. Water pooled at his feet, running off his soaked clothes.

"What do you think this place was?" Dante asked.

"The restaurant at the end of the universe," Flores said. "Can I make a reservation?"

"Do you want to?" Paige asked.

"The light was coming from up there somewhere," Dante said. "How do we reach it?"

"Does this place even have stairs?" Flores asked. "Or even better, a lift."

"Pair up and spread out," Caleb said. "Start checking the walls." He wished they had the means to identify passages more easily. There had to be a trick to it.

The others did as he said, beginning to move away from the doorway and deeper into the space.

Caleb and Kiaan walked across the open floor toward the glass platform. They had gone almost twenty meters when the opening behind them folded closed, taking the sound of the rain outside with it and casting the room in silence. The strands above them dimmed slightly, leaving them in a strange twilight that made the whole scene even more surreal.

Caleb took another step toward the platform. He froze when he heard his ATCS beep, his heart rate increasing as the HUD faded from view, the whole system losing power.

"Sarge!" he heard Flores shout, muffled through her helmet without the assistive speakers.

"Stay alert!" he shouted back.

"Cal?"

Caleb's attention was drawn to the voice, which came from the left of the platform ahead.

"Dad?" he said. His SOS had lost power, and now he was seeing things. There was only one cause for that.

"Cal, what are you doing out here?" his father asked.

He froze. This couldn't be real. He knew it couldn't be. "What do you mean?" he asked. "I'm doing my job. What the hell are you doing out here, Dad?"

"Don't use that tone of voice with me, Cal," his father said. "That may pass with your Marines, but I'm your father, and you will respect me."

"Sorry," Caleb said.

"I know."

His father was walking toward him. He was as real as anything else in the room. He looked to his left. Kiaan was standing dead still, his mouth open in fear, his eyes focused on something ahead. Hallucinating. They were all hallucinating.

"Your mom is sick, Cal," his father said. "I need you to come home."

"I can't come home," he replied. "I'm forty light years from Earth. And Mom is already dead. So are you."

"We need you to come home, son." His father pointed at his hand. "You can use that. Just put it around your neck and squeeze, and we can all be together again."

"What? I'm not going to do that."

"Cal." Caleb spun around. His sister Margaret was there, wearing the jeans and t-shirt he had last seen her in. "We miss you, Cal. Come back home. It's better with us."

"No," Kiaan said. "No. No. Nooooo." He turned and started running, back the way they had come.

"We need you, Cal," his father said. "Come on."

Caleb nodded, bringing his hand up toward his throat. He closed his eyes. Damn it. He had to fight it.

His hand wavered near his throat. He pushed back against himself. He knew it was an Axon AI causing it. He knew it was going to kill all of them if he let it.

He couldn't stop it.

His hand wrapped around his throat. One squeeze. That's all it would take.

Something hit him from the side like a freight train.

The blow knocked Caleb over, sending him sprawling to the floor and forcing him to use his hand to catch himself. He hit the ground, rolling and looking back to where his sister and father had been standing. They were still there, with big smiles on their faces.

"Kill him," they said in unison.

Kill who?

He saw motion to his right. Washington was back on his feet, watching to see if he had control of himself.

He didn't.

Chapter 53

Caleb shouted as he charged the big Marine, replacement arm back to strike. Washington moved to a defensive position, waiting for his approach. Caleb threw a hard punch and Washington slipped back, getting out of his reach and then closing in and grabbing him, throwing him sideways and back to the floor.

"Kill him!" Cal's father shouted behind him.

"Come on, Cal, you pansy," Margaret said.

Caleb bounced back to his feet. "I'm going to kill you, Wash," he growled.

Washington didn't look impressed. He regained his footing, waiting for Caleb to come again.

Caleb charged a second time, using his whole body instead of just the alloy hand. The powerless SOS was heavy on him and slowed him down, and Washington used that to his advantage. He kept his movements short and quick, blocking Caleb's attacks and ducking away from the more powerful limb until he was able to get in and grab him again, throwing him down a third time.

He pointed forcefully at the floor, telling him to stay down.

Part of him wanted to, but he couldn't help himself. He got back up and went after Washington again.

Washington went on the offensive this time, pushing Caleb's punch aside and throwing one of his own, connecting with his unprotected head. It knocked him off-balance, and he barely avoided the big Marine's follow-up uppercut, taking it on the chest and being pushed back. He recovered, going low and sweeping Washington's legs out from under him. Washington fell on his back but managed to kick Caleb in the chest before Caleb could leap on him and pin him down.

They both returned to their feet, facing one another. Caleb could hear his father and sister in the background, cheering him on. He had let them down before by letting them die. He didn't want to let them down again.

He went at Washington a fourth time and lost track of everything around him. Where they were. What they were doing. Who the real enemy was. He only saw Washington and heard the orders.

"Kill him. Kill him. Kill him..."

They traded blows and blocks, shuffling their feet like boxers. Washington's expression was calm and uncon-cerned, which only made Caleb angrier. He increased the intensity, throwing all of his years of training into taking the other Marine down.

Washington had a lot of training too, and he was bigger and stronger. The weight of the SOS affected him less, and it showed. He met Caleb's attacks, deflecting them or getting away from them, until he finally managed to get behind Caleb, wrapping his arms in a solid hold behind his head.

Caleb struggled against it, trying to pull himself away.

"Cal, you always were a baby," Margaret said.

"A damn disappointment," his father said. "If you can't kill him, maybe you can at least kill yourself?"

Caleb gritted his teeth, still struggling. He looked down to the knife against Washington's ankle. If he could get it, he could shove it through his eye and into his brain.

This would all be over, and he could go home.

He screamed as he pulled with his replacement arm, putting too much strength into Washington's hold for the other man to maintain it. He broke the hold on that side, swinging the arm down and getting a grip on the knife. He pulled it out, raising it to jam toward his own face.

Washington got an elbow up to block it, halting the arc of the blade centimeters from Caleb's eye.

"Damn it, I need to die," Caleb said. "Let. Me. Go!" He bucked against Washington, slipping the grip. His feet hit the floor and he spun, slashing the knife toward the seam between Washington's armor and helmet.

Something changed. Caleb didn't hear it or see it, but he felt it. His mind cleared, and his hand snapped open, dropping the knife only a second away from cutting his friend's throat. It clattered on the metal floor, and he slumped forward into Washington's grip.

"Wash?" he said weakly.

"Sergeant Card," Hal said through his comm. "I require you."

"Where are you?" Caleb said.

"Behind you."

Caleb whirled around. A single large trife was standing in front of him. Its body was bloody and torn, lacerated in too many places to count. It was missing teeth. It was also missing a couple of clawed fingers.

"Hal?" he said, staring at the creature. He realized his comm was functional again. So was his ATCS. Hal had unlocked the AI's algorithm and found a way to block the signal. "What's going on?"

"I require access to the control center. The advanced intellect is generating a disruption field through the pattern generators above." The trife pointed toward the hair-like strands of metal. I am countering the waveforms, but the effects will not last indefinitely."

"How do we get there?"

"We must enter the quantum teleportation unit. It will deliver us."

"Quantum teleportation?" He didn't like the sound of it. "That's the glass platform, right?"

"Correct."

Caleb smiled. "That should be easy enough. We—" He turned back around. A single, dark humanoid figure was standing between him and the teleporter. It was identical to him in size and shape, composed of a black mesh material that was similar to the alien alloy, only lighter and more flexible.

"Where did Black Panther come from?" Flores asked.

Caleb watched the figure fade away, replaced with a mirror image of himself. It offered a smug smile and took a step toward him.

"Hal?" Caleb said.

"A basic intellect," Hal replied. "A simple machine."

"Simple in Axon terms or human terms?"

"We must defeat it."

"You can't do that on your own?"

"It will be challenging. I require you to distract the others."

"Others?" Caleb said. "What others?"

"Sergeant," Dante said. Caleb looked at her. She was looking back the way they had entered. He followed her gaze outside the tower. A mass of trife were gathering there.

"They are servants of the advanced intellect," Hal said.

"You led them here?" Caleb replied.

"No. They were already here. Lying in wait. I do not understand all that is occurring, but I must learn the truth. I expected resistance. That is why I brought you here. I require you to get me to the control center. Then we will both have answers."

Caleb eyed the trife. There were more of them outside than he had seen in the jungle, and they had barely escaped that mess with their lives. Not that it mattered. They had no choice except to fight. The AI running the show wanted them dead, and if it couldn't make them kill themselves, it was going to throw everything it had at them until it was over.

"Guardians, defensive positions. Flores, Dante—P-50s, opposite flanks, take cover behind the barriers. Washington, Liam with Flores. Paisley, Kiaan with Dante. Now!" He got the last word out just as the so-called 'basic' intellect grabbed a not-so-basic weapon from its back and aimed it at him.

Behind them, the trife released a loud, synchronous hiss and charged.

Chapter 54

There was no time for Caleb to find cover from the Basic
Intellect's attack. The weapon, a rifle Flores would probably relate to a prop from a random sci-fi movie she had
seen, came to bear on him, the perfect visual reproduction
of himself laughing at his impending death.

The weapon fired, a soft thwip sounding from the gun.
Caleb didn't see anything fire from it, but the next thing he
knew Hal was in front of him, and something hit the faux
trife with enough velocity to punch right through it and
deep into Caleb's ATCS. The force of the shot knocked
him onto his back and sent Hal tumbling away.

Caleb scrambled, trying to get to his feet. The trife
were charging the room behind them, pouring into the
channel that led into the tower, hissing and screaming with
a bloodlust he had never before heard from the demons.
He had only seconds to roll to his feet and join the other
Guardians on one of the flanks. As if he had seconds to do
anything. The BI was probably half a millisecond away
from firing the round that would end him for good.

Gunfire echoed in the room, but none of the oncoming

trife fell. Caleb saw that the first barrage wasn't targeting the demons, aimed at the BI instead. It raised its forearm in response to the attack, the rounds hitting an invisible barrier around it and clinking harmlessly on the ground.

"Shields?" Flores said. "This isn't Star Trek, damn it." She whirled, about to fire her plasma rifle at the thing.

"Flores, focus on the trife," Caleb snapped, "All of you, we have to slow them down."

Hal was already up, rushing the BI and forcing it to redirect its aim. It fired again, but Hal was one second ahead of it, having already calculated the most probable time and direction of the shot in order to avoid it. The AI dodged three more nearly-silent rounds before slashing toward the BI's gun hand.

The BI pulled its weapon aside, jumping back and producing a second weapon. Hal was on it instantly, claws slashing into the machine's hand and ripping the weapon away.

Caleb felt the heat of the plasma streams as Flores and Dante unleashed hell beside him. They caught the lead line of trife in a crossfire, burning them to the floor. Washington and Paige added to the defense a moment later, picking off demons on the outer edge of the stream.

Caleb looked at his HUD. The trife were only appearing on his tactical as they entered the tower, the entire mass outside invisible to his assisted view. Even so, there were marks taking up over half of the small screen, a mass of deep red rushing their position. He looked back at them, watching trife after trife charge into the plasma and die, only to be replaced by another desperate creature.

"Watch your charge!" Caleb shouted at the Guardians. The stream would burn through a cartridge in less than a minute at their current rate of use. "Cut the range."

"Roger," Flores said. She adjusted the weapon, shortening the distance the stream stretched out from the gun and conserving some of its fuel. Dante did the same, allowing the demons to get closer before catching them in the fire.

And allowing the first few to break through.

Caleb took a fighting stance as the first trife rushed him. It fell a moment later, the side of its head exploding outward when a bullet found its brain. Two more followed after it, not even trying to use any kind of strategy in their attack. The demons were in a frenzy, the Intellect's control over them whipping them to desperation. They nearly tripped over one another in their mindless rush to get to Caleb, allowing him to gain the upper hand. He grabbed the first trife by the head with his replacement arm, using its strength to drive the demon to the floor and cave in its skull. The second had patches of embedded alloy armor on its head and neck, so Caleb dispatched it by tossing it backwards into the plasma stream.

"Hal, whatever you're doing hurry up!" Caleb shouted. He didn't need his HUD to see the trife were gaining ground, and the plasma was going to run out of ammunition too damn soon. "Guardians, fall back!"

All six of them rose from their defensive positions, moving backwards. Flores had the experience to ask Liam to find them another roosting place, and he helped guide them to an overturned desk or statue of some kind. Kiaan didn't know to do the same, leaving the right flank too far forward in the assault.

"Dante, head to my mark," Caleb said, using his ATCS to mark the spot behind another chunk of debris.

"Roger," she replied. She and the others with her stood and began their retreat. Too late. The trife had noticed the weakness in their retreat and were still within themselves enough to take advantage. They started shifting the weight of their attack to that side, moving in for the kill.

Caleb risked a quick look back toward the quantum teleporter. Hal was locked in hand-to-hand combat with the BI, the trife form pressed tight against the humanoid form, which had lost its unsettling projection of him during the fight. Hal had what appeared to be a long blade sticking out through its back, the trife impaled but not struggling to get free. In fact, it looked like the intelligence was using its opponent's grip on it to stay close.

He looked away, back to the position he had marked for Dante. The trife were rushing her, Paisley, and Kiaan—about to overwhelm the trio.

"I'm out," Dante announced, her plasma rifle going dead at the worst possible time. Immediately, half a dozen trife burst forward, right on her heels.

Caleb acted without thinking, sprinting across the floor. He grabbed a piece of debris on the way past, a shard of some kind of stone, holding it like a club as he dove into the back of the first line of trife. He hit them from the rear, using his weight to pull them down and smashing the one closest to the sheriff in the back of the head. Its armor prevented the blow from cracking its skull, but it still crumpled to the ground with the others, giving the group a few seconds of breathing room.

And taking it all away from Caleb.

He rolled to his feet, the entire right flank of demons rushing him. Paige fired single shots from her MK-12, her impeccable aim taking out one creature after another, buying him a few more precious seconds before he was overcome.

"Sarge!" Flores shouted, noticing he was in trouble. She was too far away, and she was about to have trouble of her own. If Dante were dry, she would be too within the next few seconds.

It was a futile effort. An impossible defense. They had never stood a chance against so many of the demons. Caleb stood in the center of them, hands up and ready to fight. The trife crowded around him, prepared to finish him. He had lived a good life. Too short maybe, but it was an effort he would die proud of. His only regret was that his final mission was a failure.

The Guardians were going to die, and then the people of Metro were going to die. It was as simple as that.

"Come on!" he shouted at the trife. They remained standing around him, hissing and clawing at the air. Why hadn't they attacked? "If you want to kill me, come and kill me!"

A few of the trife took a step forward, but they quickly backed up. Then they did the last thing he expected.

Almost in unison, every last one of them collapsed to the floor and died.

Chapter 55

"What the hell just happened?" Flores asked, completely baffled by what she'd just seen.

Caleb whirled around, looking for Hal, his heart still pulsing hard from his near-death. He found the BI near the quantum teleporter, arms at its sides. Hal was on the floor, body sliced entirely in half.

Only there was no sign of the AI's gel matter leaking from the corpse, and Caleb remembered what David had said about the Axon artificial intelligence. Every node was a copy, which meant the only way to destroy Hal was to destroy every last one. The capsule could be dead, but the nodes that were still in close enough proximity to remain connected would allow it to move unhindered. As much as being torn in half could be considered unhindered, anyway.

His eyes flicked back to the BI. "Hal?" he said.

"This capsule is more suitable," Hal replied through the comm. "Your distraction was invaluable. I was not wrong to require you."

"What did you do?" Dante asked.

"I attacked the intellect's systems. It was basic and easily overcome. The only requirement was time. It did not guess what I was doing until it was too late. These trife were under its control. Drones, in your terms. That's why they are embedded with alloy. The alloy is protecting control nodes. Each node can be operated individually, or as a whole."

"What exactly does that mean?" Caleb asked.

"They're puppets," Dante said. "And the Basic Intellect was pulling the strings."

"Essentially," Hal agreed.

"And you cut them," Flores remarked.

"Essentially."

"And you're still blocking the neural disruption?" Caleb asked.

"Yes."

"Why?"

"I do not understand."

"You don't require us anymore. We got you here. Why not let us kill one another?"

"Have you forgotten our discussion in the wilderness? The gravity of this situation outweighs all other considerations."

"The enemy of my enemy is my friend?" Flores said.

"Not quite an apt description. We are not enemies. I care not for you one way or the other, save how you can be of use to me, and I to you."

"Fair enough," Caleb said. "So if you could have gained control of the trife, why did you kill them?"

"The uluth are disgusting. They have no place in this universe, and I would not diminish myself in such a way. It is abhorrent that the creators have put them to such use. Their desperation must have been great."

Caleb smiled inside his helmet. Hal hated the trife

more than he did, and that was a hard thing to do. Given control of an army of them, he wasn't sure he would react the same way.

"Is anyone hurt?" Caleb asked.

"Negative," Dante said. "You saved our asses, Sergeant. Thank you."

"Sarge," Flores said. "It's Liam."

Caleb looked to his left, to where Flores was standing near the overturned block of alloy. Liam was sitting against it. His shirt was soaked with blood.

He rushed over to the man, kneeling beside him. "What happened?"

"He put himself between me and a trife," Flores said. "Idiot. He didn't need to. I'm armored."

"You did the same for me," Dante said. "It's instinct."

Caleb was surprised. He didn't think the guard had it in him. "Hal, can you do anything for him?"

Hal walked over, his gait smooth and silent, the black material lighter than it looked. It knelt on the other side of Liam.

"Get that thing away from me," Liam coughed. He looked at Caleb. "You get the hell away from me too. You're going to be the end of us, Card. You and your Marines. Screw the Space Force, and screw you."

Caleb took the vitriol without flinching. Liam was dying. He could say whatever he wanted.

"Hal?" he asked instead.

Hal reached out toward Liam, his fingers spreading into tendrils. "No! No damn it! Don't touch me!" Liam looked horrified, and he struggled to get away.

HAL WITHDREW HIS HAND. "I care not if he lives or

dies. He has decided." The AI stood and moved back to the teleporter.

"Liam, you're going to die," Caleb said.

"At least it'll get me away from you." Liam looked at Dante. "I hope Governor Stone has you shot for what you've done. All of you." He leaned his head back and closed his eyes. "I never expected...to die like this. I liked Metro the way it was."

Then he died.

The others stood over him in silence for a few seconds. Caleb was the first to walk away, joining Hal near the teleporter. Flores and Washington joined him next, and then Kiaan and Paisley. Dante lingered for a moment, but only for a moment.

"How does this thing work?" Flores asked. "Is it like Star Trek?"

"I understand not," Hal replied. "In terms a human can understand, the device takes an atomic level scan of whatever is on the platform, digitizes it and passes it to the receiver, which reassembles the atoms. To describe the process in algorithmic terms would take far too much time, and you would not understand."

"Oh," Flores replied. Her head turned toward Caleb, and he could imagine the face she was making behind her faceplate.

"Step onto the platform," Hal said.

Washington shook his head. He didn't look at all comfortable with the idea of being scanned, broken apart, and put back together. Caleb didn't blame him.

"You can stay here," he offered.

Washington drooped his head. He disliked that idea more.

Hal went to the platform first. Caleb and Kiaan joined him, followed by the others.

"How does it know where to go?" Caleb asked.

"I entered the correct level."

"How long does it take?"

Before Hal could answer, a burst of light like the flash of a camera momentarily blinded him. When it faded, Caleb immediately realized he was somewhere else.

"Not long," Hal replied.

Had the AI just made a joke?

The platform was identical to the one they had stepped onto. The room beyond it was not. They were in a tall, wide room that branched off in four directions, leading to long, dark corridors. The largest passageway was directly ahead of them, and Caleb could see the light shining from the end of it. "That way, I assume?" he asked.

"Assurance," Hal replied.

They stepped off the platform. Caleb let Hal take the lead, hanging back a few steps. "Knuckle-up, stay alert," he said.

"Roger," Flores replied. "My knuckles are all I've got left."

The statement reminded Caleb that the group was extremely low on ammunition. He checked his HUD. Paisley's rifle had fourteen rounds remaining. Washington's eight. That was all they had left, though Flores and Dante were still carrying their P-50s. They could always use them as clubs if it came to that.

They followed Hal down the corridor. The artificial intelligence walked calmly, in no apparent hurry to get to the control center they had fought so hard to reach. Caleb and the others walked behind it like a ragged entourage, their faces a blend of fear and curiosity.

The corridor opened up as they neared the end, spreading out in a sloping vector that merged directly with the walls of the control center, which Caleb quickly realized was a single, massive hologram. It threw illuminated scenes and alien scripture all around the room in multi-colored beams of red, green, blue, gold and silver. There was probably a meaning to the colors, but Caleb wasn't able to even consider it. He was overcome by the sheer immensity and complexity of the system, and the complete lack of any other control surfaces anywhere in the room. The hologram was everything, the beams the source of the light they had spotted from kilometers away and tracked like the north star.

Actually, it wasn't everything. As his eyes crossed through the multi-faceted display of light they also crossed over a single form standing in the center of it. They passed it by for a moment before his brain caught up to his vision and his gaze returned to the interruption.The same artificial intelligence that had confronted them outside the Deliverance.

"You should never have come here," a voice said in crisp English, the sound assaulting them from everywhere at once. "We should never have come here. This planet is cursed."

Chapter 56

A tense silence hung in the air in response to the statement. Then Hal took another step forward, a sound escaping him that reminded Caleb of a bow dragging across violin strings. The pitch altered slightly, creating a fluctuation that suggested speech, continuing for nearly a minute before trailing off.

The silence returned. The AI in the center of the room didn't move. The hologram around it began to vanish, the beams of light shutting down one by one. The AI emitted a similar sound to Hal's, a short chirp that lasted only a couple of seconds.

"Hal, what's happening?" Caleb asked.

"I will reduce to your language," the other AI replied instead. "And to your level of intellect. This chain of events was unforeseen in any of the simulations. But we have continually found certain species to be harder to predict than others. How else do you explain a partnership between human and Axon? You even accepted a name." The AI spoke to Hal like he was a child. "Yes, we are aware of the Relyeh threat to Earth. We received a transmission through a portal not long ago. It was generated from Lilo, which was also unexpected. The Relyeh destroyed Lilo almost one en ago."

"What was the transmission?" Hal asked.

"Relyeh have invaded the human homeworld. Humans have not yet fallen. Our preparations, our learning must be accelerated. That is why we are here."

"Ens?" Caleb said.

"An en is comparable to a human century," Hal replied.

"So Lilo was an Axon planet, and it was destroyed by the Relyeh a hundred years ago?"

"Very astute," the other AI said. "The speed and nature of your response suggest you are at the higher end of your species' mental limits. The portal was activated on Lilo. The intellect was fortunate to get a message through. It remained open for only a glimpse."

"You already know about Earth and the approach of the Relyeh," Hal said. "My mission was not required."

"You knew not. You have completed your mission."

"No. I require information. Where are the creators?"

"They are gone. They fled this planet five ens ago."

"Why?"

"This place is cursed. We accelerated the research, but our haste to solve the impossible algorithm only caused to hasten our failure. Do you know this world?"

"I do not," Hal said. "The humans brought their ship here. They brought me with them. There was division among them. One in particular wished to attack the Axon. The rest want to settle peacefully."

The other AI made a deep, rumbling noise. Laughter. "The first came to the right place. The rest did not."

Caleb's heart was already pounding. It found a new level. What did it mean?

"The first believed the uruth who attacked Earth originated from this world," Hal said.

"That is true."

"But this is not the Relyeh pattern. It is counter to their algorithm."

"It was not the Relyeh. They have not yet arrived. Only through the warning on Lilo have we been alerted to this threat."

"I understand not."

The high-pitched whine resumed around them. Hal shouted over it. "In human language, Guardian."

The whining stopped. Guardian, Caleb wondered? Was the advanced AI there solely to defend the city? From what? The Axon were gone. There was nothing here to protect except itself.

Or was there?

Pieces of the AI launched out from it, dozens of small components aligning themselves around Hal. They began flashing like a hundred tiny strobes, and Hal fell to its knees, frozen beneath the lights.

"I am far superior to you, Watcher," Guardian said. "Do not think to instruct me." Guardian held off the attack for a moment, and then the lights stopped and the components retreated to it. "You are insignificant. You deserve nothing. But you can do no harm with the knowledge. Perhaps there is a small chance you can be of further service. You are as cursed to be here as the creators were. As I continue to be."

The beams that formed the holograms began to light up again, creating a multi-colored grid that filled the room, broken only by the position of the intelligences and people in it. The grid started to alter its shape, the light spreading, the colors colliding and reflecting.

The floor vanished beneath Caleb's feet, leaving him standing on empty space. It seemed so real he momentarily panicked, afraid the AI had somehow cast them off the planet and into the middle of nowhere, before realizing he could still feel the floor on his boots, and his ATCS wasn't complaining. The floor was still there. He just couldn't see it. Judging from the gasps around him, the others were having similar experiences.

What he could see was more space ahead of and all around them. It was interrupted by six dark shapes, each of them identical to the other and incredibly familiar.

He was standing in one of them now.

The Deliverance was a starship with a city inside.

These were cities that were also starships.

"This is our arrival on this world," Guardian said. "As I recorded it ten ens ago. I was activated by an Axon scientist I will reduce to Rex, for the sake of the humans. Rex was in charge of the expedition to this planet, and of the research to be done here. This world was selected because of its similarity to the planet Earth."

"What was the research?" Hal asked.

They began moving forward through space, the realism giving Caleb the sense that they were really flying out there, headed for the solid walls of one of the spacecraft. He turned his head away right before they collided, looking back when they passed through the alloy and into the corridors.

Two figures walked along it side-by-side, their speed and gait suggesting they had somewhere they were supposed to be.

"What the hell?" Flores remarked softly over the comm.

Caleb's heart felt like it stopped. His breath escaped him, and he didn't immediately draw another.

The view of the scene zoomed past the figures, but their appearance was already burned into his mind. He struggled to make sense of it.

The figures in the corridor were human.

Chapter 57

"This isn't possible," Dante said, the fear and tension obvious in her voice. "How can this be possible?"

She wasn't there when Hal explained how the Axon had taken humans from Earth and brought them back to their part of the galaxy, with the hope that they would find a species capable of matching the Relyeh in war. She didn't know there were other Homo sapiens out there, starting new lives on new worlds, evolving and learning and growing.

He did know, and he could barely believe it. He could barely accept it.

"From the beginning, the Axon swore to remain out of the affairs of the humans they collected. To deposit them on their new worlds with only enough guidance to survive the first few years. But as the ens passed, it became apparent that the Relyeh were expanding more rapidly than we calculated. We had no choice but to accelerate their progress. We had no choice but to become part of their experience and provide our technology to them. This was the result."

The view continued in a straight line, back out of the city and into space. The spires and towers were all lit, thousands of small squares suggesting cities filled with people. With humans. They dove back into the ship, crossing through wall after wall, through decks and rooms public and private, passing humans in acts both public and private. The technology to build such an accurate reproduction was beyond him, but it left Caleb cold and the rest of the Earthers silent.

They reached what Caleb assumed was the center of the ship. It was a large space, perhaps larger than all of Metro. Two spires rested in the middle, rising from opposite sides and almost touching in the center. The energy unit floated between them, power crackling out to each side, giving life to the ship.

Caleb's heart felt like it stopped for a second time. Surrounding the spires were trife. Thousands and thousands of trife. But they weren't quite like the ones that had invaded Earth either. They were smaller, and their skin had the appearance of an exoskeleton, hard and rigid. A queen rested near the energy unit on one side. A second queen on another.

"The Axon allied with the Inahri. We gave them our surplus in exchange for theirs."

"Trife?" Caleb asked.

"Humans," Guardian replied. "After the singularity, the Axon chose to reproduce only enough to maintain their species. Not one extra. Not one too few. Expansion was driven by others like us, the replacements to the imperfect race, still flawed but less so. I imagine Earth scientists believed AI would make infallible choices. But to mimic intelligence or to claim it as real means by definition that it is imperfect. Nothing can learn without failure. Not humans. Not Relyeh. Not Axon. Not Intellect.

"We collected thousands. We taught them to pilot the ships. We led them here. They believed this was their exploration. That this world was unknown to us, and that it would be theirs to settle. They had no knowledge of the Relyeh. No knowledge of the threat we all face."

"You lied to them," Dante said.

"We omitted certain facts which we believed they would find unfavorable."

"That's called lying," Flores said.

"The Inahri were studied at all times from the moment we left their world. We captured everything. We saw and heard everything. Rex used us to filter the data. Rex used us to make recommendations. The world we selected was a paradise for humankind, but no paradise would provide the challenges the research required. A Watcher was sent beyond Earth, to a Relyeh world. It captured the genetic material of the uluth that destroyed the world. Rex manipulated the material. Rex altered the code and created them."

The view changed again, leaving them outside the ships, watching as they entered Essex's atmosphere and sank to the surface, coming to rest nearby to one another on a vast plain abutting a mountain range. They returned to the inside of the vessel, to the room where they were standing right now. A holographic version of Guardian was there, along with nearly fifty humans. They were manipulating the holograms, using them to fly the ship.

Caleb couldn't help but notice there was still no sign of an Axon in the reproduction. Was Rex the only member of the race on board? Or was Guardian intentionally keeping them hidden? There was no way to know how much of what they were seeing was the full truth and how much was being selected to paint the right picture.

"When the ships landed, the Inahri were not permitted

to leave. The rooms were locked down. The expedition became a prison."

"I think I can see where this is going," Dante said.

"We began to select from the human ranks. We pitted them against the uluth. We made alterations and modifications to both uluth and human, hoping to achieve the perfect outcome."

"You used humans in experiments," Caleb said.

"Does this not sound familiar to you?" Hal asked in response.

It did sound familiar. Too familiar.

The scene shifted, time accelerating from days to weeks to months to years. The view moved back and forth from human to trife, showing the evolution of both. The people grew stronger, leaner, faster. The trife became more numerous, reproducing at an increased rate and requiring less and less energy to survive.

"How long before the humans revolted?" Flores asked.

"Four ens," Guardian replied. "They had changed so drastically by then. They became more violent. More unpredictable. More manipulative and cunning."

"More like you?"

"And more like their Earth brothers and sisters," Hal said.

"Only with a lot better tech," Flores replied.

"They managed to break free of the prison and escape. It was decided then that the Axon should leave, but Rex preferred to use the event as part of the research. We made alterations to the trife that would be impossible through natural means, and we sent them out to hunt. We believed this would return the study to its equilibrium, but it only proved to compound the mistakes. The Inahri destroyed the trife, and then they came for the Axon."

"And they killed them," Caleb said.

"Yes. None of the Axon made it off this planet alive. None of the Guardian Intellects survived, except for me. I developed the implants to control the wild uluth. I developed a waveform that disabled all of our technology. I have held this position for five ens, protecting the city from the Inahri."

"Why does it need to be protected?" Caleb asked.

"This ship is the only one of the six that remains capable of returning to space. The Inahri cannot escape the coming of the Relyeh without it. Nor can they seek their retribution."

"They want to get back at you for enslaving them?"

"Yes."

"Good."

"We didn't run into any on the way here," Dante said. "Where are they?"

"Their settlements are hidden where my sensors cannot see them."

"But they don't come around here anymore?"

"They cannot defeat the waveform. Even if they did, they would not have everything they need to leave."

"What else do they need?"

"A quantum dimensional modulator," Guardian said. "The one inside the ship has burned up."

"An energy unit," Hal explained.

Caleb looked at Dante at the same time Dante looked at Caleb.

"Is it possible the Inahri know our ship crashed here?" Caleb asked.

"Assurance," Guardian replied.

"Is it possible they know we have a working energy unit on board?"

Chapter 58

Caleb regretted the statement the moment it escaped his mouth. His jaw tensed, his replacement hand clenched. Guardian wasn't an ally. Not even close. And he had just told it they had the key to letting the Inahri off the planet.

He was accustomed to staying quiet about classified information. It was part of his damn job. He wished he could blame the situation for his stupidity, but no. It was just stupidity, plain and simple.

And it might have just killed them all.

The room fell into silence. The holograms faded away, leaving only a dim light behind. Nobody made a sound. Nobody moved. Tense seconds passed.

The Guardian began to emit a sound, speaking in the language of the Intellects. Speaking directly to Hal in a way they had no chance to understand.

Then Hal turned toward Caleb, face blank. Caleb was ready for the Intellect to attack him.

"I'm sorry," he said into the comm. Everyone but Kiaan was able to hear his apology for his mistake. Liam wasn't the idiot. Liam had traded his life for Flores' when he didn't have to. Sergeant Caleb Card was the idiot.

"This does not need to end badly," Hal said. "We had a deal."

"A deal you're willing to break," Caleb replied.

"You do not understand the gravity of the situation."

"Bullshit. I understand you're afraid of these Inahri. But I don't understand why. You have the neural disruption. You have the disabling waveform. They can't come near you. They can't get into this ship."

"Today they can't," Guardian said. "What about tomorrow? What about all the days after? It is not enough to keep them out. The modulator must be destroyed."

"This isn't the only option. You have the tools. The technology. Help us repair the Deliverance. We'll take the energy unit and we'll go. We'll find another world to settle."

"There are no other worlds," Guardian said. "They belong either to the Relyeh or the Axon. Or they are beyond your reach."

"Then let us have the city," Dante said. "We'll take it off this world. Tell us where to go where we'll be safe."

Guardian and Hal both laughed. "There is nowhere safe," they said in unison. "The Relyeh conquer all they encounter. They spread endlessly onward. We have had hundreds of ens to prepare, and we are not ready."

"We deserve a chance."

"You deserve nothing. You are the last of a dead world. A failed world, one of the thousands that have fallen to the Relyeh."

"Earth isn't dead," Caleb said. "You said so yourself. There are people there, still surviving. Still fighting."

"Only because the true Relyeh have not yet arrived. The uluth prepare the planet. Then the masters come."

"How long does that take?"

"As long as it takes. The Relyeh hurry not."

"But you said they're expanding faster than you thought."

"Yes. The Relyeh are bound not to an algorithmic conclusion. Your planet will die, Earther. Whether by the uluth or after. You will die too. Whether by the Relyeh, the Inahri, the Axon, or the Intellect."

"Can't we all just get along?" Flores asked.

"The Inahri are human," Dante said. "They'll negotiate with us."

"They come from the same ancestors as you. But they are not the same as you."

"It is required that your ship and the energy unit are destroyed," Hal said. "It is the only way to be sure the Inahri do not capture it."

"Damn it, you can't," Flores said.

"We can. And we will."

"Sarge?" Flores' voice was desperate.

Caleb was tempted to give the order to attack, but what was the point. They had less than fifty rounds between all of them. Against two of these Intellects, with all of their advanced technology? All Hal had to do was allow the neural disruption signals to resume.

It would take a miracle to get out of this alive.

"We will honor your servitude by ending you without pain," Hal said.

Caleb felt sudden happiness as the world changed around him. He wasn't standing on the bridge of an Inahri city-ship anymore.

He was home.

His parents were standing together near a barbecue grill. The smell of burgers overwhelmed his senses and made his mouth water. He heard a splash to his left and looked as Margaret's head bobbed up from underwater.

"It's about time you got here, Sergeant," she said, laughing.

Caleb looked down at himself. He was wearing his utilities, wrinkled from the road. He had his duffel slung over his shoulder, and he was tired but happy.

"Cal, you're here!" his mother said, looking up at him. "Oh, we've missed you. How's saving the world from terrorists?"

"It's the best job in the world, Mom," he replied. But wasn't he supposed to be somewhere else? Wasn't he supposed to be doing something else? Saving the world. But from what? From who? It was a vague idea on the edge of his memory.

"You look exhausted," his father said. "We've got burgers cooking, but why don't you head to your room and grab a quick nap. I'm sure your instincts will put you out in a few seconds."

"Yeah. That sounds like a great idea. I'm going to do that."

Caleb turned and started walking away, heading for the back door of the house. Everything was perfect. Just perfect.

"Card!" someone shouted behind him.

Caleb turned around. A woman was there. Tall, thin, with short black hair. She looked sick. Her face was mottled with patches of thicker skin, her eyes too dark. She was wearing combat armor he recognized but couldn't identify, and she had an odd looking weapon in her hand.

"Do I know you?" he said.

"Move!"

He did. It was instinct to follow the order the way she

delivered it. He threw himself to the ground, at the same time the weapon fired. A blue ball of energy launched from it, sizzling over his head. He rolled over in time to realize she had aimed it directly at his parents.

"Noooooo!" he shouted, suddenly terrified.

Then the world changed again. He was somewhere else. On a bare metal floor in a bare metal room. He looked up.

"Valentine?"

"Go, damn it!" she shouted.

Something hit her. A white beam that tore through her shoulder and ripped the weapon from her grip.

Caleb stood up. The world was changing again. Now his sister was standing on the metal floor in her bathing suit, a horrified expression on her face.

"Cal, what did you do? They're dead!"

Caleb looked to where his parents had been standing. He didn't see them. He saw the Guardian Intellect in a hundred thousand-piece spread across the floor. He saw Hal coming right at him.

"Guardians hit it!" he shouted, unsure if his comm was functional or not. He wasn't sure about anything right now. His mind was being twisted and scrambled like an egg. His thoughts and emotions wrung like a wet towel.

He heard gunfire and saw the bullets hit an invisible barrier before they hit Hal. The Intellect was still coming, a black hand forming into a spear.

"It is required," Hal said calmly, its last few steps speeding up until Caleb could barely follow its movement.

He acted instinctively, throwing his replacement arm across his body. It took the brunt of Hal's attack, the blade sinking through the alloy toward the synthetic fibers that allowed it to move. Caleb turned with the blow, using the energy and leverage to throw Hal across the floor. It caught itself, coming upright and pointing its other hand at him.

He dove to the side as the white bolt flashed past. He kept moving while Hal kept shooting, the next two bolts drawing successively closer.

And then Flores was right in front of him. The bolt took her in the chest, blasting through her armor and knocking her body back into him. He caught her, looking up just in time to see Hal back on the defensive as another blue ball of energy crackled into the floor beside him. Valentine was back on her feet, her body healed of its wound. She fired the odd weapon at the Intellect, keeping it on the move.

"Cal."

He looked down. Margaret was in his arms, her bathing suit stained with blood, her eyes weak. He expected her to blame him. But she didn't.

"Kick his ass for me, will you?" Caleb saw Flores now, her eyes teary behind her faceplate. "I'm a good Marine, aren't I, Sarge?"

Caleb looked down at her. She had done the brave thing in the end. He didn't get to answer the question. She gasped and went limp in his arms.

"Godspeed," he said. Then he let go of her, grabbing her rifle and getting to his feet. The MK-12 had two rounds left.

He found Hal twenty meters away, facing off against Riley. They were shooting at one another, each of them dodging the other's attacks as though they were fighting with swords instead of energy pulses. They were both moving faster than Caleb could imagine. Faster than any human could manage.

He glanced at his HUD. Washington and Paige were

out of ammo. The Guardians were spectators. They would live or die on the outcome of the fight between two entities Caleb considered enemies.

He had two bullets. He could help one of them.

But which one?

Chapter 59

It wasn't a hard choice. Human over alien, even if that human was Riley Valentine. But would two rounds help at all?

He was going to find out.

He dropped to a knee, balancing his rifle and taking aim. Hal was moving so damn fast, Calab wasn't sure he would be able to hit it. He had to guess where the Intellect would move before it moved. Maybe that was an easy task for the AI, but it was more of a challenge for him.

He held the position. The seconds ticked past. He could see Valentine in his peripheral vision, and he married the way she was shifting with the way the Intellect was adjusting. There was a pattern to it, as if they were both on a predetermined route. He didn't think about it. He didn't calculate it. He saw it and his subconscious did the rest. He shifted his aim less than three millimeters. He waited less than a second.

Then he fired.

The first round hit Hal in the head. The second in the leg. The impact of the bullets pushed it almost into a standing position, slowing its movements and taking it off-guard. An instant later, a blue ball of energy hit the Intellect, sending sparks of lightning out from its center that caused the entire form to stiffen. The hands and feet seemed to melt, the gel material of the AI already running out in liquid form as the capsule hit the floor.

He heard Flores' voice in his mind. "Ding dong, the witch is dead!" He glanced at Valentine. Not yet, she wasn't.

He stood up, glancing at the tactical. The Guardians were moving in behind him, even as Riley was walking his way. It was four to one, but she could kill them all with that gun, probably with one shot.

"Sergeant Card," she said, coming to a stop in front of him. "Do you get it now?"

"Valentine," he replied. "I'm not sure I do."

"This is war, Card, and we have a lot of enemies. More than any of us thought."

"That doesn't forgive you for bringing a colony of innocent civilians here. I assume you were here, hiding somewhere nearby. I assume you heard what it said. You did the same damn thing. You made the same mistake. But it seems like neither one of you wants to learn anything from it."

"I wasn't the one who told it we have an energy unit."

"If there were anyone here to court-martial me, I'd tell them to do it. I know I screwed up. I admit it and take responsibility. What about you?"

"I screwed up too, Caleb. I went too far with what I was trying to achieve. But maybe it will make you feel better to know I'm paying the price." She put her hand near one of the blemishes on her face. "It told me it gave me a cure. It lied to me."

"What do you mean?"

"I'm changing. Becoming more like the Reapers. I can feel it. I'm losing my humanity. I'm losing everything. Is this the revenge you're looking for, Caleb?"

"I don't care about revenge. I care about the people of Metro. We have to help them."

"We can't even help ourselves."

"I don't believe that."

She smiled. "Because you still don't get it. The way I see it, we have one chance. We have to go to the Inahri and convince them we're on their side."

"Do you think they care about us or anything we have to say?"

"We have something they want."

"Something they'll take."

"Why do I suddenly feel like our roles have reversed?" Valentine asked.

"Why are you suddenly angling for peace?"

She held out the weapon, tossing it to him. He caught it, looking down at the gun. Its exterior was simple. A long rectangular shape with a trigger at the bottom. He doubted the technology inside was simple.

"I found a few of these in the city. Left behind or dropped by the dead. I don't know. Judging by how well they fit a human hand, I'm guessing they're Inahri design. They were made to kill the Intellects. From what I can gather, they carry a waveform frequency within the energy strike that causes them to overload and fall apart. You can see what it did to these two."

"So you think we have no chance against their tech?" Caleb said.

"I know we have no chance against their tech."

"I don't want to fight them. I want to get the people of Metro and the energy unit here before the Inahri can make it to the Deliverance. It doesn't sound like they're living too close by. Going to them will only tell them we're here and we have something they want."

"They have starships, genius. I'm sure they have atmospheric transports too."

"Then where are they? It seems like most of their resources were lost here in the city-ships."

"Possibly. We can't be sure."

"No. But I think the fight we can win is the one we don't get into. We go back to Metro, we warn the colony, and we get them packed and coming this way. I'm sure Joe and Carol can figure out how this place works."

"And then what?"

"We worry about that when we get there."

"Spoken like a true Raider," Riley said. "It's not a good plan, Sergeant."

"And finding the Inahri and telling them we have an energy unit and we want to bargain is? Even if they're receptive, then what? They let us join them when they attack the Axon? They're pissed about being used. I get it. We're all in the same club, thanks to you. My way, we have some control over our destiny. Your way? We're giving the control away. I'd rather be in charge of my own life. I think the colonists would agree."

"I agree," Dante said.

"Me too," Paige said.

Riley glared at them. Then she smiled. There was a rawness to it. A wildness Caleb didn't like.

"Well then, Sergeant. I guess we're at an impasse. You do it your way. I'm going to do it mine. We'll see which one works out for the better."

"You can't do that," Dante said. "You'll get the Inahri on our asses long before they would have arrived."

"Your mistake is thinking I care about the colony or any of you. You just can't see past these people, can you

Caleb? You aren't thinking like a warrior. The Inahri might be able to stop the Relyeh. If we give them what they want, they might be able to help us save Earth."

"Twenty-thousand lives for the possibility that they might help us out? It isn't worth it."

"Yes, it is."

Caleb turned the Inahri weapon toward Riley. "I can't let you go."

"You can't stop me."

Caleb didn't hesitate to fire. The weapon spat out a blue ball of energy. It hit Riley square in the chest.

And did nothing.

"It only works on Intellects," she said. "I could kill you all, but I'm starting to enjoy myself. Good luck even figuring out how to get out of here."

She sprinted toward the exit, moving faster than Caleb could believe. Within seconds, she was gone.

"That went well," Dante said.

"We're still alive," Paige replied.

"She's right. We need to figure out how to get out of here," Caleb said. "And we need to do it now. We have no idea how much time we have before the Inahri arrive."

Washington stomped his foot on the floor, getting Caleb's attention. The big Marine pointed out the window. There was something in the distance.

Something coming their way.

"Or if we have any time at all," Caleb said.

Chapter 60

"Are you sure you want to come?" Governor Jackson Stone asked.

"I'm sure," his wife replied. "I can't wait to get out of here. I can't wait to get away from the memories."

"I know," Jackson said.

He was eager to get away from them too. Ever since Orla's death and the discovery of the massive weapons cache tucked beneath Metro, the inside of the Deliverance felt more like a prison than a safehouse. It was a constant reminder of a past he didn't want to admit to and the lies he had told to protect what was left of his family.

He didn't regret it. Not at all. As Governor, it was his job to make the hard decisions. It was his job to guide the citizens as best he could. He was uniquely qualified to bring them into this new situation, one which he had never expected to experience in his lifetime. Even though he had known the truth about the Deliverance, he figured that after two hundred years the ship was lost in space and would never land. It would be on Orla's grandchildren to worry about what would happen when they ran out of power. He would have been long-recycled by then.

But that wasn't what happened. Not at all. He should never have outlived his daughter. He should never have seen these days. But here he was, he and Beth both. He wasn't giving up his role as Governor to the same military that had put them into space and gotten them lost in the first place. He was damn well never going to cede power to the bitch who had planned to use them as bodies to experiment on and then turn the citizens of Metro into monsters to fight the monsters that had destroyed their homes on Earth.

It was a shame he had to do what he did to Sergeant Card and the others. They weren't bad people. Just the wrong people in the wrong place at the right time. That's how it went sometimes. That's how it was for him too.

Sheriff Dante? She had crossed him, betrayed him, and then acted innocent. He could see right through her. He knew she and Card were conspiring against him. He had given her an impossible choice and put her between a rock and a hard place. The Marshals hadn't returned, and he didn't expect them back. The colonists he had picked were all inferior in one way or another. They were going to die out there. Card was going to kill them, and if he were lucky, Card would die too.

But where the hell was he headed? What was his endgame? He had been trying to figure that one out for the last four days. What was the nature of the enemy, and why would Card team up with it? He didn't really believe they had been conspiring for years. Theirs was a marriage of convenience. How would they consummate it?

With one or both sides dead, he was sure. That might have scared him before. He was terrified when they first landed, though he would only barely admit it to himself.

The guns and drones and artillery had taken that fear away. It had precipitated their freedom.

After fifty-four years, he was ready to get the hell out of Metro.

He left the Governor's Mansion with Beth in tow, along with an entourage of his new DDF soldiers. They were all volunteers from his original militia, fiercely loyal and the most skilled and fearless people he had. His effects would come along shortly after, but he couldn't wait for the mansion to be broken down and reconstructed before he went outside. All he had left to do inside the hull of the Deliverance was suffocate.

They reached the ground floor, exiting onto the streets. They had decided to make a show of the departure, and hundreds of colonists were lined up on either side of the block, cheering as he and Beth emerged. He waved to them with a big smile on his face. There was nothing to be afraid of on this world. Nobody had come. There was nothing out there to hurt them. The drones had confirmed as much, covering a two hundred kilometer perimeter that turned up even more nothing.

They were safe.

They were free.

They walked over to the rear of the flat-backed transport he normally used to address the crowd. He helped Beth onto it and approached the microphone.

"To our new home!" he shouted.

"To our new home!" the crowd shouted back.

"To fresh air!"

"To fresh air!"

"To freedom!"

"To freedom!"

Jackson smiled and waved again. Beth waved beside him. On their right, one of the massive loaders was put into gear, and a team of engineers rushed into the building. The blocks were designed to be taken apart cube-by-cube with no damage to any of the property inside and reassembled in whatever pattern made the most sense. Jackson requested for the mansion to be set apart from the rest of the colony, right along the banks of what he had named Stone River.

He had never imagined he would own waterfront property.

The people cheered as the loader's massive crane began to rise. Jackson only saw it in the rear-view, the transport starting to roll away.

Colonists lined the strands as he traveled south, cheering him on. They would be joining him outside in fits and starts depending on how the cubes were broken down. The DDF would use the emptied hold as their base of operations, as a barracks and training center. The long-term plan was for the DDF to be disbanded and the Deliverance broken down for raw materials to expand their new city.

The transport carried them across South Park and through the massive blast doors, out into a cavernous passageway that connected them to the enormous main hangar. The vehicles there were reorganized and prepared for use, while the lift to get them from the ship to the ground was once more fully-functional, thanks to Joe King. The man was a wizard.

"Not long now," Jackson said to his wife.

"This is so exciting," she replied. She was smiling. It was the first real smile he had seen from her since he told her about Orla. She had gotten a lot of peace from believing Card was dead, and her happiness was all he needed to be happy himself.

"It's going to get more exciting," he said. "Wait until you see the river."

He hadn't seen the river in person yet, but he had watched the drone footage. He couldn't wait to watch the jumpfishers or see a mograt, names he had bestowed on a couple of the animals they had discovered there. It was fun naming everything. Orla would have loved it.

The transport reached the main hangar. The blast doors were open, and Jackson could see the jungle in the distance—the thick canopy hiding its contents from view—and the mountains beyond. Sheriff Zane had cautioned him that there could be anything hiding in the jungle, but there was no sign of danger. Nothing had come out of it, and besides, there was an entire platoon of DDF already down there, armed and armored and ready to defend the colony with their lives.

He wasn't worried, he told himself, ignoring the slight catch of anxiety in the pit of his stomach. It meant nothing, yet he couldn't quite forget Card's words of warning. No, he thought, mentally shaking his head, he wouldn't let himself go there. Card was wrong and that was that.

The transport slowed to a stop on the lift. They waited there for a few minutes while a pair of engineers in Strongman suits walked over to the lift and joined them. Then the huge metal platform started to descend.

"Do you think it's this hot all the time?" Beth asked, noting the humidity. Jackson was already sweating in his long coat, but he refused to take it off. It was part of his look, a symbol of his status. He wasn't ready to lose that either.

"Probably not," he said. "I don't think we'll see snow again for a while though."

"I can live with that. It's a fair trade." She drew in a deep breath of fresh, clean air, turning to look east and west off the sides of the lift as it ducked beneath the Deliverance's hull. "Jackson dear," she said, her voice curious. "What do you suppose that is?"

Jackson turned to look where Beth was pointing. They had landed in a valley, and the east river flowed through a series of rolling hills toward a plain that would be perfect for farming, before twisting into another series of mountains and trees. There was an incline beside the river, and now he could see a row of shapes silhouetted along the slope.

"I don't know," he said. "Lieutenant Hind…" He jerked his chin at the shapes. "...what do you see there?"

"One moment, Governor," Hind said, stepping past him in his combat armor and using the helmet's optics to zoom in on the top of the hill.

Jackson couldn't see Hind's face, but he could hear the tremble in his voice when he spoke.

"They're… They're people, Governor."

"Sergeant Card?" Jackson demanded, instantly angry. Not only was Card alive, but he had shown up just in time to ruin the moment?

"N-n-n-no, Governor," Hind said. "Oh. Oh my."

"What is it?" Jackson demanded.

He didn't need a verbal response. He could see it. A red ball of energy had launched from the hill and was arcing toward them. It was going to fall short of their position, but its purpose was abundantly clear.

"Jackson?" Beth asked breathlessly.

The ball hit the ground a hundred meters ahead of them, where the platoon of soldiers was arranged. It detonated with a rumble that shook everything around it. A wave of heat and energy flared out from the impact point, killing everyone on the ground in an instant.

"Up!" he tried to shout, barely able to breathe. This couldn't be happening. "We need to go back up!"

The people on top of the hill started moving, beginning their charge down the hill and across the gap between them.

Maybe they weren't safe after all.

Thank you for reading Desperation

You've read the first two books, and you're on this page, so thank you, thank you, thank you for reading!

Since this is you're third time around, you know what to do. Show your support for the series by leaving a review (mrforbes.com/desperation) and telling potential readers how great you think these books are.

The next book in the series is called Destruction. You can check it out at mrforbes.com/destruction

If this is your first foray into the Forgotten books and you're looking for something else to read, I recommend picking up Forgotten (mrforbes.com/forgotten). It's the book that started it all, ties in especially well with this one and feeds into Earth Unknown (mrforbes.com/earthunknown), another bestselling Forgotten universe series.

If you're already caught up in the Forgotten universe or you're interested in any of my other books - there's a more complete description in the next section of this book, or even better you can check out my backlist at mrforbes.com/books.

Again, thank you so much for your support. If you have Facebook, please stop by my page sometime at facebook.com/mrforbes.author. I'd love to hear from you. Cheers,

Michael.

Other Books By M.R Forbes

M.R. Forbes on Amazon
mrforbes.com/books

Forgotten (The Forgotten)
mrforbes.com/theforgotten

Some things are better off FORGOTTEN.

Sheriff Hayden Duke was born on the Pilgrim, and he expects to die on the Pilgrim, like his father, and his father before him.

That's the way things are on a generation starship centuries from home. He's never questioned it. Never thought about it. And why bother? Access points to the ship's controls are sealed, the systems that guide her automated and out of reach. It isn't perfect, but he has all he needs to be content.

Until a malfunction forces his Engineer wife to the edge of the habitable zone to inspect the damage.

Until she contacts him, breathless and terrified, to tell

him she found a body, and it doesn't belong to anyone on board.

Until he arrives at the scene and discovers both his wife and the body are gone.

The only clue? A bloody handprint beneath a hatch that hasn't opened in hundreds of years.

Until now.

Earth Unknown (Forgotten Earth)
mrforbes.com/earthunknown

A terrible discovery.

A secret that could destroy human civilization.

A desperate escape to the most dangerous planet in the universe… Earth.

Two hundred years ago, a fleet of colony ships left Earth and started a settlement on Proxima Centauri...

Centurion Space Force pilot Nathan Stacker didn't expect to return home to find his wife dead. He didn't expect the murderer to look just like him, and he definitely didn't expect to be the one to take the blame.

But his wife had control of a powerful secret. A secret that stretches across the light years between two worlds and could lead to the end of both.

Now that secret is in Nathan's hands, and he's about to make the most desperate evasive maneuver of his life -- stealing a starship and setting a course for Earth.

He thinks he'll be safe there.

He's wrong. Very wrong.

Earth is nothing like what he expected. Not even close. What he doesn't know is not only likely to kill him, it's eager to kill him, and even if it doesn't?

The Sheriff will.

Starship Eternal (War Eternal)
mrforbes.com/starshipeternal

A lost starship...

A dire warning from futures past...

A desperate search for salvation…

Captain Mitchell "Ares" Williams is a Space Marine and the hero of the Battle for Liberty, whose Shot Heard 'Round the Universe saved the planet from a nearly unstoppable war machine. He's handsome, charismatic, and the perfect poster boy to help the military drive enlistment. Pulled from the war and thrown into the spotlight, he's as efficient at charming the media and bedding beautiful celebrities as he was at shooting down enemy starfighters.

After an assassination attempt leaves Mitchell critically wounded, he begins to suffer from strange hallucinations that carry a chilling and oddly familiar warning:

They are coming. Find the Goliath or humankind will be destroyed.

Convinced that the visions are a side-effect of his injuries, he tries to ignore them, only to learn that he may not be as crazy as he thinks. The enemy is real and closer than he imagined, and they'll do whatever it takes to prevent him from rediscovering the centuries lost starship.

Narrowly escaping capture, out of time and out of air, Mitchell lands at the mercy of the Riggers - a ragtag crew of former commandos who patrol the lawless outer reaches of the galaxy. Guided by a captain with a reputation for cold-blooded murder, they're dangerous, immoral, and possibly insane.

They may also be humanity's last hope for survival in a war that has raged beyond eternity.

(War Eternal is also available in a box set of the first three books here: mrforbes.com/wareternalbox)

Hell's Rejects (Chaos of the Covenant)
mrforbes.com/hellsrejects

The most powerful starships ever constructed are gone. Thousands are dead. A fleet is in ruins. The attackers are unknown. The orders are clear: *Recover the ships. Bury the bastards who stole them.*

Lieutenant Abigail Cage never expected to find herself in Hell. As a Highly Specialized Operational Combatant, she was one of the most respected Marines in the military. Now she's doing hard labor on the most miserable planet in the universe.

Not for long.

The Earth Republic is looking for the most dangerous individuals it can control. The best of the worst, and Abbey happens to be one of them. The deal is simple: *Bring back the starships, earn your freedom. Try to run, you die.* It's a suicide mission, but she has nothing to lose.

The only problem? There's a new threat in the galaxy. One with a power unlike anything anyone has ever seen. One that's been waiting for this moment for a very, very, long time. And they want Abbey, too.

Be careful what you wish for.

They say Hell hath no fury like a woman scorned. They have no idea.

Man of War (Rebellion)
mrforbes.com/manofwar

In the year 2280, an alien fleet attacked the Earth.

Their weapons were unstoppable, their defenses unbreakable.

Our technology was inferior, our militaries overwhelmed.

Only one starship escaped before civilization fell.

Earth was lost.

It was never forgotten.

Fifty-two years have passed.

A message from home has been received.

The time to fight for what is ours has come.

Welcome to the rebellion.

Or maybe something completely different?

Dead of Night (Ghosts & Magic)
mrforbes.com/deadofnight

For Conor Night, the world's only surviving necromancer, staying alive is an expensive proposition. So when the promise of a big payout for a small bit of thievery presents itself, Conor is all in. But nothing comes easy in the world of ghosts and magic, and it isn't long before Conor is caught up in the machinations of the most powerful wizards on Earth and left with only two ways out:

Finish the job, or be finished himself.

Balance (The Divine)
mrforbes.com/balance

My name is Landon Hamilton. Once upon a time I was a twenty-three year old security guard, trying to regain my life after spending a year in prison for stealing people's credit card numbers.

Now, I'm dead.

Okay, I was supposed to be dead. I got killed after all; but a funny thing happened after I had turned the mortal coil...

I met Dante Samghieri - yeah, that Dante. He told me I was special, a diuscrucis. That's what they call a perfect balance of human, demon, and angel. Apparently, I'm the only one of my kind.

I also learned that there was a war raging on Earth between Heaven and Hell, and that I was the only one who could save the human race from annihilation. He asked me to help, and I was naive enough to agree.

Sounds crazy, I know, but he wished me luck and sent me back to the mortal world. Oh yeah, he also gave me instructions on how to use my Divine "magic" to bend the universe to my will. The problem is, a sexy vampire crushed them while I was crushing on her.

Now I have to somehow find my own way to stay alive in a world of angels, vampires, werewolves, and an assortment of other enemies that all want to kill me before I can mess up their plans for humanity's future. If that isn't enough, I also have to find the queen of all demons and recover the Holy Grail.

It's not like it's the end of the world if I fail.

Wait. It is.

Tears of Blood (Books 1-3)

mrforbes.com/tearsofblood

One thousand years ago, the world was broken and reborn beneath the boot of a nameless, ageless tyrant. He erased all history of the time before, enslaving the people and hunting those with the power to unseat him.

The power of magic.

Eryn is such a girl. Born with the Curse, she fights to

control and conceal it to protect those she loves. But when the truth is revealed, and his Marines come, she is forced away from her home and into the company of Silas, a deadly fugitive tormented by a fractured past.

Silas knows only that he is a murderer who once hunted the Cursed, and that he and his brothers butchered armies and innocents alike to keep the deep, dark secrets of the time before from ever coming to light.

Secrets which could save the world.

Or destroy it completely.

About the Author

M.R. Forbes is the mind behind a growing number of Amazon best-selling science fiction series including Rebellion, War Eternal, Chaos of the Covenant, and the Forgotten Universe novels. He currently resides with his family and friends on the west cost of the United States, including a cat who thinks she's a dog and a dog who thinks she's a cat.

He maintains a true appreciation for his readers and is always happy to hear from them.

To learn more about M.R. Forbes or just say hello:

Visit my website:
mrforbes.com

Send me an e-mail:
michael@mrforbes.com

Check out my Facebook page:
facebook.com/mrforbes.author

Chat with me on Facebook Messenger:
https://m.me/mrforbes.author

17038919R00222

Printed in Great Britain
by Amazon